THE PERFECT MATCH

BROOKLYN SORENSON

Copyright © 2021 by Brooklyn Sorenson

All rights reserved.

No part of this book may be reproduced in any form or by any electronic or mechanical means, including information storage and retrieval systems, without written permission from the author, except for the use of brief quotations in a book review.

This is a work of fiction. Any names, characters, organizations, places, events, or incidents are either products of the author's imagination or are used in a fictitious manner. Any resemblance to actual persons, living or dead, businesses, companies, locales, or events is purely coincidental or fictionalized.

Cover designed by Brooklyn Sorenson

Photo: Depositphotos Inc.

https://brooklynsorenson.com

❈ Created with Vellum

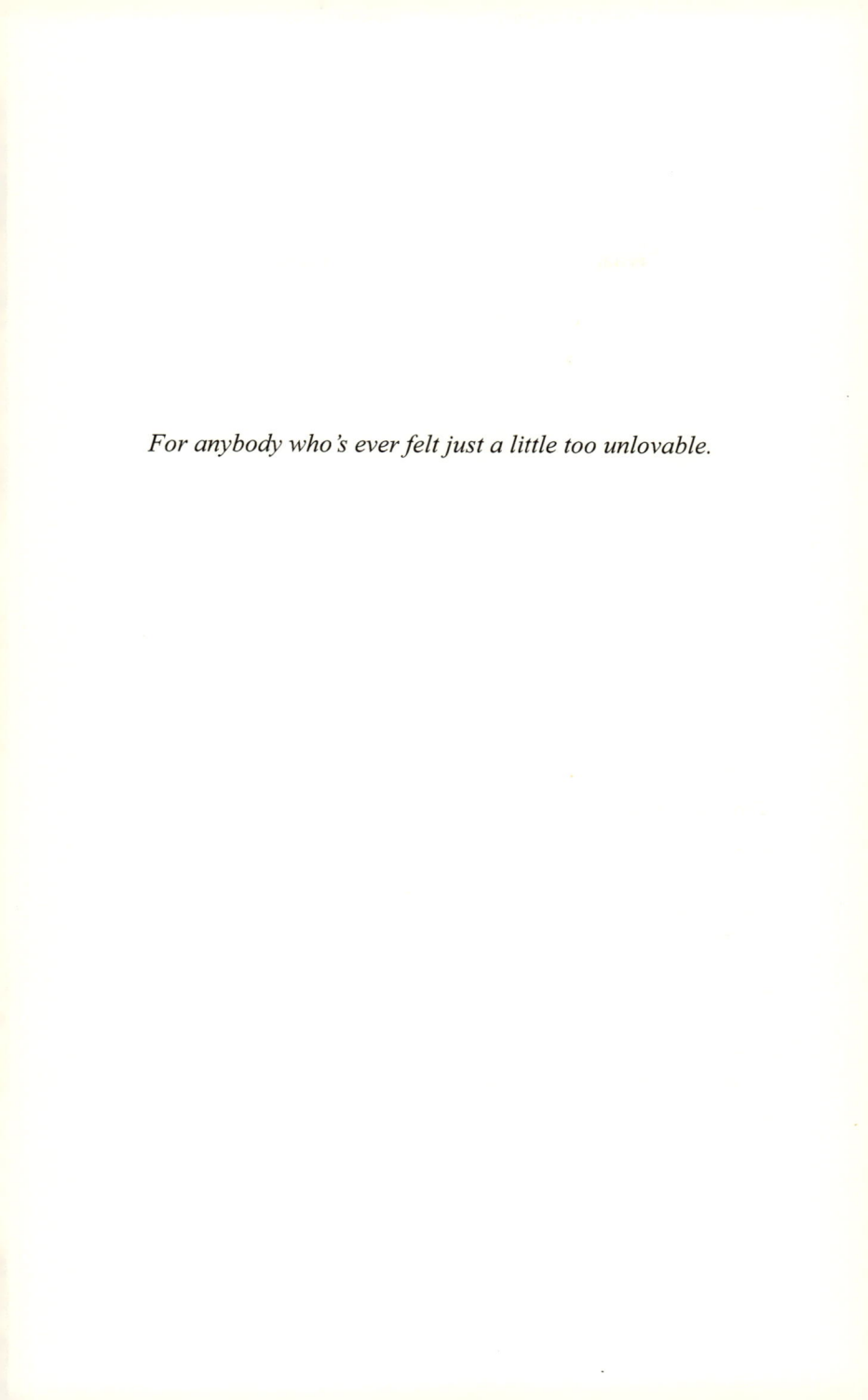

For anybody who's ever felt just a little too unlovable.

1
PARKER

The wind howls, harshly whipping between the houses that surround us. My ears fill with the sound of leaves rustling as the trees sway, bowing from the violent storm ripping through San Diego.

"Dad, come on! Run," I scream, but I'm not sure he can hear me. He's gripping the trunk of a palm tree, shaking his head back and forth as he glances around, searching for a safer place to take shelter.

"Dad, hurry! You can make it."

The sky's wrath swallows my desperate cry as rain pounds against the concrete. I'm holding the front door open, begging him to make a run for it. It's safe here.

Warm.

Welcoming.

Unlike the sudden downpour raging outside.

It was unexpected—the storm. Dad religiously checks the weather before he goes out for a run. He would have seen that it wasn't safe had the weatherman mentioned it. Which means he wasn't prepared for its severity.

Nobody was.

"Dad," I cry out one last time, pushing the front door wide open.

His eyes connect with mine as he shakes his head again.

"I can't. I'm sorry, Parker. I'm so sorry," he yells, his voice traveling to me on the wings of the wind.

I open my mouth, prepared to beg once again when an ear-splitting boom thunders through the air that separates us. My eyes widen in horror as lightning strikes the tree my dad is sheltering underneath, blinding us with the brilliance of its light.

Words trap in my throat as a second deafening crack shakes the house, the noise drowning out my scream as it rips past the lump in my throat. The tree snaps in half at the same time as my dad glances up, raising his arms to protect his head from the palm tree that's crashing down around him.

My heart seizes in my chest as I hear one last, "I love you, Parker!"

JOLTING AWAKE, I SIT STRAIGHT UP IN BED, MY HEART RACING A mile a minute. Sweat pours off me as I glance around, trying to make sense of my surroundings.

It's still dark, the shadows dancing across the walls of my bedroom indicating it's either the middle of the night or the early hours of the morning. It's been months since I've had such a vivid nightmare, reliving the horrible scene that stole my father from us all. It took years for the memory to fade enough for my subconscious to stop playing it on a loop night after night, my nightmares refusing to let me move past the tragic event I witnessed firsthand.

So why now? Why the fuck is it back, haunting me through my dreams?

Glancing to my left, I find Leigha wrapped up in my sheets,

her naked breast peeking out from under the covers. She must not have left after our wicked sexathon last night. A soft sigh falls from her lips as she twists, burrowing deeper under the sheets.

Why the fuck is she still here?

The mental fog of my nightmare lifts as I gain my bearings, and it's then that I notice her phone on the nightstand. There's noise coming from that general direction, and I finally put two and two together on what caused my mental suffering. Her white noise app she swears she needs to sleep is set to the soundtrack of a thunderstorm.

Mystery solved.

I've asked her several times to never play her stupid as fuck white noise app if she's so determined to stay overnight. Consider me unsurprised she doesn't listen for shit.

Tossing the sheet off my body, I climb out of bed and head for the bathroom. There's no way I'll be going back to sleep. My heart is still racing, and there's no doubt that if I close my eyes, I'll see that same image again—the tree crushing my dad, killing him in an instant.

Turning the shower on, I push the nozzle to the coldest setting, hoping the water will erase the emotions flooding through my chest, wreaking havoc on my mental state.

Running my hands through my hair, I bow my head and grip the back of my neck. I watch the water cascade around me as I inhale deeply, my chest expanding as air swirls in my lungs. Lips quivering with my exhale, I repeat the process, focusing on the calming technique. With each deep breath, I cleanse my mind of the last few mental images, replacing them with the clarity of what I need to do next.

I've been seeing Leigha for the last few months. I would call it casual fucking. She prefers the term "dating." Delusional, if you ask me.

Either way, it seems our time has run its course. Lucky for me,

I'm leaving for two days on a business trip. It should be enough time for Leigha to get her shit out of my house and disappear. I kept telling her to stop leaving her crap here, but I swear she's doing it on purpose. Hoping if I wake up and see her clothes cluttering up my space, I'll change my mind about not wanting her around forever.

Need I repeat, delusional?

Shutting the water off, I step out of the shower and grab a warm towel to wrap around my waist. Leigha is sitting up in bed when I exit the bathroom, looking at me with confused, bleary eyes.

"What are you doing up? Come back to bed, baby," she whines in a grating voice.

"Shut that fucking noise off and get up," I growl while tossing her shirt to her. "I'm taking off on a business trip, and you need to leave."

Her face scrunches up in displeasure, and I know I've hit my mark.

"What the hell is your problem? Can't you wait five minutes before being an asshole?"

She grabs the shirt I tossed at her and tugs it over her messy bedhead, finally covering up her perky tits. There's no doubt she's got a nice rack, but now's not the time to get distracted by her sex appeal.

"I could. But what's the point in that? It's your fault I'm already in a shit mood. I told you to never play that bullshit in my house again," I scold, my head tipping in the direction of her phone. Her eyes follow my gaze, realization dawning as the recorded thunder sounds through the room.

"Why does it make you so mad? You know I need it to sleep, and I left it on low. You could barely even hear it."

"I fucking wish that was true, but it doesn't matter. I asked you not to play it, and you didn't listen. Now you need to grab your shit and leave."

She huffs before swinging her legs over the side of the bed. I allow myself two seconds to get distracted by her body before looking away. There's a reason I've been fucking her for the last few months. She's a petite, bottle blond with nice legs, a great rack, grabbable ass. And those lips? Yeah. They were made for sucking.

My cock twitches at the thought of letting her wrap her seductive lips around my length one last time, but then I see my sweat-soaked sheets and think better of it.

Turning my back on her, I finish getting dressed, shoving my phone, wallet, and keys in my pocket before grabbing my travel bag I packed last night.

She releases a huff from those puffy little lips of hers, grabbing her few items from the bedroom as I'm ushering her toward the front door.

"When will you be back? Maybe we can have dinner and discuss our future? Tiffany got a ring last week. It's so big and beautiful. Here, let me show you a picture so you can see what I'd like when the time comes."

Pushing her phone aside, I shake my head. "That won't be necessary."

"What do you mean? Do you already have one picked out?" She glances at me, batting her wide, hopeful eyes, and I almost feel bad for how I'm about to crush her dreams of marrying my money.

Almost.

"Hell, no. There's no future here, Leigha. In fact, there's not even a tomorrow for us. I'm leaving for this business trip. And when I get back in two days, I want you gone."

Her mouth drops open, and her eyes start to shine. "W-what? I thought you said I made you happy?"

"No, I said the sex made me happy. And I can get that anywhere. I told you from the start this was never going anywhere, and I meant it. You're getting too clingy, and it's not working for me anymore."

"I'm not clingy," she whines, stomping her foot like a toddler throwing a tantrum.

"You've been here every night this week."

"Well, yeah. I've been practicing my homemaker skills! I've been here, slaving away, trying to make you happy!"

"Well, newsflash, Suzy Home Lounger, your skills could use a little work. Last time I checked, lounging around by my pool all day, sipping dirty martinis and flirting with my cleaning staff while neglecting to—I don't know—help make dinner, do a load of laundry, or make the bed, does not equate to a good homemaker."

I can see the hurt in her eyes, but I simply don't care. It's probably fake anyway, just like everything else about her.

"Parker, don't leave me! I'll do better, I promise! I love you!"

Those last three words force a shiver of horror down my spine, driving the final nail into our fuck buddy coffin. She might be in love with my money, but she sure as fuck doesn't love me.

Shaking my head, I roll my eyes and audibly snort out my disbelief. Then, just to be an asshole, I lean in and kiss her cheek one last time before walking away. Opening my car door, I step one leg inside before turning back to look at her. "Thanks for being such a good fuck. Better luck with your next sugar daddy."

Winking, I turn and sink into my leather seat, slamming the door behind me. Pressing start, the engine rumbles as I take a deep breath, the nasty smirk fading from my face once I'm alone. I wasn't always this way. I used to be a decent guy who cared about women and their feelings, but that was before I became rich and a string of women introduced me to the reality of having money.

Women flock to me. There's no use in denying it. But they usually want nothing more than my money, my cock, or a ticket straight to the front page of tabloids.

So I started seeking out casual hookups instead of girlfriends. But each new hookup stole a little more of my light, turning me into the asshole you see today. My mother would be ashamed if she ever saw the new me, but it's not enough to change my ways.

Nah. This works better. Maybe not for anyone around me, but it sure as fuck works for me.

Pressing my foot down on the accelerator, I glance into my rearview window, watching as the dust kicks up around my Aston Martin DB11, literally leaving Leigha in my dust. I have half a second of guilt as I watch the tears stream down her face, but it's gone in an instant when I remember why I'm starting my trip several hours earlier than planned.

The sting of pain in my chest reminds me of why it was necessary to cut ties. She never should've played that stupid rain soundtrack. Maybe then I would've kept her around for another week or so.

Oh well.

Her loss.

She knew where I stood, and it was never going to be at the altar. If she had shown any actual interest in me as a human being instead of just using me as a way to pay for her expensive as fuck lifestyle, things might have been a little different.

Unfortunately, she was just like the rest of the women I seem to gravitate toward: Crazy.

RETURNING FROM MY BUSINESS TRIP, I TURN DOWN MY DRIVEWAY and instantly know something's wrong. My skin prickles with anger as I see my pristine yard littered with beer cans and trash.

The thunder of music filtering out of my house can be heard inside my vehicle, and it's a wonder the neighbors haven't already called the cops to shut this shit down.

Whipping into my parking space, I cut the engine and storm out of my car, pulling my phone from my suit pants. Not wanting to spend more time than necessary on the phone, I give the police dispatcher my name and address and tell her there's been a break-in before hanging up.

I'm halfway up the steps when a couple stumbles out of what used to be my front door but is now a trashed piece of wood hanging off its hinge. The woman's eyes are glazed over, and she's barely holding herself up with the help of some dudebro who doesn't look old enough to be drinking.

"Great party, man," the woman slurs as they pass me, kicking a beer can across the lawn.

My heart thunders in my chest, anger coursing through my veins as I start to understand what the fuck's happening.

Leigha.

Taking the steps two at a time, I cross the threshold of my house and nearly faint from the sight in front of me. My once white walls are full of graffiti, my furniture is upturned and trashed, and there are unfamiliar faces everywhere I look.

I stomp from room to room, searching for Leigha with no success. Instead, I find a new disaster in every room I enter.

Someone hosted a fight club in my bedroom, destroying everything in their path and using my thousand dollar suits to clean up their blood.

There are holes in the drywall of every hallway.

The bathrooms are all flooded, the excess water seeping into my expensive carpet.

Empty beer cans and liquor bottles litter every available surface in the dining room, and some questionable white substances are found on the kitchen counters.

Stepping outside, I find Leigha lounging near the pool that didn't survive the hostile takeover, either. It's overflowing with shit.

Literal. Shit.

The fact that she's still lying beside the pool despite the horrid stench it's giving off serves to prove how trashed she must be.

A slow smile takes over her drunken face when she spots me seething on the patio. "Hi, honey. Welcome home," she slurs, waving her hand toward the destruction.

"Leigha, what the fuck have you done?"

"Whatever do you mean, darling? I was just working on improving my homemaker skills like you suggested," she says with an evil laugh, hiccuping halfway through her cackle.

My fuse blows as I turn my back on her and shout, "Everyone, get the fuck out of my house. Now!"

Several heads turn my way, but not a single one of them makes a move to leave. A cheer goes up in the middle of my living room, drawing my attention, and I push my way through the crowd, doing my best to reach the source of the commotion.

I stop dead in my tracks when I see some twenty-something loser pulling my family photos off the wall, smashing them to the ground as everyone cheers him on. He grabs the last image of my parents off the wall and chucks it to the floor, the glass shattering upon impact. He drops his pants and whips out his dick, and I see red.

Before I can lay my hands on the fucker that's urinating on my family's faces, I spot two police officers weaving through the crowd, bravely entering the chaos that is now my home.

Striding toward them, I meet them at the entrance of my living room, doing my best not to punch every drunk person I pass on the way.

"We received a call about a break-in. What the hell's going on here?" one of the officers shouts over the ruckus.

"Officers, thanks for coming. I need help getting everyone out of here."

"Is this your place?

"Yes," I shout over the music and yells of partygoers. "I just got home from a business trip. My ex-girlfriend broke in and threw this party."

"Is she here?" he asks while pulling handcuffs from his pocket. The second officer has moved to the stereo, pulling the plug from the wall and cutting the music off.

Just then, I hear a gasp to my right and turn to see Leigha standing in the living room, looking down at the trashed photos of my family. Her eyes are wide with shock, and her hands are covering her mouth as she drunkenly sways on her feet. A tear streaks down her cheek as she looks over at me.

"Parker—"

"Fucking save it, Leigha."

"Is that her?" the officer asks. Still glaring at Leigha, I nod my head, unable to speak past my seething rage.

He steps toward her and grabs her hands, placing them behind her back before slapping handcuffs on her. The other officer calls for backup and starts herding people out of my house.

"Parker, please, I-I'm sorry," Leigha hiccups, her tears falling faster now as she's forcibly removed from the room.

Turning my back on her, I bend down and pick up a photo of my mom and dad that managed to escape the asshole's stream of piss. Brushing a few pieces of glass off the image, I swallow past the lump of emotion lodged in my throat as I stare down at their happy faces. My dad has his arm wrapped around my mother at a hockey game, both of them smiling brightly at the camera. My brother Rory and I were there with them, but we managed to avoid the sappy-ass photo opportunity. Something we were happy about at the moment. Now? Not so much. It was the last game we went to as a family before he died that next week.

My mother's smile hasn't been the same since. He was her forever love, and he was ripped away from her too soon, leaving her with nothing but heartache and two rowdy kids to raise alone. We struggled for years before we came out on the other side, but we haven't been the same happy family since we lost the glue that held us all together.

"Sir," the police officer behind me says, breaking me out of my reverie. "I don't think you should stay here. You got somewhere you can go until this place gets fixed up?"

Still gazing at my parents' obvious love, forever captured in this now wrecked photo, I nod my head and release the image from my hand.

It floats back to the floor, coming to rest on top of all the other shattered memories from a past that was once so happy and full of love. Taking one last look at the destruction Leigha's "love" for me caused, I turn my back on it and walk out, leaving it all behind.

My parents might've had that one-of-a-kind love—the kind everyone was envious of—but it destroyed my mother in the end, stealing away her happiness. Which is yet another reason to avoid anything that resembles a relationship.

Love wrecked my mom. Just like it wrecked my whole goddamn house.

2

RILEY

"Okay, your profile is ready. Now all you have to do is click on their profile, glance through it, then swipe right if you like them, left if you don't, or swipe up if you think you should've had this man's baby inside you, like, yesterday," my best friend Maddie explains.

Nerves creep up my spine, wrapping around the base of my neck. My body breaks out in a sheen of sweat, and as much as I wish it did, my hesitation doesn't go unnoticed by Maddie. We're currently sitting in the living room of my apartment finishing off our second bottle of wine while setting me up on this new dating site called "Matches."

Turning to face me, she scans me from head to toe, frowning as she catches me wiping my sweaty palms on my pajama shorts. "Are you sure you want to do this?" she questions.

Am I?

I thought I was, but now…

"Do I want to be an almost thirty-year-old joining a dating app for the first time ever? No. Not entirely. But am I ready to meet someone and fall in love? Absolutely."

"Well then, pack your bags, biotch. We're getting you the hell out of SinglesVille!"

My chest rumbles with my laugh as I shake my head at her antics, grabbing my phone out of her hand to look through my profile she set up.

My extended stint as a single woman never bothered me before, but now that I'll be turning thirty in a few months and am as single as the day I was born, I'm starting to panic a little.

I want to fall in love and start a family sooner rather than later, and the dating pool seems to be shrinking every day, while my desire to be a mother grows tenfold with every lonely day that passes.

I knew from a very young age that I wanted to be a mother. My entire childhood was spent taking care of baby dolls—a phase I never grew out of. My first job as a teenager was babysitting the kids down the street, and I loved every single minute of it. I was born with a bone-deep passion for caring for humans and animals alike—nurturing them, watching them grow, loving them—it's all I want in life.

Unfortunately, life seems to have other plans for me. Plans that don't include getting laid regularly or bearing children.

"What if nobody's interested in me?" I ponder out loud, breathing life into my biggest insecurity.

"What, are you crazy?"

"No, I'm serious. Is it possible to never match with someone on a dating site? I mean, who would want me anyway? I constantly smell like animals, and I've been known to come home covered in questionable substances. Sexy, right? 'Hey, honey. I got shit on by three different animals today, and I think there's monkey blood in my hair. How was your day? Can I have a kiss?' Yeah. That would be a no, even for me."

"Oh, stop it. You're a total catch. You have a bangin' body, a pretty smile, and the cutest freckles. You have this whole air of innocence about you," she says, waving her hand around my face. "And you're obviously smart, given your medical degree. Yeah, if I was a guy on this app, I'd totally fuck you. After you shower, of course," Maddie says with a laugh, forcing one of my own.

Looking down, I try to see myself through her eyes. *Bangin' body?* I don't know about that.

My legs are decent, and my butt is still nice and firm. But there are curves where there shouldn't be and stretch marks I can't get rid of, no matter how often I coat myself in skin-firming lotion.

I have auburn hair that falls midway down my back, green eyes, and a smattering of freckles across my nose, cheeks, and shoulders. My mom used to call them Angel kisses. I, however, think they're annoying and try to cover them up with makeup as often as possible. At least on my face—my shoulders are left to fend for themselves. There's not enough makeup in the world to cover those babies on a daily basis.

I suppose I'm not a troll, by any means. But I'm also not sure I stand out enough to be chosen over the other gorgeous women living in San Diego. I didn't stand a chance in college when I was in the best shape of my life, so why would now be any different? Especially if even a quarter of the beautiful women in San Diego are using this dating app too.

Maddie fidgets in her spot on the couch, growing antsy the longer I hesitate. She's watching me like a hawk, waiting for me to start swiping.

Glancing at the screen, I notice the first guy that's popped up in my queue isn't all that attractive. His profile says his name is Carl. He's thirty-five, single—well, duh. Why else would he be on here?—and works at a grocery store as a cashier. I try not to judge his career choice, but I can't help but wonder if he'd be able to help support a family on that type of salary or if I'd be forced to carry the brunt of the financial load.

There are three different photos on his profile, all showing that he's pretty short and has a beer gut. Not only that, but he has a creepy porno 'stache and stringy brown hair that looks like it could use a good washing. Or twelve.

I think this is an obvious no, right? *Right.*

Maddie chimes in, asking me why I'm still giving this guy the time of day.

See? Even she agrees.

My thumb moves to the screen, ready to swipe left, when all of a sudden, something crashes into the wall next door. Jumping from the unexpected noise, my thumb jerks, swiping up instead of left.

"Crap, crap, crap. What did I do?"

Ding.

The notification alert sounds as the screen lights up with confetti, letting me know I just "Super Matched" with Carl and his porno 'stache, sending my heart into a panic. "Oh, my god, no. I didn't mean to do that!"

"Well, look on the bright side," Maddie laughs out. "You can stop worrying about never finding a match. You've only been on the site for five minutes, and you already super matched."

Turning a glare on her, I shout, "This isn't funny, Maddie! This guy looks like a total creep. How do I unmatch with him?"

I'm effectively losing my cool right now, while Maddie is just sitting there rolling with laughter, being unhelpful. There's sweat forming on my upper lip, and my knee is bouncing so hard, I'm probably creating a dent in my hardwood floor. Feel free to call me "Tigger" because my knee won't. Stop. Bouncing.

"Come on, Maddie, what do I do? How do I delete this match?"

Ding. My phone sounds, alerting me to a new message from Carl.

Maddie and I both stare down at my phone in complete horror.

Or at least my look is of horror. Maddie has her hands up to her mouth, hiding her squeal of...*delight?*

What the hell? Can't she see we're dealing with a DEFCON 2 emergency? I don't even know who this guy is! For all I know, he could be plotting my kidnapping right this very second.

Oh, god.

What if this turns into a scene from *The Silence of the Lambs,* and he starts demanding I put lotion on my skin?

Peering down at my legs, I notice they're actually a bit dry and could use another coat of lotion, but that's beside the point. I want to put lotion on because I *want* to, not because I'm being *forced* to.

Maddie is still giggling, so I toss my phone at her in a mixture of panic and irritation. It hits her forearm, causing her to fumble before she throws it back at me. When picturing setting up a dating profile, I never imagined resorting to playing hot potato with my phone while panicking over a message from a man I am abso-freaking-lutely not interested in.

Finally, after a few tosses back and forth, Maddie talks me off the ledge and convinces me to open his message. And she's right...what's the harm in seeing what he has to say? Besides, I shouldn't jump to conclusions. I may not be instantly attracted to him, but maybe he's a nice guy? He already liked my profile, and the dating pool *is* limited these days. I could probably settle for a nice guy, and maybe the attraction will grow later...much, much later. Like, after several washes of his hair and shaving his mustache off.

I open up the message, only to be appalled at the crass message he sent. What the hell does he think this is, the beginning of a porno? I guess the mustache makes sense now.

Gross.

After finishing her laughing fit, Maddie helps me unmatch and block the guy's profile. Done with all the excitement for the evening, I put my phone down on the coffee table, trading it for my nice, full glass of moscato.

Maddie sighs and leans back against the couch, taking her own healthy sip of wine.

"So what type of man do you want to match with? Like, if you came across a guy that was a 'no-brainer,' what would his profile look like to you?"

I sit back and ponder her question while taking a few sips of my wine.

"Who would my perfect match be? Well—" I start before she cuts me off with a laugh.

"No man is perfect. Get that out of your head right now, and you'll be less disappointed in the long run. Trust me."

"Yeah, yeah, whatever. *My* version of perfect would be someone a little older than me. Preferably with a decent career, a sense of stability, and no previous marriages or kids. He'd be intelligent. Charming. Goal-driven. Good looking, obviously. I want to find someone that jumps off that screen screaming, 'I'm the guy for you!' Does that make sense?"

Maddie barks out another laugh and shakes her head at me. "Honey. If you find a man like that, make sure he has a twin brother. I could use a little loving too."

"Oh, please. You get enough 'loving' for the both of us combined."

"Not from anyone that matters," she mutters under her breath, bringing her glass of wine to her mouth and polishing it off.

Her comment confuses me, but before I can question it, she places her wine glass on the coffee table and stands. She has a crazy work schedule, being an emergency room nurse and all, so I know she needs to head home and get some sleep before her early shift tomorrow.

With a quick hug, she wishes me luck, tells me to keep her

updated, and heads out, leaving me to question whether this dating app was a good idea after all.

THE NEXT DAY AS I'M WALKING INTO WORK, I FEEL A SURGE OF positive energy. It's a beautiful spring morning, and I can't wait for my first appointment of the day. I'm one of four full-time veterinarians at the Shoreline Safari Zoo in San Diego, and today I get to perform the first check-up on our new tiger cubs, Mikko and Zeke.

After getting settled into my office, I quickly go through my work emails to see if any immediate cases need to be added to my schedule or if there are any updates on our pregnant giraffe. She's due any day now, and I hope I'll be working when she goes into labor. Watching a new life begin is one of my favorite parts of my job, but unfortunately, it doesn't look like that'll be today.

Once my inbox has been thoroughly sorted and my schedule is set for the day, I gather my phone, lab coat, and clipboard and head to my first appointment.

Allie, my friend and veterinary technician, is busy setting things up when I enter the room, but she turns and smiles when she hears me walk in. Her beautiful smile is so big, the skin at the corners of her bright blue eyes crinkles with happiness. Her naturally blond hair is pulled up into a perfectly styled messy bun—something I've never been able to pull off—and her face is free of any makeup, thanks to her flawless skin. She's a petite little thing, my five-foot-four height towering over her four-foot-six, slender frame. A little ray of sunshine, she's one of the reasons I love my job. We've been working together for a year now, and I consider her to be one of my best friends, despite me technically being her boss.

Mikko and Zeke are brought into the room by their caretakers, and we start the process of administering their check-up. As we work, I fill her in on last night.

"So...I did something potentially crazy."

"Oh, boy. What'd you do?"

"I finally got tired of being single and let Maddie set me up on that new dating site, 'Matches.' I haven't matched with anybody yet, at least not intentionally, but I'm excited to see where it goes!"

"Oh, wow! That's exciting. I never really took you as the dating app type, but hopefully you find what you're looking for."

"Yeah, I was a little skeptical too. But I'm almost thirty and haven't met anyone in a natural setting, so why not give it a shot, you know?"

Mikko is currently switching back and forth between taking swipes at my stethoscope and trying to gnaw my hand off while I check his heart rate. Zeke, on the other hand, is climbing Allie like a tree, sweetly trying to lick her face.

"I understand. It's tough out there in today's dating world," Allie says while trying to place Zeke back on the exam table. "I'm really lucky to have Trevor. Did you know we met on a dating site?"

My forehead scrunches in confusion. I knew they were college sweethearts, but I always assumed they met at a college party or something.

"No, I didn't know that, but I'm glad to know it's possible. I've always admired your relationship. You both are always so happy together and make it seem so easy."

"Of course, there's hope. But don't be fooled; it wasn't always this easy. We faced a unique set of problems due to meeting on a dating site."

My nerves spike again, wondering how dating on an app would be different than meeting someone on my own. I'm so far removed from the dating world, I don't even know what to expect. "Oh? Like what?"

"Well, I was always worried he was still using the app to keep his options open, and I think we both went through the initial fear that we weren't who we said we were in our profiles. Cat-fishing is a real problem, so make sure you go into this with open eyes."

"That's fair. But can't that also happen without an app?"

"Of course. It's just easier when you're hiding behind a screen, ya know? If you match with someone, make sure you always, always, always meet the guy in public for the first few dates, just to be safe. Be smart about it, but have fun while you're at it. You never know who you could meet."

Nodding my head, I smile and thank her, storing away her advice for future use. We fall into a natural silence as we focus our attention on the adventurous cubs, doing our best to stay on schedule.

One appointment quickly flows into another, and before I know it, another grueling day of work has come to an end. Finished with my end-of-day notes, I hop in my car and slowly cross town, cursing the heavy traffic like always.

Once I finally make it home, I kick off my dirty scrubs that smell like the zoo and change into a tank top before raiding my dresser drawer, looking for my favorite cotton shorts. I have an ungodly extensive collection of silly cartoon pajamas, but I finally find my favorite ones and tug them on. They were a gift from Maddie and are covered in cacti with the words "Pain in the Rear" across my butt, making me laugh every time I wear them.

I grab my leftover chicken and rice from the fridge and reheat it while picking up my phone, checking the dating app to see if I have any new matches.

Once the home page of the app loads, my stomach sinks to the floor. The screen flashes, showing "Zero New Matches." An overwhelming sense of disappointment grips my heart as I read those words, so I pick my phone up and call Maddie to see what she thinks of this update. *Or lack-of, I guess.*

"Hey, Riles, I was just thinking about you. How many dates do you have lined up? Do I need to buy you a bat so you can start fighting off all the men who want that hot ass of yours?"

Cringing, I interrupt her tangent before she digs the hole any deeper. "Maddie, stop. I haven't gotten a single match. I told you this was a bad idea."

"Uh...what? Not a single match? Are you sure you're doing it right? How many men have you swiped right on?"

"Um...only one, I think. But he was so cute! And he loves animals, which is obviously a good match for me."

The other end of the line falls silent, and I have to pull the phone away from my ear to make sure I haven't dropped the call.

"Maddie? Are you still there?"

"Um, yeah. I'm here, Riles. Did you say you've only swiped right on *one* guy...?"

"Well, yeah. How many guys do I need? I'm just looking for 'The One,' you know?"

"Rii-leyyy," Maddie sighs, dragging out my name. "That's not how this works. You'll probably have to go on several dates before you meet the right guy. You can't limit yourself to just *one* guy in the beginning. That's like...only picking one donut at the bakery after seeing several different kinds, only to get home and take a bite out of the donut and realize you picked the wrong one, and it tastes horrible. Now you're stuck at home with no donuts. You can't do that. You have to sample several donuts *at* the bakery before picking your favorite. Then you still have to buy more than one. The more donuts, the better. Duh. Everyone knows that."

Huh. She has a point. Also, I should totally pick up donuts tomorrow morning for the clinic. That'd be a nice little treat.

But anyway, "Crap, you're right. I guess I didn't think of it that way. I'll look through a few more profiles tonight."

"You're damn right, I'm right! Alright, I gotta go. There's a tub of ice cream calling my name, and you have some swiping to do. Catch ya later, Sexy Beast."

Laughing, I set my phone down after I hear the call end. Finishing up the last few bites of my dinner, I grab a glass of wine, filling it to the rim before heading to the bathroom to run my nightly bath.

Pouring a generous amount of vanilla and lavender bubble bath into the tub, I light a few candles to get in the right frame of mind for picking out a potential future husband. After making sure my wine is easy to reach, I lower myself into the steaming hot water, instantly sighing as relaxation takes over.

While soaking, I pull up the app and start reading through the profiles as they pop up.

First up, "Hmmm. Stanley," I ponder out loud, talking to myself. "Not bad looking. Decent job. *Oh.* He has a kid. A cute kid, but still. That's not really what I'm looking for."

Don't get me wrong, I love kids. But I wouldn't just be dating the man and his child; I'd be dating him, his kid, and the kid's mother—assuming she's still part of the picture. She'll always be a part of their life, and she should be, but I don't want to spend my time competing against a woman I know I'll never win against. I've spent far too long doing that already. I don't want to do it forever.

Grabbing my glass, I take a sip of my moscato before pulling up the next profile.

"Thomas. Oh. Well, that's an...interesting beard. What's up with men and their weird facial hair these days?" Scrolling to the bottom of his profile, I find a hidden nugget of information. "Ughhh, no job. Can't have that."

I swipe left and continue to swipe through a few more

profiles, taking several gulps of my wine—each bigger than the last—losing interest the longer I swipe.

"Barney? What the heck kind of name is that?" I question, my voice bouncing off the walls of my bathroom. "I don't want to be thinking of a big purple dinosaur every time I yell his name out during sex. Hello, mood killer." *Goodbye.*

After looking through several more profiles without a single swipe right, I get discouraged and drain the tub, opting to call it a night and take my tipsy ass to bed.

3
PARKER

Standing in my temporary apartment, I raise the glass of bourbon to my lips, using the burn of alcohol to mask the irritation of being in an unfamiliar place.

In terms of a place to live, it's not terrible, considering the whole two minutes I gave my assistant to find the place. She could've done worse, just to spite me, but I'm glad she didn't. She will be, too, when she sees the bonus on her next check.

That being said, it's still a shitty place to be in. The new couch is uncomfortable, the layout is smaller than I'm used to, and the walls are basically paper-thin. Rhett helped me move this couch in yesterday and damaged the drywall when he carelessly bumped it into the wall.

I'm also used to my privacy, which is severely lacking here. If I have to listen to my next-door neighbor's shitty taste in music for the next month, I might be likely to set the place on fire.

How the hell did I end up here?

I'll tell ya how—fucking women. Good-for-nothing, crazy-as-hell women.

At this point, I'm not any better. I'm the fucking dumbass that keeps giving women chances they don't deserve.

The police dragged Leigha out of my destroyed home that night, but for some idiotic reason, I decided not to press charges on the condition she be shipped off to rehab, followed by counseling to deal with her...*issues.* I knew she had a slight drinking problem, so that's on me. But I didn't realize she had levels of craziness this high until I walked into the mass destruction she orchestrated.

So her ass is sitting in some posh rehab facility meant for celebrities while I had to relocate to a temporary apartment so my house could be completely remodeled. Not to mention the underground pool. Thanks to the fuckers who used it as a giant toilet, the filtration system was destroyed beyond fixing, rendering the entire pool useless. Who fucking knows how long it will take to rip that out and replace it with a new, shit-less oasis.

The thing better rival a goddamn luxury resort for the trouble it's causing. Not that I can blame anybody—except fucking Leigha—I didn't want to drain the shit-filled water, either.

On the bright side, when all is said and done, the remodel will triple the value of my home. I'd be tempted to send Leigha a thank-you note once it's completed, but she'd probably misconstrue the gesture as an invitation to slip her crazy ass back into my life.

Hard pass.

On some rational level, I can understand why she did what she did. I was a dick for how I dumped her. But that's not breaking news. I was an asshole during our entire stint as fuck buddies, and I'll continue to be an asshole if it keeps me from delusional women that believe in the "L" word. I don't have time for scorned heart bullshit.

But despite how I treated her, it wasn't grounds for destroying my whole house. Maybe a suit or two. Hell, I could even forgive her for trashing my mattress, or dumping out all my dressers, like a normal human might do after a "break-up." That would be easier to clean up. Cheaper too.

But no, she had to go full-on psycho and take it out on the whole house. And regardless of how clearly I understand that alcohol played a part in her decision, it doesn't make it forgivable.

An obnoxious knock lures me out of my miserable sulking. Opening the door, I come face-to-face with Tweedledee, making me wish I would've ignored the knock. Sulking in misery would've been better than having to deal with company.

Wesley—otherwise known as Tweedledee—forces himself past me, stumbling through my entryway.

"What's up, man? Brought beer."

With a heavy sigh, I flick the door closed, following after him. "What the hell are you doing here?"

"I told you," he jests, raising his hand holding the case of alcohol. "I brought beer."

Jesus, this fucking idiot. Why am I even friends with him?

"Why?" I demand, my voice dripping with irritation.

He stops, his head tilting to the side as he considers my question. "Huh. I don't know. I guess I decided spending my night with my grumpy-ass friend was better than sitting at home alone."

"Feel free to change your mind. Door's right where we left it," I huff, my thumb pointing behind me. His annoyingly loud laugh makes me roll my eyes. I wasn't kidding.

He plops down on my couch, pulls a beer out of the box, and pops the top off, flicking the lid to the floor.

"How'd you find my place?"

He picks up my remote, pointing it at my flatscreen. It powers on, the screen coming to life with the latest sports highlight reel.

"Rhett gave me directions. I invited Colton, but the loser was busy with work."

Fucking Rhett.

Wes, Rhett, Colton, and I all met in college, back when I was more...what's the term the guys use? Oh, yeah. *Fun.*

Now I can't seem to get rid of them, no matter how much of an asshole I am. I shouldn't complain, honestly. Running my own multibillion-dollar company doesn't leave much time for me to relax, but when I do, the boys are always there, pulling me into their immature bullshit. *Like now.*

Accepting defeat, I settle on the other end of my couch, kicking my feet up onto the coffee table.

"Heard about Leigha. Bummer, man."

Not wanting to talk about it, I simply grunt, my arms folding against my chest as I recline in my seat. The TV screen flashes with game updates from around the National Hockey League, catching Wesley's attention, but not for long.

"Hey, I hooked up with a fuck-hot model last week. Girl was wild and just your type. Want me to send her your way?"

"Hard fucking pass. I'm done with women."

"The fuck does that mean?" he questions like the idiot he is.

"It means I'm done with women. Done dating. Done fucking. Done mingling. Done with it all. If it's not my hand, I don't fucking want it."

Wes sits there silently, his forehead furrowed in confusion as he stares at me. He waits for me to say I'm joking, but I'm not. Up until last week, I thought I was a professional at picking out women who were fine with no-strings-attached sex.

Fuck, was I wrong.

Now I need a goddamn break from crazy. So from here on out, it's strictly a life of celibacy for this asshole and his palm.

Shaking his head, Wes declares, "Well...that sounds fucking stupid."

My chest vibrates as a sarcastic laugh bursts from my mouth. I knew he wouldn't understand. Rhett wouldn't, either. Colton is probably the only one in our group with enough sense to understand why I need to steer clear of all women for the foreseeable future.

Tipping my glass of bourbon up, I swallow the last of my smooth liquor, the ice in the glass clinking as I place it on my side table. "Mark my fucking words. You keep sticking your dick in everything that breathes, and you're going to reach a day you regret it too."

"Hey, now," he protests, bringing his palms up in a halting gesture. "I have more standards than just that. They have to breathe *and* have a pussy." Being the douchebag that he is, he breaks out in obnoxious laughter, making me wish he'd just fucking leave already.

4
PARKER

I'm sitting at my desk, scanning through last quarter's fiscal reports, when a sharp knock on my office door breaks my concentration. The door creaks open and Haylee, my personal assistant, pops her head into the room.

"Have you seen the tabloids?"

Goddamn it. The fucking tabloids. Apparently, I was wrong when I said this shit wasn't breaking news. I should've known it would only be a matter of time before it blew up in my face.

"Of course I have, Haylee. Some people make it their fucking mission to make sure I see them," I sneer, my voice dripping with sarcasm as I toss the reports back down to my desk.

She rolls her eyes and dishes my shit right back to me. "Just wanted to make sure you were aware the city of San Diego still sees you as their resident asshole. Congratulations! Title is still yours."

The corner of my mouth tugs up in a slight, unwanted smirk at her comment. Her snark, although somewhat annoying, is one of many reasons she's the best PA I've had in years. She doesn't take crap from anybody—myself included—and she never drops the ball, no matter how hectic things get around here.

She's never late, rarely takes a day off, and her loyalty knows no bounds.

It helps that she's not half bad to look at, either. With her long blond hair, big blue eyes, shapely legs, and a round ass constantly hugged by tight skirts, she's a fucking bombshell, alright. But I value her skill set and loyalty over her looks any—and every— day of the week.

Thank fuck, her sex appeal never affects our work. Hell, she's never even hit on me. Not once. If I hadn't caught her mooning over photos of the Hemsworth brothers a few months back, I'd assume she was into women.

But in all reality, her refusal to hit on me is yet another plus in her column. In the early years of starting my company, I had a few too many assistants that couldn't get a single thing done because they were too busy trying to get their hands down my pants.

I'll admit, some of them succeeded in doing so right before they were shown the door. That led to a few HR nightmares, but damn. I needed someone to keep my schedule and do my busywork, not throw themselves at me and sabotage my company with their lack of work ethic.

But other than the occasional ass-ogling, she's never shown any interest, which is why we work so well together.

Doesn't mean she escapes my ray of fucking sunshine personality, though. "Shouldn't you be working? I'm not paying you to read trashy magazines," I bark out in an angry tone.

She smiles and bats her eyelashes, her tone coated in false sweetness when she replies, "It's lunchtime. You're not paying me regardless of what I'm doing."

Point made.

With that, she leaves, slamming my door behind her. Leaning my elbows on my desk, my head falls to my hands, my fingers doing their best to massage away the headache that's brewing.

I fucking knew the tabloids would paint me as the bad guy here, despite the fact it's my house that was demolished. Doesn't matter what the fuck I do, I'll always be the bad guy, which is why it's so much easier to just play the part at this point.

I lean back in my office chair before swiveling around to face my floor-to-ceiling windows. Being the owner of my own company affords me some fan-fucking-tastic perks, one of which is this view. I can sit and watch the ocean waves crashing against the shoreline from my corner office on the forty-third floor of my building.

As I study the rhythmic motion of the ocean in an attempt to calm down, I fall into deep thought about the past.

The last few years haven't been easy, but all the long days, hard work, and thousands of headaches have definitely paid off.

Ten years ago, I was fresh out of college, working as an assistant at Fast Fit—a floundering outdoor sportswear company. I had so many ideas on how to pull the company back up into the black, saving them from going bankrupt.

Unfortunately, my dumbass of a boss was packed to the brim with stubborn pride and refused to take any advice from a "young peon straight out of college that wouldn't know how to find his way out of a wet paper sack using a flashlight and a map."

The company went under two months later and had to close its doors. I, however, went on to use my "young peon" ideas to start Parker Solutions, a consulting company that specializes in business management. We do everything from restructuring and rebranding to calculating financial risks. And when a company is beyond saving, I simply buy them out, liquidate their assets, and rebuild from the ground up. But that rarely happens. I'm a genius when it comes to dissecting an issue until I find a solution.

Since the start of my company, I've saved thousands of businesses from having to close their doors. And last time I checked, Parker Solutions was worth billions while my old boss is working on the ground level of a business that has already sought me out for help. *Twice.* He barely clears $60K a year, and I'm raking that in every other week.

Guess he should've listened to this young peon's ideas. He could've still been at the head of his company instead of barely making a livable wage in San Diego. *Who's the peon now, fucker?*

My phone rings, the shrill tone vibrating against the walls of my office, breaking me out of my reverie. Swiveling around, I snatch up the phone, not bothering to check the caller ID.

"Parker," I growl out, barely concealing the irritation I'm feeling.

"Now, is that any way to answer your phone? What if I was a high-profile client?"

My shoulders dip in a heavy sigh, my mother's familiar voice an instant calming balm.

"Sorry, Mom. Caught me at a bad time."

"Are you okay? Your brother and I heard about Leigha. So sorry, dear."

"Heard about it or read about it?" I snap, knowing they most likely saw the fuckery in the tabloids.

"Watch your tone, Mister," my mom chides, filling me with shame. She doesn't deserve my wrath, nor is she to blame for my troubles. But that doesn't lessen the embarrassment of my mother seeing my failures splashed across every tabloid in the city. "If you must know, I heard from your brother. I don't know how he found out, but you know I don't pay any mind to those trashy magazines."

"I know, I'm sorry. I didn't mean to snap at you," I sigh, my fingers pinching the bridge of my nose.

"Rory said he knew of an excellent construction crew if you need one. Said he's used them before, and they'd be perfect for the job. Costly Construction. Have you heard of them?"

"No, and what the hell kind of name is that?" My eyes narrow at the suggestion, suspicion trickling through my veins. I know my mom just wants to fix things, but it's a well-known fact that my brother and I don't get along these days, so why would he be suggesting anything that would help me?

"I don't know, but he's just trying to help. Please let him," she begs. "Maybe this is his attempt to mend the broken bridge between you two."

Warning bells sound in my head, telling me this is a bad idea, but I'd do anything to please my mom. I know she hates that Rory and I no longer get along, so if using a stupid-ass construction crew with a stupid-ass name will make her happy, I'll do it. Besides, maybe she's right, and he really is coming to his senses. I highly doubt it, but you never know.

"Okay, Mom. I'll give them a call."

"Thanks, honey. Anyway, you'll never guess who I ran into the other day!"

Her excitement is practically palpable through the phone, and a low growl rumbles up my throat, already knowing where she's going with this. I don't give a fuck who she ran into. It's not happening.

"No."

"What?" she asks with fake innocence.

"Don't even go there, Mom. I'm not meeting anyone."

"Parker, come on. Let me set you up with a nice girl."

I love her, but her whining has zero effect on me right now. Especially after the last woman she tried to set me up with. "Thanks, but no."

"Why not? My heart is just sick over what these women have been putting you through lately. Let me find you a nice, good girl. I just want to see you happy and loved."

"Do you not love me?" I question sarcastically, causing her to huff out in annoyance.

"Of course I do, Parker, but—"

"Then that's all I fucking need," I insist, cutting her off.

"Parker! Watch your language."

Sighing, I bite my tongue at her angry tone. I'm a grown-ass man and should be able to say whatever the hell I want, but apparently, my mother doesn't see it that way. She seems to hold this idea that I'm never too old to have my ass whooped, despite the fact I have over a foot and a hundred pounds on her.

Haylee knocks on my door and peeks inside, tapping her wrist while mouthing the word "meeting." Grateful for an excuse to end this train wreck of a conversation, I tip my head up in acknowledgment.

"Sorry, Mom, I have to go. I have a meeting in five. Please don't worry about me, I'll be just fine on my own. Have a good rest of your day. Love you."

Sighing softly, she concedes, "Okay. Love you too, honey."

The phone clicks off, and I stand, gathering everything I'll need for my meeting in the conference room. I'm halfway to the door before guilt assaults my conscience. My mother is the most important person in my life, and despite how shitty my life is right now, she didn't deserve my attitude on the phone.

Changing course, I walk back to my desk, knowing full-well I'll be late for my meeting, but I don't give a fuck. They'll either wait, or they won't—whatever. This is more important.

Pulling up the website for a trusted flower shop, I scour their page, a small smile tugging on my lips as I find what I need. It's a simple bouquet of white and yellow daisies in a bright yellow coffee cup. There's a smiley face painted on the side of the mug, which is cheesy as fuck, but I know my mother will love it.

I have half a second of hesitation, considering sending her a bouquet of roses or something more expensive like she deserves, but it's pointless. They wouldn't mean the same.

Ever since my dad died, I've been buying my mother daisies. I still remember coming home from school one day shortly after dad passed. My mom had fresh tear tracks staining her cheeks, but she did her best to hide her sadness from us. Not knowing what to do, I hugged her and ran outside to play, leaving her to grieve in peace.

I was kicking a soccer ball with Rory when I noticed the neighbor's bed of flowers on the side of their house. With my mother's sadness at the forefront of my mind, an idea had sparked to life.

At least once a month, our dad would bring home beautiful flower arrangements. He'd walk in, hand them to our mom, and kiss her on her cheek before whispering in her ear. Her face would light up with a smile, and though I always thought it was gross as a kid, I loved that she was so happy.

Wanting to bring a smile back to my mother's face, I snuck next door and plucked a few flowers from their garden. They were nothing like what our father used to bring home, but at twelve years old, I wasn't in a position to do better. I ran inside, finding my mother in the kitchen. I tapped on her shoulder and handed her the flowers when she turned around, a mask of innocence covering my face. She gasped with surprise, her hand shaking as she grabbed the pathetic excuse for a bouquet. I was still too short to reach her cheek at the time, so I wrapped my arms around her in a tight hug and whispered, "Love you, Mom."

She smiled and told me she loved me too, and ever since then, I've been sending her daisies. As much as I want to spoil her with something different, it's not the price of the bouquet she loves. It's the sentiment and the memories they provide. The reminder that she's loved. Besides, roses were her and dad's thing. Daisies are ours.

Clicking order, I stand and head out of my office, ready to get back to work. Regardless of whatever else this day brings, at least I'll know my mother is smiling.

5

RILEY

Walking into the restaurant for my date, I immediately spot Oliver. He's dressed to impress in a full suit with a silk button-up shirt underneath. A little flashy for my taste, but at least he resembles his photos on his profile.

He sees me standing here and walks toward me, going straight in for the hug. While he's attractive and smells nice, I stiffen a little. A handshake would've been more natural, especially since we barely know each other.

After being guided to our table by the hostess, we settle into our seats. Looking around the restaurant, I can't help but notice the romantic ambiance. It's adorable, but I wonder if Oliver is a frequent flyer at this cute little date-night restaurant or if it's his first time here too.

"Thanks for agreeing to meet me tonight for dinner. I'm so sorry I had to cancel last night, but I'm thrilled we were able to reschedule so quickly. I appreciate you being so understanding of my needs."

"Of course. It was no problem," I lie. When he texted me twenty minutes before our date last night, claiming to have an emergency, I was incredibly annoyed. After a week of agonized waiting, Oliver was my very first match on the dating app. The level of excitement I experienced when the notification for a new match crossed my phone was downright embarrassing. Then I wasted time shaving my legs and getting dressed up, just to sit at home alone when he asked to reschedule. He's lucky I was desperate to get back into the world of dating. Otherwise, I would have told him where to shove it.

"Did everything turn out okay with your emergency?" I ask with mock sweetness, trying to hide my annoyance.

"Oh, yes. It was touch and go for a while there, but I was able to pay a little extra to ensure my nail technician could squeeze me in on such short notice."

Um...*what?* Did he just say...*nail technician?*

"I'm sorry, I must have misunderstood you. Surely you don't mean you canceled our date to go to a nail salon?"

Oliver looks at me with a serious expression, frantically nodding his head. "Oh, yes. I was leaving work when I noticed my nails were long enough to snag my custom-tailored silk work shirt. And I can't have that! I live and die by my nail trimming schedule. My nail technician, Shannon, is usually on top of these things. She schedules my mani-pedis regularly enough that I rarely have to worry about this type of situation occurring. But she dropped the ball this month. Can you believe that? How unprofessional. I had to dock her tip by a whole five dollars."

Staring at him with a blank expression, I have to actively concentrate on closing my gaping mouth. This has to be some sort of prank, right? I've never heard of someone being so high maintenance they had to cancel a date to get a manicure.

"Um, sure," I stutter out, barely concealing my disgust.

Trying to find some common ground, I suggest, "Maybe if things go well between us, we can go to the nail salon together. I haven't had a pedicure in so long, I could probably use one."

"Oh, absolutely not. I like to go by myself. It's my 'me time.'

Besides, I have to concentrate on what Shannon is doing. If I'm going to pay that much to have my nails done, they better be up to my standards, you know? Having a date at the nail salon would just distract me from what's really important—my nails."

My forehead starts to cramp from being furrowed for so long, so I clear my throat and try to steer the conversation in a different —less weird—direction.

"Okay. So…your dating profile says you work at Golden Health Enterprises? Tell me more about that. Do you conduct medical research? Or are you on the marketing side of the business?"

"Actually, I'm the Waste Management Connoisseur," he answers smugly.

"Oh, that's fascinating! What does that entail, exactly?"

He sits up, proudly puffing out his chest while saying, "I handle the dumping of every trash can in the building. When the researchers have trash they need removed, they call me. When the CEO requires a fresh liner for his waste paper basket, I'm his guy. When the President of the Board is stopping by, and the company needs to make sure the building is in tip-top shape and void of all trash, they bring me in. I'm kind of a big deal."

"Oh. So you're a garbageman? You have to wear custom-tailored silk shirts for that?"

"No, no. Not a garbageman. I'm levels above that. I'm the Waste Management Connoisseur of Golden Health Enterprises. I take my position very seriously, and I make sure to dress the part."

Again, with the smug smile. *Is this guy for real?*

"Okay, let me get this straight. You dump people's trash. Correct?"

"Yes, that's basically what I do, if you must play it down."

"Alright, so…You're a garbageman. In a fancy shirt."

Oliver's smug smile drops completely, replaced by a stern

glare. "No. Are you hard of hearing? That's not my title at all. Say it with me. Waste. Management. Connoisseur."

Excuse my French, but.

This. Motherfucker.

You have got to be kidding me with this shit. He's a—say it with me—Garbage. Man.

Don't get me wrong, I have nothing against that profession. Every major company needs them, and I highly respect them for the job they do.

In fact, I absolutely adore our recycling and garbage removal crew at the zoo. I would not want their job, but they always do it with a smile and a friendly joke or two when they pass by. All that trash baking in the San Diego sun? Trust me, it's hard work keeping the zoo from smelling like a garbage dump mixed with animal feces, and I commend them for their efforts.

But, if you're a garbageman, just own it. There's no need to lie or talk yourself up. I would have respected him for at least having a job he clearly enjoys.

"Okay. You're a Waste Management Connoisseur. In a fancy shirt. Got it. Why don't we go ahead and order our food."

Where the hell is our waitress?

I need food and wine if I'm going to finish this date. In fact, maybe I should forego food and drink my dinner instead. Might make this date a little more bearable.

Catching the attention of our waitress, she scurries over to take our order. I choose the chicken parmigiana and order a bottle of their house merlot. After giving me a side-eye for asking for a bottle rather than a glass, Oliver requests the eggplant lasagna and makes a big deal about sticking with water.

The waitress leaves our table, and I silently pray she brings the bottle of wine over right away.

Risking a glance at Oliver, I see he's sitting there staring at me with a crazed smile. I'm not sure if he's trying to make me uncomfortable or not, but he's excelling at it.

Thankfully, the waitress returns to our table with the bottle of wine and pours my first glass for me, telling me our food shouldn't take too long. Right as I'm picking up my glass to try the wine, Oliver clears his throat rather loudly.

"Are you sure you should be drinking a whole bottle of wine tonight? It is a work night, you know."

What is he, my mother? "Thanks for your concern, but I think I'll be alright. The carbs in my dinner should balance out the wine."

"Oh, that's right. You ordered the chicken parmigiana. Maybe you would have been better off ordering the eggplant parmigiana? Fewer carbs, you know. It would do wonders for your waistline."

Sucking in a deep breath, my eyes widen at his bold statement.

"I'm sorry, what are you implying?" *Is this guy trying to get smacked?*

"Oh, nothing! If you're happy with your current waistline, then, by all means, eat the carbs."

He picks up his glass of water and tries to initiate a cheers with my glass of wine, but since I'm already taking a drink, all he does is smash my glass into my mouth—hitting my teeth with the rim.

"Mmph," I groan out as wine dribbles down my chin from the impact.

"Oh, sorry. I didn't realize your teeth were so big. Otherwise, I obviously would have waited," he says as I do my best to clean the wine off my chin.

Thankfully, our waitress arrives right then, bringing our food and an extra napkin to clean up the rest of the wine that was unfortunately wasted in our mishap. She tops my wine glass off before scurrying away from the table, probably sensing that this is a date from hell.

As we dig into our meal—which is carbolicious, by the way—the conversation turns to slightly less annoying topics. Emphasis on slightly.

Oliver tells me all about his life growing up.

Where he got his trash compactor.

What TV shows he's currently watching.

The best trash bags to use.

Where he does his clothes shopping.

Which scented bags are best for masking the smell of trash.

I've mostly been sipping wine like it's a bottomless glass, nodding my head and wondering how fast I can unmatch with this guy. *Is it too impolite to just get up and walk away?* Probably.

After a few seconds of unnatural silence, I look up and notice Oliver's attention is glued to a lady walking by our table. Or, more aptly, glued to her feet.

He looks a little green around the gills when he turns his attention back to me. "Did you see her toenails?"

Oh, boy. Here we go. "No, I didn't. Was there something wrong with them?"

I'm not sure he can nod his head any harder, but he might try. I wouldn't put it past him.

"Uhm, yeah! How could you not notice? Her toenail polish is chipping so bad, she might as well not be wearing any. What an eye-sore. Can't she see people are trying to eat here?"

Oh. My. Gosh!

I'm mortified for this guy. What is his obsession with nails? I thought he was just obsessed over his own nails, but this is a step past the level of crazy I'm willing to deal with.

Shoveling my food into my mouth, I try to finish my meal in a hurry, wanting to get out of here as soon as possible.

"Can I see your toenails?"

Did you hear that? The sound of a record scratching?

Glancing around, I make sure I didn't miss a DJ setting up in the corner of the restaurant.

Nope. No DJ. It was all in my head.

"Um. I don't think that's really appropriate right now."

"Well, when else are you going to show me your toenails? I need to make sure you take good care of your nails before committing to a second date or any type of future with you. I know you're probably already planning our wedding, but I can't move forward with you until I see the appearance of your toenails."

"Trust me, I don't think it's going to be an issue."

"Why? Did you just have a pedicure done? What color did you choose for your nails?"

"No, no pedicure. Like I said earlier, I haven't gotten my nails done in a long time. My job doesn't allow me to wear nail polish because it could be harmful to the animals if there was an emergency, and I didn't have time to grab surgical gloves. So I just don't wear nail polish at all. Not even on my toes. Saves time and money."

Oliver looks crestfallen at my lack of toenail polish, but it's me that's totally taken back by his next statement.

"Well, I could help you find a new job? Something less hostile that doesn't keep you from taking care of your nails. I'm kind of an expert on finding wonderful jobs."

No words. There are absolutely *no* words that could possibly come out of my mouth right now that my mother would approve of.

"Um. Thanks, but I think I'll stick with my job."

The waitress finally comes around to collect our dinner plates and asks if we would like to order dessert. I want to end this date sooner rather than later, but I've been eyeing the desserts all night. And at this point, what're another fifteen or twenty minutes added to this horrendous date?

"Oh, the triple-layered coconut cake looked delicious, but I'm not sure I could finish the entire slice. What do you think, Oliver? Would you like to split a slice?"

Oliver looks at me with utter disgust before saying, "Coconut shavings look like nail clippings, and I absolutely will not put something so grotesque into my mouth."

I. Am. Speechless.

Hell, even the waitress looks mildly disgusted when I look at her.

"You know what? I think we'll just take the check. Thanks."

Oliver agrees, nodding his head enthusiastically like he's the one that's suffered through the worst date of his life. Before the waitress can leave the table, Oliver grabs her attention again.

"Make sure you split the check down the middle. I may be the Waste Management Connoisseur at Golden Health Enterprises, but I'm still not making the big bucks just yet."

Did he just wink at me? I have to get out of here.

6

RILEY

Walking through the apartment door after my date from hell, I kick my heeled boots off and head to the bathroom. My feet are killing me, and I can't wait to soak in the tub. As I'm walking down the hallway to start my bath, my phone dings with a new message from the dating app.

I open up the app to see who's messaging me and instantly regret doing so, the sensation of heavy rocks dropping to the bottom of my stomach assaulting me. Praying that he's just messaging me to tell me there won't be a second date, I open the message and read it through squinted eyes—as if that could possibly make his message any easier to stomach.

Oliver: *We never did get the chance to take a peek at your toenails. Would you mind sending me a photo of your feet? I want to make sure there's nothing funky going on down there before scheduling our next date.*

Ugh. I think I just threw up in my mouth a little bit.

Although, that could just be a side effect of too much wine. Either way, he can't seriously be thinking we'll be going on a second date, can he? He tried to lean in for a kiss as we were standing in front of the restaurant, and I stepped back so fast I nearly landed on my ass. That should have been a clear sign I wasn't interested, right? Well, obviously not.

Riley: *I'm sorry, Oliver. There won't be a second date for us. I don't think we were a good fit, but I wish you all the best with your future dates. I'm sure there's a woman out there for you with beautiful toenails. Good luck!*

As soon as I see the message has been read, I hurry and exit out of the chat box and bring up his profile, hitting the unmatch button.

Looking at the clock, I wonder if Maddie is still awake. I bet she'd love this story.

Riley: *Are you up?*

As I wait for her to respond, I run my bath, pouring in more lavender bath salts than necessary. I'm in definite need of some stress release, and apparently, I won't be getting that from the male variety tonight. Not that I was really aiming for that, though.

Okay, yes. I kind of was.

It's been way too long since I've seen any romantic action. And I don't just mean a few months. I'm talking several years. So I was hoping tonight would be full of romance, caressing touches, and soft kisses that lead to second or maybe even third base.

Instead, I was faced with…*Oliver.*

My phone dings with a text from Maddie, saving me from my current misery.

Maddie: *Yeah, I'm up. But if this is your version of a booty call, I'm sorry to tell you I still don't swing that way. You're gonna need to work on your game a little more if you really want to hook this sexy fish.*

Riley: *LOL. Don't worry. Just because I'm still not getting any doesn't mean I'm ready to convert to lady love just yet. Although, after the disastrous date I just went on, I might be closer than ever to making that leap.*

The sleepy effects of wine are slowly taking over, so I drain the dirty water and turn the shower on to quickly wash my hair and body before stepping out of the tub. Just then, my phone dings with another incoming text.

Maddie: Disastrous date, you say? Hold on, I need popcorn for this.

Maddie: Actually, why don't we get together for a girls' night, and you can remind me why I'm happily single then.

Riley: That's a fantastic idea! I have to work late tomorrow night, but how does Saturday work for you? I'll bring the wine, you have the popcorn and snacks ready?

Maddie: Oof. Saturday. The Snipers play at 7:30 that night. It's a make it or break it for the playoffs. BIG GAME, RILES! But if you can shove your mouth full of popcorn until the commercial breaks, we could probably make that work.

Her text makes me roll my eyes, but I shouldn't be surprised. The San Diego Snipers are our local NHL team. I'm not really into hockey, but Maddie is a diehard Snipers fan. She has season tickets and watches every away game. I don't think I've ever met a more dedicated sports fan. She schedules life events around the hockey season, has several official jerseys, and her house is decorated with fan paraphernalia.

It's a bit over the top, but I love her—rabid hockey fan and all.

Crawling into bed, I fluff my pillows and set my alarm before sending out my last message.

Riley: I wouldn't dream of interrupting you and your precious Snipers. ***Wink Emoji*** *I'll bring enough wine and magazines to keep me occupied. See you Saturday!*

Maddie: Awesome. Night, Riles.

Saturday night rolls around, and I'm getting ready to leave my apartment to head over to Maddie's. I'm running late after being called in for emergency surgery on one of our zebras this afternoon. The poor girl was found lying in the zebra pasture, barely moving and taking rapid, shallow breaths.

According to the caretakers, she had been acting out of character the last few days, constantly pawing at the ground and laying down, just to stand back up. Why they didn't call us to check her out sooner, I'll never know. The vet tech in the office today was able to get the zebra's heart rate and temperature and noticed both were significantly elevated, so they called me in since I'm the vet on-call this weekend.

I immediately rushed to the zoo, still dressed in my cut-off shorts and a tank top. Luckily, I was at least wearing tennis shoes. I was able to quickly diagnose that the zebra was suffering from extreme colic—a gastrointestinal condition that causes severe pain—and needed to be rushed to surgery.

The procedure went off without a hitch; however, the zebra isn't out of the woods yet. Now we have to watch for infection at the incision site or any signs of adhesions from the surgery. With any luck, she'll make a full recovery and be back to her normal, healthy self soon.

After getting home from the emergency surgery, I jumped in and out of the shower to rinse off the clinical smell of antiseptics mixed with the signature zoo scent. But even with rushing to get ready, I'm still running an hour behind.

I texted Maddie when I left my office to let her know I'd be late, but the game's already started, so I don't expect a text back.

Gathering up all of my things, I head to the front door. My arms are full with my purse, three bottles of wine, and a bag of clothes, just in case I need to sleep off the alcohol at Maddie's. I even packed my pair of cotton pajama shorts with pizza cutters and slices of pizza all over them. They say "Cutting Carbs" on the ass, which is rather appropriate for the story I have to tell her.

Walking out of my apartment, I struggle to get the door closed behind me without having to set all of my stuff down, but finally manage after a few hook and pulls with my foot. Turning down the hall, I notice a stunningly handsome male standing in the elevator. He has his phone up to his ear and his other hand tucked into the pocket of his suit pants.

With midnight black hair and eyes that rival the bluest of oceans, he practically oozes sex. Something about him seems oddly familiar, a tingle of recognition running up my spine, but I'm sure I've never met him. That's not something I'd be likely to forget. So he must be new? Or visiting. Or...*wait.*

Could this be my new neighbor? No, there's no way I'd be that lucky.

Juggling the stuff in my arms, I hustle down the hall, trying not to drop anything. The doors to the elevator start to close, so I yell out, "Hold the door, please!"

The mystery sex on a stick looks up, and we make eye contact before he turns his back on me, continuing his phone call while the doors close—without me inside.

What a freaking jerk!

Good looking or not, I can't stand people who think they're too good to help others. How hard would it have been to hold the door open?

Setting the bottles down, I push the elevator call button while trying to tamp down my anger. When it finally makes its way back to my floor, I gather all my things again and head down to the lobby, somehow managing to make it all the way to my car without dropping anything. I don't see the mystery man in the parking lot, which is probably a good thing. Saves me from having to curse at him.

I make it to Maddie's house in record time and fumble my

way up her porch steps. The sound of her TV blaring reaches my ears through her front door, and I know there's no way she'll hear me knocking.

Sure enough, after a few well-placed kicks to her door with no answer, I set everything down again so I can grab her spare key from my key ring.

Unlocking the door, I grab all my stuff and walk into her house, kicking the door shut behind me. Maddie's standing in the middle of her living room, wearing an oversized Kingston Turner jersey, yelling at the TV with popcorn stuck in her hair. How she managed that, I have no idea, but it definitely matches the crazy fan appearance she's pulling off.

Cupping my hands around my mouth, I yell out, "MADISON!"

She jumps about a foot in the air, yelping as she turns around and drops into a piss-poor impersonation of a karate stance. Once she sees it's me, she straightens up, giving me her best death glare.

Yeesh. She might've shaved a year or two off my life with that look.

"What the hell, Riles! Haven't you heard of knocking?"

"Yeah, but who needs to knock when I have a spare key and can catch you doing…whatever that was." I joke, barely able to contain my laughter. Turning back to the kitchen, I grab two glasses and continue yelling at her while pouring our wine. "Why do you have the sound so loud? I think half the neighborhood can hear what's going on in this game!"

Walking back into the living room, I find Maddie facing her TV again, doing an odd sort of dance. She's hopping back and forth from foot to foot, her knees raising toward the ceiling while shoving handfuls of popcorn into her mouth.

Although, that's a bit of a stretch. For every kernel that makes it into her mouth, seven plummet to the floor, creating a giant mess.

"Maddie, did you hear me?"

She ignores me, her attention focused on the screen, leaving me no option but to grab a handful of popcorn from the bowl on her end table. Throwing it at her, I shout, "Madison!"

She startles, spilling more popcorn from her bowl.

"Huh? What? I told you, you have to wait to talk until the commercial breaks. This game is a nail-biter. If we don't start scoring soon, we can kiss the playoffs goodbye."

"Maddie, I'm—"

"No! SHH! The second period is almost over. You can talk then." She goes back to watching her game, and I sit down on the couch in a huff.

While waiting for the intermission, I pull out my phone to continue reading through the most recent online issue of the *Journal of Zoo and Wildlife Medicine* that I started earlier today.

Eventually, the period ends, and Maddie takes a seat on the couch. She picks up her glass of wine and chugs the whole thing in one go before turning to face me.

"Okay, you have seventeen minutes before the final period starts. Talk fast."

I launch into a recap of my date with Oliver, and as predicted, Maddie is in hysterics by the end of it.

"Wow, Riles. I didn't know it was possible to find someone so weird, but you done did the damn thing. I can't believe he wanted photos of your feet. What a creep!"

"I know, right? I felt a little bad blocking him at first, but he just wouldn't take a hint."

"No, you were absolutely right to block him. He probably would've tried to sell the photos of your feet online for a quick buck."

"Oh, my god, gross. I'm honored you think my feet are nice

enough to make money off of, but that's a nightmare waiting to happen."

Maddie laughs before shooting off the couch, running to the bathroom. She has a nervous bladder that always kicks in during her games.

I get up and refill our glasses, sitting back down just as the final period starts. Maddie turns back into her frantic self, yelling at the TV before the puck has even touched the ice. I watch the game for a little bit before I get bored and pick up my phone to scroll through my social media apps for a while. Next thing I know, I've watched six videos of animals doing cute shit.

When my last video ends, I glance up at the game. There are only a minute and forty-five seconds left in the third period, and the teams are tied at two. The whistle blows, and there seems to be some sort of scuffle on the ice.

I'm not really sure what's happening, but Maddie stands up and throws a heaping handful of popcorn at the TV while yelling at the referee. She's tossing out curse words like a sailor leading a ship-wide riot.

"Jeez, Maddie. You get mean when you're watching hockey. What's going on?"

"They're sending Kingston to the sin bin! It was a bullshit call, though. How was that slashing? His stick didn't even touch the other player! Fuck!" She's gripping her hair so tight, she might be bald by the end of this game.

I decide it's probably best for both of our safeties for me to sit here quietly until the clock runs out. I don't want to get murdered, and Maddie probably can't afford bail money.

She's so focused on the game, I think a robber could come in and hold me at gunpoint, and she wouldn't realize there was an issue unless it was occurring on the ice.

Picking my phone back up, I pull up Matches to scroll through the queue. I've matched with a few other men in the last week, but most of them don't seem interested in talking. They either don't respond to my messages at all or "ghost" me after the first few exchanges. It's almost like they swiped right just to add another notch to their match list, not because they actually wanted to meet me.

As I'm scrolling through the dating app, I receive an alert that Zach, a recent match, has sent me a new message, proving me wrong. Right as I open the chat, I'm greeted with a hideous photo of his dick. It's small and hairy and probably shouldn't be that color. I scream out at the same time Maddie does.

"Oh, my god! What the fuck is that?"

"Oh, my god! They fucking won!"

She turns and jumps on the couch, spilling my wine into the bowl of popcorn sitting on my lap.

"We're going to the playoffs, baby!"

Ignoring the mess she's making, she continues to jump up and down on the couch, shouting with excitement. That is, until she gets a good look at the image still pulled up on my phone.

"Uh, Riles? What the *hell* is that?"

"I don't know," I yell, dropping my phone. "This Zach dude just sent me a photo of his disgusting penis with a message that said, 'I sent you one, now it's your turn. It's the naked pic quid pro quo.' Gross! His penis looks like it belongs in a horror movie. Seriously, it looks like it's about to get up and scurry away. Why would he think it's a good idea to send this? And who the hell just sends a dick pic out of nowhere?"

"Grade-A douchebags, that's who. Give me your phone, Riley."

She holds her hand out to me with a crazy look in her eyes, and I'm genuinely afraid for this man's safety.

"Wh-Why? What are you going to do with it?"

"Look. My boys just clinched a playoff spot, and I'm in the mood to celebrate, starting with showing this guy who's boss.

Now. Give me your phone, so we can handle this and move on to the bottles of celebratory wine."

I hand her my phone, partially shaking from the disturbing image I may never be able to scrub from my mind, and somewhat out of fear for how she plans to "handle" this.

Maddie is furiously typing on my phone with her tongue peeking out from between her lips. I hear the message sending "whoosh" right before Maddie looks at me with an evil gleam in her eye.

"Oh, boy. What did you say to him?"

"Oh, nothing really. I just told him I was an undercover FBI agent who created fake dating profiles to catch perverts who send unsolicited photos of their male appendages to unsuspecting women. Then I told him the FBI considers that as distribution of pornography without a permit, which is a felony in the state of California, punishable by ten years in prison. I also might've said if we catch him doing it again, he'll be sent straight to prison without the possibility of parole."

I look at her with complete and utter awe. Where does she even come up with this stuff?

"Is that even true?"

"I don't know, I failed criminal justice. But the douchebag has already taken it upon himself to delete and block you from the app. So he probably took it seriously, and look at that. Now we don't have to deal with him anymore. Hopefully, he learned his lesson and won't subject another innocent woman to that repulsive sight."

She's examining her nails like she didn't just impersonate an FBI agent to scare away a pervert, something that might legitimately be a criminal offense.

I love her, but...when did she turn into a psycho? A lovable psycho, but still...

"So now that that's out of the way, what should we do? Do you want another glass of wine?"

She steals my glass out of my hand before jumping up and rushing to the kitchen. While she's gone, I question whether this whole dating app was a mistake. So far, all it's done is make me lose faith in the male population.

I had visions of romance and happiness, but instead, I've been more miss than hit, leaving me no choice but to doubt the likelihood of finding my perfect match.

7

PARKER

Rifling through the stack of papers on my coffee table, I pull out the last three years' worth of tax documents I downloaded off the website for The Helping Haven. Being a non-profit organization, they're required by law to have the information available to the public, along with their meeting minutes, but they weren't easy to find. Tucked away at the bottom of a seemingly useless page on their site, I wouldn't have found them had I not known what I was looking for.

Scanning the page, I mentally crunch numbers and wonder how they haven't gone bankrupt already. Judging by the minutes from the last few meetings, coupled with their recent tax documents, they're damn near closing their doors, which means it's the perfect time for me to swoop in and offer them a deal.

Grabbing my laptop, I power it on and navigate to the website for The Helping Haven, scrolling through their mission statement while taking notes. Based in California, the non-profit organization helps families get back on their feet after they've suffered a loss.

The loss itself doesn't matter. It could be the loss of a spouse, the loss of a job, the loss of a home. Whatever the loss may be,

The Helping Haven steps in to lend a hand in whatever capacity they're able to.

I've had my eye on them for a while now, watching from afar as they do what nobody did for my family when we suffered our unimaginable loss. I often wonder how different my life would be today had someone stepped in with helpful resources.

Would my mother be happier?

Would Rory and I still be close?

Would I have worked so hard for everything I have today?

Would I be less of an asshole?

There's no way of knowing—other than that last one. Odds are I'd still be the same prick I am today. But what I do know, without a doubt, is the tables have turned, and now it's The Helping Haven that needs a hand. Families across the state are bleeding the organization dry. It's a simple lesson in economics. The demand is there, but the money supply is short.

My phone buzzes, vibrating in my pants pocket with an incoming call. Glancing at the clock on the wall, I immediately know who's calling me. There are only three people in the world that would be bothering me this late at night.

My douchebag friends.

Pulling my phone out of my pocket, I confirm my suspicions. I consider letting the call roll to voicemail, but the thought has barely crossed my mind before I nix it. It'd be pointless. The annoying bastard will keep calling until I answer.

"What do you want?" I growl by way of greeting.

Music blares from the other end, sending another snap of irritation through my veins.

"Where the fuck you at, man? Get your ass to Club Onyx," Rhett shouts over the noise. Usually, he's pretty successful at convincing me to do shit I don't want to do, which is probably why they made him call instead of the other two, but tonight he can fuck right off. There's no way I'm going to a club right now.

"Not tonight. I have shit to do."

"Like what? Rake in more money you'll never spend?" *Quite the contrary, actually.* When I don't respond, he tries a different tactic. "Come on, man. The club is crawling with sex tonight. You'd have your pick of any woman here."

"Pass. That's the fucking last thing I need right now."

Rhett covers the receiver, muffling his voice, but I can still hear him yelling to Wesley over the music. "He's being a little bitch and doesn't want pussy."

There's more rustling over the line before Wesley's dumbass yells into the phone. "There's plenty of dick here, too, if that's what he wants."

Obnoxious laughter fills the phone, followed by Rhett's booming voice hollering, "Nice one, bro!" Rolling my eyes, I remove the phone from my ear and hit the end call button, cutting off their childish bullshit. I'm sure Colton is there with them, but he's the more mature one in the group and rarely gets involved in their ridiculous banter. He's more reserved and would rather pack a punch with class.

As soon as I toss the phone on the coffee table, it lights up with an incoming text, causing a sigh to bubble up my throat. The phone vibrates twice, forcing me to pick it back up.

Rhett: *Stop being lame and come have a drink with us.*

Wesley: *He doesn't know how to not be lame.*

Parker: *Can't. Need to get this proposal done.*

Wesley: *Told you!*

Colton: *There's more to life than work.*

Wesley: *What he means is…Stop being a bitch baby. We'll keep you from sticking your dick in anything too crazy.*

Parker: *If I come down, I'll make it my mission to steal every girl you talk to tonight. Don't make me cock block you.*

Wesley: *You wouldn't.*

Parker: *I would. And you already know they'd pick me over your ugly ass.*
Colton: *He's not wrong.*
Wesley: *Fuck you!*
Parker: *I'll pass on that too. Now leave me alone. And wrap it before you tap it.*
Rhett: *Yes, Dad.*
Wesley: **Gif of a soldier saluting**

Tossing my phone back down on the table, I grab the remote and flip the TV to a hockey game for some background noise. It's not a Snipers game, so I know I won't get too distracted, but it's enough to drown out the silence ringing in my ears.

My attention returns to the website in front of me, and after collecting all the information I need, I pull up all three of my bank accounts and start calculating what needs to be done next.

Nobody knows about this business venture I've been considering. Not even Haylee. This decision has nothing to do with my normal business practices. It's personal, which is why it's been kept a well-guarded secret. Nobody can fuck up your plans if they don't know about them.

Rhett wasn't wrong earlier. I've made more money than I can hope to spend in this lifetime unless I want to take up poor spending habits. Which is exactly why I'm sitting here, alone in my temporary apartment on a Saturday night, contemplating this wild decision.

8
RILEY

The next morning, I wake to the enticing aroma of fresh coffee. My mouth feels like it's full of cotton, and my head is pounding harder than a jackhammer at a construction site. Compliments of the wine, I guess.

Dragging myself out of Maddie's spare bed, I zombie walk to the kitchen. Maddie's sitting at her kitchen island, coffee in hand and sporting her unnaturally bright smile.

Ugh. Why can't she wake up feeling like death like the rest of us regular people with hangovers do? She's so happy and perky, I could punch her and not even feel bad about it.

Probably.

Okay, I'd feel a little bad, but dammit, why can't she just be a normal human for one day?

"Good morning," she practically yells at me. "Help yourself to coffee, you big grump ass."

Seriously, how is she so full of energy? Didn't we have the same amount of wine last night?

I roll my eyes before setting my phone down on the island in exchange for grabbing a mug from her cupboard, filling it to the brim with straight deliciousness. If I could inject it into my veins,

I would. But unfortunately, Maddie isn't using her nursing career to the best of her ability and sneaking IV's home for me to use for coffee.

Bitch.

Turning around to face her, I bring my cup of coffee up to my lips, preparing to take the world's largest drink. Before the coffee can cross my lips, my phone dings with a notification from the dating app.

Lowering the mug, I eye my phone with apprehension. Not Maddie, though. She looks at me expectantly, practically bouncing in her seat with giddiness.

"Aren't you going to check that?"

I eye my phone again, trying to settle the nerves wreaking havoc on my stomach.

"I don't know. At this point, it feels like nothing good comes from that dating app. Every time I get a new message, my dating life takes a turn for the worse."

"Oh, stop it. It hasn't been that bad," she argues while laughing. "You've only been on one date. Dick dude doesn't count. I handled that more than you did. In fact, we should consider him my match. You didn't even have to interact with him. So erase him from your failed matches column and forget that ever happened."

"Ugh," I groan out. "As much as I would love to, I'm not sure I can erase that image from my mind. I think I'll wait a few days before giving the app another shot. I need a cleansing of my soul before I can tolerate another match."

Maddie rolls her eyes before reaching out to grab my phone. I shoot my hand out, trying to grab it before she does, but I don't stand a chance. *When the hell did she get so fast?*

I watch her open the app and pull up the new message before I force myself to look away, avoiding another ungodly sight.

Instead, I take my first drink of coffee and practically melt from the liquid crack hitting my soul.

"Aww, Riley! I think we caught a good one this time. He seems like a real gentleman. And his photos are smoking hot. We have to give this one a chance."

We? What's this "we" shit? The last time I checked, I suffered through Oliver's date alone.

She tosses my phone over to me, and I peek down at the screen with one eye closed. Not that I don't trust her, but she *has* been known to jump the gun on handing out the "gentleman" title.

Liam: *Hey, beautiful. I'm sorry it took so long for me to reach out to you. I had some things come up with work that kept me rather busy, but I was hoping you'd like to go on a date sometime? Maybe some night this week, if you're free?*

I look up at Maddie with a small smile tugging at the corners of my lips and butterflies fluttering in my stomach.

"Okay, you're right. He seems sweet. I think I'm free on Tuesday night. Should I accept his date?"

"On Tuesday? No way. You don't want to come off as desperate. Come on, Riley, I thought I taught you better than that? Tell him you're free on Wednesday."

Rolling my eyes, I snort at her ridiculousness. Like a whole day is going to make that much of a difference on the scale of desperation.

Riley: *Hi, Liam. I'd love that. How does Wednesday night work for you?*

Maddie and I start talking about what I should wear on our date while I try not to stare at my phone, eagerly awaiting Liam's response. After a few minutes, my phone dings, and Maddie squeals with obnoxious delight.

Liam: *Wednesday's excellent. If you feel comfortable with it,* *send me your address, and I'll pick you up at 6:00. See you then, beautiful.*

Maddie claps her hands and giggles when I read the message to her.

"See! I told you you were fuckable. No doubt, this guy is digging you. *Hard.* Just like he will be when he sees your outfit."

Laughing, I shake my head, trying to act nonchalantly but secretly praying she's right.

"I DON'T UNDERSTAND, MADDIE. HE SAID HE HAD A WONDERFUL night and would contact me soon. There's no way the interest was one-sided," I whine over the phone.

It's Sunday night, and I haven't heard a single word from Liam since our date on Wednesday. When I checked the dating app to see if I somehow missed a message from him, I saw that he unmatched with me on the app, and all of our previous exchanges had completely disappeared.

It was almost as if it never happened at all, and that hurt my heart more than I cared to admit.

We never exchanged phone numbers, either, so I have no way of contacting him unless I want to send him an email using the address I found on his company directory—but that feels way too desperate.

"I don't know, Riles. From everything you told me, it seemed like he was into you. I don't have the answers for why he's ghosting you now, but as much as I hate to tell you this, sometimes that's just what happens. He could've been acting, for all I know. But what I do know is you can't keep dwelling on this. You have to let him go and move on."

"I'm not dwelling," I lie.

She had to work this weekend, so I did nothing but lounge

around in my apartment for the last two days, watching the latest season of *Married at First Sight* on Netflix. I analyzed our date every which way I could think of to try and figure out why he decided he wasn't interested in me anymore, but I'm still at a loss.

"Riles, don't lie to me. I can practically feel your despair seeping through the phone. Buck up! Liam wasn't the be-all, end-all. There are plenty of other donuts at the bakery. Dust off his crumbs and head back to the donut display."

I don't want to, but I can't help myself from laughing. "Why is everything always about donuts for you?"

"DoNut hate. Donuts are life. Either get on board with the deliciousness, or DoNut talk to me," she states seriously.

I roll my eyes at her double pun before sighing, knowing she's right. I can't force anybody to want to be with me, and I shouldn't have to.

Thanks to the self-esteem issues I developed in college, I've spent the last several years learning to love myself just as I am. Teaching anybody else how to do it isn't at the top of my list of things to do. I want to find someone that will want me and love me all on their own, and I guess Liam isn't the man for the job—despite how well he seemingly fit the role.

Sensing my turmoil, Maddie sighs before saying, "I know you want to find love, Riley. And you will. But you have to remember that while you were focusing your attention on school, shunting all the boys to the side, the rest of us were going through what you're experiencing now. Only, we went through it over a span of years, not weeks. You were never going to find your perfect match right off the bat. It takes time sifting through all the wrong men. But when the right man does show up in your life, you're going to know without a doubt that all the bad dates and piss-poor matches were worth it to find that everlasting love."

She pauses briefly, sighing once again before her voice travels down the line, her tone softer than before. "You're worthy of a man miles above these duds you've been handing out chances to. So don't give up, or you'll never find him."

A tear quietly cascades down my cheek as I listen to her spiel. Other than the terrible secret I've been keeping from her for all these years, she knows me so well. She's already guessed that I would fully accept the fault for this failed date, even if it's not mine to bear.

Wiping away a few errant tears, I whisper, "Thanks, Maddie. I know you're right. My perfect guy is out there, and I'm sure I'll find him one of these days."

"That's the attitude I'm looking for! And who knows, maybe you're looking at the wrong guys. Maybe the guy you're meant to end up with will surprise you with how different he is from all your expectations. You just need to open yourself up to a wider variety of men instead of picking out your perfect man before you've even met him, limiting yourself to a small pond when there's an entire ocean out there, right outside your apartment."

"So you think I should start swiping right on every guy on the app?"

"Woah, woah, woah. I didn't say that. Don't invite the crazies in. Just...stop swiping left because they don't meet every single one of your criteria. If they at least check one or two boxes, give them the chance to surprise you with how they create new boxes for you."

"You know, you give awfully great dating advice for someone who rejoices in her singleness."

"I'm single because I want to be, not because I don't know how to date. Have you forgotten our college days?" *How could I?* "While you were holed up in our room studying, I was out meeting new guys, learning the ropes of dating, and swimming in the deep end with all the playboys. I did all that so I could teach you how to navigate the dating world later in life. You're welcome."

Forcing a laugh, I do my best to cover the fact her words aren't funny to me in the slightest. If she had any idea what her "dating life" did to me in college, she wouldn't be so cavalier about needing to help me now.

"Nice try, but we both know you were just sowing your wild oats and basking in the pleasure of your harem. No need to bring my dating life into your promiscuous choices in college," I counter, praying it doesn't come off too snarky.

"What? I was a good girl. I don't know what you're talking about."

Yeah, that's the problem.

Just then, I hear a distinctly male voice whispering to her in the background. I can't hear all of what he says, but I do catch the words "bring your sexy ass back to the bedroom."

My chest tightens with the same type of jealousy I felt all those years ago, knowing she has no issues finding men who want her. But at least now she finds them on her own, without my help.

A rustling sounds over the line, almost like she's trying to cover the mouthpiece with her hand, and I hear her shush him before chiming out, "Sorry about that. What were we talking about? Oh, yes! I was an angel in college. I don't know why you would suggest anything different."

"Whatever you say, Maddie," I concede, forced humor coating my voice. "I'll let you go, so you can continue being an angel with whoever your guest is. I need to get some cleaning done before bed, anyway. Talk later."

I hang up before she can catch the hitch in my voice as all the feelings I've been clinging to over the years do their best to escape. She doesn't deserve to be on the receiving end of my jealousy or my despair. It's my own fault for lying to her all these years—hiding how much she and her "playboys" in college destroyed my self-confidence.

Switching gears, I pull up Allie's message thread and send her a text, hoping she's still awake. She's listened to me complain about Liam's silence all week, so at least I don't have to repeat everything I've already told Maddie.

Riley: *Still no word from Liam.* ***Sad Face Emoji*** *But I did match with another guy. Sending you a screenshot of his profile. What do you think? Should I message him?*

She responds right away, thankfully. I'm a little hesitant to move forward with this stupid app, given all the issues I've had so far, but I'm also not ready to give up. So when I saw I matched with Benjamin, a new spark of hope flared to life. His profile didn't necessarily fill me with butterflies—unlike when I matched with Liam— but maybe they're just in hiding after too many false alarms?

His page said he's thirty-four, loves a home-cooked meal, thinks being financially responsible is smart, and strives to save money any way he can. He also appears to love a good thrill, has a few photos with a lady I'm assuming is his mom, and a few pictures of him dressed up, sporting a friendly smile. I remember thinking he seemed nice when I initially saw his profile, and I'm hoping that holds true.

Allie: *Yes, go for it. You'll never know unless you try, right?*

Riley: *Right. Okay, I'll message him now.*

Allie: *Good luck! I'm heading to bed. Tell me what happens tomorrow.*

Riley: *Okay, thanks! Goodnight.*

Taking a deep breath, I exit out of my messages and switch to the Matches app, bringing up Benjamin's profile again. After re-reading his biography, I draft up a simple message and send it off to him, doing my best to not give in to my anxiety after the message is delivered.

Riley: *Hey, Benjamin. Nice to meet you.*

Luckily, he responds right away, leaving me very little time to freak out. We send a few messages back and forth, breaking the ice a little before settling on a date for Wednesday night.

Releasing a sigh of relief, I plug my phone into my charger and settle into bed. I'm excited to give Benjamin a chance. He's not exactly what I'm looking for—at least I don't think so—but maybe that's for the best. At the very least, he doesn't seem like the type of guy that will ghost me after one date.

9

RILEY

My phone lights up with a text from Benjamin, letting me know he's downstairs in the parking lot. Slipping my shoes on, I grab my purse and keys before leaving the apartment, giving myself one last pep talk as I make my way downstairs.

I'm not going to let my previously failed dates ruin this date.

Benjamin isn't going to end up like the others.

We're going to have a wonderful time, and everything will be great.

Taking a deep breath, I glance at my reflection in the lobby entrance mirror. My hair is curled. My lips are stained a deep red. The black, off-the-shoulder top is slimming, and these jeans make my legs and butt look fabulous. I'm feeling sexy, and I'm ready for a great date.

Pushing the front door open, I immediately spot a man sitting on a sexy, black crotch rocket. The thing looks dangerously fast, and I realize Benjamin wasn't lying when he said he enjoys a good thrill. I was a little irritated when he texted me, but now it makes sense why he didn't want to turn the motor off to come up to my door like a gentleman.

I've never been on a crotch rocket—or a motorcycle of any

kind—and the butterflies that have been noticeably absent finally make an appearance at the idea of getting on the back of his bike.

Benjamin's helmet covers his whole head, and the visor is blacked out, making it impossible to see his face. He's wearing a black leather jacket and tight jeans, and I swear he couldn't be sexier right now if he tried. The idea of wrapping my arms around his torso as the wind blows through my hair has me incredibly turned on.

Turning his head toward me as I walk closer to his bike, he revs his engine a few times, and I swear my panties instantly grow wet.

Suddenly, the crotch rocket shoots forward and races out of the parking lot—without me on it.

What the hell?

Did my date just bolt at the mere sight of me? I glance back down at my outfit but don't see anything out of place.

Nope.

I know I look good, so why did he just leave without so much as a word?

Just then, I hear a car honking. Glancing up, I see the vehicle that was parked just behind the motorcycle, blocking my view of it.

There's a man that looks a lot like Benjamin's profile photos hanging out of the window of a beat-up minivan. He's waving at me excitedly and gives an extra honk of his horn—like I could possibly miss his obnoxious waving.

Realizing I won't be getting on the back of a motorcycle tonight, I deflate like a popped balloon, my shoulders dropping with a sigh. I reluctantly step closer to the minivan that has a different colored sliding door on the rear driver's side, enough dents to resemble a cratered moon, and sounds like it's on its last leg.

Benjamin leans out of his window again, begging me to hop

in the van so we can get our date started, and suddenly, I'm having flashbacks to when I was younger, and my mother always told me to never get in a van with people I don't know. Is this what she meant?

While it's true this was a scheduled date, I don't really know Benjamin. Hell, I don't even know if he prefers to be called Benjamin or Ben. Am I about to be kidnapped and held hostage in this beat-up minivan?

Fear grips me, sending tingles up my spine as alarms blare in my head. But just as I'm about to run back to the building, Benjamin smiles at me and says, "It's okay, look! None of my door locks work. I promise you won't get trapped in here with me. See, watch." His hands fly to the lock button, pressing it several times to prove the locks are, indeed, broken.

For some odd reason, this calms my racing heart, but just in case, I send out a cautionary text to Maddie.

Riley: Leaving for my date with Benjamin. Probably no need to worry, but if you don't hear from me later tonight, send help. I'm sharing my phone's location with you now, just to be safe.

Once the message has been sent, I open the passenger door and climb in, securing my seatbelt once I'm settled. Moving my purse to my lap, I make sure my pepper spray is within reach, just in case anything sketchy happens.

My phone buzzes with a new text just as Benjamin cheers and puts the van into drive.

Maddie: Uh. WHAT. What the hell is going on that you felt the need to send out a pre-SOS?

Riley: Nothing, really! Just being careful. It's a crazy world out there, you know? You can never be too cautious.

Maddie: Huh. Okay, then. Got your location. Let me know if Benny Boy decides to turn you into human taco meat. I'll show up with guns blazin', don't you worry, boo.

Feeling slightly relieved, I put my phone away in my purse,

turning my attention to the road. I'm closely watching where we're going but still can't figure out where he might be taking me.

"So, Benjamin, where—" I start to ask before he cuts me off.

"Ben."

"Excuse me?"

"Ben. You can call me Ben. Or Benji-Bear. That's what my mom calls me. You can, too, if you'd like," he says with a smile aimed my way.

"Oh, okay. I'll stick with Ben for now, but I'll, uh, keep that in mind."

He nods his head and smiles, and I realize I probably misjudged him. He gives off a warm, bubbly vibe. Too nice to be a serial killer. Probably.

"Anyway, where are we headed tonight?"

"Well, as my profile stated, I love me a home-cooked meal. So I thought we would pop on over to Thyme to Cook and see how well you handle a hot kitchen."

"Oh, that sounds like fun! I love cooking, but I've always wanted to take a class to fine-tune my cooking skills."

"Well, this oughta be the perfect date for you, then, yeah? Man, I'm good at pickin' 'em out."

I'm laughing now, but by the end of the night, I'll think back on this moment and hate myself for not seeing the signs. I should've known when Ben said he was good at picking out dates that things weren't going to go well, but you know what they say. Hindsight's always twenty-twenty.

"No freaking way. Then what happened?" Maddie asks, enjoying yet another story of my dating app failures. We're hanging out at her house after a Saturday afternoon Snipers game.

They won today, so she's over the top excited about...well, *everything*.

We've both been so busy the last few days, we haven't had the chance to catch up over my date with Ben, so now she's hounding me for all the gory details.

"He just sat there! He watched me cook the entire meal by myself, then didn't want to eat the lasagna while it was still hot. Said some crazy crap about loving cold lasagna. I wanted to bolt then and there, but the meal I had just slaved over was too good to leave."

"Yeah, I wouldn't let the food go to waste either. Good choice."

"I know. But then things got worse. Turns out, Ben still lives with his mother—"

"No way," she yells with a laugh, shoving popcorn in her mouth.

"Yep. At thirty-four! Said he loves to save money, and apparently he wants his next serious girlfriend to move into her basement with him."

"Oh, dear Lord. You sure pick some duds, Riles."

"You're telling me. His idea of a thrilling adventure is sitting at home on a Friday night, watching action movies with his mother. According to him, she makes a batch of—get this—chocolate chip-less, chocolate chip cookies, and they share them and watch movies all night," I say with a deadpan stare.

"Uhh...aren't those just sugar cookies?"

Tossing my hands into the air dramatically, I shout, "That's what I said. But, apparently not. I don't know, Maddie. He was really nice and kind of funny, but I don't think I can entertain the idea of a second date, knowing he'd eventually want me to move in with him and his mom."

"Nope, don't do it. It's a trap. And I refuse to ring his mother's doorbell to save you from their basement."

Laughing, I take a sip of wine before remembering the photo she sent me after my date. "I forgot to ask, where the hell did you get that outfit from Wednesday night?"

When I made it home from my date with Ben, Maddie sent me a photo of her wearing a trench coat, a red bandana, and a hard hat with a multicolored feather sticking out of the top. She also had a plastic children's tool belt around her waist with water guns shoved in the belt loops like some sort of crossover between a Bob the Builder and a knock-off gunslinger.

She claimed it was her superhero, friend-saving outfit. It was absolutely ridiculous, and I loved every inch of it.

"Don't ask questions you don't want the answer to. Trust me. That's a need-to-know only situation."

Meaning her current *"friend"* probably has a kid. Which is actually interesting. She usually avoids those types of situationships like they're the plague.

Laughing, I shake my head. "Only you would sleep with a man just to borrow his kid's play tool belt."

She shoves me back and laughs before sobering up, hitting me with a serious look.

"You know what you need, Riles?"

"I need a lot of things. A new potential boyfriend, another glass of wine, and a massage wouldn't be the worst thing in the world, either."

"No. Well, yeah. But no, that's not where I was going with this. You need a one-night stand!"

"Oh. Um…I don't know, Maddie. Isn't that a bit reckless?"

She sighs dramatically before saying, "I love you to death, Riley. But you could definitely stand to be a little more reckless right now. Loosen up a bit and have some fun, you know?"

"What? I'm loose! I have fun…"

"Umm, probably don't go advertising that you're loose. That's not going to attract you very many guys. At least, not any guys you want."

I give her another shove while giggling, "Shut up. You know what I meant."

"Well, fun or not, you need someone to come clean out the pipes. A palate cleanser, if you will. Someone to rock your world so hard they knock the cobwebs right off that dungeon of yours."

One look at my scowling face, and Maddie starts cackling, her head shooting back with laughter.

"It's not a freaking dungeon," I lie. The poor thing hasn't seen any action past my trusted vibrator in years. "But, I guess you're probably right. A one-night stand wouldn't be the worst idea."

"Hell yeah," she cheers with an over-the-top fist pump. "Okay, here's what we're going to do. You're going to hand me over the rights to your dating app for the night—because, let's face it, you can't be trusted to pick out a good match at this point—and I'm going to set up your one-night stand. While I'm doing that, you can start the beautification process so you're good and ready for some dick. Okay? Okay. Let's do this thing!"

She holds out her hand and slaps her fingers to her palm, making a "gimme, gimme" motion.

Reluctantly, I hand her my phone, nervous about how fast this is all moving. She picks up her own phone and shoots off a quick text before diving into my dating queue.

As she flips through the dating profiles, I sit here and drink my wine. My glass is halfway to my mouth when the rest of her plan registers in my brain.

"Um, Maddie?"

"Hmm?" She responds without looking at me.

"What do you mean by the beautification process?"

She peers up at me with a look of innocence I already know doesn't belong on her face.

"Hmm? Oh, you know. Just the normal process most women go through. It's nothing major, so don't worry."

"Cut the crap, Maddie. What are you talking about?"

She rolls her eyes and sighs before saying, "Okay, fine. What level of ladyscaping do you usually maintain?"

"Uh...lady-wha?"

"Exactly. No need to worry, though. I texted my lady, and she's on her way over with all the supplies we'll need."

"Wh-what supplies? What lady?"

Just then, her doorbell rings. Maddie jumps off her couch to answer the door, leaving me to sit here alone, shaking in fear for what's about to happen. Knowing Maddie, it's not going to be pleasurable.

"Hi, Justine. Thanks for coming over. Living room's this way."

Maddie points my way before running to the kitchen. The lady from the front door—Justine, I suppose—walks into the living room, her hands full of bags, and...*is that a wax pot?*

Oh, hell no.

Justine unloads her stuff, and sure enough, there are wax beads, wax strips, a few different types of lotions and after-care products, nail polish, and a slew of other beauty supplies.

I'm going to KILL Maddie.

Speaking of the devil, she must sense my rising panic. She scurries over to me and tries to placate me with another glass of wine.

"Don't freak out. It's gonna be okay. Justine's just going to groom you a little bit, and we'll be done in no time. A little bit of pain now for weeks of beauty. It'll be worth it, trust me."

A squeak flies out of my mouth when she says a little bit of pain. I don't do pain. Me plus pain equals mega tears. It's true. Call me a bitch baby, if you will. *I don't. Like. Pain.*

Justine looks at me with a glimmer in her eyes, and judging by that look, she probably gets off on torturing people.

This is not what I signed up for when I came over here today. But apparently, there's no arguing with Maddie. She's pulling me down off the couch by my arm and pushing me toward the blanket Justine has spread out on the floor.

"Okay, what are we starting with first? Legs, underarms, or the lady bits?" Justine questions.

"LADY BITS? OH, HELL NO," I screech out, shaking my head back and forth. *No.* No, no, no.

No freaking way.

"Oh, hush. You'll be fine. I do this all the time, and I'm still alive. Just calm down and drink your wine."

She turns to Justine and whispers, "I think we better start with the jungle down under. Get that out of the way first, don't you think?"

"JUNGLE DOWN UNDER?" I shout, sputtering out my wine. "Screw you, Maddie, it's not that bad. I do shave, you know!"

I'm in full-on panic mode. I can't believe my own best friend would willingly sign me up for this torture.

What a bunch of bullshit.

I attempt to edge away, slowly crawling backward. I'm eyeing my purse, wondering if I can make a run for it out the door before either of them catches me. Unfortunately, my best friend seems to have eyes in the back of her head. She reaches out and grabs my ankle, pulling me back toward the waxing station with a strength I didn't know she possessed.

This is starting to feel a lot like a hostile takeover, and I'm not ready for it.

Justine tells me to strip down and lay back, and I swear I see stars. I'm about to pass out, and we haven't even started.

Maddie, knowing me as well as she does, knows I'm not

about to remove my own clothes in front of this stranger without a bit of encouragement. "It's okay. It's nothing she hasn't seen before. We're all women here. There's nothing to be ashamed of."

Eyeing her with apprehension, I slowly undress, resigned to my upcoming torture. While the idea of pain doesn't sit well with me, I can't deny that not having to shave for a while would truly be a blessing.

When I'm down to nothing but skin, I hesitate, crossing my arms over my body in an attempt to hide my nudity. Maddie rolls her eyes before pointing to the blanket. I close my eyes with the idea that, if I can't see her, she can't see me, and lie back on the floor, tightly squinting my eyelids shut.

Suddenly, my skin starts to tingle with a burning sensation as Justine rubs something cold and wet all over my...*lady bits*. She tells me she's just cleaning the area of any oils or moisture, but I'm too scared to speak actual words, so I just nod and squeak out a few incoherent grunts.

Then, the sensation of hot goo spreading across my bikini line replaces the cold gel, and I know there's no going back. There's a short pause before Justine's hand pulls my skin tight. And then...

"SONUVABIT—" I scream out before Maddie clamps her hand over my mouth, muffling the rest of my curse.

"Jesus, Riley, do you want the police to show up? My neighbors are going to think someone's being murdered over here."

"They are," I protest, my voice muffled by her hand. "My lady bits are being sent to the seventh circle of hell!"

A few tears slip down my cheeks before Maddie removes her hands from my mouth, replacing them with a kitchen towel.

"You're so dramatic. Here. Bite down on this if you need to. But just hold still. Justine is fast; she'll be done before you know it."

Over the next forty-five freaking minutes, I'm poked, prodded, and stripped of damn near all my body hair. Maddie has gone back to scrolling through my dating queue, no longer entertained by the horrendous torture session going on down on her living room floor.

Right when Justine finishes up with my underarms, Maddie shouts out, "Oh! I think I found the perfect guy. He's sexy AF, only twenty-eight—so you know he's still got some power behind those hips—and his profile says he's DTF. He's perfect for what you need."

I look up at Maddie from my position on her floor and ask, "What does DTF mean?"

Both girls look at me with confusion before Maddie takes pity on me. "Oh, Sweetie. It means he's down to fuck."

"Oh, wow. Jesus. He just put that right there on his profile?"

"Yup. Make things easier when you know right off the bat what they're looking for."

Huh. I guess that's true—no sense in wasting everybody's time.

Maddie resumes typing on my phone, and Justine announces that she's done waxing and orders me to get dressed. I'm all too happy to oblige, so I jump up and dress faster than a man caught in bed with a woman he shouldn't be sleeping with.

Fully clothed again, Justine orders me to pick out my nail polish. She's a bit pushy, and it's no wonder she and Maddie get along so great.

"Oh, I can't wear nail polish. It's against our clinic's policy at the zoo."

Without looking up from my phone, Maddie groans out, "Stop being such a rule follower. You can wear nail polish for one workday. Just wear gloves all day if you have to, then you can remove the polish after your hookup."

"But, how do you know it will only be one day?"

She gives me an evil grin before announcing, "Because I just set up your one-night stand with Sebastian."

"What?" I screech out, dropping the red nail polish I picked out. "I haven't even seen him yet. What if he isn't my type?"

"Honey, he doesn't need to be your type. This isn't a date. It's a modern-day version of the Cum and Go. You'll never see this dude again after Monday night. All that matters is he's hot—which he is, obviously. I picked him out—and if he can get you off, even better, but no guarantees. If anything, this will just get you back into the game."

"She's right, girl. Don't get your hopes up too high on the orgasm, though. Half these young men wouldn't know how to find your clit if they had a map and a giant neon arrow pointing to it," Justine adds.

I'm trying so hard not to show how horrified I am at the idea of this one-night stand, but they aren't painting a pleasing picture, and I'm not so sure I'm up for this anymore.

"Don't even think about canceling on Sebastian, Riley James. I'll know. Don't think I won't."

What the…what is she, a mind reader?

"Okay, sheesh. I won't cancel. But can I at least see the guy I'll apparently be sleeping with?"

"No, not yet. I'm not done with him yet."

"Fine. When will I meet him?"

"Monday. He's out of town for work right now. So you're going to his place Monday when you get off work to Netflix and Chill. I just scheduled you an appointment online with my hairstylist to get a blowout over your lunch break. You're going to look smokin' hot."

"Well, that's…cool. What am I supposed to wear to a Netflix and Chill? I have a cute new pair of PJ shorts. Should I wear those and a cute sweatshirt?"

Justine stops painting my nails, and I feel both of their stares burning me at the stake. Heat radiates through me as my blush spreads from my chest up to my face, setting my skin on fire.

Maddie knows how inexperienced I am, but Justine has never met me. She probably thinks I'm twelve with how clueless I am in the sex appeal department.

"Jesus, Riles. No. You're going to go out and buy some super sexy lingerie tomorrow. I'll go with and help. And I have an adorable tank top you can wear with your black skinny jeans. Just because it's a night in doesn't mean you can show up looking like a slob. The goal is to get laid, not cuddle up to watch a movie. If you aren't fucking halfway through the movie, you're doing it wrong."

Shaking my head, my eyes dart to the floor, avoiding eye contact with either of them. My body is throbbing where I've been de-haired, my heart is racing with nerves, and my skin feels two sizes too small thanks to the comfort box Maddie is doing her damnedest to push me out of. I've reached my capacity for discomfort, and I'm ready to go home and freak out in peace.

I know I said I was ready for some fun. But having sex with someone I've never met seems extreme. As does the "beautification process" I've gone through tonight. My mom would probably have a heart attack if she knew what I allowed Maddie to talk me into. Lord knows I feel like I'm about to.

10

PARKER

"Just get it the fuck done," I yell into the phone before slamming it down on the receiver. I'm so sick and tired of all these bullshit excuses.

I fucking knew I shouldn't have listened to my mom when she said Rory recommended this construction company. I swear he picked the worst construction company in the yellow pages just to spite me. Costly Construction. *What a fucking joke.*

He's not shy about announcing his hatred toward me these days, so I'm not sure why I expected anything different. Asshole can't let go of a grudge.

Doing my best to temper my anger, I force my attention back to my computer screen. My fingers drum in a rhythmic cadence against my desk as I scroll through the updates in our ongoing projects this quarter, making sure things are running on schedule.

A few minutes later, an annoying buzzer sounds through the room, my progress once again interrupted by the intercom on my office phone. I swear one of these days, I'm going to rip that fucker out and chuck it at the wall.

"Sir, Costly Construction is on line one again. There appears to be some sort of issue with the flooring materials now," Haylee sighs.

I let out a harsh growl and mash my finger down on the intercom button, ready to shout back at her. Before I can rip her head off, though, I release the intercom button and take a few deep breaths. It's not her fault this construction company is incompetent.

Rory may have convinced my mother that Costly Construction was known for their excellent renovations, but the only thing they're costing me is a giant fucking headache. That's the last time I try to please my mother by taking my immature brother's advice.

Pressing back down on the intercom, I bark out, "Fire them. I don't care how you do it, but make sure they know their crew and all of their shit needs to be out of my house by five pm, or I'll donate it all to a start-up construction company that could probably run circles around this joke of a crew." I let go of the intercom button before another thought occurs to me.

"And get me a new list of the top-rated construction companies in the area within the hour."

Haylee doesn't answer, but I know she heard me. She's probably rolling her eyes at my attitude, but fuck it. She knows the score. Nobody gets shit done by being nice.

Thirty minutes later, there's a knock on my door, followed by Haylee entering the room. She stalks toward me, barely looking up from her notepad before she slaps a piece of paper down on my desk and starts rattling off information.

"Here's a list of all the top-rated construction companies in the area. I went ahead and called each one to check their availability. The companies with an asterisk by them are the ones that could begin immediately or within the week, but I circled the crew I think would be best for the job. They aren't available right away, but they are the best in terms of quality work."

I push the list back toward her, not bothering to look at it. "I trust your judgment. Call them back. Offer them double their hourly rate if they can have me back in my home within a month. But make sure they know I'll destroy them if they take my money and don't follow through on that request."

She rolls her eyes before nodding her head, moving on to the next item on her list. "Your next appointment will be here in fifteen. I've emailed you a recap of their business goals, where they're falling short, and the proposal we had put together to turn their numbers around. You have a conference with the bookstore at four to discuss their grand re-opening. I'm still waiting on your suit selection for next week's gala, and…" she pauses to turn her notebook over, "…your mother called. She wants to know if you can still get her two tickets to the Snipers playoff game this week."

Silence fills the room, forcing me to look up from my computer. Haylee's looking at me expectantly, one eyebrow raised to the heavens. Her attitude induces my own eye roll.

"Got the email, reviewing it now. Give me a ten-minute warning call before the bookstore conference. Put an order in for a new grey Armani suit, black dress shirt, black tie. And let my mother know I bought her tickets."

I pause before blurting out, "Wait! No. Don't call her. I want to see her excitement in person, so I'll swing by and surprise her once I grab them from Colton. That'll be all, Haylee."

Returning my attention to my computer once again, I scroll through the proposal she just sent me. The annoying sound of a throat clearing seconds later forces me to look back up at Haylee's expectant face. Her hand is on her hip, and she's lightly tapping her foot, signaling her impatience. I let out an annoyed growl before rolling my eyes, snapping out, "Thanks."

She giggle-snorts—how unattractive— and turns on her heel to leave the room.

Right before she shuts my door, her head peeks back into the room. "Oh, and Sir? Next time, I recommend not being such an asshole when ending things with your fuck buddy. Especially before leaving town. I'd rather not have to spend my valuable time hiring a construction crew for you again."

One look at my angry face, and she bursts out laughing before shutting the door, leaving me no chance to respond.

11

RILEY

Standing outside of Sebastian's apartment, I pace back and forth, doing my best to calm my racing heart. I can't remember the last time I was this nervous, but I know without a doubt my sex life and I need this.

Badly.

My skin is hairless and as smooth as a baby's bottom. My hair has been professionally blown out, and my nails are a vibrant red. I'm wearing the most daring lingerie I've ever seen, and my outfit is on point.

Too bad I'm probably ruining my perfectly applied makeup by nervously sweating, despite the cool evening air.

Maddie finally let me see a photo of Sebastian, and I have to hand it to her—he's super hot. But what if he sees me and decides I looked better in my photos? Or worse yet, what if I completely suck at sex and he laughs at me? It's been so long, I'm not entirely sure I remember what to do with my hands.

I take a deep breath in, hold it, then slowly let it out.

Then I proceed to do that twelve more times before ripping the bandaid off, strutting into the apartment building with fake confidence. Anymore lingering, and the cops probably would've shown up, wondering how I escaped the asylum I clearly belong in.

Reaching Sebastian's floor, I remind myself this is just a practice round for my future boyfriend. I'll brush the dust off my vagina and make sure I still know how to use the damn thing before taking my next boyfriend to the bedroom. After tonight, I'll never see this guy again. So if I suck, I suck—no big deal.

My knuckles rap against the wood door, the sound ringing through the empty hallway, bouncing off the walls with an echo. My palms are sweating, and I'm half a second of doubt away from bailing on this mission when the door swings open.

No going back now.

Sebastian is standing before me in grey sweatpants and no shirt. His muscles are on full display, and boy-howdy, I think I remember how to use my vagina now. I don't remember telling my feet to move. They just took the reins and led me straight into his sex den all on their own—probably at the command of my needy vagina.

He offers me a beer while leading me to the living room, but I ask for water, not wanting alcohol to cloud my memory of this man's body. *And those eyes.* They're a startling green, standing out against his dark olive skin and chocolate brown hair. Maddie hit the jackpot with this one.

We sit on the couch, each taking an opposite end. He's further away than I'd like him to be, practically sitting on the arm of the couch, but maybe he's just as nervous as I am?

"I picked out *The Proposal*. Have you seen it?" he asks me in a deep, raspy voice.

Odd choice, but..."I have, but I'm okay with watching it again."

He nods, clicking start, and the next thing I know, we're half an hour into the movie, and he's still sitting as far away as he can get. How does he plan to make a move from all the way over there? Or does he want me to?

Shit. I don't know what to do!

Another twenty minutes go by as I wage an internal debate, fidgeting in my spot on the couch. Eventually, I get to the point where I'm too uncomfortable sitting here in all of these clothes and lingerie and decide to just go for it.

Standing, I grab Sebastian's hand, pulling him up from the couch. He asks me what I'm doing, but instead of answering him with words, I lead him down the hall. Opening the first door on the left, I pull him into the—whoops—bathroom. *Definitely not having sex in here.*

An awkward giggle shoots from my mouth as I turn and shut the door, leading him to the next room instead.

Ah, yes. This is more like it. There's a king-sized bed in the middle of the room just begging to be used.

Pulling us through the doorway, I turn around and kick the door shut before facing Sebastian. He walks backward as I stalk toward him, keeping a foot of space between us. The back of his knees hit the bed, where he falls to the edge with a look of...*apprehension?*

Shit. Was Maddie wrong about this being him being down to, um...freak? He doesn't seem too into this right now.

"Are you...okay?"

Despite his wide, alarmed eyes, he nods his head. "Yeah. I'm just, uh, nervous."

Refusing to let his nerves derail my mission to get laid, I nod and strip my clothes off, piece by piece. I'm nervous too, but maybe our nerves will disappear once I'm naked.

My tank top tangles in my hair as I'm removing it, causing me to stumble until I get freed, and I damn near fall over removing my pants. I was physically prepped for every aspect of this night, but apparently, I should've practiced stripping, too, because this is anything *but* sexy.

When I'm down to just the lingerie, Sebastian eyes me up and down, his eyes widening as they rake over every inch of bare skin this daring lingerie shows.

That's better.

Sebastian crawls backward up the bed, and I follow after him, slowly climbing up his body in what I hope is a seductive move. He hasn't said a single word this whole time, so it's hard to be sure, but I think he likes what's happening so far. Otherwise, he'd stop me…*right?*

Leaning down, I softly brush my lips across his neck as I settle my now wet and throbbing pussy on top of his…

Wait. *Shouldn't he be hard by now?*

I glance up, trying to gauge his reaction, and am shocked to see a horrified expression contorting his face. My mouth falls open to ask what's wrong, but he beats me to the punch.

"OH FUCK. THERE IT IS. I'M DEFINITELY GAY. NO DOUBT. WHAT THE FUCK IS THAT, AND WHY IS IT PULSING?"

My ears definitely heard his announcement. *How could they not?* I think the whole block heard my Matches date come to this unfortunate and ill-timed conclusion.

Unfortunately, my pussy did *not* get the memo. She's still tingling, thinking we're finally going to get lucky. She's ready for her trip to Pound Town. Packed her bags. Bought a ticket. Threw her celebration.

She.

Is.

Ready.

But Mr. Babble McBabbleson is still having his coming out of the closet moment, and I think I'm starting to hyperventilate. *Why does this shit keep happening to me?*

Just when I think it couldn't possibly get any worse, he opens his mouth again.

"My mom told me I just hadn't found the right woman yet. But I'm lying here staring at your bare kitty cat, and all I can think is it's about to swallow my dick whole, and I might never get it back. I have no idea how deep that cave is or what's lurking in the darkness up there, and I think if I stick my P in your V, my balls are going to shrivel up inside my body, seeking an escape. And I'm rather attached to my balls, you know?"

He takes a deep breath before continuing on with his rant, "I thought maybe I was just a late bloomer. Twenty-eight isn't too late, is it? Everyone thought it was weird that I was still a virgin, but holy fuck, now I know why I was never interested in sex. This is bad. This is really bad. I knew I thought my neighbor's biceps were sexy. And those abs! Am I right, or am I right? Anyway, can you get that thing off my dick? He's about half a second from entering into hibernation."

Um...*what?*

Did he seriously just imply that my vagina is a cock-seeking monster that's going to eat his dick for dessert? Excuse the fuck out of me, but my lady cave is a classy bitch. She only accepts willing sacrifices.

And—wait. Did I really just think of my vagina as a lady cave? My god. It's time to cut my losses and run. But first... "YOU'RE A VIRGIN?"

Yeah, Riley. Because that's what's important here. My mouth and my brain need to have a lengthy discussion about priorities.

"You said you were just nervous," I screech, my heart hammering in my chest as embarrassment floods through my system.

His voice cracks with a hint of hysteria, his pitch like nails on a chalkboard when he cries out, "Well, I am!"

Scurrying off him, I jump down to the floor, eagerly searching for my clothes.

I find my tank top and end up putting it on backward, but I'm in too much of a hurry to get out of here to care. Grabbing my pants, I hop on one foot while shoving my other leg through the pant hole. I lose my balance—because, of course, I do—halfway through and end up stumbling into his nightstand, bumping his lamp off the edge.

It goes crashing to the floor, shattering into a million pieces—just like my dignity.

Fully dressed, I hightail it to his front door, only stopping to grab my purse and keys off the living room floor. I'm halfway out the door when I realize Sebastian is still in his bedroom, having a rather hysterical coming out of the closet moment, bitching about not even wanting his friend to set him up on this app in the first place.

That explains so much.

If I were in a better place in my life right now, I'd stop to talk him through this. There's absolutely nothing wrong with being gay. Unless you're me right now and were expecting to finally get laid.

Shaking my head, I silently wish him luck and dash out of his building so I can lick my wounds in private.

While on my way home, I repeatedly call Maddie so she can talk me off the ledge. But she's on my shit list right now because not only did she pick me out a gay one-night stand, she isn't answering her damn phone when she knew I was meeting up with this dude tonight. What if this was an emergency and I was being murdered right now?

But no—no murder for me. It's worse than that. I've been lady blue-balled by a man that couldn't even help it. I'd be an asshole to be mad at him, but it would've been nice if he figured out he was gay *before* I stripped down naked for him.

Entering my apartment, I dial Maddie's number one last time, letting out a wounded battle cry and throwing my purse against the wall when she doesn't answer.

My asshole of a neighbor picks that exact moment to bang on our shared wall, trying to silence me. Not in any kind of mood to be told what to do, I stomp over to the wall and use my fist to bang right back, hitting the wall twice as hard as he did. Honestly, it's a miracle my fist doesn't plow right through the drywall with how much anger and humiliation I throw into that knock.

The realization that my wall's getting plowed harder than I did tonight sends me into a bigger spiral, spurring on an avalanche of angry tears.

I start stripping out of my clothes for the second time tonight, only this time, it's to change into my brand new pair of cotton pajama shorts. I grab a raggedy old college sweatshirt and put it on, but because I'm too busy crying and yelling about cock-seeking vagina monsters, I don't notice it's inside out and on backward. *Again.* Clearly, I've lost the ability to dress myself after my humiliation this evening.

I'm in the middle of cursing out loud and pulling on my hair, wondering why God has been punishing me lately when I hear a knocking on my door.

Ignoring it, I pull out my phone, bound and determined to delete this stupid-ass dating app that has ruined my life.

"Fuck this. I'll just adopt a cat tomorrow. Who even needs a man? Not me, that's fucking who. Just me and my cat. Best of friends!"

Unfortunately, the tears running down my face are clouding my vision, and I can't find the disable account button. Using the back of my hand to wipe the tears away so I can see the screen, I try again but get distracted by the mess of black covering my hand.

"Argh," I scream out, mad that even my mascara is conspiring against me tonight.

The knocking on my front door starts back up, causing my eyes to cross and my shoulders to bunch up around my ears. Anger, disappointment, and humiliation take over my body, fighting for the top spot as I growl, hiccuping halfway through.

Without a care in the world as to what I currently look like, I stomp over to the front door and swing it open, shouting, "What do you want? Can't you hear I'm in the middle of a breakdown?"

My breath catches in my throat as my blurry vision clears, allowing me to see who's at my door. Eyes widening, I gasp, damn near choking on my own spit.

Holy. Freaking. *Shit!*

12

PARKER

It's late by the time I walk into my apartment. After wasting half my afternoon talking to several construction companies that don't sound too promising, I got held up at the office finishing a proposal.

As hard as she tried, Haylee wasn't able to convince BK Construction, her first choice crew, to take the job on such short notice with the time frame I demanded. They insist it will take a minimum of two months to fix all the damage and renovate the pool area.

I'm exhausted and frustrated over this entire ordeal. Is it too much to ask to get my goddamn house fixed?

If I had known then what a headache this would turn into, you could bet your ass I would've pressed those charges against Leigha. As it turns out, being "nice" isn't all it's cracked up to be.

Shedding my suit jacket and tie, I roll the sleeves of my white button-up shirt to just below my elbows and empty my pockets, tossing my wallet, keys, and phone onto my kitchen counter. Grabbing a tumbler out of the cupboard, I pour myself two fingers of bourbon to take the edge off.

Pacing back and forth across my living room, my mind is

racing, trying to figure out a way to incentivize BK Construction to take the job and finish my house in one month instead of two. Lifting the glass to my lips, the smoky scent of bourbon burns my nostrils, making my mouth water. I'm about to drain the contents when I hear a thump against the wall, followed by my neighbor yelling obnoxiously next door.

Fucking hell. This is exactly why I can't wait to get back to normal life in my own house. First, it was annoyingly loud music a few weeks ago, and now it's a full-blown meltdown. Does the insanity ever end?

I can't make out what she's saying, but whatever it is, it's annoying as fuck, and I'm in no mood to deal with this lady's hysterics tonight.

Not for the first time since moving in, I walk over to our shared wall and start pounding on it, yelling for her to shut the hell up. That's clearly not going to work this time, though. Her yelling grows louder, and I'm shocked as hell when she has the nerve to pound back on the wall.

Whipping around, I stomp to the kitchen, grabbing my cell phone off the counter while debating my options. Calling the cops seems a little overboard, even for my grumpy ass. This chick might be crazy given the fact she's yelling her head off at... looking over at the clock, I realize it's only half-past nine. Irritation creeps through my veins, knowing it's not late enough to involve the police—yet.

Changing course, I dial the building super's number, but my irritation spikes to rage in a hot second when I'm sent to voicemail. *Of-fucking-course.* Hitting the end button, I toss my phone back on the counter, not bothering to leave a message. I'd bet my entire year's salary the worthless fuck won't return my call anyway.

Raking my hand through my hair, I grip the ends tightly as another shriek sounds next door, my head pounding with rage.

Fuck this. Downing the last of my bourbon, I slam the empty glass on the counter, the leftover ice clanking against the glass, before storming out of my apartment.

As the door slams behind me, I take a few deep breaths, filling my lungs to capacity in hopes of slowing my angry heart, so I don't lose my shit on this lady. She's clearly having a bad day—just like me. But you don't see me causing a disturbance to my neighbors, do you? No. She can cool her shit and handle this like any other *normal* adult.

Bringing my fist up to her door, I give it a good, solid pound, using the side of my fist for maximum sound, ensuring she'll hear me over the racket she's causing. When there's no immediate answer, I pound again, prepared to break the door down with force if I need to. The longer she makes me wait out here, the higher my temper rises.

Just when I'm about to pound on her door for a third time, it swings open, bringing a mascara monster into view.

"What do you want? Can't you hear I'm in the middle of a breakdown?"

Oh, I can fucking hear, alright. I just don't give a damn.

Her face is red and twisted in anger, matching mine, but she has no right to be the angry one here. She's the one fucking up my night, not the other way around.

A gasp escapes her pretty little mouth as recognition dawns on her at the same time it hits me. We haven't officially met, but there's no doubt I've seen her around.

The first time I noticed her, she was walking to the elevator with her hands full, begging me to hold the door for her. I thought about it, but I was on the phone with Costly Construction and knew it would be a heated call, so I turned my back on her and let the doors shut so I could continue the call in private.

I'm fairly certain I saw her again a few nights ago when I left on my Ducati. She was leaving the apartment building, looking hot as fuck and eyeing me like she wanted to take a ride, but I didn't stick around to take her up on her desire. I shot out of the parking lot like a madman the second an unexpected spike of lust traveled up my spine, heating my blood to a boil.

While she stands in her doorway in a daze, I take a moment to rake my eyes over her, taking in the finer details I missed before. With dark red hair falling across her shoulders, wide, vivid-green eyes, and full, pouty lips shaded a deep red, she's good-looking—if you can move past the makeup she has running down her face. Hell, she even has a smattering of freckles peeking through the mascara caked to her cheeks.

A face pretty enough to bring a grown man to his knees. But...*what in the actual fuck is she wearing?*

Her sweater seems to be hiding some decent curves if I remember correctly, but it's on inside out and backward. She's wearing cotton pajama shorts covered in cartoon avocados that are...hugging? Dancing? Hell if I know, but they're fucking weird.

She's still standing in the doorway, babbling on hysterically, but I ignore that, tuning her out as I continue on with my visual sweep.

My tongue acts on its own volition, darting out of my mouth to sweep across my bottom lip as I take in her long, lean legs. A brief image of them wrapped around my hips as I fuck her into the next century pops into my head, sending the blood rushing to my cock. Shaking my head, I do my best to clear the unwanted image from my mind, but my lonely dick isn't ready to simmer down.

Needy bastard.

She's a hot fucking mess, and I have zero business thinking about her and sex right now. It ain't gonna happen. I refuse to break my celibacy pact. Not even for a pair of sexy legs.

When my eyes finally make it down to her feet, I have to

shake my head, blinking my eyes a few times to make sure I'm seeing things correctly. Why the hell is she wearing high heels with pajamas?

I'm about to ask her exactly that when she thrusts her hand out, forcing her phone into my chest. I nearly drop the thing when she lets go and pulls her hand back, but just barely catch it halfway down my torso.

"Can you delete this? The whole thing. Just…get rid of it."

The fuck?

She turns around and stumbles away from me, leaving me standing in her open doorway, confused as fuck with her phone clutched in my hands.

From this view, I can see the words "Let's Avo-Cuddle" written across her ass, clearing up my earlier confusion on what the hell the avocados were doing.

Rolling my eyes, I glance down at her phone to see what's going on and find a dating app called "Matches" pulled up. I've heard of it, but I've never needed to use it for myself. Women have never been in short supply in my life. Quality? Complete shit. But I can't complain about the number of women I've bedded in my lifetime.

The sound of glass clinking draws my eyes back up in time to see this lady pulling a wine glass down from her kitchen cupboard. She turns and opens the fridge, grabbing a brand new bottle of wine before slamming the fridge door shut hard enough to make the contents rattle.

I watch with amusement as she struggles to uncork it, then, instead of pouring herself a glass of wine, she lifts the bottle to her lips and starts chugging it.

What the fuck was the point of getting a glass?

Shaking my head, I bring my gaze back to her phone. While she's preoccupied with her bottle of wine, I take the time to snoop through her profile, finding out her name is Riley James. She's a twenty-nine-year-old veterinarian at the Shoreline Safari Zoo, which I hate to admit is kind of neat. At least I know she has some brains in her, despite what her behavior tonight is telling me.

According to her bio, she enjoys cooking, reading, time spent on the beach, and is looking for her happily ever after. Jesus. Is she serious with this shit?

Silence rings through her apartment, drawing my attention away from her phone. Her ranting and raving have quieted down, which I'm not mad about, but now she's sitting on her couch, staring at the wall. The hand clutching her bottle of wine raises to her mouth, and I watch with a mixture of disgust and admiration as she drains half the bottle in one gulp.

Who the fuck is she matching with that's pushed her to alcoholism? Flipping through her profile again, I find her matches and put two and two together. She's got some real losers in here.

I click on her most recent match and scan through his profile. Sebastian. *Huh.* How the hell did she match with this dude? He's clearly into men.

Shaking my head, I locate the account button and select disable. A message pops up, asking me why I'm deleting my—or her—account. I type in, "Total trash," and hit send. Seems accurate enough.

I take a few steps into her apartment to give her back her phone and find her passed out cold on her couch, still wearing her high heels. The bottle of wine resting on her lap is empty and in danger of falling to the floor.

Sighing heavily, I rub my hand against my chin that's now sporting a five o'clock shadow. Walking over, I gently shake her shoulder, trying to wake her, but she gives a mighty snore and rolls over, the empty bottle of wine tumbling to the floor, clinking as the glass hits the hard surface.

Whatever. She's not my problem anymore. Tossing her phone

down on the couch next to her, I turn to leave, happy to be done with this nightmare.

I'm halfway to her front door when I spot her keys on the entryway table, bringing me to a halt. Alarm bells clang in my head, causing my heart to stutter in my chest, sweat forming along my hairline as I realize my crucial mistake. My eyes fall closed, and an angry growl rips from my throat, knowing my phone and apartment keys are both inside my now locked apartment. My dumbass was so focused on ending the madness happening next door, I went and stormed out without grabbing my shit.

When Haylee suggested this apartment building, I was a fan of the added security it offered, hoping it would keep the crazies out. But now that I'm locked out of my apartment, I'm regretting ever moving into a building with apartment doors that lock automatically because the only one it's keeping out is me.

Turning back around, I stalk to the couch, pickup up Riley's phone with a huff. Thankfully, it doesn't have a passcode on it. I search through her contacts for the building super's number and hit dial, but it's as useless as when I tried earlier. The longer the phone rings without connecting, the harder my fist clenches in anger, coming dangerously close to crushing her phone in my grip.

After calling three times in a row, I bring my hand up to the bridge of my nose, massaging away the tension my anger has caused. I should be showered and lying naked under my covers by now, but no. This annoyingly sexy—*sexy?* Where the fuck did that come from? No—this *crazy* chick had to go and derail my entire night with her drunken hysterics.

Still clutching her phone in my hand, I stare at the blank screen, attempting to work through the issue, but my options are pretty limited here. Without my phone, wallet, or keys, I can't exactly escape to a hotel room until the incompetent building super decides to answer his goddamn telephone and let me into my apartment.

I can't call Haylee to come get me. God forbid I memorize a phone number.

My buddies live too far for me to walk to at this time of night, and there's only a twenty percent chance they'd be home if I did.

My office is also across town, but the security officer could let me into my office if I could get there.

Walking across the room, I peek out her apartment window and find—fucking rain. *Of course.*

I guess that only leaves me with one option.

The blinds snap back into place as I retract my hand and turn around, eyeing the drunken woman passed out on her couch. Glancing around her apartment, I take in her lack of a second couch. She has a reclining chair, but there's no way my six-foot-two frame will fit comfortably on that small ass chair.

I'm not about to sleep in her bed—who the fuck knows what goes on in there—so…Floor it is, I guess. But fuck if I'm gonna sleep on it bare.

Locating her linen closet, I grab a few sheets, blankets, and pillows and set up my makeshift bed as far from the couch as I can get while still keeping her in my line of sight. Standing back up, I look down at what promises to be a horribly uncomfortable bed for the night. This is not how I pictured my night going.

Before lying down, I give Riley another shake, just to make sure there are no chances of me returning to my heavenly bed tonight. When she doesn't stir, I growl out a few expletives before reaching down, relieving her of her high heels. I grab a throw blanket she has draped across the back of the couch and throw it over top of her before picking up the empty wine bottle, setting it and her cell phone on the coffee table.

Good enough.

This woman doesn't mean jack shit to me. If she wants better than this, she should've thought about that before getting drunk and falling asleep with a complete stranger in her apartment.

Turning the lights off, I hesitate, questioning whether I should remove my own shoes, pants, and shirt or if I should accept complete misery tonight. Looking over my shoulder, I confirm my one-night roommate is still passed out cold before shrugging my shoulders, saying fuck it.

Undressing to my boxers, I fold everything and set it next to my bed before crawling under the covers, praying for the hours to slip by quickly. The faster morning comes, the faster I can get the hell out of here.

13

RILEY

A stream of light sneaking through my curtains causes me to stir the following morning. I try to roll to my other side to avoid the devilish light but am met with resistance in the form of…a cushioned wall? *What the heck?*

Peeling my eyes open, I blink a few times to clear away the sandpapery grit clinging to my eyeballs. I must've fallen asleep with my contacts in. Great. I'm going to regret that all day. And what is that smell?

I huff out a deep sigh and freeze. *Oh, god.* It's my breath. I sweep my tongue across my teeth and am met with disgusting sugar remnants caked to my teeth. It's bacteria heaven in there, and I am *not* here for it.

My eyes slowly take in my surroundings, understanding dawning that I'm on my couch. I don't remember falling asleep here last night, but judging by the taste in my mouth and the pounding headache I'm battling, I have wine to thank for the holes in my memory.

Swinging my feet down off the couch, I struggle to my feet but nearly fall back on my ass when I notice a bed of pillows and blankets across the room. Fear snakes its way up my spine, slithering through my veins at the sight of an adult-sized lump under the pile of blankets.

My heart races, beating double-time, and my stomach turns over dangerously, threatening to spill its contents. Although, I can't tell if that's from the hangover or because there's an intruder in my apartment, and I have no idea how they got in here or why they're sleeping on my floor.

The sound of deep, rhythmic breathing reaches my ear, telling me my floor dweller is sound asleep. I tiptoe across the room and peek over the wall of blankets, my eyes landing on an outrageously handsome face.

Wait a damn second—I know this face!

His hair is more rumpled than the last time I saw him in the elevator, and I can't confirm the color of his eyes, but I'd recognize that facial structure anywhere. Even covered with morning scruff, I can tell it's the sharpest jawline I've ever seen. His unfairly long eyelashes are resting against the top of his cheeks, and his skin is flawless. Just like the last time I saw him, I can't help but think he's the hottest man I've ever seen.

But, still, why is he here?

I look down at myself to gauge my own appearance and groan at what I see. This man didn't just materialize out of thin air in the middle of the night, so there's no way he didn't see me in my cotton, cartoon avocado-covered pajamas. Not to mention the fact that my sweatshirt is still inside out and backward. How embarrassing.

Slowly stepping back, I scan the room, finding my phone sitting on the coffee table. I pick it up and…Dead. *Of course.* Dashing to the kitchen, I plug it into a charger, impatiently shifting from one foot to the other as I wait for it to power on.

Once my screen comes to life, I debate my options. I could

call the cops and have them remove the stranger. Although, that could get a little weird since all signs point to him not actually breaking in. The doors lock on their own from the inside and are damn near impossible to get into without keys. Which means I had to let him in. But when?

Thinking back on last night, I review my mental timeline. I remember fleeing Sebastian's after finding out he was gay—yeah, that's still a shock—and coming home, I tried to call Maddie, threw a temper tantrum that could rival a three-year-old on their worst day...and then what?

Ugh, think, Riley.

I bring my fingers up to rub my temples, squeezing my eyes shut and focusing all my attention on last night's events while also ignoring the angry noises coming from my upset stomach.

Then it hits me—the door. Someone was knocking on my door during my emotional breakdown. I answered, and the asshole from the elevator was standing there. Did we exchange words, though? I don't remember inviting him in, or really anything after the bottle of wine I started drinking.

The panic rises again as I realize I can't exactly call the cops over this. So what should I do?

Chewing on my bottom lip, I stifle a groan. I'm going to catch so much shit for this, but as much as I don't want to, I'm going to have to call Maddie. She's the only person I can think of that will know how to get a strange man out of my apartment.

Pulling up my contacts, I'm about to hit call when the tingling sensation of being watched washes over my skin, the hair on the back of my neck standing at attention. Straightening my back into a ram-rod position, I slowly turn toward the living room. *Yep.* Mr. Elevator Asshole is awake and staring at me with an amused look, a slight smirk tugging at the corners of his lips.

He stares at me; I stare at him, neither of us making any

sudden movements. My level of discomfort climbs to dangerous levels, and I'm starting to wonder if this is how zoo animals feel —constantly being watched day in and day out.

I shift back and forth from one leg to the other, trying to dislodge the prickling sensation of hysteria climbing up my spine from this stranger watching my every move in my own apartment. When the silence becomes too much, I panic and blurt out, "What?"

His smirk grows into a full-blown taunt before he snorts and says, "Nothing. Just waiting to see if you're going to break out into hysterics again, or if last night was a one-night-only kind of show."

Oh, great. He's still an asshole.

He shifts on his bed, and the top of his blanket falls, revealing his bare, muscular chest. Hold up. Is he naked under there? Why isn't he wearing a shirt?

Oh, shit. Did I sleep with him?

No, surely I'd remember that…right? I squeeze my thighs together in a sneaky maneuver to determine if there's any soreness between my legs, but judging by how fast his eyes snap down to my legs, I'm going to guess that wasn't as subtle as I was aiming for.

His eyes dance with wicked humor, and my embarrassment skyrockets. The room fills with his booming, conceited laugh, probably assuming I'm rubbing my legs together with desire. And just like that, my embarrassment recedes, snapping into full-blown anger.

"Did we have sex last night?" I harshly whisper, disdain dripping from my tone.

The humor in his eyes fades as the laugh dies in his throat, his face transforming into a steely glare that rivals my own.

"Honey, if we had sex last night, you'd know it. And I sure as shit wouldn't be sleeping on your floor. I would've woken up in my own heavenly bed instead of with a goddamned crick in my neck."

He's still glaring at me, but that didn't explain why the hell he *is* on my living room floor right now.

"Okay, then…did we fool around?"

He has the nerve to roll his eyes at my question. "I didn't touch you. I prefer my women to be coherent when I take them to bed for any reason at all. Besides, I've had enough crazy to last me a lifetime."

Rearing back, my eyes widen in shock before narrowing into slits. "What the fuck is that supposed to mean?"

"Your hysterics last night could be heard a mile away, disrupting everyone's peaceful night. Next time, I recommend toning it down a few levels. Leave the crazy for the bedroom if you want an actual shot at a relationship worth a damn."

Who the fuck does this guy think he is? "If you aren't here because we fooled around, then there's absolutely no reason I should have woken up to you on my floor. I don't recall inviting an asshole for a sleepover, so feel free to leave."

His eyes narrow into a hard glare, an intimidating growl rumbling through his throat as he stands. The blanket previously covering his body falls to the floor in his haste to jump to his feet, revealing his sexy-as-sin body, covered by nothing but a pair of boxers.

He bends to pick up his clothes, leaving me with no other option but to stare at every single rippling muscle that flexes as he moves. Despite the anger flowing through my veins from how much of a jerk he is, I can't help but drool over his physically fit body. He's without a doubt the biggest asshole I've ever met, but *damn,* is he sexy.

Finally dressed, he turns to face me, catching me mid-drool.

With a smirk, he steps closer to me, forcing me to retreat, my back bumping into the kitchen counter.

"I slept on your living room floor last night because you were too preoccupied with your meltdown to notice that I was still standing in your doorway with your cell phone in my hands when you started drinking. Next thing I know, you were irresponsibly passed out drunk on your couch with your apartment door wide open and a stranger lurking in the doorway. You started making weird noises, and I was worried. So instead of leaving you drunk and alone, I slept on your living room floor to make sure you didn't die in your sleep from alcohol poisoning. Next time, I'll leave you to fend for yourself."

With that, he turns on his heel, stalking toward the front door as I stand here with my mouth gaping open. He manages to make it three steps before my brain fires up, knowing I didn't drink *that* much.

A giggle bubbles up my throat, spilling past my lips. Two seconds later, I'm laughing hysterically as the asshole comes to a dead stop, turning to glare at me over his shoulder.

"You really are a basket case, aren't you? What the hell is so funny about nearly dying?"

"Y-you got locked out, di-didn't you?" I choke out around my laughter, my hands pressed against my stomach that's screaming with pain, courtesy of this morning's hangover.

Growling, he stomps forward, ripping open my door. My laughter follows his retreat but dies in my throat when he stops short of slamming the door, turning back to look at me as he says, "I'm sure you had fun with Sebastian last night, but I deleted the dating app like you requested, saving you from a miserable existence full of failed dates. You're fucking welcome."

With that, he leaves, slamming the door behind him.

I stand there in shock with a gaping mouth, the tears from my laughter still leaking out of my eyes as my brain registers his parting comment. Picking my phone up, I close out of my contacts, moving to my page of apps. Sure enough, the Matches app is nowhere to be found.

Embarrassment creeps into my cheeks, but it will have to wait until later. I yelp at the time, booking it to the bathroom to shower and get ready for work. Needing to remove my contacts, I face the mirror and let loose a scream, startled by my own reflection.

I have mascara running down my cheeks, and my foundation is caked together from last night's tears of anger and frustration. My hair resembles a bird's nest, and I'm pretty sure those are drool spots on my shirt. *Great.* I can't believe this is how he got to see me.

Not that I really care what some asshole thinks of me, but dammit! No wonder he thinks I'm crazy.

"He was such an asshole! I've never disliked someone so fast in my life."

Allie and Maddie sit in the booth across from me, sipping on their cocktails as I fill them in on what happened last night and this morning.

Maddie texted me earlier, apologizing for missing my calls last night, and asked if I wanted to get drinks tonight. Since there was no time to fill her in at work, I invited Allie along, making it a girls' night out.

We're at a bar called Prohibition Lounge. It's a speakeasy with a hidden entrance and a specialized menu to reflect their 1920s theme. The lighting in here is dim, usually giving off a reddish hue that feels sexy and intimate. There's a pretty decent crowd this evening, all waiting for the live band to start up around nine.

"I think it was sweet that he stayed to watch after you," Allie coos, swooning over my neighbor's lies.

"Allie, he was lying. He didn't stay because he was worried about me. He stayed because he got locked out and didn't have anywhere else to go."

"Well, still," she huffs out. "Maybe you should bake him cookies. Try to smooth things over."

"Screw the cookies," Maddie chimes in. "You should jump his bones the next time you see him."

I suck in a sharp breath, scrunching my face in disgust at her suggestion.

"What? You said yourself he was the sexiest man you'd ever met. I would've jumped on that opportunity faster than—"

"No," I yell, cutting her off. She doesn't need to remind me how fast she'd jump on a hot, single guy. "You don't get a say in this, Maddie. This is all your fault anyway."

She sputters, giving me a look of confusion. "How the hell is it my fault? I didn't lead the man to your apartment and tell him to stay. Although, that's not a bad idea. I'll tuck that away in case your dry spell doesn't end soon."

Ignoring the last part of her comment, I slap the table and shout, "Because! You're the one that demanded I set up a dating app in the first place. Then you convinced me to say yes to Liam when I should have just called it quits after Oliver and Mr. Dick Pic. And then you send me on my way to fuck a gay guy, which led to my massive breakdown, bringing the asshole to my door."

"Okay, yeah. My gay-dar is usually way more accurate. I must've been distracted by the sheer hotness in Sebastian's profile. He blinded me with muscles, so it's not my fault I couldn't see past that to catch the gay vibe he was giving off."

"She's got a point there," Allie agrees. "I probably would've been distracted by the muscles too."

They high-five each other and laugh, my eyes rolling with a

huff. Taking a sip of my cocktail, I ignore my friends, casting my eyes over the people milling around the bar. I'm in the middle of checking out a rather cute guy when my attention is snapped back to the table.

"I still think you should bake some cookies for your neighbor. You should never be enemies with those who live next to you. It never ends well."

"Or you can just offer to service his needs, if you know what I mean," Maddie interjects with a wink.

Thankfully, the band begins their set, saving me from having to answer. We sit there for another hour or so, our conversation taking a back seat so we can listen to the band's jazz performance.

After a while, Allie leans across the table, shouting over the music that she needs to go. Maddie glances at her phone and nods her head, so we all get up to pay our tab and leave.

On my way home, I pass a late-night bakery, and without conscious thought, I turn into the parking lot. I do my best to convince myself I'm not here to buy my neighbor cookies—they're for me. I love cookies, and I deserve them after the hellish few weeks I've been through.

But that's a lie. As much as I would love to stick to my guns and hate the sex on a stick, I simply can't. I hate conflict. So without overthinking it, I grab an assortment of cookies, pay, and book it out of the bakery before I can change my mind.

Walking into my apartment, I drop my purse by the door and run to the bathroom to relieve myself of the drinks from earlier. As I wash my hands, I stare at myself in the mirror, making sure I don't have smeared makeup or crazy hair this time.

Deeming myself acceptable, I head back to my front door, picking up the box of cookies on my way. I've barely stepped into the hallway when I slam straight into a brick wall, stumbling backward from the impact.

"Watch it," the wall growls at me, a tingling current flowing through my arms where his hands grip me, keeping me from falling.

Looking up, I stare into his electric blue eyes that are pinning me to the spot. He's wearing black dress pants and a slightly rumpled, baby-blue button-down shirt, the sleeves rolled up to his elbows again. His tie is halfway undone, hanging loosely around his neck, and his hair is in disarray. I have a sudden urge to run my fingers through his messy strands to see if they're as soft as they look, my fingers twitching with desire, but refrain at the last minute.

He tightens his grip on my arms and narrows his eyes, his glare snapping me back to reality. Clearing my throat, I shake my head and take a step back, putting some distance between us as I clutch the box of cookies tightly in my hands.

"S-sorry. Um. For running into you. And for last night." Shoving the box of cookies in his direction, I continue to fumble over my apology. "I picked these up for you...to apologize. Not for running into you, obviously. Um, for last night. For bothering you last night. They aren't poisonous or anything."

Oh, my god, why would you say that? Now he's definitely going to think I poisoned them.

My cheeks burn with heat over how stupid this man makes me feel. I have a medical degree, dammit. Good looks and mesmerizing eyes shouldn't zap me of my brain cells like this.

He looks me up and down, his eyebrows quirked as he judges my outfit before scoffing, his face clouding with annoyance.

"If you kept your hysterics to a minimum, there wouldn't be a need for cookies—poisonous or not. But hey, at least you no longer look like a drowned rat. Props to you for cleaning yourself up."

His hands join in a slow golf clap, then he turns on his heel, forcing his keys into his door before walking into his apartment.

The door slams shut behind him, the sound echoing around me as he leaves me standing in the hall alone—speechless yet again.

Backing into my apartment, I slam the door before growling with anger, tossing the box of cookies into the kitchen before stomping to my room, doing my best to make as much noise as possible, just to spite him.

What a fucking jerk!

14

PARKER

The door to my apartment slams shut behind me, leaving Riley standing alone in the hallway. I drop my briefcase by the door and kick off my shoes.

Cookies. *Ha!* What a fucking joke.

Walking to my bathroom, I whip my tie off as I go. It's late—a hell of a lot later than I intended on getting home this evening—and all I want is a hot shower to rinse off this god-awful day.

Reaching into the shower, I turn the handle as far left as it can go. Steam immediately fills the bathroom as I strip off the rest of my clothing, tossing them in my dirty clothes pile in the corner.

Stepping under the boiling stream, I immediately sigh. The heated water hitting the back of my neck is doing wonders to soothe the pulsing headache that's been building all evening.

I wash my hair first, then grab my body wash from the shower caddy, squirting a good amount in the palm of my hand before placing the bottle back on the shelf. Working the gel into a good lather, I run my hands along my arms and up into my underarms, giving them a good scrub. My eyes close, a heavy sigh releasing from deep in my chest as my hands flit across my body, making their way down to my abs. The lower I go, the more my dick stirs, twitching with excitement.

He's been feeling a tad neglected since I gave up sex, causing me to pop a semi at the briefest of bodily contact. He doesn't even give a shit that it's my own hand doing the caressing.

My hand slowly lowers, grabbing my semi-hard cock and giving it a few cleansing strokes before moving to my balls. Between my own man-handling and the hot water cascading down my body, my dick throbs with need.

Knowing a good jerking would help chase away the last pulses of this tension headache, my hand drifts back to my shaft, gripping the base before stroking up to the tip. After a quick twist around the head, my hand glides back down, tightening my stroke with each pass—my cock fully hardening in my firm grip. Wanting to finish this quickly to get some food, I flip through my mental spank bank.

Bracing my free hand against the shower wall, I circle the head of my dick, paying special attention to the sensitive underside while I picture a busty brunette giving me head. Using the aid of the hot water and a tight grip to mimic a warm mouth, I stroke my dick in time to her imaginary mouth wrapping around my length, bobbing up and down. Cupping my heavy balls in her hand, she takes me deep down her throat, a moan slipping through my lips as I wish this was real.

She gags a little, pulling her mouth off my shaft and replacing it with her fist. She strokes my entire length, her thumb rubbing my slit and gathering my pre-cum before moving her fist back down to the base of my shaft, spreading the moisture. The pads of her fingers skate across the sensitive vein bulging with pleasure.

I imagine the water streaming down her chest, her tits glistening as they heave with her efforts. Her hard nipples skim against my thighs, the muscles flexing with each kiss of her stiff peaks. A harsh groan vibrates through my chest as my balls draw tight to my body, my impending orgasm rushing to the surface.

Suddenly, my fantasy shifts without permission. Instead of a brunette, I'm looking down at my fist wrapped up in auburn hair. Vivid green eyes peer up at me as her freckled face drips with water. Her pink, pillowy lips part as her tongue strokes up the underside of my hard-as-stone cock before she wraps her lips around the tip, sucking hard.

My orgasm slams into me, cum spurting from my slit and coating the shower wall. My shaky legs threaten to buckle under me, weak from the powerful orgasm that just zapped all of my energy.

Where the hell did that come from? And why in the actual fuck did I just think of Riley? The woman does nothing but piss me off and annoy me endlessly.

Slamming the water off, I step out of the shower and dry off, the mental mind-fucking stealing my post-orgasm euphoria. I wrap the towel around my waist and head into my bedroom, grabbing a fresh pair of briefs and my favorite grey sweats.

While I'm busy scrounging for food in my fridge, my phone beeps with a new text. Pausing my search efforts, I pick up my phone to see if it's anything important or work-related. *Nope.* Just a new text from Colton in our group chat.

Before I can open the message, both Wesley and Rhett respond. They'll probably spend the next few texts bickering. Might as well let them get that over with while I heat up my dinner.

A few minutes later, I'm sitting in front of my TV with the latest hockey highlights playing on the screen. I'm about to take a bite of my leftover beef and broccoli bowl when my phone alerts me to yet another message in the group chat, the screen showing nine new texts. Jesus Christ.

Colton: *Hey, fuckheads. Ice is open tomorrow night. Setting* up a pick-up game against the Whalers. Puck drops at 6:05. You boys up for a night of whooping some ass?

Wesley: *I'm game. Although, you better leave the ass-whooping to me. Wouldn't want you to break a nail.*

Rhett: *Yeah, okay. You couldn't land an ass-whooping if you were paid to do it, Wes.*

Rhett: *Count me in, though. Someone needs to be there to secure a win.*

Wesley: *Fuck you guys. I could win the game blind-folded without any help from you jackwagons.*

Rhett: *Get real. You couldn't hit the back of the net if your stick had a laser pointer on it.*

Rhett: *Parker, you game? We might need an ice girl. Position is yours if you're free.*

Wesley: *Sends GIF of cheerleader*

Colton: *I'll bring my nephew's snow shovel. Should be the perfect size for his baby hands.*

Rolling my eyes at their bullshit, I check my schedule for tomorrow. I have a meeting at three forty-five, but it should be over early enough to make it to the arena on time.

Parker: *You pussies need to work on your trash talk before tomorrow night. I've heard better chirps from a dead bird. See you fuckers at 6.*

Rhett sends a middle finger emoji, Colton doesn't respond, and Wesley sends back a gif of some dude swinging his dick around—whatever that means.

MY MEETING RAN LATE, SO NOW I'M RUSHING TO THE ARENA FOR our game. Being late isn't an option. The Snipers organization only allows us so much time on the ice for these pick-up games. They had an afternoon practice since they have a playoff game tomorrow, but the crew will still need to prep the arena for tomorrow night's game, meaning we have to be cleared out by eight-thirty.

Arriving at the arena minutes before puck drop, I throw my gear on and rush through a few stretches, skating on to the ice with just enough time for a few warm-up laps around the boards. The only equipment we're required to wear is a helmet and skates, but if you've ever been hit with a puck after a slap shot, you think twice about not wearing hockey pads during a game—no matter how annoying they are.

"Nice of you to join us," Colton teases, smirking at me with raised eyebrows as I stop next to him.

"Got held up in a meeting, but don't worry your pretty little face. I'm here to deliver the ass-whooping you ordered."

Just then, Rhett and Wesley join us, each slapping my back in greeting. There's not much time for anything else as the ref signals for us to take our positions for the puck drop.

I skate to center ice, preparing for the face-off. I'm a center for our team, Rhett and Wes are wingers, and Colton is our goalie. The two defensemen on my line this week are Colton's coworkers. They work for the Snipers and are the reason we're able to schedule ice time.

The rest of our team are friends of Colton's or people he's met through his job. I don't know any of them, and I don't care to. All I care about is winning this game.

The team we're playing is full of assholes. They live for dirty hits and crappy chirps, no matter how bad we annihilate them every game. As we're waiting for the puck drop, their center, Brad, sneers at me, hissing, "Nice gloves. Do they make those in men's sizes?" He thinks he's funny, but he's too busy hurling piss-poor insults to realize the puck is being released by the referee.

Fucking idiot.

I beat him on the drop, swiping the puck back and passing it to Rhett before Brad realizes what's going on. And just like that, the game is off to a fast-paced start.

It only takes us three minutes to score, giving us a 1-0 lead. Brad gets his panties in a bunch over his fuck up, cross-checking me every chance he gets, but he's such a little bitch, I hardly feel a thing.

After his fourth check, I whip around, skating backward so I can see his face when I bark out, "Is that all you've got? I've seen bigger hits in the Juniors."

His face turns red with anger as he charges for me, dropping his gloves on the way. I welcome his advance, a cocky smirk covering my face. Between the stressors with my business, my wrecked house, and not getting laid, my testosterone is through the roof lately, with no chance of a release outside of my own fist. A good fight is exactly what I need.

He plants one good hit to my face before I lay him out, raining punches across his face. My hand stings with pain from connecting with his helmet, but it's not enough to stop me.

When the blood from Brad's nose drips to the ice, our teammates step in, helping the refs split us apart. Rhett eyes me with confusion before releasing my shoulder, skating off toward the other end of the ice. I'm not usually one to participate in fights, but tonight it was abso-fucking-lutely needed.

We each get two-minute penalties, sending us to the sin bin and leaving our teams to battle it out 4-on-4. When our penalty ends, I skate across the ice to our bench, joining Rhett and Wesley while waiting for our next shift.

Grabbing my water bottle, I squirt some in my mouth before swishing it around and spitting it back on the ice while Rhett and Wes both stare at me.

"What?" I grunt, my voice still tinged with pent-up anger.

Rhett raises his eyebrows at me before saying, "What the fuck's crawled up your ass?"

"Nothing. Just stressed out."

"Because you're not getting laid, or what?" Wesley pipes in.

"No," I grunt, the lie falling flat on my lips.

"You sure? Because nobody's holding you to your stupid experiment but you. If you need to get laid, just do it and move on."

"Fuck, no. This has nothing to do with me not getting laid and everything to do with my house still being fucking wrecked, work stressing me out, and my next-door neighbor annoying the absolute shit out of me with her lack of respect for those she shares a wall with."

"Huh," Rhett grunts out, sharing an annoying look with Wes. "Is your neighbor at least hot?"

Mulling it over, I consider lying again, but what's the point? It's not like the fact she's fuck-hot really matters. "I guess. Not in a normal sense, though. Her sexiness sneaks up on you. Too bad she's got a flare of crazy in her."

Wesley's bitch ass is the first to respond, shouting out, "Dibs! I like them a touch crazy. Makes the sex ten times hotter," he says while smirking, leaning across me to give Rhett a fist bump.

A weird sense of discomfort settles in the pit of my stomach when he stakes a claim over Riley. *Not sure what that's about.* I can hardly stand the woman, but the idea of Wes sleeping with her makes my skin crawl.

"Back off," I growl out in anger. "Nobody gets her. In fact, she's off-limits. I have enough problems with her already. I don't need my friends making the situation worse by fucking and ducking."

They both share another quick glance while smirking, but I ignore them, focusing on the game. My eye is starting to swell, as are my knuckles, the pain radiating up my forearm. I might have to cancel any face-to-face meetings tomorrow, but fuck, was it worth it to release my pent-up frustration.

A fourth-line winger sends the puck flying into the back of the net, bringing us up another point. I'm a bit distracted as I haul ass over the boards to take the ice, my thoughts clouded by a certain little redhead. Just as doubt creeps in, questioning if I've been too much of an asshole, an image of my wrecked house pops into my head. While I know she wasn't responsible for the destruction, I can't ignore how crazy she seems.

Yeah, nope. I don't have room for any more crazy in my life. It's best to keep her at arms-length, and the only way I know how to do that is to continue with my cold front. She'll get the message and stay the fuck away. *I hope.*

15

PARKER

The game ends with a score of 4-1, and after our team gathers at center ice to celebrate our win, we skate off toward the locker room to shower and change.

As I'm shoving my skates in my gym bag, Colton slaps me on the back, holding out two tickets to tomorrow's playoff game.

"For your hot mom, as promised."

Grabbing them from him, I shove them into a locker. He laughs, unbothered by my unspoken threat. The guys have always lusted after my mom, but they all know I'd slaughter them if they ever tried to act on it. Shouldering my bag, I give him one last glare, his laughs following me out of the locker room.

Fifteen minutes later, I'm letting myself in the front door of my childhood home. My mouth waters as I yell out, "Mom? Smells great in here."

My body tenses, ready for battle as the sound of a glass slamming against the table rings through the air, followed by chair legs scraping across the wood floors. Seconds later, my brother Rory appears in the hallway, wearing his signature scowl.

"What the fuck, Mom. You said he wouldn't be here," he shouts over his shoulder, his voice carrying toward the kitchen.

"Hey! Don't talk to her like that, you asshole."

Ignoring my demand, he smirks, his chin tipping up at my face. "Nice shiner. Looks like I'm not the only one that thinks you're a prick."

He shoves past me, knocking me in the shoulder on his way by. Our mother rounds the corner, hurrying into the hallway. She's twisting a towel in her hands, her face scrunched up with worry, cutting off the insult sitting on the tip of my tongue.

"I didn't think he was coming, but you're both always welcome here. Please don't leave, Rory. I miss both of my boys."

He shoves his feet inside his shoes and grabs his keys off the entryway table, ignoring her desperate pleas. "You know I can't stand to be in the same room as him. Not after what he did. Call me when he's not around."

Sparing a glare in her direction, he walks out, slamming the door behind him. One glance at my mom's drooping shoulders and broken-hearted face, and I'm following him out the door, ready to beat him to a pulp for upsetting her.

Rory's halfway to his car by the time I catch up to him. Grabbing his shoulder, I spin him around to face me. He immediately tenses up, his fists curling in anger.

"What the fuck's your problem, man?" I demand, keeping my eyes on his fists. I'm not in the mood to add another bruise to my battered face.

He scoffs, stepping closer as he harshly spits out, "You know exactly what the fuck my problem is. Don't act like an ignorant little twit. It doesn't suit you."

My head rears back, my eyebrows raising at the venom in his words. I know he's been angry with me, but aside from that one punch—or five— to my face, he hasn't been overtly malicious about the misunderstanding we had last year.

"You're still mad about that? Jesus, it's been over a year. You've gotta let it go, man. I didn't even know!"

"Don't tell me what to do," he growls at me. "You don't know jack shit about the damage you've done in my life."

"For the last time, I didn't fucking do anything. You never told me how you felt. Had you been a man and spoken up, I could have changed things. But you acted like a little bitch and kept a lid on it until you blew. And that's nobody's fault but your own."

He opens his mouth, ready to respond when he's cut off by our mother's harsh tone. "Boys! That's enough. You're causing a scene."

Sure enough, I glance around, noticing a few neighbors watching us. Rory huffs, shaking his head as he turns on his heel and stalks toward his car. I have half a mind to trip him, so he falls flat on his face, but think better of the idea. With his current attitude, he'd probably try to pin some bogus assault charge on me.

He slams his car door and peels out of the driveway moments later. Shaking my head, I turn back to the house, almost running straight into my mom. Her face is a perfect picture of disappointment at the sight of Rory's tail lights, filling me with guilt.

The corners of her mouth tip up in a bleak smile as she ushers me into the house, but I no longer want to be here. I hate upsetting my mom. Her life has been hard enough the last twenty years without me adding to her unhappiness.

Call me a momma's boy, I don't care. I've always shared a special bond with my mother, both before my dad died and especially after. She was the only parent I had left, after all. So it kills me to know that this ridiculous feud between Rory and I is hurting her. But he's a stubborn prick and won't give me a chance to fix what broke between us. Not that there's anything I could really do now. He should've been more honest and upfront with me years ago. Maybe then things wouldn't have escalated the way they have. And that thing with his fiancée? *Yeah, didn't see that coming, either.*

My mother brings her roast, carrots, and potatoes to the table and sits next to me. We dish out the food in silence, Rory's absence a mountain of discomfort between us. I know she doesn't blame me for him storming out, but regardless of his actions, we both know he'd still be here if I hadn't shown up.

I shovel a few bites into my mouth before complimenting her on the delicious meal, but it does nothing to improve her mood. She aims a doleful smile my way and continues to push her food around her plate, never taking an actual bite. After a few minutes of silence, she sighs, pushing her chair away from the table. "I'm sorry, Parker, I'm not feeling well. I think I'm going to turn in for the night. Will you lock up on your way out?"

Swallowing the lump of guilt in my throat, I nod, wishing like hell I could go back in time and change my decision to come over tonight. At least then, she would've had a good night with Rory. "Of course, Mom. Love you. Sleep well."

"Thanks. Love you too, honey." She pats me on the shoulder with another half-smile before heading upstairs. Her bedroom door softly clicks shut, the ensuing silence casting a blanket of gloom across the room.

Glancing around, my eyes catch on the family portrait hanging on the wall behind what used to be my dad's spot. The longer I stare at it, remembering the type of close-knit family we used to be, the more the ball of emotion solidifies in my stomach, settling like a boulder.

This is the table we used to share every meal; Rory and I often talking over each other while excitedly sharing stories of our day.

The couch in the living room across from me is where we all used to sit, crammed together for Friday night movies, nothing separating us but a bowl of popcorn.

My back faces the sliding glass door that leads to the backyard where my dad used to grill our summer feasts while Rory and I ran around, shooting each other with nerf guns. Our battles almost always turned into wrestling matches, fighting over the last pack of foam darts before our mom would lean out the door, yelling at us to cool it.

Rory and I used to do everything together. We were practically inseparable. And in the times our closeness caused arguments, our parents were always there—a united front—with some new creative way of forcing us to squash the tension.

Now there's a mountain of disdain between Rory and me, a fortress of grief surrounding our mother, and no father to bring us all back together. Glancing around the now empty table, I've never felt so...*alone.*

Having lost my appetite, I grab my plate and toss the rest in the trash before loading the dishes in the dishwasher. Taking the tickets for tomorrow night's playoff game out of my back pocket, I set them on the kitchen counter by the coffee maker where I know she'll see them.

Disappointment swirls in my stomach, knowing I won't get to see the joy on her face when she sees them, but that's what I deserve after rising to Rory's anger. I just hope she enjoys the game. She deserves to have fun.

While driving home, I think about everything I need to fix in my life: my house, my relationship with my brother, and my mother's happiness. There's simply no room for any other drama in my life. Especially not in the form of a crazy, redheaded storm.

16

RILEY

The last week and a half passed by in a blink of an eye, and by some act of God, I've managed to completely avoid running into Mr. Grumpass next door.

Well—almost completely. There was that embarrassing run-in last Friday when he was leaving the apartment building with a motorcycle helmet tucked under his arm as I was getting home from work. After stopping at his vehicle, he turned and started walking toward my car, and I somewhat panicked.

Okay, that's a lie. I *completely* panicked.

Wanting to avoid any sort of interaction with him, I ducked down in my seat, trying to hide. Unfortunately, I failed to realize his bike was parked in the stall right next to my car. I had glanced around, desperately looking for something to cover myself with, but luck wasn't on my side. I didn't have so much as a paper bag to throw over my face, leaving me with no choice but to try and crawl clear down to the floor as he reached the side of my car.

It almost worked too. But my nose betrayed me, choosing that exact moment to sneeze, attracting his attention. He glanced behind him—directly into my window.

We made eye contact for what felt like years before he shook his head and looked away. He secured his helmet, swung his muscular leg over the bike, and turned the key. Without sparing me another glance, he revved the throttle and shot out of the parking lot.

Once the coast had been clear, I tumbled out of my car, falling to the hard pavement. With my face tomato-red, I jumped up, brushed the dirt off my pants, and booked it inside, where I continued to avoid him for the next eight days.

Now it's Saturday afternoon, and I'm getting ready for the Paws-itive Adoptions gala this evening. My dress is hanging up, wrinkle-free, my shoes are sitting out, and my make-up and hair are done to perfection, but I'm nowhere near ready to attend this event.

The no-kill shelter, Paws-itive Adoptions, rescues homeless cats and dogs from the streets, providing them with any medical attention they need before sending them to their forever homes. They also re-home family pets for free, saving them from a life on the streets or being placed into a bad home. Since they're a relatively small shelter, they don't have the veterinarian staff they need to help some of the neglected animals that come in needing extreme medical attention.

That's where I step in. I volunteer my vet services once or twice a month—depending on my availability—to administer any vaccines needed or perform any surgical procedures.

So when the owner, Macie, called me last weekend, asking if there was any way I could attend their fundraising gala and give a speech, I knew I couldn't say no. My heart physically hurt when she admitted Paws-itive Adoptions had been struggling financially for the last few months and were close to having to shut down. These animals have held a soft spot in my heart for so long, it was a no-brainer to set my fear of public speaking aside to help keep a roof over their heads.

Thankfully, a consulting firm felt the same way and stepped

in, offering to help them turn things around, pro-bono. Macie said the company owner had a soft spot for animals and didn't want them to shut their doors, but they needed more than just his help. Hence, tonight's gala.

I just pray I'll make it through this night without butchering my speech, worsening their situation.

WALKING INTO THE EVENT, MY EYES WIDEN AS THEY TAKE IN ALL the tasteful decorations. The firm hired to save Paws-itive Adoptions spared no expense this evening.

The gala is being held in one of the spacious meeting rooms at the Fleet Science Center in Balboa Park. Thousands of twinkling fairy lights hang from the ceiling, giving the room a soft glow. The tables are draped in beautiful, cream-colored cloth, topped with elegant floral centerpieces and the finest china I've ever seen. Tripods holding digital displays line the room's perimeter, each screen showing a different animal ready for adoption. It's absolutely brilliant.

After confirming that I'm on the list for this event, the door attendant directs me to table thirteen. Gathering my dress in my left hand so it doesn't drag behind me or cause me to trip—made that humiliating mistake before—I head in the direction she pointed out.

Arriving at my designated table, my eyes fall on the back of a well-dressed man standing in front of an empty chair. A steel grey suit covers his tall, muscular frame, his pants hugging his ass so perfectly, I'm practically salivating. With dark black hair expertly slicked back, professionalism radiates off him in waves.

A tingling sensation sweeps up my spine, the hair on the back of my neck standing at attention as he picks my name card up off the table. My smile slowly fades, exchanging for a furrowed brow as the man flicks the card between two fingers, slowly shaking his head back and forth as it flutters back down to the table.

That's odd.

Clearing my throat, my voice is subdued as I greet him. "Hello. Looks like I'm your seat neighbor." I plaster on my brightest smile right before my tablemate turns around, stealing my breath the second his face comes into view.

My smile drops in an instant, transforming into a deep scowl. My traitorous body, however, doesn't seem to care that we hate this man because wetness pools between my thighs at the sight of his handsome face.

He narrows his eyes at me, and I stand up straight, pointing my finger at him before whisper-shouting, "No! What the hell are you doing here?"

He raises an eyebrow at my greeting, offering no explanation. I rip my card up off the table, double-checking that it does, in fact, have my name on it. Then I snatch his card from the table, not even caring that my manners have flown out the window. I'm sure we're gaining some unwanted attention from the other attendees, but I can't bring myself to care.

With his card cradled between my fingers, I stare down at his name, wishing the letters would magically rearrange into "Chris Hemsworth," or literally *anybody's* name but his. When that doesn't happen, I repeat his name out loud, testing it on my lips.

"Parker Adams." What the hell kind of name is that?

Okay, fine. There's nothing wrong with the name. It's just *him* there's a problem with. I glance back at my jerk-off of a neighbor, hoping this has all been a figment of my imagination.

Nope. He's still standing there, looking at me with his stupid, smug face. Other than his raised eyebrows, he's looking awfully calm, his hands stuffed in his pockets as I continue to freak out. I look back down at his name before whipping my head back up in his direction, whispering, "Parker Adams."

Pushing my arm out, I shove the card in his face before demanding, "Are you sure this is you?" Adamantly shaking my head, I don't wait for his answer before bringing the card back into my line of vision. "No, there's no way fate would be this cruel."

He scoffs before responding, "I don't know about fate, but my name is definitely Parker Adams."

I glance back down at the table, refusing to believe this is who I'll have to sit beside for the next several hours. "You're absolutely sure this is your seat?" I ask, pointing at the seat directly next to mine, praying—again—that there's been some sort of mistake.

"Well. The card says, 'Parker Adams.' And I am, indeed, Parker Adams. Got the name at birth. I've become pretty acquainted with it. It's probably mine to keep. So yeah. This is my seat." He rips out the chair directly in front of him and sits, leaving me standing there with my mouth gaping wide open.

He grumbles something under his breath, but I'm so busy fuming, I miss what he said. "I'm sorry, what was that?"

Turning to face me, he harshly spits out, "I said you're welcome to exchange seats with someone else. Or I can see if there are any open chairs in the hallway if you prefer. I know I do."

Growling at him, I turn on my heel and stomp away, heading toward the bar I spotted on my way to the table. I'm going to need alcohol if I have any hope of making it through this evening.

17

PARKER

Settling into my seat at the table, I wave down a waiter, demanding a glass of bourbon. I'm going to need it to tolerate sitting next to that woman for several hours. He scurries away to fetch my drink, leaving me to try and put the pieces of this shit-tastic puzzle together. *Seriously, what the fuck is she doing here?*

I don't have to wait long for an answer. Macie, the owner of Paws-itive Adoptions, stops at the table to see if I've met Riley—the shelter's volunteer veterinarian giving tonight's speech. What are the fucking odds?

Barely concealing my snarl, I inform her we're well-acquainted. She squeals with delight before explaining why she sat us next to each other, believing we'd get along perfectly since we're both passionate about saving the animals.

Ha. Joke's on her. Or maybe it's on me? Hard telling at this point.

The waiter shows back up with my drink, and Macie excuses herself to mingle with the other guests, leaving me to sip my drink in peace.

A short while later, Riley returns to the table. She's carrying a glass of champagne, but judging by the way she stumbles while pulling out her chair, followed by unceremoniously plopping down into her seat, I'm going to guess she had something stronger at the bar.

Thank fuck, nobody else seems to notice our Boozy Betty over here. She better sober the hell up, though. Macie is counting on her to deliver a speech worthy of donations. And frankly, so am I.

Obviously, I know it's not just up to Riley to bring in the donations. Hell, she's not even a paid employee of the shelter. That being said, her speech still matters. It's the only major speech being given tonight.

The rest of the donations will hopefully be a result of the sad as fuck digital displays I had Macie strategically place around the room. Each display shows a different animal currently up for adoption at the shelter. That was a stroke of genius if I do say so myself. It's physically impossible to get to the bar or a table without seeing at least three of the displays—something I'm hoping will help a few of the animals find their forever homes.

Dinner is finally served and not a moment too soon. Things were getting awkward as fuck with the silent tension growing between the gorgeous woman sitting to my right and me. *Yeah, I said it.* She's absolutely radiant when she's not scowling. But hell, even that's kind of cute, which only serves to piss me off more.

As soon as dinner ends and the plates have been cleared, Riley excuses herself from the table. I fight it for all of seven seconds, but that's as long as I can hold out. Subtly shifting in my seat, my eyes track her like heat-seeking missiles as she struts across the room. I hate that I can't take my eyes off her, but for some inexplicable reason, my body responds to her. That dress clings to her sexy as fuck curves, making it impossible to look away.

I'm not the only one, either. With a quick glance around the room, I spot several men watching her, their eyes feasting on her curves. She doesn't seem to notice, though, and I can't help but wonder if she realizes her sex appeal.

Eventually, I'm able to un-glue my eyes from her ass long enough to talk to some of the gala attendees. Mostly because she left the room, but that's beside the point. I make my rounds, securing a few donations from some of San Diego's wealthiest fuckers while sipping on some top-shelf bourbon. Riley bounces back into the room a short while later, but I try like hell to keep some distance between us. Now's not the time for a teenage-esque boner.

A few different ladies sidle up to me, latching on to my arms while slamming a lid on my unwanted lust. None of them are terrible looking, but I don't need glasses to see they only want one thing from me. I ignore them for long enough, and they all slither back to their own corners, leaving me to handle some business.

After an hour or so of schmoozing, Macie pops up on stage to introduce Riley for her speech. The crowd politely claps as she takes Macie's place behind the podium, hiding from my view. She's no longer stumbling, though, so that's a plus.

Riley clears her throat several times while fidgeting, clearly uncomfortable with speaking in front of a large group. Then, just when I think it was a mistake to put a microphone in front of her, she opens her mouth and proves me wrong, blowing me away in the process.

Color me fucking surprised—she's got beauty *and* brains.

Riley absolutely captivates the audience. They laugh at her stories of childhood pets, tear up when she describes the state some of the rescued animals are in when they're brought to the shelter, and "ooh" and "aww" over success stories.

She waxes poetic as she explains how their donations will help give these animals a better temporary home within the walls of Paws-itive Adoptions, and I watch as several people start pulling out their wallets. She clearly has a gentle, animal-loving heart that shows through her heartfelt words. That, or she's a phenomenal actress. But if that's the case, she's got me and everyone else fooled.

Women are wiping away tears, and the men are hiding their emotions behind their drinks. She's single-handedly changing the animal shelter's future with her speech, and my own animal-loving heart can barely handle it.

She wraps up the end of her speech and thanks people for their time and money. As soon as she clears the stage, there's a split in the crowd—half of them rushing to her side to speak with her, and the other half rushing to the donation table.

Mission: Accomplished.

AFTER MINGLING FOR A WHILE LONGER, I DROP MY ENVELOPE IN the donation box and slip outside, retiring for the night. Before the gala started, I stuck a blank check and a letter in an envelope, instructing Macie to use it to match the balance of tonight's donations.

I could have skipped all this fanfare in favor of writing her a check to keep the shelter open, but I wanted to make sure she was serious about saving the shelter. I got all the proof I needed tonight and plan on having Haylee set up a yearly donation. Whatever it takes to save the animals.

I'm only several feet from where I parked when I stumble across Riley standing next to her car. Her back faces me, and it's dark outside, but there's no mistaking those fuck-hot curves draped in emerald green silk. The closer I draw, the clearer her distress shows. She's pacing back and forth, her cell phone glued to her ear while her free hand frantically waves through the air with wild gestures.

What the hell's her problem now?

She hangs up the phone just as I stop behind her. Stomping her foot, she tosses her head back and releases a shriek, resembling a wounded animal.

Fucking Christ. I thought we moved past this, but I guess she can still be dramatic as hell despite her intelligence.

She bows her head and slumps her shoulders, growing silent as the seconds tick past us. I consider scooting past her, continuing on to my car, but decide against it at the last second.

"Problem?" I ask, my harsh voice splitting the quiet air between us, startling her.

She whips around with crazy in her eyes, quickly squatting low, bringing her fists up into a fighting stance. Her purse slings back, and it looks like she's seconds away from throttling me with it.

As recognition dawns, she straightens up with a growl, lowering her purse to her side. Her face is still coated in hatred, but apparently, she doesn't see me as a threat. Great news for me and my balls. They were ready to retreat to avoid a possible attack.

Riley sighs dramatically, her shoulders slumping in defeat as she turns back to face her car. "My tire's flat, and AAA can't replace it until tomorrow."

Leaning around her, I glance at the tire with zero life left in it. "What about your spare? That should get you home."

She hangs her head and kicks at a rock on the sidewalk, quietly admitting, "I forgot to get it replaced after my last flat tire."

Rolling my eyes, I run my hand across my chin, debating what to do. I could put her in a cab. But that's a level of assholery I should probably avoid, given the fact we live in the same building.

Of course, I could feign having plans, but the idea of leaving her standing here alone in the dark makes my skin feel uncomfortably tight. I may be a giant dickhole, but if something happened to her because I walked away, I'd hate myself forever.

Sighing with annoyance, I accept my fate. "Let's go."

Without waiting for her to answer, I pass her and continue walking. If she doesn't follow, that's her problem, not mine.

I'm a few steps from my car when I hear her high heels rapidly click-clacking against the sidewalk. Despite my reluctance to be cooped up in a car with her, I can't help the smug grin that crosses my face. I knew she'd chase after me—the ladies always do.

We climb into my car, each of us putting our seat belts on. I turn the stereo on and turn it up enough to ward off a conversation. She doesn't seem to mind, though. Her fingers drum against her thigh, perfectly in time with the beat of the song.

Fucking joke's on me. Her fingers dancing across her thigh like that is distracting as hell. My cock twitches in my pants as my head fills with images of skating my fingers up her thighs, following their path with my tongue.

Shaking my head, I ward off the unwanted images. Seriously, what the hell has gotten into me? Just because she showed a different side of herself tonight doesn't mean I suddenly like the woman. And it's not like she's a threat to my celibacy pact. I have zero desire to sleep with the woman.

Nope.

None.

Except....

My attempts to ignore her are failing. Her perfume permeates the air in my car, annoying me beyond belief because...*Fuck*. She smells divine. I'm torn between rolling down the window to clear my senses and leaning closer, embedding her smell into my nostrils.

She shifts in her seat, the slit in her dress parting, revealing a sliver of her tan, toned leg. Gritting my teeth, I clench the steering wheel tightly with both hands, my knuckles white from my effort to refrain from reaching over to test her skin's softness.

My dick takes note and tries to stand up—because of-fucking-course it does. *Christ.* You'd think I've reverted to my teenage years with the way my cock hardens at a simple glimpse of her upper thigh.

I attempt to subtly rearrange the situation in my pants before she notices and forms the wrong idea. *Or the right idea?* Hell, I don't even know anymore.

Thankfully, I have this fancy-ass sports car and can press the pedal to the metal, cutting this trip in half. The faster I get us home, the faster I can get away from the Devil's temptation.

Noticing the change in speed, Riley turns her head, scowling in my direction. "In a hurry?"

Not wanting to explain that I'm seconds away from pulling the car into an empty lot to fuck her brains out, I simply nod my head, spitting out, "Yup."

Crossing her arms, she scoffs, turning her body toward the door. Her dress shifts with her movement, revealing more of her legs, and my traitorous eyes dart from the road to that slit, hoping it will fall open a few more inches. *I wonder if she's wearing underwear?*

Groaning in frustration, I force my eyes back to the road. Just because it's been a while since I've been properly fucked doesn't mean I need to plant myself between Riley's legs.

On the other hand, the angry hate sex would probably be off the charts.

Dammit. NO. I'm stronger than this.

Probably.

Kind of.

FUCK. Are we there yet? I'm losing my goddamn mind.

Thankfully, Riley isn't in much of a mood to talk or even look at me, so I don't have to worry about her witnessing my raging hard-on that just. Won't. Quit.

After what feels like a century, we finally pull into the parking lot. She has her seatbelt off and her purse held in her hands, hopping out before I've put the car fully in park. Now who's in a fucking hurry?

I climb out of the driver's side, finding her standing near the hood of my car, digging in her purse. Presumably for her keys, but fuck if I really know. Right before she storms off toward the building entrance, she turns to me, mumbling, "Thanks for the ride," before quickly facing the building.

She rushes forward, clearly trying to get away from me. Well, then. She can just fuck right—*oh, shit.*

Her heel catches in a crack in the sidewalk, snapping off the shoe. She teeters, completely off balance from her now missing heel, as her arms wave around, spilling all kinds of shit from her purse. I dash forward, catching her just as she falls to the side.

Two wide, vivid green eyes peer up at me, her lips parted from a startled gasp. Everything around us falls silent, and I swear to you, in that exact moment, I go full-on stupid. My arms tighten around her, loving the way she feels while cradled in my embrace, and my gaze darts to her still-parted lips, admiring their fullness.

Her tongue peeks out, swiping across her bottom lip, and the last ounce of blood in my brain drains, funneling straight into my cock. Desire grips me by the balls, the desperation to taste her mouth defeating my self-restraint.

Dipping my head, I'm centimeters away from molding my lips to hers when a car honks, startling the shit out of both of us. Riley jerks in surprise, and I'm too lust drunk to react quickly enough. Her head pops up way too fast, slamming straight into my nose.

Fuck, that hurt.

I immediately drop her, my hands flying to my nose,

attempting to staunch the blood. With a yelp, Riley falls to the ground, just as the first few drops of red soak into my brand new Armani suit.

She rolls to her knees, grabbing a pack of tissues that fell from her purse during the commotion. "Oh, my god, I'm so sorry. That car came out of nowhere!" Ripping the package open, she reaches in, grabs a few tissues, and violently shoves them under my nose. My face jerks back from the sting of pain as she hits my nose —again.

Gritting my teeth, I rip the tissues from her hand before she breaks my fucking nose with a third hit and rise to my feet. The car from earlier honks again, and I turn my back on Riley, directing all my pain and anger at the honking car as I flip them off. They jerk their wheel to the right and skirt around us, the driver returning my hand gesture as they fly out of the parking lot. *Fucking assholes.*

"Are you alright?" I demand, snarling the words though my gritted teeth, my back still facing her.

When she stammers back that she's fine, I grunt and walk away, needing to get upstairs to take care of my nose. My mother would beat my ass if she found out I left this chick outside with a broken heel and her shit scattered across the pavement. But I already fulfilled my good deed by bringing her home, and she went and damn near broke my nose as a thank you. So, no. Me, myself, and my stupid-ass confusing thoughts are done for tonight.

Slamming my apartment door shut behind me, I stalk to the sink. Turning on the faucet, I angle my face down, sticking it under the running water, the cold water soothing my throbbing nose.

What in the actual fuck happened tonight?

The logical side of my brain knows we don't actually like Riley. In fact, we are perfectly content with our new single life and the lack of drama. However, the part of my brain that produces hormones is at war with the logical side, trying to convince me she isn't all that bad.

And then there's my dick. He fucking thinks he runs this show and is convinced Riley's sexy ass is all we need in life. He's doing a stand-up job of making shit real hard here. Pun intended.

It's two against one, and I'm actually worried the logical side of my brain is losing. In fact, I think my celibacy pact is in real fucking danger.

18

PARKER

The sun shines through my office window, beating against my back as I finish up a call with Macie. I don't always work on Sundays, but after last night's gala, we wanted to hit the ground running. We have a few last minute things to wrap up before I switch gears, focusing on my secret project. One of them being the finalized list of donors and their contributions she emailed me within hours of the gala ending last night. I told her we'd form a plan for where to allocate the funds, which is why my ass is currently planted in this seat.

When I offered to help her business pro-bono, she was overcome with tears, but I still had my reservations on whether she'd be one to listen to my advice or not. Sometimes business owners are stubborn assholes that think they need to hold the title of "Captain" in a death grip, no matter how far they've sunk their own ship. Not Macie, though. She cares too much about the animals to let her pride steer her off course, which makes this job a hell of a lot easier.

Just as I hang up with Macie, Haylee bounds through my door without so much as knocking. She's dressed down today in skinny jeans and a light blue blouse, which I choose to ignore, considering I pulled her away from whatever she usually does on a Sunday afternoon.

Her eyes are fixed on the stack of papers she's holding, barely glancing at me before dropping her gaze back to the pile as she struts toward my desk. I know the minute she registers my black eyes, her head whipping up in a double-take as she pulls up short, her jaw dropping open. Her eyelashes flutter with rapid blinks before she pulls herself together, blurting out, "What the hell happened to you?"

"Watch your fucking language," I snap back, dodging her question.

She snorts and rolls her eyes, plopping down into the empty seat in front of my desk. "Seriously, what happened? Did you and Rory get into another fight?"

My brow furrows in confusion as I shuffle a few papers against my desk. *Why is she asking about Rory?* Our arguments haven't been violent since last year's "incident." I'm more likely to earn a shiner in a pick-up hockey game than from a fight with my brother, something she should already know after my black eye a few weeks ago. *Weird.*

"No. Riley's hard-ass head made friends with my nose last night, and now, here we are. Did you bring me the new ads for the shelter?"

The second I mention Riley's name, a flashback of last night flits through my brain. Seeing her stare at me with those gorgeous eyes and fuckable lips has my dick stirring again, twitching against the zipper in my pants. My mouth waters as I remember how close I came to kissing her. What the hell is that about? It's like I'm not in control of my own body anymore.

"What's that look for?"

"Huh?" I huff, shaking out of my lustful memories.

Tossing the ads down on my desk, she smirks, her back

resting against the chair as she gets comfortable. "Why'd you make that face a minute ago? You looked all sex-crazed."

See? Clearly, I've lost all control.

"There was no face," I grunt out in irritation.

"Whatever you say, boss. Why were you with Riley? That's your neighbor lady, isn't it? I thought you hated her."

"She was at the gala last night. She had a flat tire, I gave her a ride home. Then she broke a heel, almost fell, I caught her, she nailed me in the nose with her head. End of story." Before I can think better of it, I open my mouth again and make things worse. "And I don't hate her. She's different than I thought she was." *Shut the hell up, idiot.*

Haylee peers at me with a calculating look, her eyes slightly narrowing before her face breaks out in a taunting smirk. "Sooo, you went from hate to date overnight? And here I thought women were the indecisive ones."

"Hold the fuck up," I chide, my hands rising in a halting motion. "I didn't say I want to date the woman. But it would probably be..." I hesitate, figuring out how to finish my sentence. "Beneficial...if we could at least be friendly."

What? It's not a total lie. I *don't* want to date her, but I can't very well admit to my assistant that after last night, I want to fuck this woman so hard she forgets what day it is. I spent all night tossing and turning, my head full of thoughts about getting closer to the vixen next door, coming to the conclusion she won't disappear from my thoughts unless I face the situation head-on.

Preferably with the "head" in my pants.

What's one tiny break in the celibacy pact, right? We can fuck the hate out of our systems, then go back to being nothing but cordial neighbors, and my brain can return to focusing on shit that actually matters.

Like The Helping Haven.

"Riiiight. Beneficial to be friends. I think you've got the

phrase a little jumbled, but let's go with it. Any ideas on how you're going to transition from the biggest asshole she's ever met to beneficial friends?" She questions with a snort and raised eyebrows, the little smart-ass.

Rolling my eyes, I swivel in my chair, facing my floor-to-ceiling windows. Running my hand across my chin, I stare out at the shoreline. She's right—fuck, I hate admitting that—I've made a mess of shit with my particular brand of assholery. But it's nothing I can't fix. *Probably.*

"I was hoping you'd be able to help with that. I might need a woman's touch here."

"I'm not a miracle worker. From what I've gathered from your bitching, you've already shown her you're an asshole. If she has any brains in her at all, she'll avoid you like the plague."

I lift my arm in the air, flipping her off over the top of my chair, not bothering to turn around. She snickers before falling silent, leaving me to my thoughts as I debate how to fix things. I don't think whipping my dick out—no matter how impressive it is —will work in this situation.

"Oooh, I have an idea!" Haylee's excited voice cuts through the silence, my eyes widening with an ounce of fear.

This oughta be interesting.

19

RILEY

Mondays are typically my favorite day of the week. It never matters how bad last week ended or what horrors transpired over the weekend—because, let's face it, weekends usually aren't that good to me—Mondays are a fresh start.

Plus, I always wake up full of excitement, itching to return to my zoo animals.

This Monday, though? Yeah, it's not off to a great start.

Between the disastrous ending to the gala Saturday night and spending my Sunday fixing my tire, I must have fallen into bed without setting my alarm last night.

I'm right in the middle of a drool-worthy dream featuring an attractive, muscular man with raven hair and sapphire eyes when a pounding on my door wakes me with a start.

Disoriented and confused, both from dreaming about *him* and from wondering who would be visiting in the middle of the night, I bolt straight up in bed, casting my wide, sleepy eyes around the room. Glancing at my alarm clock, I panic when I realize it's closing in on eight a.m.

With a shriek, I jump out of bed, immediately falling to the floor thanks to the stupid sheets wrapped around my legs. I disentangle my legs before hopping up, kicking the sheets across the floor with a grunt for good measure.

I'm distracted by the sting of pain in my chin after it bounced against the floor and am halfway into the bathroom before knocking booms through my apartment, reminding me of why I'm awake in the first place.

Grabbing my robe from the bathroom, I shove my arms in the sleeves while hurrying to the front door, ripping it open to find —nobody.

What the hell?

I know somebody knocked—I heard it loud and clear—so where'd they go? Stepping out of the doorway, I scan up and down the hall, searching for my ghost of a visitor. Two steps into the hallway, I stumble as my foot catches on a box sitting on the floor. I hop, skip, and jump, my arms flailing, trying to avoid falling for the third time in as many days.

What the hell is happening to my life?

Righting myself, I bend down and pick up the bakery box with my name stamped across the top. Did I sign up for some sort of bakery delivery and forget about it? No, surely not. That's not something I would forget.

Wondering who would be sending me baked goods, I carry the box into my apartment to investigate. Carefully setting it down on my kitchen table, I take a few steps back, tilting my head to the left as I stare at it for…admittedly, way too long. I'm not sure what I'm expecting to happen, but something about this feels wrong.

So I stand there, staring at the bakery box, and it sits there… well, not staring at me. But it's definitely taunting me. With a shake of my head, I force myself to get a grip and step forward. I gently grab the edge of the box, inhaling deeply and holding it. Surely, nobody would put a bomb in a cardboard bakery box…right?

Closing my eyes, I rip the lid off and jump back, bracing for impact. A few seconds of silence pass as I gather the courage to peek out of squinted eyes. Nothing exploded or jumped out at me, so that's a good sign.

Stepping closer, I peek at the contents of the box, my mouth pooling with drool as the delicious scent of cinnamon and sugar fills the air. Four perfectly frosted cinnamon rolls taunt me, steam rising from the centers as if they were just removed from the oven.

Hypnotized by the aroma of deliciousness, I almost miss the message written on the inside of the bakery box, reading, "Breakfast is on me." Beneath that, there's a postscript that says, "Not poisonous."

A spark of rage races up my spine as a hazy memory pops into my head—my prick of a neighbor telling me he didn't want my poisoned sweets. I'm practically shaking with unbridled fury at his audacity. Who the fuck does this guy think he is?

After every single rude encounter we've had, he thinks he can just smooth things over with breakfast like he didn't deny my apology cookies weeks ago?

Well, screw him.

I may have almost broken his nose, but he was an asshole the whole way home Saturday, then left me alone in the dark parking lot, scrambling to pick up the contents of my purse with a broken heel and a bruised ass. Not to mention all the times he's been a prick since the day he moved in. He and his guilt rolls can go to hell.

Picking up the box, I close the lid and dump the whole thing straight into the trash. Brushing my hands off, I rush to the bathroom to shower before work.

Two Days Later

Okay, fine. It's only been two minutes, and I'm already scurrying back to the trash can to dig the bakery box out like a starving raccoon. Truth be told, I'm surprised I lasted two whole minutes. I may hate Parker with the fury of a thousand suns, but that doesn't mean these cinnamon rolls should go to waste. There are starving people right here in California. No need to spit in their faces by throwing free food out.

Tearing one side off, I pop it in my mouth, practically melting into a puddle of happiness right then and there as the perfect combination of cinnamon and sugar explode on my taste buds. Alternating between shoving bites into my mouth and licking frosting off my fingers, I waltz back to my bedroom to finish my morning routine. Shooting off a quick text, I let the other vets know I'm going to be late as I finish the last bite of my breakfast and hop in the shower.

Forty minutes later, I walk out to the kitchen to fill my travel coffee mug, eyeing the bakery box resting on my table. I really shouldn't have another one. *Definitely not.*

On the other hand, I might have to skip lunch to make up for being late, so…Grabbing my lunch box, I gently place an extra cinnamon roll in an empty container, making sure the lid doesn't touch the frosting. I snap the lid shut before tossing in an apple and some crackers. I can practically hear my mother's voice in my head, chiding me for my unhealthy lunch, but what she doesn't know won't hurt her. Might hurt my waistline later, but I'll cross that bridge after I eat that second roll.

Snatching my keys and purse, I hurry out the door, scowling at Parker's door on my way to the elevator. If I had the time, I'd give him a piece of my mind. I wouldn't give the cinnamon rolls back or anything, but I'd make sure he knows I don't forgive him. People who can't apologize face-to-face don't deserve my forgiveness.

By the time I get home from work, I'm exhausted and stressed out. Within a few hours of being at the zoo, it was clear my day wasn't going to turn around. We were busier than we've been in weeks. The animals were feisty as hell and wanted nothing to do with being seen by us, several emergency procedures popped up, and nothing ever seemed to calm down. I never got to eat my "lunch," and even Allie seemed a bit harried over the complete dumpster fire that was this Monday.

Kicking off my shoes, I undo my braid, shaking my hair out and massaging the pain from my scalp. Sighing in relief, I'm about to reach into my scrub top to unsnap my bra when I'm interrupted by a knock at the door. I consider ignoring it, not in the mood to deal with anybody right now, but curiosity takes me by the hand, leading me to the door. As it swings open, I'm surprised to find a delivery man dressed in a tan uniform staring back at me. Glancing down at his clipboard, his deep timber voice questions, "Ms. James?"

"Yes, that's me. But I didn't order anything."

He shrugs his shoulders before holding his clipboard out to me. "Sign here, please."

Remembering my surprise from this morning, I sigh in irritation and sign my name before handing the clipboard back to him. He bends and picks up a tall, white gift box, holding it out for me to take. I hesitantly reach out, grabbing it from his hands. It's donned with red ribbon, crafted into a large, pretty bow on top, and isn't nearly as light as I was expecting. The delivery man tips his hat at me and turns on heel, stalking away.

Curiosity and annoyance battle it out for my dominant emotion as I kick the door shut behind me and carry the box to my kitchen counter. Tugging the bow undone, I pop the top off and pull out the contents, floored by what I find inside—a 2016 bottle of Joseph Phelps Insignia wine, already slightly chilled. The label is gorgeous, but I've never heard of this wine, so I pull out my phone to do a little research.

Typing the name of the wine into my search bar, I bring up the first results on the page and nearly choke on my own tongue. It's a three hundred dollar bottle of dessert wine.

What in the actual shit?

There's a gift tag attached to the top of the wine bottle, catching my attention. Pulling it off, I read, "Mondays: when a wine-down is better than a meltdown."

That. Jerk!

One time. I have a meltdown *one time,* and he thinks he can throw it in my face all willy-nilly whenever he wants? And why is he still sending me shit? Wouldn't it be easier—and cheaper—to just come over and apologize to my face?

God, why are men so…irritating?

I go straight to my cupboard to pull down a wine glass, pouring a small sample of the wine. Bringing the tumbler to my lips, I take a sip, damn near buckling to the floor at the decadent taste.

Well, shit. It's the best damn wine I've ever had.

I fill the glass and am heading for the couch when I notice the bakery box still sitting on my dining room table. Changing course, I grab the biggest roll in the box, and make my way to the living room, sinking down into my couch to lose myself in mindless television for the night. Normally, I wouldn't dare to drink anything I didn't buy myself, but after the day I had, nothing seems likely to steal away my stress quite like wine and a cinnamon roll.

While I'm still not overly fond of my neighbor, and am quite wary of what the fuck he's up to, I have to admit that I hate him just a teeny, tiny bit less, thanks to him supplying my breakfast *and* dinner. But he better not get his hopes up or anything. He can't just buy my friendship with expensive gifts. I deserve a lot better than that, and flaunting his wealth doesn't impress me. I make my own money and can buy my own stuff.

What would impress me is if he was a real man and could admit he was wrong to be an asshole and apologize. But until then, I'll sit back and enjoy this lovely little surprise after a day from hell.

20

PARKER

Sitting on a bench on the corner of Hudson and Spes in Anaheim, California, I watch the people coming and going across the street. I've been sitting here for the last two hours, doing nothing but observing how many families The Helping Haven sees throughout a typical day.

The building is a multilevel brick warehouse that's seen better days. From the outside looking in, I'd never guess it was a place of hope, a place to get your life together, without the aid of the sign hanging above the entrance reading, "The Helping Haven."

Each person that walks through the front glass doors differs significantly from the next. Some are happy and hopeful, some are hesitant to walk through the doors, and some are downright struggling, seemingly weighed down with troubles. The single parents with a kid or two in tow hit the hardest, though. They all look the same—like they've seen better days.

As a bead of sweat travels down my temple from the California sun beaming down on me, I stand from the bench and cross the street, ready to meet Sarah for my tour of the building.

Entering through the glass doors, I'm taken back by how vastly different the inside is compared to the worn-down exterior.

Everywhere I look, it's bright and cheerful. Two of the walls are exposed brick, but the other two are painted a bright yellow with vinyl motivational quotes plastered to them in big, bold fonts. There are tables placed strategically throughout the room, and a food bar set up at the back with a line already forming. A snack rack stands off to the side with everything from bags of chips and crackers to bagged cookies, all easy to grab and go.

To my right stands a long, mahogany counter with a cheery-faced brunette standing behind it, looking at a computer screen. She notices me standing here with my hands stuffed in the pockets of my expensive-ass suit. Using a blank expression, I do my best to hide the emotions flooding my system, trying to peek through my tough exterior at the sight of so many broken families standing in line for food.

The brunette steps around the corner of the counter and bounces over to me with a friendly smile plastered to her face. "Hi! You must be Mr. Adams? I've been expecting you."

Reaching my hand out, I grasp hers in a firm shake, nodding my head once. "Ms. Tilling. Shall we start the tour?"

"Please, call me Sarah," she pleads with a twinkle in her eye.

She steps further into the room, and I follow close behind, taking everything in with my well-trained business eye, doing my damnedest to leave my emotions at the door. I won't lie and say it's easy, but it's a necessary evil when making business decisions.

"As you can see, this is our cafeteria of sorts. Anyone enrolled in the program is welcome to come and go as they please, as long as they sign in at the front door. They can come in and sit for a hot meal, take a boxed meal to go, or simply grab something from the snack rack as they pass through. We are proud to help anyone that passes through our doors, as long as they can prove they've lost something of importance. We specialize in single parents and widowed spouses—kids or not—but we also accept individuals that have lost their jobs or homes and are at the end of their ropes.

"We do our very best to verify that those passing through the program are desperately in need, to not waste resources, but we also try not to turn people down that clearly need our help. In our six years of being open, we've only had a handful of proven scammers."

Nodding my head, I listen closely as I observe everything from the people in the room to the finer details of organization and cleanliness. After a few minutes, she leads me to a staircase off to the side, climbing the stairs to the second level. Her hips sway exaggeratedly as she takes the steps ahead of me, and I can't help but roll my eyes. Her looks are nothing to scoff at, but she's no fiery redhead, which means her chances with me are zilch.

Reaching the next floor—this one with orange walls and areas sectioned off with cubicles—she waves her hand around the room, pointing out a few significant details. "This is our work resource floor. We hold weekly training sessions for job qualifications and specific certification courses for various fields. There are stations to aid with building resumes, and stations with mock interviews for practicing purposes. We intended to begin six-week night classes for various career fields, but unfortunately, the funds fell through, and we had to table the plan."

Maintaining a blank face, I store that information for further use and silently follow her to the third floor, where I find a much different setup. The walls up here are a light purple, with a circle of chairs in the middle of the room. There are fake palm trees in the corner, hovering over a cream-colored chaise that faces a white armchair—an identical setup in the opposite corner. A distinct calming scent swirls through the air on this floor. I can't quite put my finger on what the smell is, but whatever it is, it's rather soothing.

"This is what we refer to as our healing floor. We hold group meetings twice a day—one in the morning, and one in the evening. There are also two separate areas, as you can see, for those needing private sessions," Sarah points out, motioning to the furniture in the corners. "The meetings are mostly focused on grief and surviving the loss of a partner or child, but they are open to anybody that's suffering a loss, no matter what it may be. We do our best to be inclusive of everybody's grief here. We also encourage our people to meet here on their own, outside of the meetings. It's a place to come together to share our burdens. Here at The Helping Haven, we understand that sometimes, our loads are just too heavy to carry alone, and when that happens, we're here to offer a place to set your burden aside, giving your shoulders and your heart a place to rest."

My heart squeezes with her explanation of what the room offers those who enter. After nights of silently sitting outside of my mother's en-suite bathroom, listening to her cry behind closed doors, I wish like hell she would've had a place like this to turn to. She was always so strong, hiding behind a formidable suit of armor. But at night, when she thought we were sleeping—blissfully unaware—she'd let that shield down, releasing her grief. But I knew. *I always knew.*

For years, I'd sit next to her bathroom door, my hand plastered to the door in an unseen display of solidarity, wishing I could add her grief to my own, carrying it for her. My throat would constrict with emotion, silent tears tracking down my cheeks as her quiet whimpers of pain escaped through the crack at the bottom of the door. Every night, without fail, I'd wait until the shower turned off to leave my post, returning to my bed, so she'd never feel embarrassed. And every morning, without fail, she'd meet us in the kitchen for breakfast, ready to face another day with a brave smile covering her face. She'd pretend to be alright for our sake, and I'd pretend I didn't spend the night before silently sharing her grief.

Looking around this room, with its lavender walls and calming vibe, I fucking wish like hell it existed when we needed it the most, and I'll be damned if I see it taken away from others who need it now.

Turning my back on Sarah, I march to the staircase, climbing to the next floor, escaping the memories this one fills me with. Sarah's heels click-clack behind me as she hurries to catch up, once again taking the lead on our tour as we step onto the landing.

"This is the final floor of the building, and as you can see, it's split into two sections. The section in the back is the sleeping quarters, used by anyone who's recently lost their home, and the front section is used as a daycare for any families needing childcare as they pull their lives together. Community volunteers run the daycare, as well as any parents that are in-between jobs, waiting to hear back from completed interviews. Our members are also allowed to volunteer in the cafeteria or help with housekeeping duties, all of which cut down on the organization's costs."

Dipping my chin, I nod with understanding. I raise my hand up to my chin, rubbing it against my weeks' worth of scruff as I consider whether or not I'm ready to do what comes next. Wanting some time to process what's been revealed on the tour, I turn to Sarah, dismissing her for the time being.

"I'd like to be alone for a while, please."

She eyes me with a questioning look, her eyebrows slightly furrowed. "Oh, um. That's not really allowed, but I suppose I could leave you be for just a bit. But, um. Know that we do have cameras."

Doing my best not to scoff at her implied warning, I simply nod my head in her direction. *Does it fucking look like I need to steal anything from here?* When she makes no move to leave, I hit her with an impatient stare, my eyebrow quirked in annoyance.

"Oh. Um, right," she mutters, clearly flustered. Nervously wringing her hands, she turns to leave, heading toward the stairs.

When I made the appointment for the tour, I gave no explicit reason, alluding to a possible interest in being a donor. They have no idea I'm actually here to buy out the organization, so her hesitancy is probably justified, no matter how annoying.

As I'm walking around the area, processing today's information, my attention catches on a young boy and his mother, hiding in the corner of the sleeping quarters. The mother is young—early twenties, if I had to guess—and is squatting down in front of the boy. I'm not around kids enough to know for sure, but he's probably six. Maybe seven. His hair is messy, his clothes a bit baggy, and his dirty face is coated in a stream of tears.

Doing my best to hide my piqued interest, I slowly walk around a few of the bunk beds, pretending like I'm examining each area's setup. With my head bowed, I peek up through my lashes, watching the scene unfold.

"I don't want to stay here! I want to go home. I want dad," the young boy yells, his little foot stomping hard on the floor as tears roll down his chubby cheeks.

The mother drops her chin to her chest briefly, her body shaking with emotion. When she looks back up at the boy, her watery voice wavers as she murmurs, "I know, baby. I want that, too, but you know that's impossible."

"Why?" he screams, his own voice muddled by tears.

"Because, baby, daddy's in heaven. You know that."

The boy's foot stomps hard on the floor, unimpressed with his mother's words. My own heart stumbles in my chest, fully understanding how this young boy is feeling, even if he's not sure of it himself. He's probably too young to know what heaven means.

I was old enough to understand my dad was gone forever, and I still struggled with the concept. This young boy probably has several years of confusion ahead of him yet—years he'll spend yearning for a father that can never come home, despite how much he'd probably like to if he had a choice.

I watch as the young mother leans in, trying to wrap her arms around her son, but he pushes her away, running to the bathrooms in the corner instead. Her hand rises to cover her mouth, muffling the sob that rips from her throat as he runs from her.

With the sudden urge to give the mother her privacy, I silently make my way toward the stairs, heading down to the level below in search of Ms. Tilling. If anything, what I just witnessed solidified my decision. The people across California need this place, and I'll do whatever it takes to give it to them.

Descending two floors, I find Sarah down on the resource floor, straightening a cubicle at the front. Clearing my throat, I wait until her attention is focused on me before stating, "I've seen everything I need to."

Her eyes shine as she smiles brightly, her hand reaching out, settling on my bicep as she cheers, "Oh, that's great! What did you think? Are you ready to help the families of California?"

Sure as fuck am, but not in the way she thinks.

"As a matter of fact, I am. Everything I've seen today convinced me of my decision. I've done my due diligence, and I know your organization is in danger of closing its door. I'm here to make an offer to buy out the organization."

Her face pales as my words sink in, the smile slowly fading from her lips. "Wait, what? You're not here to become a donor?"

"No."

"O-oh. Um. Oh," she stutters, shocked by my admission.

Pulling an envelope from the inside of my suit jacket, I hand it to her, placing it in her shaking hands. "Everything is outlined in here. I'm trusting you'll get it into the right hands. If not, I have a copy ready to be sent to every contact email listed on the website. I'll be waiting for a call."

With that, I dip my head and turn to the doors, leaving her slack-jawed and speechless in the middle of the resource room.

21

PARKER

Six hours later, I'm sitting in the hotel restaurant, flipping through work emails over dinner, when my screen switches to an incoming call from a local number.

"Parker speaking," I answer in my curt business tone.

"Mr. Adams, this is Noelle with The Helping Haven. I've received your offer from Sarah, and I have to say, I'm rather taken back. The news that we're nearly bankrupt has yet to go public."

"I've been in this business long enough to not need public news to know when a business is floundering."

A few moments of silence pass as she digests my statement, probably wondering how I know what I know. With a clearing of her throat, she responds, "Very well. I must say, your offer is very generous, but you must understand it's a decision that can't be taken lightly. This organization is very dear to my and the board's hearts, and we've been clinging to the hope of bringing in more donors rather than selling out or closing."

"I understand that, and I'll have you know, your mission is very dear to my heart, as well. This is more than just a business decision—it's personal and will be treated as such. I'm prepared to buy you out today, on one condition."

"And what is that?"

"That this remains anonymous—both the sale and my name."

Silence greets me on the other end of the line, not that I'm surprised. A takeover rarely happens quietly, and I'm sure she's questioning my motivation behind that. Odds are, she'll be googling me as soon as we get off the phone, if she hasn't already. It won't take a fucking genius to understand my reasoning—my reputation in the press is shit. I just hope it doesn't cause issues with the purchase, but I'm prepared to fight dirty if I need to. They aren't in the best position to turn down my offer. Unless they genuinely don't care about keeping their doors open.

"I will take that into consideration, along with the rest of your offer."

"Good. While I have every intention of dissolving the board and replacing it with my own staff, transforming it from a board-ran, non-profit organization to a partner-ran company, I want to assure you that your principles, organization name, and current mission will remain the same. Naturally, some practices will need to change to meet my vision for expansion—"

"I'm sorry, expansion?" she questions, cutting me off mid-sentence.

"Yes. Expansion," I repeat, doing my best to keep my irritation from my tone. *I fucking hate being interrupted.* "It's my goal to slowly expand The Helping Haven until there's one in every state."

A surprised gasp travels through the phone, followed by prolonged silence. Finally, Noelle gathers her wits, her voice slightly wavering as it travels down the line. "Wow. That's an impressive goal. What about funding? If you're looking to buy us out, surely you know the organization is on its last leg, barely keeping its head above water."

"Funding is not an issue," I state, dismissing her concern quickly. "Not only do I have the determination to take over the founding organization and bring it back to a healthy state, but I also have the funds to do so, without any help from donors. Past the flagship warehouse plans, I have already begun securing a portfolio of wealthy donors interested in bringing the expansion to life.

"My previous experience with running a company and restructuring failing businesses lends me the necessary tools to conduct successful fundraisers, which will be essential in the expansion moving forward. I assure you, Noelle, I fully understand the passion your current organization stems from, and I'd hate to see you have to close the doors on such a wonderful program. I'm simply ready to take over the reins and breathe fire into your dwindling embers, and I'll do so with every ounce of love and integrity I possess."

"Very well," she sighs after a brief hesitation. "You've given me quite a deal to consider. We'll need some time to process everything."

"I understand. Take the time to discuss my offer with your board, and make sure they're aware of their imminent dissolution should you move forward with the sale. As seen in the offer, they'll be compensated well for their efforts thus far. This is my personal number, and I'd appreciate it if it's the only number used to contact me moving forward. I'll be waiting for your call."

"Yes, thank you. Goodbye, Mr. Adams."

Tapping the end call button, I disconnect, my phone screen turning black as I take a minute to breathe—to feel the unfiltered emotion coursing through my veins—before locking that shit down tight.

Pulling up Haylee's contact information, I shoot her off a text, ignoring the late hour. I hated to leave in the middle of smoothing shit over with Riley. I didn't want to lose ground while I was away on business, so I trusted Haylee to coordinate the delivery of my hand-selected gifts until I return.

Parker: *Status of today's delivery?*

Haylee: *What the hell kind of question is that? I said it would be delivered by noon, and it was. Take a chill pill, man.*

Her response annoys me to no end, my fist clenching tightly around my phone. Taking a deep breath, I ignore her sass, moving on to the next order of business.

Parker: *Is tomorrow's ready?*

Haylee: **Eye Roll Emoji**

Parker: *What the hell kind of answer is that? Is it ready or not?*

Haylee: *Yes, BOSS. It's ready and will be delivered on time. Now, if you don't mind, I'd like to return to my reality TV show since, you know, IT'S AFTER HOURS.*

Rolling my eyes, I smirk before sending her another work-related text, just to be a smartass.

Parker: *Did you send off the notice of asset liquidation to Wicks and Bricks today? And what's the status of the Blue Line Design proposal? Don't forget to send out a meeting request with the accounting department for next week, either.*

My phone rings in my hand, the screen lighting up with an incoming call from Haylee. With a snort of humor, I hit ignore before powering down my device. I don't need to listen to her bitching at me as she confirms the completion of her work. I already know she got everything on her list done and more. And while I might trust her, that doesn't change anything. She's still my employee, and I wouldn't be me if I weren't an ass who pushed her buttons, just for the hell of it.

22

RILEY

"Please, for the love of God, tell me you didn't actually do that," I joke, wiping the tears of laughter from my eyes. Maddie and Allie are hanging out at my place, having a girl's night. Music plays softly in the background as we sit here laughing over Maddie's latest sexcapades.

I snort into my glass of wine, courtesy of Allie's trip to Napa Valley last weekend, when Maddie responds, "Oh, I totally did." She stands and demonstrates, thrusting her hips while fake moaning.

Allie and I howl with laughter, unable to contain ourselves as Maddie continues to reenact her dismissal of last week's fuck buddy. Plopping back down on the couch, she huffs on her nails before fake-shining them on her shirt. "I think it's safe to say he won't be contacting me again."

I open my mouth to respond but am cut off by a knock at my door. A sense of dread instantly assaults my stomach at the sound. Considering the two women in this room are my only friends, I can easily guess whoever's behind that door is about to shit on my plan to avoid all things Parker tonight.

He's been sending me little surprises for a week now, something I have yet to share with either of my friends. Partially because I don't want them to get any ideas, but also because I barely understand it myself, so I know they won't either. When he sent me an edible arrangement to the vet clinic, Allie was standing right next to me. I felt horrible when I lied to her and told her it was from my parents, making up some bogus excuse for why they were sending it, but I wasn't ready to talk about the absurdity going on between my neighbor and me—I'm still not.

Standing, I hesitantly cross to the door and open it, doing my best to block whoever it is from Maddie and Allie's view. I sigh in relief when I see a young, gangly teenage boy wearing a Papa's Pizza hat, holding six large pizzas that clearly aren't for us.

Shaking my head, I say, "Sorry, you have the wrong apartment." He looks down at the receipt and back at my door number with apparent confusion as I quickly smile at him before closing the door. I make it two steps down the hallway before another knock sounds, drawing Maddie and Allie's attention again.

Oh, for the love of... Sighing, I turn back around, swinging the door open to see what he needs. "Yesss?"

He clears his throat and looks at me like I've lost my mind. "Sorry to interrupt, Ma'am. The address on the receipt matches your apartment. Are you not Riley James?"

Stunned, I peer down at the receipt, and sure enough, it has my name and address on it. He thrusts the pizza into my hands, tells me it's paid for and turns, briskly walking back down the hallway before I can refuse the pizza again.

Closing the door, I carry the six freaking boxes to the kitchen table. Knowing it's pointless, I still ask, "Did one of you order pizza and forget how much we can actually eat?"

They both jump up from the couch, joining me by the table. "I'm hungry as hell, but even I know we can't eat six pizzas. I would have needed to wear my turkey-day pants for something like that," Maddie jokes with a laugh.

A sickening sense of realization dawns on me just as Allie picks up the receipt and says, "Wait. There's a note here at the bottom."

I snatch the receipt out of Allie's hands, crumpling it into a ball before she can read it, knowing exactly who it came from. Looking at the wall behind me, I'm tempted to take the pizza and toss it at his door, but when I look back, Maddie's already shoving a slice of supreme into her mouth, groaning with satisfaction. I'm sick and tired of this man throwing gifts at me, hoping it will be enough to make me forgive him.

Allie watches Maddie with a mix of horror and skepticism as she chomps away on the pizza. Turning to me, she asks, "Do you think this is safe to eat? Who sent it?"

"It's safe," I answer, rolling my eyes with a sigh. "Probably. It's from my neighbor." Yeah, that could've been paired with a record scratching, given the ensuing silence.

Allie stares at me with her mouth wide open, and Maddie's lips are turned up in a cheesy-ass smile as she wiggles back and forth like a dog shaking its ass in happiness.

"Have you been holding out on us? Did something happen between you two? I thought you hated each other?" Allie asks, firing off rapid questions.

"Hell yes! I knew it," Maddie shouts, fist-pumping the air. Turning to face Allie, she shouts, "You owe me twenty bucks."

Allie's cheeks flush as she dips her head, avoiding my eyes.

"What? Why does she owe you money?"

"I bet her at Prohibition that you two were going to bone. All that tension and hate? I could practically smell the future make-up sex."

Slightly offended, I roll my eyes before hissing, "Ew! That's gross. And anyway, you're wrong—we didn't have sex, and I still dislike him. But apparently, he's trying to change that."

Plopping down on the couch, our plates piled high with pizza, I fill them in on everything I've been hiding, starting from the gala and ending with his sudden outpouring of gifts.

"You lied to me," Allie accuses, her eyes shining with hurt.

"She lied to both of us," Maddie corrects, aiming a glare my way.

"I'm sorry. I just...wasn't ready to admit what was going on."

"And what, exactly, is it that's going on?" Allie asks.

Picking at my pizza, I avoid their eyes as I admit, "I don't know."

Their hushed whispers meet my ears, but I ignore them, lost in thought over what all this means.

After learning his name at the gala, I let curiosity get the best of me. I shamelessly googled the shit out of him, right after I stripped off my dress and cleaned up from my tumble in the parking lot. I ended up falling into a rabbit hole of photos showing him standing next to beautiful, skinny, model-esque looking women. Each image showed a new woman that could outshine me on their worst day, so it's safe to say he couldn't possibly be interested in me in a romantic way. Not when I'm so plain and ordinary looking, and certainly not when he looks the way he does and is used to the type of women in those photos.

So what gives? What other reason could he possibly have for sending all these gifts? *Guilt?* He doesn't seem like the type, but I've been wrong before.

Although—there was that moment in the parking lot. I swear, seconds before I was scared half to death and nailed him with my head, he was leaning in to kiss me. *Wasn't he?* I wasn't drunk—hell, I wasn't even tipsy by then. So I know I didn't imagine it. *Nope.* I'm sure of it. He was going to kiss me. And worse yet, I was going to let him.

I had felt a tingling deep in my core the minute his gaze landed on my lips. It felt so damn right to have him staring at me like that, all lust-drunk and hungry. The closer he drew to my lips, the more the excitement grew. A feeling of desperation stole over me—desperation to feel his lips against mine, to know what his scruff felt like against my face. His arms tightened around me, and the strangest thing happened. I felt like I was finally home. Right up until he dropped me, that is. Kind of ruined the moment, you know?

Anyway, none of my other matches made me feel that way on our dates. Not even dreamy Liam. I wanted Liam to kiss me, sure, but I wasn't consumed with that same desperation to feel his lips on mine. So why did I feel that way with Parker? I don't even like the man.

He may be attractive, but he's the furthest thing from my type, personality-wise. We couldn't be more different if we tried. In fact, the only thing we do seem to have in common is our love of animals. And though that's a huge point in his column, it's not enough to overlook every assholeish thing he's done since meeting him.

Which circles us back to—*why the gifts? What does he want from me?*

Maddie shoves my shoulder, shaking me out of my internal investigation and bringing me back to reality.

"I'm sorry, what'd you say?"

Maddie snorts in irritation before repeating her question. "I said, aren't you going to go thank him for the pizza?"

"What? Hell no. If he wanted a thank you, he should've delivered them in person, along with an apology."

"Why are you being so stubborn? Forgive the man and move on already."

"Yeah, you need to give that man a chance. Clearly, he's

feeling sorry for everything you two have been through," Allie adds.

"He can be sorry all he wants. He should be! But that doesn't mean shit to me until he actually apologizes—with words. He's been a mega jerk for weeks for absolutely no reason. And instead of apologizing like a real man, he's hiding behind gifts. Nope. Hard pass."

"But it's a step in the right direction," Allie pleads. "He's at least trying. Maybe you need to teach him how to appropriately apologize. He's a man, after all. They're clueless and need all the help they can get."

"He's a grown-ass man. How would I teach him how to apologize? And why should I even have to? Isn't that something his mother should've done?"

Ignoring my last question, Maddie unhelpfully suggests, "Apologize first. That's how you can teach him. Lead by example, and all that shit we learn in elementary school."

"I tried to," I shout with exasperation. "He scoffed in my face and denied the cookies."

"But he's trying now," Allie emphasizes, once again defending the enemy, my frustration building as the two of them team up against me.

Maddie smirks, and I already know I'm going to be annoyed with whatever comes out of her mouth next.

"You should give him *your* cookie."

Yep. Knew that was coming.

"I am not giving him my *cookie*," I whisper-shout, glancing at our shared wall, worrying he can somehow hear this absurd conversation.

"But imagine how hot the angry, make-up sex could be. I bet it'd be wild."

"Have you ever even had make-up sex? I feel like you need to be in a relationship to experience that. And we all know you're allergic to those. Besides, angry make-up sex doesn't even make sense."

Ignoring my rebellion, they share an evil glance before they both stand and grab an arm, pulling me up from my comfortable position on the couch.

"What the heck are you guys doing?"

"Helping you. You're going to go talk to him, even if we have to drag you the whole way and knock on the door for you."

"It'd be helpful if you didn't make us do that, though. Come on. Be the bigger person here and just go thank the man," Allie pleads.

"Okay, okay, fine. Let me go."

Releasing my arms from their grips, I straighten my clothes, narrowing my eyes at them in an evil glare. I wrench my door open and stomp the few feet over to his apartment, knocking on his door before I lose my nerve.

And then, I wait. And wait. *And wait.*

After standing there for another thirty seconds, knocking with no answer, I turn to walk away, stoked things worked out in my favor, and I didn't have to talk to him.

But just as I take the first step toward my apartment, his door swings open.

Cursing my luck, I sigh and turn to face him, damn near choking on my own tongue. He's dripping wet, wearing nothing but a towel that's hastily draped across his lean hips. Gripping the door with one hand, he uses his other to hold the towel together, his hand positioned just above a considerable bulge—is it growing?—that hints at a damn good time. His muscles are on full display, rippling with every small movement, and if I tilt my head to the right, I can see a tattoo peeking out over his ribs.

He clears his throat and starts talking, but I'm too busy admiring the masterpiece standing in front of me to hear what he's saying, the buzz of desire drowning out his words. My eyes catch on a drop of water that's gliding down the skin at the base of his throat. I watch, hypnotized, as it weaves a path down his sternum, right between his muscular pecs. The water droplet glistens as it continues to slide down the valley of his six-pack abs, finally disappearing into the towel, right above his bulge that's *definitely* growing.

Holy Mother of God.

23

RILEY

"Wet," I mumble under my breath, my eyes tracing every inch of his body, wishing like hell he'd drop the towel he's clinging to.

"Excuse me?" Parker chokes out around a laugh, snapping my eyes back to his.

Clearing my throat, I open my mouth and blurt out, "I'm wet," while gesturing to his body.

Oh, shit. That's not what I meant to say. "Wait, no. Crap. You're wet, not me. Obviously," I stammer out, heat filling my cheeks. Although, I'm most definitely wet too. My panties are drenched with desire from the visual heaven standing before me, making this situation even more uncomfortable.

His eyes sparkle with humor as he peers at me with an amused grin. *I'm glad someone thinks this is funny.* The hand gripping his door flexes, the movement rippling his bicep muscles once again. Drool pools in my mouth as my eyes fixate on the defined muscles, my fingers flexing with the urge to run my fingers along the bulging vein in his forearm.

"The pizza for thanks," I stupidly murmur before slamming

my mouth shut again. My brain is obviously short-circuiting. I can't form a coherent sentence to save my life.

"You're welcome, I think," he taunts, adding a wink to his smug tone. My brain floods with naughty images, cycling through like a movie reel; me licking the water off his body, me running my hands up his muscular thighs, me gripping the monstrous bulge hiding under that towel.

Swallowing harshly, the flush in my cheeks heats to an inferno as I use my last working brain cell to force myself not to fan my face.

Without another word, I turn and walk away on shaky legs before I do something crazy—like jump into his arms and dry hump him.

What the hell is happening to my body? I know it's been a while since I've had sex—a long, *long* while—but, damn. I didn't know that would turn me into a dog in heat the minute I'm faced with temptation.

Darting into my partially open apartment door, I slam it shut behind me. Pressing my back against the door, I close my eyes, trying to tame my haggard breathing while simultaneously committing the image of his wet, hard, muscular body to my memory for future use.

Someone clears their throat, and I wince, remembering I have an audience. Slowly opening my eyes, I find two sets of eyes staring at me from the living room. Maddie has her eyebrows raised, looking at me in amusement with her arms crossed and her foot tapping against the hardwood.

Thankfully, Allie is acting normal, standing there smiling sweetly at me.

"Well?" Maddie demands. "Did you thank him?"

Still unable to form words, I simply nod my head. My eyes are bugging out, and I'm still blushing like mad when I blurt out, "Naked." *Still struggling with words, I see.*

Clearing my throat, I try again. "I mean, he was naked. Not that I thanked him naked. I mean, he had a towel on, but otherwise, he was naked. And wet. So, so wet," I ramble out while licking my lips. I shouldn't have done that, though, especially in front of Maddie. But I couldn't help it; I had to make sure I wasn't drooling.

They both surge forward, each of them grabbing one of my arms, hauling me to the living room couch. As soon as my butt hits the cushions, they bombard me with questions.

"Is he muscular?" Allie questions.

"Is he fuckable? Tell me he's fuckable," Maddie demands.

"Does he have chest hair?"

"Could you see any tattoos? Piercings? Please tell me his nipples were pierced. Fuck, that's so hot," Maddie groans out.

"Ooh, did he have that little V thing? Those are so sexy. I wish my husband still had his."

"Stop," I yell, overwhelmed by their barrage of questions. I take a few deep breaths, still trying to calm the tingling in my… lady area.

"Yes, he was muscular. He had a dusting of chest hair and a tattoo on his ribs, but I was too blinded by the very, very deep V he had to notice what the tattoo was of."

They both squeal, leaving me with no doubt that Parker can hear us next door. The cocky jerk probably knows we're talking about him.

"Oh, my god. Oh, my god. Okay. Wow," Maddie chants while fanning her face. "You didn't answer my question, though."

My brow furrows as I look at her with bewilderment. Pretty sure I answered all of their questions—at least all the ones I could hear.

She leans closer and raises her eyebrows. "Well? Was he fuckable?"

Oh, for the love. This woman.

Clearing my throat, I look everywhere but at her.

I can't believe I'm about to admit this, so I'm sure as hell not going to make eye contact while doing so. "Mmmaybeprobablyeah," I quickly mumble under my breath.

"I'm sorry, what was that?" Maddie demands, leaning toward me with her hand cupping her ear as Allie tosses her head back with a laugh.

"I said, 'yeah,'" I shout, embarrassed to admit I'm attracted to the enemy.

Maddie pumps her fist in the air, way too excited over my obvious discomfort. I'm saved from having to respond when Allie glances at the clock and shoots off the couch.

"Oops! I didn't realize it was getting so late. Trevor doesn't like to go to bed until he knows I'm home safe, so I should get going."

Grabbing her empty plate and wine glass, she hurries to the trash can and tosses her trash before setting the glass in the sink. Swiping her purse off the table, she rushes to the door, calling out over her shoulder, "Thanks for tonight! Good to see you, Madison. See you tomorrow, Riley."

The door barely shuts behind her before Maddie sinks lower into the couch, pouting. "Ughhh, I should probably go too. Five a.m. comes way too early."

Wincing, I take a sip of my wine. "That sounds horrible. I'm so glad I don't have to get up that early for work."

Maddie picks up a throw pillow from the end of the couch and playfully hits me with it, "Real helpful, thanks."

Laughing, I toss it back at her. "Anytime."

She laughs and shakes her head before groaning again as she stands to gather her stuff. I'm about to call after her, telling her goodnight, when she whips around with crazy in her eyes.

"Oh shit! I can't believe I forgot. I have an extra ticket to the

Snipers playoff game this weekend. Will you go with me?" she begs.

Usually, I'd say no. Maddie gets a little crazy at these games, and I don't really like the extra attention she draws. I'm always worried she's going to get us kicked out of the game. But she's hitting me with her best puppy dog eyes, and I can't seem to form the word no.

"Um, sure. When is it?"

She bounces up and down in glee before answering, "Saturday night at seven, but the doors open at six. It's game seven of the Western Conference Final, so we'll need to get there early. It's going to be wild."

I plaster on a smile, trying hard not to show the nerves creeping in at her statement. I'm well aware that playoff games are extra exciting, but game seven? She's not exaggerating. It *is* going to be wild.

"Can't wait. I'm sure it will be great," I squeak out.

"Hell yes! Oh, my god, I can't wait. Don't forget to wear the jersey I got for you." She runs over to hug me, damn near squeezing the life out of me as I internally panic, wondering where the heck I put it after wearing it last. Releasing me from her death grip, she plants a kiss on my cheek and squeals, "Love you, Riles! See you Saturday."

She turns around and hustles back to the door, slamming it shut. A click rings through the now silent room as the automatic lock engages, my shoulders slumping with exhaustion now that I'm alone. I clean up our mess before hurrying through my nightly bath, dressing in a tank top and cartoon cotton shorts once I'm dried off. These ones are covered in tiny gnomes, all posing in silly positions with the words "Sexy and I Gnome It" written across my butt. I can't help but giggle every time I wear them, especially knowing they came from my mother.

Crawling into bed, my thoughts stray to earlier in the hallway. The tingling in my core sparks back to life as I envision running my hands up and down Parker's sexy-as-sin body. His blue eyes were darker than I've ever seen them, swirling with a hint of mischief and lust I could easily lose myself in.

My hand scorches a trail down my abdomen, setting my skin on fire as I imagine it's Parker's hand caressing my skin. The cotton material of my tank top drags against my pebbled nipples, a sigh slipping past my lips as my other hand darts out, eagerly searching my nightstand for my trusty vibrator.

Wrapping my hand around the familiar toy, I click the power button, the vibrations shooting up my arm as I tug my shorts down, leaving myself bare. Sparks of desire shoot up my spine the second I make contact with my throbbing clit. My breathing grows heavy, and my back arches from the pleasure radiating through my body. It's been so long since I've had a release, I know this won't take long.

Tingles crawl up my legs, warning me my orgasm is drawing near. My muscles clench in anticipation, my heart racing as a lightning bolt of ecstasy strikes my core. Thoughts of swirling my tongue around Parker's erection, filling my mouth with his hard length flit through my mind, my desire peaking. My body feels like it's about to rocket into outer space as my hand shoots out, trying to grab hold of the headboard to ground me.

Lost in my lustful thoughts, I hardly notice when my hand bumps into my bedside lamp, sending it crashing to the floor mere seconds before a loud moan rips through my throat, echoing against my bedroom walls. I'm a handful of vibrations away from my orgasm slamming into me full force when a pounding on my front door jars me from my heated imagination. My orgasm flees into hiding, embarrassed over being caught in the act.

"Nooo," I whine out loud, slapping my hand dramatically against the bed. "I was so close!"

With a huff of frustration, I tug my pajama shorts up and climb out of bed, desperate to quickly get rid of whoever's knocking at my door.

24

PARKER

Wearing nothing but my favorite pair of grey sweats, I lounge on my couch, replaying what transpired about an hour ago.

I was in the middle of showering when I heard a series of loud knocks on my door. Shrugging my shoulders, I ignored it. Nobody knows I live here, so I figured it was just a lost visitor. I grabbed my shower gel off the shelf and lathered it up in my hands before running them all over my body, enjoying my steamy shower. I had just started rinsing the suds off when another round of knocks reached my ears over the water.

After groaning with annoyance, I finished rinsing off and stepped out of the shower. Ripping a towel off the rack, I stormed to the door, irritated that the most relaxing part of my day was being interrupted.

The look on Riley's face changed from irritation to desire in the blink of an eye as I ripped the door open and came into view. I watched her eyes rove over every inch of my body, gazing at me like she wanted to devour me for dessert, and my cock was happy to rise to the occasion. I'm probably lucky she turned and left when she did. I wasn't confident in my towel's ability to contain my hard-on for much longer.

When Haylee suggested I send her small gifts, I thought she had lost her goddamn mind. It was the dumbest idea I ever let her talk me into. Not only did I want to avoid setting precedence for constantly spending money on her, leaving the door open for her to use me, but I also didn't want Riley to think I was just some arrogant asshole trying to buy her affection. But after the way I treated her over the last few weeks, I was at a loss for better ideas.

Now, though. *Fuck*. Now, I'd send her pizza every day if it meant she'd look at me the way she did in that doorway. She was so overcome with blatant lust, she could hardly form a sentence. I let her stumble over her words, not wanting to break the dazed spell she was under. I know I look good. I work damn hard for this body. The least I could do after everything I've put her through is let her salivate over me for a few minutes. Plus, it gave me a chance to stare at her tits without her noticing.

Thanks to the paper-thin walls in our apartments, I heard her friends leave about thirty minutes ago, and it's been quiet over there ever since. I wonder what she's doing now and if she's still thinking of me like I am her. Part of me was hoping she'd come back over after they left, but I knew that was a long shot. I figured once her lustful hypnosis ended, she'd be right back to avoiding me.

Sighing, I abandon my post on the couch, moving to my bedroom to handle the raging hard-on I've had since the second Riley licked those plump lips of hers. Settling against my pillows, my hand snakes under the waistband of my sweats, wrapping around my hard, pulsing length. I'm a few strokes in when a sudden, sickening crash sounds next door, followed by a loud moan.

Not thinking straight, I jump out of bed and run straight for

Riley's apartment, worried she's been hurt. I rapidly bang my fist against her door, anxious to make sure she's okay. After a few agonizing minutes, the door swings open, presenting me with a view I wasn't prepared for. *Goddamn, this night keeps getting better and better.*

Riley stands before me in a tight, low-cut tank top and a tiny pair of ridiculous cartoon shorts. She's a goddamn vision with her flushed cheeks and glassy eyes. Her hair's slightly messier than when I saw her earlier, almost like she—or someone else?—has been running their hands through it.

Fuck. Is someone here with her? I didn't hear anyone enter her apartment after her friends left, but maybe they were quiet? Peeking over her shoulder, I search for evidence of another guest in Riley's apartment. My fists curl in anger, the thought instantly boiling my blood. There fucking better not be anyone else here.

Sighing with relief when I don't see or hear anyone else, I look back at Riley, scanning her body from head to toe. There's no question she looks aroused. Was she…pleasuring *herself?*

Holy fucking fuck.

This girl is going to be the death of me.

The tops of her breasts strain against the edge of her tank top with every labored breath, swiftly unraveling my control. My eyes latch on to her tits, praying to every God known to man they'll escape their prison on her next breath so I can see what color her nipples are. *Are they a dusty pink or a dark brown?* Fuck, I'm about to explode in my sweats like a goddamn teenager.

What is this woman doing to me?

Her breathy voice breaks through my concentration, my gaze snapping up to hers. "Sorry, did you need—"

Her sentence cuts off with a gasp, her jaw dropping open as her eyes widen. I follow her gaze and find that her eyes are zeroed in on my painfully hard erection. It's pressed tightly against the material of my sweats, giving her a perfectly clear outline of my boner.

If I had any blood left in my brain and was capable of thinking straight, I'd probably be embarrassed at the fact that there's even a small wet spot at the tip of my dick, effectively showcasing my desire for the vixen standing in front of me.

She inhales sharply, the rising of her chest attracting my eyes once again. Her nipples pebble under her tank top as she groans quietly, licking her lips.

And I. Fucking. Lose it.

Growling, I surge into her apartment. My hands find her hips, gripping them tightly before slipping around her back, filling themselves with her ass. Her eyes widen as my leg kicks back, connecting with the wide-open door, slamming it shut behind us.

She gasps in surprise but wraps her hands around the back of my neck, pulling me toward her face. I slam my lips down on hers, reveling in how soft and pillowy they feel against my demanding mouth. Her hands tighten around my neck before drifting down to my shoulders. She pauses briefly, goose bumps rising along my flesh as her nails dig into my skin. Tingles shoot through my arms as she trails her fingertips down to my biceps, her grip tightening against the straining muscles.

My hands squeeze her ass, her nipples scraping against my hard chest as the moment brings her body flush against mine. Bending my knees, I drop my hands to the back of her smooth thighs, hoisting her up. Her legs wrap around my hips as I turn and slam her back against the wall behind her door. My aching shaft presses tightly against the apex of her thighs, the heat from her center radiating through her cotton shorts, driving me wild with lust.

She moans, and I take full advantage, thrusting my tongue past her parted lips. With my cock pressed against the front of my sweats, I grind my hips against Riley's; my knees damn near buckling at the delicious friction. My grip tightens around her thighs, holding her up, and *goddamn*. They feel just as sexy as I imagined they would wrapped around my hips.

Gritting my teeth, I hiss with pleasure as she tilts her hips and grinds against my dick, adding to the mess of pre-cum already staining my sweats. If she keeps moaning and rubbing against my dick like that, I'm going to bust before I get the chance to feel her warm center wrapped around my throbbing cock.

Done with the teasing, I throw my arm out, using it to clear off the top of her entryway table. Her belongings crash to the floor as I sit her down in their place. Reaching down, I twist my hands into the waistband of her shorts, pulling them down and flinging them over my shoulder.

She gasps as I run my hands back up her legs, pushing her thighs wide open. Kneeling, I catch my first glimpse of the sexy pink between her legs. My mouth waters at her intoxicating smell, dying to get a taste. I dive forward, my tongue plunging into her wet heat. A growl tears from my throat as she tangles her fingers in my hair, her thighs closing around my ears in pleasure. I'm holding nothing back, alternating between thrusting my tongue as far as it will go inside her and swiping up her wet slit to circle her clit. I've never tasted a pussy so sweet, and I know at that moment, I'll never get enough of her.

Riley rocks against my tongue as I apply more pressure to her sweet bundle of nerves. Her thighs quiver around my face, a moan falling from her lips, and I know she's close. Needing to speed this along before I blow in my sweats, I flick her clit with the tip of my tongue, keeping a steady rhythm that matches the electric desire pulsing through my own veins. My dick twitches, begging for a taste of her, but there's no time. She tenses around me, the sexiest moan crossing her lips as she bursts against my tongue.

She's still twitching and shaking as I stand, gathering her up in my arms and carrying her to the couch. Laying her on her back, I rip my sweats down, kicking them across the floor. I have a split second of rational thought, realizing I don't have a condom with me, but the second her legs fall open, it's gone, fluttering away from my mind.

Swiping my cock up and down her slit, I coat myself in her juices before sinking my hard length into her tight, wet pussy. A growl rips past my lips at the intense pleasure gripping my balls from her heat. I thrust into her hard and fast, knowing I won't last. It's been way too long since I've had a pussy this sweet bared to my cock.

Reaching up, I yank her tank top over her head and toss it to the side, revealing perfectly pink nipples, begging to be sucked. With a heavy groan, I lean forward, sucking one into my mouth, biting down hard before soothing the sting with my tongue.

"Oh, god, yes!" Riley cries out with pleasure. Her fingernails rake down my back, no doubt leaving a mark that will last for days. With the next powerful thrust of my hips, she screams out my name, her velvety walls fluttering around my cock. Her arms tighten around me, bringing her body flush against mine as she shakes with the second orgasm that just slammed into her, and that's it.

Game over.

My balls draw up tight as I slam into her one last time. "Fuck," I yell out, almost forgetting my cock isn't wearing a coat. I pull out, wrapping around myself with a tight fist. With a few last jerks of my cock, I paint her tits with my cum, releasing every ounce of pleasure pooling in my balls before slumping with exhaustion. My eyes fall closed as I rest my head against the back of her couch, her legs stretched out across my thighs.

Other than our haggard breathing, her apartment is silent, neither of us daring to speak. Blood returns to my brain as my cock deflates, the realization of what the fuck just happened plowing through my mind. Daring to open my eyes, I roll my head to the right, finding Riley peering at me through barely open slits. A hint of a smile crosses her lips but fades with the next slow blink of her eyes.

Her breath evens out as my hand mindlessly travels up and down her calf, enjoying the softness of her skin against mine. My body is exhausted, ready to fall into a deep, blissful sleep, but my mind races on as I continue to stare at her.

Ever since the first woman I took to bed, sex has always been either a tool to relieve stress or just something fun to do while bored or horny. It's always been pleasurable, sure, but it's never felt like *that*.

"I still don't like you, you know. This doesn't change anything," Riley whispers with her eyes closed, breaking the silence between us. My chest rumbles with a chuckle, despite the way my gut twists with her words. *We'll fucking see about that, babe.*

I don't bother with a response. I'm too relaxed to pick a fight right now. Instead, I move her legs and reluctantly stand, walking into her kitchen. After opening a few drawers, I find a kitchen towel and get it wet. I clean myself up, then rinse it out and head back to the couch, where I find Riley sound asleep, soft snores passing through her pretty little lips. Doing my best not to wake her, I gently clean between her thighs before moving up to her chest.

Groaning, I wipe away the last remnants of our desire. Riley was beautiful before, but coated in my cum? Fuck, she's hot as hell. She may think this is it for us, but I have other plans for her. I don't care what it takes to change her mind about me. No matter what, this won't be a one-time deal. Not if I have anything to say about it.

Searching her apartment, I locate her phone sitting on her

bedside table. I pick it up, thanking everything holy she still doesn't have a password on this thing. Opening her contacts, I store my information before shooting myself a text off her phone. A slow, wicked smile transforms my face, knowing she can't escape from me now.

25

RILEY

My alarm clock blares beside me, jolting me from a pleasant dream. Sighing, I reach over to hit the off button and am met with a glorious soreness in muscles that haven't been used in way too long. My thighs, my abs, my...*lady bits*. You name it, it's sore.

Maddie was right. Hate sex really is in a league of its own.

Speaking of which, who knew I'd be so turned on by a dominating alpha male? The way he stormed in and took control was like a fantasy come to life. I've never been pushed up against a wall like that, nor have I ever had a man act like he was incapable of resisting me. Remembering the look in his eyes before he sank his dick inside me sends a shiver down my spine. And that tongue of his?

Oh. My. *Gosh.*

The things he did with that sinful tongue deserve a trophy. Heck, that's not even good enough. He deserves a whole freaking monument.

I haven't been with many partners in my life, but I'd like to think I know good sex when I'm having it. And holy crap, does Parker know how to do the sex with that giant cock of his. The thing should probably have a name, brain, and life of its own with how big it was. I'm probably going to be sore for *days*.

Stretching my legs out, my foot connects with a pillow that ended up at the foot of my bed, pushing it off the edge. Instead of hearing it softly hit the floor, a manly grunt echoes around the room.

My eyes shoot open, the sex fog I've been basking in lifts as I realize that, while last night was amazing, I don't remember moving from the couch to my bed. I also don't remember Parker leaving. He did leave, though...*didn't he?*

Another quiet groan sounds from my floor, and I shoot into a sitting position, peeking over the side of my bed. *Yep.* There's a man on my floor—again.

Panicking over my new frequent floor flyer, I kick my legs around to untangle from the sheets and end up dislodging another pillow. I watch in silent horror as the pillow falls off my bed, hitting Parker square in the face before sliding to the floor.

He jerks awake, frowning at the pillow with confusion before slowly moving his eyes up to meet mine. They narrow at my panicked face, almost like he's silently accusing me of ambushing him with a pillow.

"I didn't throw that at you. It fell," I squeak out, my voice betraying me as it comes out sounding guilty as hell. He glances at the second pillow lying next to him and looks back up at me, his eyebrows rising with doubt. Pointing at it, I shout, "That one fell too."

His gaze instantly drops to my chest when I raise my arm, fire burning in his eyes. A blast of cool air assaults me, goose bumps rising on my skin. Time seems to slow to a crawl as I glance down with horror, realizing I'm still naked from last night.

Gasping in shock, I reach for the sheet to cover myself up again, but it's too late. Parker's eyes are burning holes in the bedding, and a certain appendage of his salutes me from under the towel he used as a blanket.

Clearing my throat, I force my eyes away from his enthusiastic cock soldier. He's still staring at me—Parker, not his dick—his eyes roving every now-covered inch of me. Squirming under his heated gaze, I wrack my brain for a way to break the tension and blurt out the first thing that comes to mind. "Why are you sleeping on my floor again? Is this normal behavior for you?"

He gently shakes his head back and forth while blinking rapidly, almost like he's trying to shake himself from a daze. Is it possible he's just as affected by me this morning as he was last night? I thought for sure that was just a fluke—a situational horniness. There's no way he would still be attracted to me in the broad light of day.

Right?

"You passed out in a sex coma on the couch," he starts, his voice heavy from sleep. "I carried you to bed."

The word, "Oh," slips from my lips on an embarrassed whisper, my cheeks heating at the thought of him tucking my naked body into bed. But, wait. That didn't explain…"Why'd you stay?"

Parker tilts his head to the left, quietly observing my every move. He sucks his bottom lip into his mouth, chewing on it as he drops his eyes from mine, glancing around the room like he's lost for words.

A soft chuckle works its way out of my mouth as understanding dawns. "Locked out again?"

His eyes snap back to mine, still so full of heat. "Yes," he growls. I shake my head, unsure if I'm disappointed in his answer or amused by it, but have no time to decide before his next words nearly stop my heart. "But that's not why I stayed."

"Oh. Then…why did you?"

"Because I wasn't ready to leave."

My breath stalls in my throat as my eyes widen in shock. I

swallow once. Twice. Three times, before I'm able to whisper, "Oh."

He chuckles—god, even that's sexy—and responds with, "Yep."

I cautiously eye him on the floor, wondering where we go from here as I take in his slightly disheveled hair, the thick stubble covering his chin, and his darkened eyes, heavy with sleep. Everything about him is annoyingly sexy, making me feel self-conscious of my bedhead and makeup-free face. Clearing my throat, I avert my eyes before asking, "Why are you on the floor, then?"

"It's not where I started out. But somewhere around four this morning, you started thrashing around like a fish out of water. I took a knee to the junk and rolled off the edge of the bed to avoid another blow. I must have fallen asleep somewhere between trying not to vomit from the pain and praying you didn't just strip me of my manhood."

Oops.

"Sorry. I've been told I'm a wild sleeper," I mumble, the blush in my cheeks slowly creeping down my neck. Parker's eyes narrow, and my eyes flash to his hands as they form into fists, tightly gripping the blanket. I'm waiting for him to lash out in anger over his pain, but it never comes. He just sits there, quietly staring at me.

He's making no move to get up and leave, and I really do need to get ready for work. Not to mention, my bladder is currently protesting, demanding to be relieved. My eyes dart back and forth from Parker to the bathroom, trying to figure out what to do. Obviously, he saw all the goods last night, but something about the vulnerable position of me walking past him naked while he's lying on the floor has me too scared to get out of bed.

"I should probably go," I blurt out.

"This is your apartment."

Shit.

"Um. Yeah. I just mean…Um. I have to work today."

He snorts with humor but still doesn't make a move to leave. He's either unaware that I'm trying to kick him out, or he simply doesn't care. "Yeah. Me too. It's Wednesday."

Right.

"What are you doing Saturday morning?"

Caught off guard by his line of questioning, my brain stalls out, answering before I can think better of it. "Huh? Nothing. I don't work Saturday morning."

His stupidly handsome face transforms into a smirk as he softly shakes his head, standing from the floor. "Good. I'll pick you up at ten."

"Huh?"

Without answering, he turns to leave but halts halfway through the bedroom door. His head drops to his chest as he grabs the back of his neck, inhaling deeply before facing me.

"One other thing."

Gulping, I peek up at him from under my lashes, nervous about where this is going. "Yeah?"

"Are you on birth control?"

His question punches me in the gut, reminding me of how irresponsible we were last night. I can't believe I forgot about protection. That's never happened to me before.

"Oh, um. Yeah. I am."

"Are you clean?" he questions, eyeing me carefully as he braces himself against the door jam.

A sudden bout of anger courses through my veins at his audacity. If there's anybody in this room that should be worried about that, it's me. The man has probably slept with half of San Diego, but he's concerned about *me?*

"Yes," I snidely huff out, irritation lacing my tone. "Are you?"

He has the nerve to smirk at me again, his arms crossing

against his chest. I do my best to ignore his sex appeal, but it's useless. The anger running through my veins changes course, transforming to lust the longer I stare at him. No man has the right to look so damn hot in grey sweats.

"Yep," he states, his ocean blue eyes darkening like a storm the longer he watches me. My skin heats to an inferno as his eyes leisurely track up and down my body, pinning me to the bed. He licks his bottom lip before glancing at the alarm clock on my nightstand.

His eyes close for a brief second before reopening with a shake of his head. "Fuck," he groans under his breath. "I need to go. See you Saturday morning."

"Okay," I whisper, my eyes locked on his.

He turns and leaves, breaking the spell I'm under as my front door slams shut behind him.

Wait. What the heck did I just agree to?

SETTLING INTO MY OFFICE CHAIR, I DROP MY PURSE ON MY DESK and bring my computer to life. It immediately dings with an email from my colleague, letting me know there's been an emergency in the cat complex, and she and Allie will be unavailable most of the day. Looking over the schedule, I re-arrange a few things to make up for being down a vet and a tech.

As I'm staring at my screen, the blocks of appointments blur, my focus shifting from work to the last twenty-four hours. Waking up with Parker on my floor was definitely a shock to the system, but it's the events that led to that that have my mind in a jumble. How did we go from hatred to life-altering sex so quickly? *And why the hell did I agree to a date?*

My stomach rolls with nausea as my head swims with all the ways this could end in disaster. Heck, I don't even think we're on the same page. I'm looking for someone who's ready to settle down and start a family, and maybe I'm judging him too harshly, but Parker just doesn't seem like the type to want to change diapers and wipe snotty noses. Something about him screams anti-settling down, which is exactly why I'm freaking out over Saturday. Not to mention the tabloid stories he's been featured in the last few months. The last thing I need is my picture splashed across magazines when this ends in a dumpster fire.

With my nerves eating at me, I pick up my phone, shooting off a quick message to Maddie, praying she'll know what to do.

Riley: *Hey, so… I kind of did something insane last night, and I need your help to unravel the mess I've suddenly found myself in.*

She texts back almost instantly, but my office phone rings before I can open her text. There's an emergency with one of our panda bears. He's suffering from volvulus—otherwise known as a nasty bowel obstruction—and I'm needed right away. Two emergencies within the first hour of our day doesn't bode well, and if I was more religious, I'd swear this was a sign from up above.

Shaking away the thought, I toss my phone in my purse, tug my white coat on, and head out to the Asian Passage. Maddie and my mess with Parker will have to wait.

A few hours later, I plop down into my office chair to eat a quick lunch. Fishing my phone out of my purse, I'm greeted with a handful of messages from Maddie, the last one coming in just over a minute ago.

Maddie: *You've come to the right place. I tend to find myself in the middle of messy things all the time. Hit me with it, girlfriend.*

Maddie: *Wait a damn second. I just left your apartment less than twelve hours ago. What could you have possibly done since then?*

Maddie: *Did you go to a nightclub after we left and not invite me? Rude.*

Maddie: *Were you kidnapped by the mafia, and now you're locked in a sex dungeon?*

Maddie: *Bet they wanted to see if the drapes match the curtains, huh. *Wink Emoji* Just go with it, sweetheart. Mafia or not, you need a good dicking to pull you out of your drought.*

Maddie: *Are you not answering because you're tied to the bed?*

Maddie: *That's so hot. Get it, girl!*

Maddie: *No? Hmm. Did you join a circus, and now you're trapped in a train car covered in monkey shit?*

Maddie: *Because if so, you're on your own. I just got my nails done, and I don't want to mess them up with animal poo, no matter how much I love you.*

Maddie: *Okay, okay. For real. Are you okay, or do you need me to save you from the Girl Scout Underworld? Have you been force-fed so many Thin Mint cookies you can't escape on your own now?*

Maddie: *If so, snatch me a few before I roll you out of there. Those cookies are bomb.*

Reaching her last message, I laugh at her craziness before typing out the real issue. I don't know where she comes up with this crap, but I bet her mind is a very fun place to be.

Riley: *I had sex with Parker.*

The minutes tick by as I stare at my screen, anxiously waiting for a response that's not coming. Not that I can blame her. She's usually the one with the wild stories, not me. She probably thought I was going to tell her I was late paying my credit card bill or something similarly insignificant. I doubt she was expecting me to say I actually did something crazy…Like sleep with the enemy.

Ten minutes later, my phone buzzes with her response, but I should have known she wouldn't believe me.

Maddie: *Dreams don't count as actual sex, babe.*

Rolling my eyes, I consider not responding, but I really need help, and who knows how long Allie will be busy today.

Riley: *No, seriously. We had crazy hot sex, then I passed out on the couch. He carried me to bed and was still there when I woke up this morning.*

Riley: *Well. Kind of. He was on my floor again, but still. Then before he left, he basically told me we were going on a date this weekend. My stupid mouth betrayed me, and I agreed, but I'm not sure I should go through with it.*

Maddie: *Well, holy shit. My vagina is celebrating for yours!*

Maddie: *But also, why the hell not? Isn't this exactly why we downloaded that dating app for you? So you could get back out there, meet some hot guys and start dating again?*

Maddie: *And don't you dare say it's because you hate him. We're past that.*

Riley: *We're *mostly* past that. But I still don't think he's my type.*

Maddie: *That man is everybody's type, Riley. Stop kidding yourself.*

Riley: *Physically, yeah. But that pretty package probably comes with a side of heartache. I can feel it in my bones, and I'd rather cancel now than risk a broken heart when I find out he's just using me.*

Maddie: *You don't know for a fact that he's using you or that he's going to hurt you. For all you know, he could be your soulmate, but you don't even want to give him a chance.*

Riley: *And for good reason! The man might as well come with a warning label.*

Maddie: *Is there a warning label? Or are you running because loving him wouldn't be easy?*

Her question stuns me, my mind reeling as I pick at my food. I'm nowhere near ready to think about the "L" word with Parker —I'm still trying to ditch the "H" word— but there's no doubt a relationship with him would be a challenge. Especially if he remains the same asshole he's been from the start. But relationships, in general, are hard, and that's not deterring me from looking for my soulmate. So is it him or my fear of being hurt again that's driving me to cancel this date?

Riley: *I don't know for sure. But the idea of dating a man like him scares me.*

Maddie: *I understand that. But you can't live like that, Riley. You can't keep chasing after the safe options because you're scared of getting your heart broken. You have to unlock the cage you've shoved your heart into and set it free. Give it the power to love, and love fiercely, despite the what if's and possible consequences. Because I hate to break it to you, but even the safest option can utterly destroy you. They, too, have the choice to leave you for the person that sets their heart on fire.*

Maddie: *Set your heart free, Riley, and know that all-consuming love is worth any pain and suffering you might feel in the end. Whether we like it or not, everything ends—either by choice or in death. But only you can choose to let it begin.*

A single tear slides down my cheek as I read her words. I know she means well, but her words take me back to our college days, during a time when I gladly would have set my heart free. In fact, *I did*. But all that got me was heartache and a bruised ego, knowing every guy I tried to date left me because they wanted someone I could never be.

Parker reminds me of all those guys that used me in college. I don't know him well, but between his rude attitude and his overwhelming alpha-male confidence, he exudes a playboy vibe, and that's the last thing I want to get involved with.

Been there, done that.

But…what if Maddie's right? What if he's not who I thought he was?

When I don't answer right away, she sends another text, sprinkling her brand of humor into our heavy conversation.

Maddie: *Give the man a chance. A REAL chance. Maybe he'll surprise you. And if not…If I'm wrong, and after a few dates, he really is still a complete asshole, let me know. I'll help you pull a "Goodbye Earl" and we'll bury his ass if he hurts you. Deal?*

Riley: *Okay. Fine. I'll try.*

Maddie: *Good. That's all you can do. Now, delete that last message, so your pre-assigned FBI agent doesn't indict us for murder charges before his body is even cold. Gotta go. Duty calls. Love you.*

Keeping it short, I send her back a text saying, "Love you too," before sitting back in my office chair, thinking over everything she's said. My computer chimes, drawing my attention as it alerts me to my next appointment. Cleaning up my food, I pack what's left into my lunch box before getting back to work, doing my best not to overthink things. Because as much as the idea scares me, I guess I have a date with Parker this weekend.

26

PARKER

My cell phone feels like a heavy boulder when I pick it up, rotating it over and over in my hand as I debate my options. Inhaling deeply, my chest expands, the seams on my shirt threatening to burst before I blow the air out with a heavy sigh. Navigating to Riley's name in my phone, I draft a quick message. My thumb hovers over the send button as I stare at what I wrote.

Parker: *Unexpected meeting popped up on Saturday. Sorry, need to cancel.*

Growling, I delete the message, the cursor sprinting backward as each word erases. Tossing the phone down on my desk, I rake my hands through my hair as frustration fills my veins, only to pick the phone up and try again.

Parker: *Sorry, but something popped up for Saturday morning. Raincheck?*

The longer I stare at the words, the harder I want to kick my own fucking ass. When I woke up on Riley's floor, her wide, sleepy eyes staring back at me and her hair a tangled disaster, my heart clenched in my chest, aching with the desire to see her like that every morning. She seemed so vulnerable—so unapologetically real—in that moment, and that's something my past...relations...have been missing.

With that realization at the forefront of my mind, my brain took a temporary trip to insanity, telling my mouth to demand a date before I could remember why I put dating on a shelf in the first place. My goddamn dick didn't help matters, either. If he could shake his head in agreement, he'd have us winning a million bucks on "Dick's Got Talent" for how fast he jumped on board with the idea of dating Riley.

Stomach swimming with doubt, I harshly rub my hands up my face, pressing the heels of my palms roughly into my eyes as I contemplate what to do. Now that I haven't seen her in two days, my rational thinking has kicked back in. I have a heart to protect, a company to run, another business to take over, and a brother I'm feuding with over complete bullshit. I have zero business trying to fit any more into my life—especially a relationship.

Besides, I already fucked her. Broke my own rule and took her sexy ass to bed—couch? *Whatever.* We fucked. And while it was the hottest sex of my goddamn life, shouldn't that be enough? Can't we just leave it at hot sex and call it a day? Who the hell says I have to date her too?

Well...nobody. But every time I try to send this message to cancel our date, my brain loses its ability to command my thumb to press send, and my stomach swirls with nausea.

I've never had this reaction to a woman before. Not even with Sadie, the woman I thought I was going to marry years ago. And ever since that blew up in my face, I've had zero issues turning women down or kicking them out of my bed without an ounce of guilt or hesitation. I'd wipe my hands clean and move on to the next woman before my last fuck finished drying her tears.

So what the hell is my deal now?

Women fall at my feet every week, tripping over themselves just to get close to me. But not Riley. Hell, she barely even likes me—said so herself two nights ago, right after we fucked. *I still don't like you, you know. This doesn't change anything.* A smirk tugs at my lips as her words ring through my brain for the millionth time since that night. I shouldn't find her aversion to me so sexy, but I do. Whether it's the challenge in her words or the simple fact that she isn't blatantly obsessed with me that's driving my interest through the roof, I'm not sure. But whatever the reason is, the chick's been fucking with my head for weeks now.

I told Haylee those gifts I'd been sending her were just to smooth shit over, to end the hostility between my neighbor and me. But now I'm not so sure. Maybe my fucking heart knew what it needed before my brain did—which is exactly why I should be canceling this date. That fucker has steered me wrong more than once and shouldn't be given the reins of power.

Moving my thumb, I hover over the send button, my brain in an all-out war for dominance. My heart clenches with fear when I twitch, damn near hitting send. With a throat-rumbling growl, I allow the battle to continue, jerking my thumb down to erase the message once again.

Opening a desk drawer, I toss the phone inside, slamming the lid on my indecision. Odds are, it'll still be there when I finish with my work.

WALKING INTO MY MOTHER'S HOUSE FOR DINNER, MY NOSTRILS fill with the tantalizing scent of homemade spaghetti. My mom makes the best meatballs in all of San Diego, so when she sent me a text asking if I wanted to come over for dinner, I wasted no time reserving my spot at the table.

"Smells good, Mom," I yell out, dropping my keys on her entryway table. I kick off my shoes and head in the direction of the kitchen, smiling when she comes into view.

"You're just in time," she exclaims with a face-splitting smile, nodding her head at the pot on the counter. "Bring the noodles to the table, and let's eat."

Doing as she says, I follow her into the other room, setting the food down on the table.

"How was your day?" I ask, taking the seat next to her. Her face lights up with happiness, warming my cold heart a few degrees.

"It was good. Went to lunch with a few friends and had a great time, then got a few things done around the house. And now that you're here, it's even better."

Her answer brings a small smile to my face, making me happy her day was better than mine. I'd suffer through a million shitty days as long as my mother could have a good one.

As we dish out our food, she starts in with her twenty questions. "Any plans for the weekend?"

I debate lying to her but decide against it. Like a shark in the water, she sniffs out lies like they're coated in blood. "I have a date planned for Saturday morning, but I'll probably cancel. Colton invited me to the Snipers game Saturday night with the boys. He's got box seats, believe it or not. Other than that, probably just work."

"Does the game interfere with your date plans?" she asks, her brows furrowing with confusion.

Clearing my throat, I break eye contact as I admit, "No," before shoving a meatball in my mouth.

"Oh. Then why are you canceling?"

Taking a second to mull that over, I try to find an honest explanation but can't. Hours later, I still don't have one.

Swallowing my food, I take a sip of the water she poured for us before I arrived. Keeping my gaze focused on my food, I huff out, "Now's not the time to add to my plate. Besides, I've been an asshole, and she doesn't seem to like me."

"First off, watch your language, mister," she scolds, her voice taking on a hint of irritation. "Second, we'll come back to your behavior." *Great.* Can't wait. "But what's this about not adding to your plate? That's no way to view a relationship."

"First off," I respond with sarcasm, mocking her words. She narrows her eyes at me, and I know I'm seconds from being smacked upside the head, which I probably deserve. "I never said the word relationship. I said date. Singular. Don't start forcing wedding bells at me just yet."

Waving her hand, she brushes off my warning. "Semantics. There's no point in going on a date if the end goal isn't to form a relationship. Now, what's this about being rude?"

With a heavy sigh, I push the last three meatballs around on my plate, avoiding eye contact as I explain everything from my first night in the apartment to the night Riley and I officially met. I leave out the dirty details of our night together, but she gets everything else. From pounding on her wall—twice—while yelling to turn down her music, to refusing her fresh cookie peace offering, and every fucked up thing I've done in between. I explain it all, making sure she has every piece of the assholish puzzle I've been building since night one.

Chancing a glance, I find her staring back at me, a mix of anger and disappointment coating her eyes. "Parker Lee Adams," her voice explodes, bouncing around the walls of the dining room as I wince.

Oh, fuck. Never good when she breaks out the full name.

"How dare you treat that poor woman with such hostility. She did nothing to warrant that, and I raised you better!"

"Fuck, I know," I yell, slamming my fist down on the table as frustration takes over. *That's going to cost me a daisy or twelve.*

Resting an elbow on the edge of the table, I rake a hand through my hair, roughly gripping the ends. She's not telling me anything I haven't already figured out, but it's too late to change shit now.

Slamming her own hand down on the table, her voice rings through the room as she berates me, her menacing tone raising the hair on the back of my neck. "You listen to me, and you listen well. You will go on that date, and you will act like a gentleman, you hear me? If for no other reason than to make up for your childish behavior. If she's not actively falling at your feet, she's a good one for you. Might bring you down a peg or two," *fuck, hasn't she already?* "Which you clearly deserve if you're going around treating women with disrespect just because you've been burned lately."

Picking at the last of my food, I silently process her request. She's not asking for much. One date. I already demanded one, so what's the harm in following through? It's not like Riley can wreck my world with only one date.

Right?

Fucking wrong. She's already ripped my celibacy pact to shreds and is now screwing with my head before the date even starts. She absolutely could destroy my life with one date. The real question is, would it be worth it?

The silence stretches between us as my mother wisely gives me time to mull shit over. She knows me better than I probably know myself, so she knows when to push and when to hold her tongue.

When I finally have a handle on my thoughts, I glance back up at my mother. Her eyes dart back and forth between my own, the anger slowly fading from her face as she must recognize the unfamiliar emotion flickering in my gaze. She softens her tone, but it still feels like a punch to the gut when she asks, "What are you so afraid of, Parker?"

"I'm not afraid of anything," I insist, my voice harsher than I intended as the lie shoots past my lips. I'm fucking terrified of making another mistake, of adding to my list of regrets and getting hurt in the process, but I can't tell anybody that. Least of all her. I'm San Diego's resident asshole. The second someone realizes I have a heart, it's game over for me.

She stares at me, her eyes narrowing as she silently calculates the truth of my statement. Her head slowly shakes from side to side as she easily detects the lie and latches on to it.

"Then why not give her a chance? Just because you haven't been great at picking out women in the past, doesn't mean this one is destined to fail too. They're not all Leigha."

"You're not wrong. Leigha is a breed of her own. But you said it yourself; I've never been good at picking out women. Who's to say this one isn't a mistake too?"

Her eagle eyes peer back at me, her face a picture of concentration as she considers my question. Finally, her voice dips into sweetness as she murmurs, "It's not. I have a good feeling about this one."

Her voice holds all the assurance I'm lacking, but I'm still not sold on her response. "How? You've never even met her."

With a shrug of her shoulders, my mother joins the list of insane women in my life as she responds, "I don't need to. Your behavior tells me everything I need to know. I've never seen you act like this over a woman, which tells me she must be special. Give her a chance—a real chance," she intones, dipping her head and glaring at me from beneath her long lashes. "If after the first date, you're still not sure, then don't pursue her. Let her down gently and move on. But don't knock her just because others have knocked you. I taught you better than that."

She stands from the table, gathering our empty plates before walking into the kitchen, effectively ending our conversation. Her parting words have my mind scrambling again, reminding me why I've been struggling with the thought of canceling.

Obviously, a part of me wants Riley—wants to find all the

ways she's different from the other sharks in the dating waters. I can't say I knew that from the beginning since I was too busy giving her my signature cold shoulder. But I knew from the first time my dick entered her sweet canal that she was special.

Okay, fuck, that's not true either. It was after that—when she told me she still didn't like me as she was falling into a sex coma. That's when I knew Riley was special. She solidified that the next morning when we woke up, and she tried to kick me out. I acted like I had no idea what she was trying to do, but I've kicked my fair share of women out of my bed. I knew she was trying to give me the brush off, which is exactly why I knew she deserved a real date.

Not to mention the fact I still crave her. Badly. I was stupid to think I could fuck the woman out of my system. It would seem having sex with her only made shit worse. Now that I know what it feels like to have her naked skin against mine, to feel her silky heat hugging my cock, there's no way I can give her up. Which can only mean one thing.

Why the hell are mothers always right? It's goddamn annoying.

Standing up, I grab the last of the dishes off the table and join the know-it-all in the kitchen, kissing her cheek as I say goodbye. It's taken me entirely too fucking long, but after some shared wisdom and a verbal kick in the ass, I finally know what I need to do.

There's a wall of hate between us, but I'm ready to tear it down.

27

RILEY

Saturday morning dawns bright and early, but I've been awake since long before the sun rose. Lying in bed, I stare at the ceiling, debating canceling on Parker for the millionth time, but when I turn my head, my eyes find the spot on my floor where he sat the other morning, watching me. Butterflies swarm my stomach as the memory of his handsome face taunts me. Picturing his signature smirk as he told me to be ready by ten sends a spark of excitement racing through my chest.

I have no idea how today will go or what will come next, but at the very least, maybe it will quiet all the questions I have about the man.

Crawling out of bed, I get ready, keeping in mind I also have the Snipers game tonight. Dressing in my best pair of jeans, a cute black tank top, and some simple Keds, I lay my Kingston Turner jersey out on my bed so it'll be ready to go for tonight. I've just finished applying one last swipe of lipstick when a series of knocks echoes through my apartment.

Walking to the door, I stop a few steps short, my stomach tying itself in knots. The only thing standing between me and possible heartbreak is that door. I could ignore it, pretend like he never mentioned the date—is this even a date?— and move on with my life. Or I can open the door, give him a chance, and pray every bit of hesitation and doubt I'm feeling is a lie.

Another set of knocks sound, jolting me into action. Reaching out, I grab the handle and open the door, my body making the decision before my heart can protest any further.

My breath stalls in my throat as Parker comes into view. He's wearing a tight, black leather jacket, holding a similar version in his hand. His dark-wash jeans hug his muscular thighs, and he's finished the bad boy look with tousled hair and black boots. Excitement courses through my veins at what his attire could possibly mean. The only time I've seen him dressed this way, he's been coming or going on his bike.

He looks me up and down, his eyes glittering with an unfamiliar emotion. His tongue peeks out, swiping across his lower lip as he looks me up and down. "Goddamn, Riley. You're a sight for sore eyes," he growls in his deep baritone voice.

You took the words right out of my mouth, I think to myself, thanking everything holy my mouth behaved this time. Blushing from head to toe, I nod my head before murmuring, "Thanks. You look good too."

With a quick wink, he holds out the leather jacket he's been holding, handing it over to me. "You're gonna need this."

I take it from his hands, the leather sliding against my hands like butter. "Are we going for a ride?" My voice trembles with excitement, hoping he says yes. I don't know why else he'd be handing me a leather jacket, and I've wanted to climb on the back of that beast since the first time I saw it.

"You fuckin' bet. Perfect weather for it," he states before pausing, taking in my expression. His face clouds with apprehension, his eyebrows narrowing as he questions, "Unless…you don't want to?"

"Oh, no, I do! I really do."

His face clears, his signature smirk reappearing as he nods his head.

I slide my arms into the jacket, the cool material fitting perfectly. Tugging the jacket closed, I peek up at Parker and catch him staring at me. His eyes have darkened to a midnight-blue, transfixing me to the spot. Butterflies storm my stomach at his look, waiting for him to make a move, but instead of mauling me like a few nights ago, he shakes his head and steps back.

I try not to let the disappointment of his retreat steal my excitement of what we're about to do, but I'm not too successful. It was stupid of me to get my hopes up. I'm not exactly his type, despite what happened the last time we were together.

"Let's go," he demands, his voice deeper than it was a second ago. I nod my head and step out of my doorway, following him to the elevator.

The next thing I know, I'm wearing a helmet and am sitting on the back of a crotch rocket. Parker reaches back, grabbing my hands and wrapping them tight around the front of his midsection, bringing me snugly against his muscular back. My nipples harden, and the second he revs the throttle, I damn near combust from the vibrations shaking my body.

Without further warning, we shoot forward, maneuvering out of the parking lot and on to the street. My hands tighten around his abs, holding on for dear life as he rockets us along the coast. The cool ocean breeze rushes past us, and I close my eyes, tipping my head back into the wind and smiling as the sun hits my face. A strong sense of peace steals over me as I realize I've never felt so unrestrained and carefree.

I'm jolted out of my peaceful moment when I feel Parker run his hand from my calf up to my thigh. His hand climbs further and further up my leg, shooting a rush of pleasure straight to my core. The adrenaline of being on the bike, mixed with his bold move, has my pulse racing, my heart hammering in my chest. He seductively rubs my thigh a few more times, squeezing it before returning his hand to the handlebar.

Embracing the lust Parker spiked, I gather my courage and allow my hands to wander from their position on his abs. They glide up his chest to caress his pecs before slowly slipping back down past his abs, heading further south.

I'm about to move my hands to his outer thighs when Parker reaches down, grabbing my right hand. He guides me to the noticeable bulge between his thighs, proving he's just as turned on by my wandering hands as I am. He squeezes my hand once before removing his hand, focusing on the road again.

Abandoning all rational thought, I continue to caress his hardness through his jeans, alternating between squeezing and rubbing my hand along his considerable length. My thighs tighten around his waist as I grind my front against his back, reveling in my heightened desire.

I'm squeezing his cock firmly when he slows down, coming to a stop. Confused, I look up at our surroundings, noticing we've left the coastal highway and are stopped at a side street stoplight. My hand is still thoughtlessly rubbing his dick when I turn to the right and see a police officer stopped next to us. He turns his head in my direction, making eye contact before following the path of my arm to where my hand is still indecently fondling Parker.

Humiliation shoots through me, forcing me to rip my hand off Parker like his cock has burned me. I bury my head against his shoulder, shielding my view from the officer. Parker's back rumbles against my cheek, and it takes me a minute to realize he's laughing. *Laughing!* We are seconds away from being arrested for public indecency and reckless driving, and he's laughing.

What the hell?

Before I can react, the light turns green, and Parker rockets ahead, leaving the officer in our rearview. A couple turns later, we pull into a parking spot outside of The Green Way Café. Parker shuts the bike off before twisting around to offer me a hand. I grab his hand and awkwardly swing my leg over, kneeing him in the back before stumbling to the ground. I fidget with embarrassment as Parker expertly dismounts the bike, but thankfully, he doesn't mention my clumsiness.

Instead, he turns to me and helps me remove my helmet. Reaching up, he gently swipes a few rogue hairs off my cheek, tucking them behind my ear. "Fucking sexy," he murmurs, gazing into my eyes. My knees—already unsteady from our ride—go weak, threatening to collapse if I don't get a hold of myself. He drags his hand down my cheek and cradles my chin, his thumb seductively swiping against my lips.

My tongue bravely peeks out, gliding against the pad of his thumb, and I watch as his eyes flash to an inky blue, desire crashing in like a wave. A hoarse growl rips from his throat before he tugs on my bottom lip, releasing me with a pop. Leaning in, his lips brush against my ear, sending shivers down my spine as he whispers, "Do that again, and we won't make it through brunch."

He turns to stow away our helmets, leaving me a breathless mess on the sidewalk. I don't miss how he readjusts the bulge in his pants or the way his shoulders are rigid with tension, which does nothing to temper my lust. *Maybe he is attracted to me?* Taking a deep breath, I close my eyes, willing my pulse to slow.

I always knew Parker was dangerous, but I just assumed it was my heart that needed protecting. Apparently, I prepped the wrong organ for this date.

28

PARKER

Opening the café door for Riley, I gesture for her to head in before me. I'd like to say it's me being a gentleman, but really, I'm just looking for another opportunity to stare at her delicious ass in those jeans. Her curves are fucking deadly. My hand twitches with the urge to grab her ass, but I think better of it, my mother's voice ringing through my head, chiding me to be a gentleman.

The door shuts behind me, and as soon as I drag my eyes off Riley's backside and take a look at our surroundings, I have half a mind to turn the fuck around and leave.

I'm going to murder Haylee.

With an open floor plan and white-washed brick walls, decorated with wood shelves, vivid green plants, industrial lamps, and black and white art pieces, the café she suggested is girly as fuck. Everywhere I look, there's a hint of elegance and romance. The beams are all exposed, with string lights and plants hanging from them, and the tables are all dark-stained wood with lit candles for centerpieces. I've never felt so out of place in my leather jacket and black boots.

My skin crawls, urging me to grab Riley's hand and haul her

ass to somewhere better suited for my taste, but when she turns to me with a brilliant smile covering her face, I know my ass is staying put. I'll deal with being uncomfortable as long as she's smiling at me.

There's a sign that says to seat ourselves, so Riley leads us to a table near the back window, overlooking the busy street outside. I watch as a few heads turn her way when she walks past, but one menacing look from me, and they all avert their eyes. I doubt Riley even realizes the effect she has on people, which only makes me want her more. She's clearly not after attention, something I'm not used to in the women I...*date.*

The word still feels unfamiliar on my tongue, and my stomach clenches with nerves that this is a mistake, but I push them aside. I promised my mother and myself I'd give Riley a real chance, and that's exactly what I intend to do. I'll worry about the consequences later.

A waitress hustles over as soon as we sit. I can tell from my peripherals she's probably decent looking, but not enough to steal my eyes from the beauty sitting across from me, her hair resembling a glowing fire as the sunlight peeks through the window, kissing the top of her head.

"Hello, welcome to The Green Way Café. Can I get you started with a coffee or water?" Her perky voice grates on my nerves, reminding me too much of Leigha's annoyingly fake voice, making it easy to keep my focus on Riley. She's watching me closely, almost like she's waiting for me to give the other chick my attention.

Crossing my arms, I lean back in my chair and pin her with an intense stare. When she doesn't immediately order, I grunt out, "Coffee, black."

Riley blushes and breaks my stare, glancing up at the waitress with a smile as she orders a large orange juice and water. I hear the waitress huff in annoyance, but I'm too busy admiring the way Riley's cheeks fill with heat to give a damn. I wonder how deep that blush can go. Would it spread to her tits as I suck on her nipples? Her apartment was too dark for me to fully appreciate the way her skin pinks under my gaze.

Riley fidgets as I watch her, my mind wandering with all the naughty things I'd love to do to her and all the positions I can't wait to put her in. She clears her throat and looks around, her lips pursing before she says, "This is such a cute little place. Have you been here before?"

As much as I'm loving picturing her naked and writhing against me, I'm thankful for the distraction her words bring. Things were getting a little uncomfortable in my jeans, and walking out of here with a busted zipper wouldn't help my already tarnished reputation in the press.

"Never," I grumble, my voice harsher than I expected, thanks to the lust I'm barely restraining. "My assistant, Haylee, suggested it, and I stupidly took her advice. She failed to mention it was so…" trailing off, I look around, unamused by everything I see. "…*Girly*."

Looking back at Riley, I catch her eyes dropping to the table, her face paling slightly. Confusion sweeps through me at her reaction to my words, but before I can question it, the waitress appears at our table to take our order.

I know what I want to eat, but unfortunately for me, she's not on the menu. Not right now, anyway. So after a quick glance at the options, I find my go-to breakfast meal and wait for Riley to make her decision.

My chest tightens with nerves, waiting to see what she's going to order. Her eyes are frantically searching the menu, and I swear, if she orders a salad or some healthy bullshit, I might die inside. Spending another meal being forced to watch a woman pick apart a salad, barely eating, will drive me to the brink of insanity.

"I'll have…um…" she hesitates, sucking her bottom lip

between her teeth. She briefly peeks up at me beneath her lashes before averting her eyes. Her voice is almost a whisper when she chooses, "The biscuits and gravy, please."

Fuck yeah. I knew she was different.

My shoulders sag in relief, but not for long. The waitress has the nerve to scoff at her choice, a deep blush spreading across Riley's cheeks as she closes the menu and sets it to the side. Anger pulses through me at the derisive sound, and I have half a mind to cause a scene. How fucking dare she insult my woman— wait. My woman?

Hmm. *Yeah.* My fucking woman.

"I'll have the same. Extra gravy. And a side of bacon."

Tossing my menu aside, I dismiss the waitress, focusing my attention on Riley again. I'm about to ask her if she's okay or what caused her reaction before we were so rudely interrupted, but she beats me to the punch, still refusing to meet my eyes as she questions, "Does your assistant normally plan your outings for you?"

I don't miss how she doesn't label this a date, but we'll circle back to that later. "No."

"I see," she whispers, nodding her head as she lifts her glass to her mouth, taking a drink of her orange juice.

"I've never needed her help with a woman until you came along."

She chokes on her drink, juice dribbling out of the corner of her mouth as she stares at me with shock. My mouth waters as I consider leaning across the table to lick the juice from her lips, but she steals my chance. Her tongue sweeps across her lips before she opens her mouth, only to close it again, clearly stunned by what I've said.

"I'm sorry, what?" she finally manages. Her words are breathy, and I swear my cock is going to punch through the zipper of my jeans at any moment now.

"I'm not used to apologizing to a woman. In my experience, they've never been worthy of one. So when I realized you were, I needed my assistant's help navigating that bitch of a wave."

She chuckles, which isn't the reaction I was expecting, but fuck it. At least she isn't mad. "I see. Well, that explains the book, then."

My eyes narrow at her words, alarm bells ringing in my ears. I didn't send a fucking book. So either she has some other asshole sending her shit. Or...

No. She wouldn't fucking dare.

Looking around the café again, I realize, yes. *She fucking would.*

"What book?" I demand, barely concealing my irritation.

"There was a book called *How to Deal with the Jerk in Your Life* mixed in with a few of your gifts last week. I thought it came from you, but now it makes more sense."

My chest vibrates as a growl rumbles up my throat, my hand clenching my napkin, forming it into a wad of trash. "Color me unsurprised. I should've known she'd find a way to embarrass me. Although, everything else was from me. She might've handled the deliveries while I was out of town, but the gifts were mine—mostly."

She nods her head, rolling her lips between her teeth, and something about the emotion swirling in her eyes has me on the edge of my seat.

"I never did thank you for the gifts. They were nice, but they weren't needed. I'd much rather have you apologize to my face than try to buy my affection with expensive gifts. I can buy my own stuff, but I can't apologize for you."

Fuck.

"It was never about buying your affection," I counter, doing my best to keep the anger from my tone. Why can't anything be simple with this woman?

My father's memory flits through my mind, reminding me of the advice he gave me when I was too young to understand it. *The right woman won't be easy, son. She'll make you work for it. But that's how you'll know she's the one.*

Taking a deep breath, I add, "I just needed a way in. You were avoiding me at every turn, so I figured one of the gifts was bound to force you to talk to me. Took longer than I expected, but I won't lie and say I didn't enjoy how things played out." I add a wink at the end, hoping that makes my explanation sound playful rather than irritated.

The food shows up at our table before she can respond, giving us a much-needed reprieve from the tension circling us. I'm not sure what Riley's thinking, her face giving nothing away, but I hope she understands my intentions. I had a feeling sending her gifts was the wrong thing to do, but fuck me if I had any other ideas.

We dig into our food, and every time Riley moans with appreciation, my cock twitches, wishing he was the one ripping that sound from her throat.

Needing another distraction, I steer the conversation in a new direction. "Tell me about your family."

She visibly brightens, her eyes glittering with joy as a smile takes over her face. I mentally fist-bump myself, happy as fuck I could still make her smile despite our...*misunderstanding* with the gifts.

"Well, I'm an only child, but I'm really close to my mom and dad. They're happily retired and living in Maine now, but we still talk on the phone and FaceTime at least once a week."

The urge to learn everything about this woman consumes me, but before I can fire off any more questions, she beats me to it.

"What about you? What's your family like?"

Her question feels like a roundhouse kick to the chest, but I should've seen it coming. *Doesn't make it hurt any less, though.* I could lie. Or simply omit some details. But what's the point? She'd find out eventually.

The emotion crushing my windpipes forces me to clear my throat, but my tone is still as rough as gravel when I answer, "Well. I have one younger brother. We're pretty close in age, but that's about the only closeness we share these days. My mom and I, on the other hand, are as thick as thieves."

"Ah, a momma's boy, huh?" Her voice is playful and full of humor, but if I'm not mistaken, a flash of fear crossed her face too.

"Something like that."

She forces a laugh, confusing me further. "That's cool. At least you don't live with her. Or…did you? Before you moved to your apartment?"

My head rears back as my forehead furrows in confusion. "Fuck no," I belt out in disgust. "I do my best to see her a few times a month if I'm not swamped with work, but I moved out the day I left for college."

"Good. That's, um. Yeah, that's great," she mutters with a sigh, her shoulders slumping in relief. *Who the heck has this woman been dating?* "And your dad?"

"Excuse me?" My head spins from the redirection in our conversation.

"You mentioned a brother and your mom, but what about your dad? Are you close to him?"

Silence descends on our table as I mull over her words. I was hoping I'd escaped having to talk about this, but Riley's not the type to let shit slip past her. She's too intelligent for evasive games.

"I used to be. He was closer to my brother Rory, but we had a solid bond too. I was his firstborn son, after all."

The happiness drains from her face as she reads between the

lines. Her words are barely a whisper in the air between us as she asks, "What happened?"

"He passed when I was twelve. Rory was barely ten at the time. He went out for a run one day and got caught up in an unexpected thunderstorm. Lightning hit the tree he was sheltering under, splitting it in half. One half collapsed on top of him, killing him instantly."

Riley's wide eyes fill with tears as she reaches across the table, settling her soft hand on top of mine. Tingles shoot up my arm at the contact, momentarily distracting me from the pain in my chest. It seems no matter how much time has passed, that pain is always there—the ghost a reminder of what could've been.

"Parker, I'm so sorry. I can't imagine how hard that must have been."

"Yep, but I didn't have a say in the matter. We were dealt some pretty shitty cards, but that's just part of life. A loss like that…It can either destroy you, or you can destroy the fuck out of it. It was hard as hell in the beginning, and still is some days, but we manage."

She squeezes the top of my hand, and before she can withdraw her own, I flip mine upside down, joining them in a comforting embrace. Her hand feels so small against my own, but something about it feels so right. It feels like…*fuck*. It feels like home.

"Was it lonely? Being an only child?" I ask, my question coming out as a plea, desperate for another redirection.

She takes the cue, pursing her lips as she thinks on it for a moment before answering. Tipping her head back and forth, she admits, "Sometimes. But I like to believe my parents made up for that void. We did a lot of stuff together as a family, and honestly, I was rarely ever bored as a child. All I needed was the animal channel or an animal magazine, and I was happy."

My chest fills with an unexpected warmth as I picture a young, nerdy Riley curled up on a couch reading a magazine.

Riley reaches for her water, taking a drink before she adds, "Besides, once I started college and met Madison, she filled that sister role almost instantly. She was my roommate, and although we were complete opposites, we formed a tight bond. She's the wild to my mild and forces me to have fun, whether I want to or not."

In an attempt to keep things light, I joke, "Ah, the best friend, Madison. And when will I get to meet her?"

29

RILEY

Never.

The answer pops into my head too fast for me to stop, and I immediately feel guilty for even thinking it. I've seen the tabloids, though. All those leggy blondes and busty brunettes—I already know Maddie is Parker's type, and the thought of losing him to her sends my heart into a tailspin.

Not that he's mine to lose, but watching another guy I'm interested in—or at the very least, a guy I've slept with—fall for my best friend might literally kill me. I can't do it again.

I know Maddie would never intentionally steal him from me, especially knowing I've slept with him. But that won't stop him from falling for her anyway, and judging by the fact I'm sitting here in this café with him, he's incredibly persuasive. Would she be able to resist his temptations? Or would she succumb to his will, just as I have?

The fact I'm so unsure is reason enough to keep them away from each other. At least for now, until I know for sure what his intentions are.

"Um," I mutter, a strangled laugh forcing itself out of my throat. "Who knows."

Parker's forehead furrows slightly, confusion coloring his face, but instead of expanding on my awkward answer, I use another question of my own to distract him. "What about you? If I were to meet your best friend, who would it be?"

The hand not holding mine lifts off the table as he brings it to his face, rubbing it along his scruffy chin. "It'd be a toss-up between Colton, Rhett, and Wes. I'm not sure I'd call them my best friends," he jokes with a playful wink, "but they're the only fuckers I make time for, outside of my family. Other than that, I stay too busy with my company and all the bullshit that goes along with being in the public eye to have much of a social life."

The moment he says public eye, a catalog of tabloid images filter through my mind, reminding me of all the women I've seen him next to in photographs at one social event or another, each woman prettier than the last. I wonder if he considers them part of his social life or if booty calls and relationships fall under a different category?

The cafe waitress appears, breaking me from my negative thoughts as she sets our check down on the table. Parker immediately reaches for it, releasing my hand from his warm embrace. He slaps a few bills into the folder and closes it, handing it back to her.

"Keep the change," he states, his deep, authoritative voice pebbling my nipples. I tug on the lapels of the leather jacket I'm still wearing, making sure they're hiding my blatant lust for the man sitting in front of me.

As the waitress ambles away, her hips swinging in an exaggerated sway, I roll my eyes. Mainly at the waitress, but also at myself for thinking I could possibly hold Parker's attention when there are hundreds of women begging for it every day.

"Should we head out?" the man in question asks, leaving the decision up to me.

With no excuse to prolong our time in the café, I softly nod my head with a, "Sure."

Pushing in our chairs, we head back the way we came. Before we climb on the bike, Parker questions, "Do I need to take you straight home or do you have time to spare?"

Looking at the time on my phone, I realize I still have plenty of time before the game, with no real plans for the rest of the afternoon. "I have plans tonight, so I just need to be home around four."

"Four. I can do that," he nods with a sexy wink.

"What else did you have in mind?"

"You'll see." He tosses his leg over the bike, turning the key and revving the throttle before offering me a helping hand. We drive a short distance, pulling into a crowded lot near the oceanfront.

"The boardwalk?" I question, my brow furrowing in confusion as we dismount the bike. Once again, I'm shocked by his choice of location. Given his usual prickly demeanor, he doesn't strike me as the type to enjoy being surrounded by people.

"Yeah. I like to come here when I'm feeling overwhelmed with scrutiny. There's something calming about walking down a street full of people you don't know. It's one of my favorite places to escape to. When you're in the public eye more often than you want to be, the opportunity to blend into a crowd is hard to pass up. Makes you feel like you're just another nobody, you know?"

"I guess I don't. I've never really been the object of people's interest, so I've never had a need or reason to blend in. It just happens naturally, wherever I go."

His head turns in my direction, his eyes slowly trekking up and down my body before he says, "For some reason, I highly doubt that."

Parker stalks forward, leading me into the Saturday afternoon crowd. We walk down the boardwalk, side by side, an occasional brushing of our shoulders the only point of contact between us. I peer inside windows into kitschy little shops, and we stop at vendor booths, admiring all the touristy trinkets and graphic tees with illustrations of the Coronado Bridge.

The noise level makes it difficult to talk much, which isn't all that bad. We've done quite a bit of talking today. Now it's nice to just enjoy each other's company without feeling the need to fill the silence between us.

Walking past a snack shack, Parker stops, grabbing my attention with a quirk of his eyebrow, his head nodding toward the shack. Never one to turn down sweets, I smile brightly, moving us toward the line.

I order a Mint Chip cone, Parker a Cookies N' Cream cone, and after a bit of reluctance on his end, I manage to pay for our desserts. It's the least I can do after the man showered me with gifts over the last week.

Parker doesn't make another move to hold my hand. In fact, he hasn't since our moment at the table, which fills me with self-doubt. He seems so hot and cold...like he wants to be intimate, and then doesn't. The back and forth is so confusing.

It's possible what happened in the café was just a moment of comfort, given the heaviness of our conversation. Maybe it meant nothing at all. Friends hold hands all the time.

But then, what about the sex? Or his wandering hands on the bike? His compliments? Why are we even here? Together?

We continue to meander through the crowd, each lost in our own thoughts, silently enjoying our ice cream. We stop every now and then to take in the ocean view, or a vendor of some sort, before eventually making our way back toward the bike as the time inches closer and closer to four.

It truly is a beautiful day, but the closer we draw to the end of our time together, the more uncomfortable I grow, a sense of unease filling my stomach as we head back home. Something just feels...*off*.

It could be the seductive glances I caught on the face of every female we passed or the questioning looks I received from more than one passerby when they saw Parker and I standing together.

Or possibly, it's because there are still so many unanswered questions surrounding Parker. What was this? Where do we go from here? Was it a one-time thing?

He never specifically said it wasn't a date. *He never said it was, either.*

He paid for brunch. *You paid for dessert.*

He bought me a jacket. *Maybe it's on loan.*

He said you were sexy. *He probably wants more sex.*

The little voice in my head has a counterpoint for every argument, doing nothing but driving my uneasiness higher the closer we get to the apartment.

Everything has been so easy between us today—*natural.* He opened up a little, shedding that asshole armor he wears so well, even if only for a short while. I saw a whole new side to him, but I'm still not entirely convinced we have a lasting connection, which scares me beyond belief.

Sure, the physical chemistry is unrivaled by any I've ever felt before, but that could fade over time. Lust doesn't last forever, and it's certainly not a foundation to build a relationship on. But does he even want a relationship? Or is he just after a new booty call? I can't deny the accessibility would be convenient. Doesn't get much easier than being right next door.

However, that's not what I'm looking for. I'm ready to settle down and start a family. Settling for being someone's booty call or friend with benefits won't fulfill this ache inside me to be a mother, no matter how attractive the friend is or how hot the benefits are.

I genuinely don't think we're on the same page, which means it's best to end this before it goes too far—before he hurts me, just like every man before him.

30

PARKER

Pulling into the parking lot, I back us into my usual spot before shutting the ignition off. I've barely turned the key, cutting off the roar of the bike, before Riley swings her leg over and hops off the bike without any assistance. She pulls her helmet off, revealing wide, panicked eyes, and thrusts it into my hand before backing away from me, filling me with a sense of dread.

I open my mouth, about to ask her if she's okay, when she gives me a nervous smile, a short wave, and turns, briskly walking toward the apartment building.

What the fuck?

Ripping my helmet off, I jog to my car, tossing both of our helmets into the passenger seat before chasing after her. By the time I make it through the lobby doors, she's in the elevator, the doors closing after her.

The irony isn't lost on me as she doesn't hold the door, and fuck if I don't deserve that. A growl of frustration rips through my throat as I rush to the stairs, climbing the steps two at a time 'til our floor. *Thank fuck I'm in good shape.*

I've never had to work so hard for a woman in my life, let

alone chase after her, which does nothing but prove she's worth it. If she was as easy as all the other women I've bedded, I wouldn't be interested in her.

I thought things went pretty well today. I dug deep, sharing things with her I normally keep to myself. I did my best to not go overboard with my physical touch or sexual advances, despite the chemistry sizzling between us being hot enough to burn down a forest. I gave it a real, honest to God chance, just like I told my mom I would. And as always, my mom was fucking right about Riley being exactly what I needed.

So why the fuck is she running from me?

Arriving on our floor, I burst through the stairwell entrance, barely breaking a sweat. Riley is just walking into her apartment as I jog down the hallway. Frustrated with her attempt to escape from me like this has been the world's worst date—it wasn't. Not even fucking close—I growl and reach my hand out, slapping it against the door she's closing. Startled, she jumps back, a squeak falling from her lips as her eyes widen in shock.

"Jesus, Parker. You scared me."

"Why are you running from me, Riley?" I demand, my tone rough with irritation.

"I-I don't know. I just...I don't know what this was, and I wasn't ready for you to tell me it wasn't a date." Her eyes churn with doubt, forcing a growl to rumble through my chest. *I thought I made this shit pretty clear.*

"It was definitely a date. And it wasn't over yet."

Stepping into her personal space, I wrap my hand around the back of her neck, pulling her toward me. She releases a high-pitched squeak from the sudden motion before I slam my mouth against hers, smothering any other squeaks of protest.

Swiping my tongue against her lips, she opens up for me, her body sagging in relief against mine, melting in my arms while I kiss the ever-loving shit out of her. My right hand tangles in her wind-swept hair, courtesy of our ride, while my left hand leaves the door and snakes around her waist, pulling her flush against my body.

The same spark of electricity I felt the other night shoots from our joined lips, traveling down my spine to settle deep in my balls. My cock hardens against my jeans, but now's not the time. She has shit to do.

Reluctantly peeling my lips off Riley's, I step back, dropping my hands from her body. Her eyes are still closed, her lips parted seductively as she gently sways without my hands holding her up.

"Now it's over," I grunt, my voice dripping with need.

Before I can do something stupid, like beg her for another date, I turn my back and head for my apartment, leaving her standing in her doorway, dazed from my kiss.

Tossing my keys on the kitchen counter, I grab a beer from my fridge and settle on my couch. I turn the television to ESPN and lift the beer to my lips, relishing the taste of the amber liquid sliding down my throat.

My phone pings with a text, and when I tell you I've never transformed into a teenage girl faster, I fucking mean it. My heart races as my hand dives into my pocket, desperately fishing my phone out to see if Riley's texting me already. *Maybe I was wrong about her not being eager to see me.*

Colton: *Emailing you your ticket now. Use the Southwest entrance. Deke will be there to escort you to the box. Don't be late, fucker.*

Shit. My heart drops in my chest—for more reason than one. I can't believe I forgot that was tonight. I've been so wrapped up in my head over Riley and work, everything else faded to the background.

Tonight is game seven of the third round of hockey playoffs, and I told Colton I'd go with him and the boys. If the Snipers win, they'll be conference champions headed to the Stanley Cup finals. If they lose, well...we won't talk about that.

Parker: *I'll be there.*

Quickly finishing my beer, I jump up from the couch to shower before the game. Looking at my watch, I see I don't have much time before I need to get on the road, which means it'll be a quick shower. The incessant hard-on Riley left me with will have to wait until later. Game-day traffic is a bitch to navigate.

Freshly showered and dressed in a Snipers t-shirt, I'm leaving my apartment when I remember I have a bone to pick with a certain blond-haired weasel.

Parker: *What the fuck was that with the café, Haylee. Are you TRYING to get fired?*

She responds immediately, almost like she was expecting my message. Admittedly, I should have done some recon of my own before settling with her suggestion. But she's never steered me wrong before, and the little sneak was probably banking on that.

Haylee: *Whatever do you mean, sir?*

Parker: *Don't fucking "sir" me. You know exactly what I'm talking about.*

Haylee: *Alright, alright. Keep your panties on. I knew it was a gamble, and you'd probably be pissy. But she loved it, didn't she?*

Parker: *That's beside the fucking point.*

Haylee: *I knew it! Yay!*

Parker: *Don't celebrate too much. She may have loved the place, but I could have done without the girly shit. Prepare to be repaid in full this week at work for your little stunt.*

Haylee: *Worth it. I wish I could've seen you sitting in that plant-filled café in what I'm assuming was your leather riding jacket. Hahahahaha. Priceless. See ya Monday, boss man.*

Kingston Turner races up the ice with the puck, dodging two Vegas players on his way to the net, sending a cheer through the arena. So far, the game has been intense, but we're ahead 2-1 heading into the third period.

Taking a swig of my beer, I glance up at the jumbotron as it switches from the second period highlights to the kiss cam. Rolling my eyes, I start to turn toward the boys when a flash of red hair pops up on the screen. My head snaps back to the jumbotron as my eyes zero in on a familiar face. The kiss cam is focused on the couple sitting in front of her, but there's no doubt that's Riley sitting in the row behind them.

A beautiful brunette sitting next to her points at the screen, bouncing in her seat with joy before she whips her face toward Riley. The brunette grabs Riley's face in both hands and hauls her toward her, planting a giant kiss directly on her lips.

The couple in front of them leans in for a kiss, but the camera zooms in on Riley and the brunette instead. The arena goes crazy over their kiss, men swinging their playoff towels in the air and cheering them on. Can't say I blame them. Two fuck-hot ladies kissing? Yeah, the arena isn't the only thing going crazy, if you catch my drift.

A rare laugh bursts out of my throat at Riley's obvious discomfort. Prying her friend's lips off her tomato-red face, Riley sinks down in her seat, hiding from the cameras as her friend stands and encourages the crowd's uproar. If I had to guess, I'd say that's her friend Madison. Riley said she was wild, and that was certainly a bold move.

Rhett is sitting next to me and dares to open his goddamn mouth, proving exactly why he's Tweedle-fucking-dumb. "Damn, look at those bombshells. Where are they sitting? I bet I could talk them both into coming home with me."

Growling, I grab his shoulder as he starts to stand, forcing him back into his seat. "Shut the fuck up, numbnuts. That's Riley."

"*That's* Riley?" he shouts, his face twisting back to the screen for another look. She's not having any luck hiding from the cameras, and the blush extending down her face, disappearing into her cleavage, is giving me and my dick some ideas. We want to feel the heat of her blush while her body presses against us. "Hot fucking damn, dude. You weren't kidding. She's fuck-hot. Are you done with her yet? I wouldn't mind taking her for a ride."

My face contorts into anger and, without thinking, I draw my fist back, ready to plant my knuckles straight into his teeth. He bursts out in obnoxious laughter, holding his hands up in defense as he jumps up from his seat. "Chill out, fucker. I was just kidding. Hey, Wes. Wes...Wesley!" he yells, trying to get our douchebag friend's attention. He's been too busy trying to swindle some blonde out of her panties instead of watching the game.

Wesley pulls his attention away from the blonde, nodding his chin at Rhett.

"We were fucking right. Our boy Parker here is whipped by the fiery redhead!"

Shoving him, I growl out, "I'm not fucking whipped, you jackass. But I already warned you she was off-limits."

"Whatever you say, man. How about that brunette? Can I have her? She looks like a fun time," he jokes, suggestively wiggling his eyebrow up and down.

"I think that's her best friend, Madison. And I don't know. Her relationship status never came up on our date today."

"Date?" Colton roars, tuning into our conversation. He's been busy talking to a few of his coworkers that are sharing the suite with us.

Annoyed, I huff out, "Yeah. Date. I took her out today. Let it the fuck go."

"Oh, man. He's totally pussy-whipped," Wesley states.

Rhett, being the fuck head he is, agrees. "Yep. We've officially lost him to the sea of love."

Ignoring Rhett and Colton's bullshit, I refocus on the jumbotron that's currently showing an instant replay of the kiss cam excitement. Riley looks beautiful in an oversized Kingston Turner jersey, but something doesn't sit right with me at having some other man's name splashed across her back. Yeah, not too crazy about that at all.

And, no. That doesn't make me "whipped". It makes me a goddamn manly man that doesn't want his girl wearing some other douchefuck's name.

The third period starts, but I'm too busy focusing on what Rhett said to pay attention to the game. They may have just been busting my balls, but they were right about one thing—I'm falling for her. I've never felt like this before, nor have I ever felt like punching someone over a female, so I don't really know what to think. But I sure as fuck can't get the woman off my mind.

Searching the crowd, I'm determined to find her in the sea of red and black. After several minutes of scanning each section, I find them behind the home bench, thirteen rows up. Now that I know where she's sitting, it'll make finding her after the game easier, which is exactly what I plan to do. She may have tried to slip away from me this afternoon, but I'll be damned if I let her get away so easily twice in one day.

From the moment Riley's skin touched mine, every molecule in my body slowly shifted, forming a pattern they were always meant to take. My plans of staying a single man went up in flames the second her body pressed tightly against mine in her doorway this afternoon. She set my soul on fire, and I'm not sure I'll ever be the same. Hell, I'm not sure I want to be. Which is a real fucking pain in the ass, given her determination to keep me at an arm's length.

But I've yet to face a challenge I couldn't overcome. And I'll be damned if that starts with her.

Settling in for the rest of the game, I stop drinking, switching to water. I need to have a clear head if I want to convince Riley to spend time with me after the game. The boys and I were planning on hitting up the bar after this, but they can fuck right off. I have more important things to do now that I've seen Riley's beautiful face again.

31

RILEY

The end of the game buzzer sounds, and half the arena sits there in silence, while the other half thunders with cheers. *What the heck just happened?*

Looking over at Maddie, I find her standing in front of her seat with her hands folded on top of her head, her mouth gaping wide open. She's practically catatonic, and I can't say I blame her. I'm not a die-hard fan like she is, and even I'm shocked at what just happened down on the ice.

We were winning by one point with only forty-five seconds left in the game. You could practically taste the excitement in the air at the probability of being conference champions. Then, the fuckery happened.

A missed pass by the Snipers turned into a 2-on-1 breakaway for the Vegas Gold Miners. They scored on the play, tying the game at two.

Not a big deal, right? There were still thirty seconds left, and we were the best in the league at scoring first if it went into an extra period.

Wrong.

The Gold Miners won the face-off, controlling the puck in the

Snipers' zone. The clock dwindled down as they passed back and forth, looking for a scoring opportunity. And boy howdy, did they get one. With ten seconds to go, one of our defensemen got caught up trying to defend the net against the Gold Miners' winger. He tripped and went down to the ice—*hard*—leaving an opening for the Vegas center, who expertly accepted a pass and sent the puck flying toward the net with a slap shot.

The goalie couldn't see through the Gold Miners' screen and didn't have a chance to drop his pads to the ice before the puck soared through his five-hole, straight to the back of the net. The goal buzzer lit up mere seconds before the end of the game buzzer rang through the arena, announcing that the Snipers just lost their ticket to the Stanley Cup finals.

Maddie drops into her seat, her head falling into her hands as her shoulders shake with emotion. She's not the only one. The Snipers fans just went from picturing the team as conference champions moving on to the Stanley Cup Finals to being relegated to the playoff graveyard, all in less than a minute.

Sinking into my seat next to Maddie, I wrap my arm around her shoulders, trying to console her as the fans around us move to the exits. A few of the fans Maddie has made friends with throughout the season pat her on her back as they scoot past us, filing out to the aisle. They all know she's a rabid fan and are probably just as aware as I am that she's about to fall into a post-playoff depression. She's been waiting for the Snipers to hoist the Stanley Cup her whole life, and this is as close as they've ever been.

We're still sitting in our seats several minutes later as the last of the fans exit the arena. The cleaning crew moves through the rows, cleaning the mess left behind by fans of both teams. The back of my neck tingles, and I feel like I'm being watched. *I probably am.* I'm sure the cleaning crew is wondering how long we're just going to sit here.

"Maddie? You okay?" I ask in a gentle voice. She doesn't answer me, though.

Worried we're going to be escorted out by security if we don't leave soon, I turn my head to glance around the arena. A deep sigh pulls my attention back to Maddie. She stands and gathers up her drink and popcorn before silently leading us to the end of the row.

Climbing the stairs, she looks up at the concourse opening, a slow smile spreading across her face. "Well, if that's not a consolation prize, I don't know what is," she purrs, perking up considerably, given the loss she just suffered.

Confused, I glance to the top of the aisle and stop dead in my tracks, my heart falling to my feet. *What the heck is he doing here?*

Maddie fluffs her hair, her signature seductive smile firmly in place. She's on the prowl, and every inch of my skin tightens, my gut clenching with nerves at the idea of Maddie meeting Parker.

Without thinking, I reach out and grab on to her arm. She stumbles to a stop, her head whipping toward me in confusion, and I falter. I don't know what I was planning on doing. It's not like I can hide her—he's already seen us.

"Riley? You okay?"

Sighing in defeat, I let go of her arm. Maddie suffered her loss, and now it looks like I'll be suffering mine.

"Yeah, um. Th-that's Parker."

She whips her head back around, her eyes bugging out in Parker's direction. He's flanked by three guys now, all of them standing there looking like they were plucked straight from a GQ Magazine.

"That's Parker?" She screeches, loud enough for them to hear us. *Neat.* "Wow. He's even hotter in person." Her tongue is practically hanging out of her mouth like a dog, and I'm about to slap her before grabbing her tongue, rolling it up, and shoving it back in her mouth. The way she's looking at him fills me with rage and self-doubt.

Finally snapping out of her lustful staring, she shakes my hand off her arm before reaching down to grab it in her hand, yanking me up the stairs. Right before we reach the men, she turns her head toward me and ominously whispers, "I apologize in advance for what I'm about to do. But I'm doing it for your own good."

A sense of dread fills the pit of my stomach as my mind travels back to our college days, wondering if that was all for my own good too.

Stopping in front of the group of men, I briefly make eye contact with Parker before my eyes shoot to the floor with nerves. I spent the majority of the game reminiscing on that kiss he left me with this afternoon after confirming that we were, in fact, on a date. The kiss was full of heat and desire, leaving me wanting more.

But now that I'm standing in front of him again, with Maddie by my side, I can't help but feel self-conscious. This is always the point where the man's desire for me shifts to Maddie, which is exactly why I didn't want them to meet yet.

"Pork Sword Parker. We finally meet."

My head snaps up, my jaw dropping in horror at what she just said. When have we ever called him that?!

One of the guys with Parker chokes on his beer, his head barely turning in time to not spray his mouthful all over us. The other two guys stand there slack-jawed, staring at her with wide eyes. Parker, on the other hand, crosses his arms, looking at her with a twinkle in his eyes. *I knew it.*

"Ah, you must be Madison. I was hoping I'd get the chance to meet you. Didn't think it'd be so soon, though."

My heart falls in my chest at his words.

"I hear I have you to thank for finally breaking the chains off my girl's vagina. I was about ready to sign her up for stripper lessons just so she could get a little pole action, if you know what I mean."

Oh.

My.

God.

I can't take this bitch anywhere!

My face turns an embarrassing shade of red, and I'm seconds away from moving to Maine with my parents, so I never have to see any of them ever again. I can't freaking believe Maddie just announced to everyone that I've been in a sex drought.

Unfortunately, the embarrassment doesn't end there. Turning to the other guys, Maddie continues on with her obnoxious ways. "And who are these fine pieces of man meat?"

I swear, each of them stands up straight, puffing out their chests as Maddie looks at them. If I wasn't so mortified over everything that's happened in the last few minutes, I'd probably laugh at their peacocking. Not that I'm surprised. Maddie has a way of making men want to show off.

With a chuckle, Parker gestures to his friends, pointing out, "Colton, Rhett, and Wesley." Turning to me, he winks, adding, "These are the fuckers I mentioned earlier today."

The corners of my mouth briefly turn up in a small smile, but it's short-lived as Parker turns his attention back to Maddie and his friends. Maddie and Colton discuss the game, Maddie's hand gestures growing more wild by the second. The other two boys and Parker stand there watching their conversation like it's a tennis match, their heads swiveling back and forth.

I welcome their distraction, taking a second to release the air that's been trapped in my lungs. My eyes travel over Parker, cataloging every inch of him and storing it away in my memory. He looks damn near edible in his black Snipers t-shirt, the sleeves clinging tightly to his bulging biceps. His hair is wind-swept and unkempt, filling me with an urge to drag my fingers through it. He's wearing different jeans than he was this morning, these ones lighter, complimenting his dark t-shirt.

He's the type of man you'd expect to see standing next to Maddie, not me. With her beautiful chestnut hair, naturally highlighted from the San Diego sun, her thin, toned body, porcelain skin, and beautiful hazel eyes that often change from light brown to gorgeous green, depending on her surroundings, she's stunning. As much as I hate to admit it, they'd look perfect standing next to each other.

"Speaking of being a die-hard fan," Maddie announces, breaking me from my thoughts. "I have a five to seven business day depression to sink into after that loss. Parker, do you mind getting this babe home tonight? Thanks."

Without waiting for an answer, Maddie slaps him on the chest before storming toward the exit. She shoves popcorn in her mouth, obnoxiously fake crying as she walks away, leaving the rest of us to watch her dramatic exit in appalled silence.

Wesley is the first to speak, drawing our attention away from Maddie. Well, mostly. He's still staring at her ass when he says, "I don't know what the hell just happened, but I think I'm in love."

Colton stands next to him, his head tilted in amusement as he watches Maddie strut through the doors.

"Fuck off, man, I called dibs in the suite," Rhett argues, his booming voice startling me. "Besides, your hands are already full. Where the hell did that little blond babe you were practically undressing during the game go?"

Doing my best to ignore the men and their comments about Maddie, I turn to the side and pull out my phone, desperate to get out of here. I'm just pulling my Uber app up on my screen when a strong presence leans over my shoulder. My head turns to the right, my eyes connecting with Parker's. His forehead furrows, his eyebrows dipping dangerously low over his eyes as he glances at my screen.

"What are you doing?" he questions, his deep voice dripping with accusation.

"Ordering an Uber. Sorry about Maddie. It's not your job to get me home. Besides, I don't want to interrupt your night with the boys."

"The fuck you are," Parker grumbles, quickly reaching over my shoulder, plucking my phone right out of my hands. I turn, staring at him in horror as he tucks it into his pocket.

With a wink, he settles his hand on my lower back, right above my ass. Glancing back at his friends, he tips his chin up and says, "Catch you ugly fuckers later."

Using his hand, he applies enough pressure on my lower back to push me forward, leading us toward the exit. Two of his friends start laughing, but one of them—Wesley, I believe—calls out after us.

"Wait, what about the bar?" he whines.

"Fuck the bar," Parker barks over his shoulder, his eyes never leaving my face. His deep, masculine voice sends a shiver down my spine, my heart tripping over itself at his alpha-like demeanor.

The boys call out obnoxiously behind us, imitating the sound of whips, which I don't fully understand. Glancing at Parker out of the corner of my eye, I catch him rolling his eyes, which only confuses me further. Are they saying he's whipped? Because there's no way that's true. Although, I am a little shocked he's taking me home, especially after meeting Maddie. That's never happened before. And speaking of Maddie…I can't believe what she put me through tonight. She's going to pay for that, I swear.

32

RILEY

A short while later, we arrive back at our apartment building. It's a beautiful summer night, a slight breeze rippling through the air, giving us a reprieve from the California heat. Nights like these make me wish I had a balcony I could sit out on, cuddled up with a good book.

One of my coworkers recommended a new read to me this week. A romance called *Fight Song*, I believe it was. She spent hours ranting and raving about the new author and how wonderful her debut novel was, convincing me to download it. I don't read romance very often, usually it fills me with too much sadness. Men don't love me like they do in those books. They never have. But tonight seems like as good a night as any for it.

I don't have a balcony to sit out on, but I do have a comfy couch and a bottle of wine chilling in my fridge. I also plugged my Kindle in to charge before I left for the game, so everything should be ready for a night of reading romance before bed.

Arriving on our floor, I expect Parker to stop at my door, but he doesn't. He passes it, stopping in front of his own instead. Facing me, he pulls his keys out of his pocket, reminding me my phone is still in there too.

"Oh, I almost forgot. You still have my phone."

"I know. I'm holding it hostage."

"What? For how long?" *What could he possibly want with my phone?*

"Until you come in and have a drink with me."

"O-oh. Okay," I stutter, his answer taking me by surprise. *I guess my book will have to wait.*

He unlocks the door and escorts me inside, his hand caressing the base of my spine again. A flush steals over my body at the contact, filling me with a warmth I've come to realize only happens when I'm around Parker.

Leading me into his living room, he gestures to the couch. "Make yourself comfortable. I'll be right back." He saunters off in the direction of his bedroom, leaving me staring after him.

When he disappears through the doorway, I glance around his living room, taking in the lack of personality. I'm not sure what I was expecting, but it wasn't this. His apartment layout matches mine, but that's the only sort of resemblance. His furniture looks brand new and barely used, his walls are bare, and there are hardly any personal touches. It looks barely lived in.

The epitome of a temporary home.

The thought flits through my mind, bringing me back to reality. Remembering that tabloid I read about his multimillion dollar estate, I guess it is. He won't be my neighbor forever, and I'd do well to remember that. This...*thing*...between us might be fun, but that's all it'll ever be. Fun. Because sooner or later, he'll go back to his real home and his real life, leaving me behind as a distant memory of "that time I hooked up with my next-door neighbor."

Sounds more like a dramatic tragedy than a romantic happily ever after, which is precisely why I tend to avoid romance novels. That shit just doesn't happen to me. I'm more like a romance trope gone wrong. Or a stepping stone to the happily ever after.

The men always leave me for my best friend—if they notice me at all.

Parker waltzes back into the room, holding a t-shirt in his hands, breaking me from my depressing thoughts. He meets me in the middle of the room where I'm still standing and hands me the shirt without a word. I glance down, looking to see if I spilled something on myself at the game, and didn't notice, but I don't see any stains.

My brow furrows as I peer back at him, my eyes swimming with questions. "What's wrong with what I'm wearing?"

"I don't want to stare at another man's name on your back all night."

My eyes flare wide, and my abdomen flutters with wild butterflies at his possessive words. I've never been attracted to dominance before, but Parker's alpha tendencies send an exciting thrill coursing through my blood.

"Bathroom's down the hall if you'd like some privacy to change, but I'm more than happy to accept a floor show too."

My cheeks heat with a blush at his seductive wink, and I tuck tail, practically running to his bathroom. As much as I love the boost in confidence he's given me, I need a reprieve from his intensity.

The material of his shirt is soft between my fingers and smells divine, a mixture of cedar and laundry soap—perfectly him. Taking a moment to settle my nerves, I close my eyes, slowly inhaling his scent as I slip the t-shirt over my head, exchanging it for Turner's jersey. Checking my reflection in the mirror, I admire how his oversized shirt fits my frame, hanging loosely off my shoulder. I've never felt super thin, especially since filling out a bit since college, but with the way his shirt drapes across my torso, I can't deny that his muscular build makes me feel petite.

With a deep breath to calm the butterflies raging in my stomach, I leave the bathroom, sauntering down the hallway with renewed confidence. Parker is busy pouring our drinks when I enter the living room. His eyes snap to mine before quickly dropping to my feet, slowly traveling up my length, perusing every inch of me from my skin-tight jeans to his shirt hanging off one shoulder. Desire flares to life when his gaze connects with mine, his gorgeous eyes three shades darker with his lust.

I roll my bottom lip between my teeth, chewing on it with nerves. His navy blues track the movement, a subtle groan falling from his lips. With a shake of his head, his hand briefly dips below the counter before coming up to grip the glass as he finishes pouring our drinks. When he moves from behind the counter, strutting my way, it's impossible to miss the bulge threatening to bust past his zipper.

Hope blossoms in my chest, my heart racing as I dare to believe he still wants me, despite meeting Maddie earlier. Maybe, just maybe, he'll be the one to prove me wrong.

Placing our glasses on his coffee table, Parker settles on his couch, patting the cushion next to him. I move to sit on the opposite end, but he's having none of that. His arm shoots out, grabbing me around the waist, pulling me flush against his side. He grabs a remote before kicking his feet up, propping them on the coffee table. His left arm snakes behind me, coming to rest on my waist as the other hand flicks the television on, bringing up the screen for Netflix.

My chest dips as the memory of my last "Netflix and Chill" flits through my mind, but with Parker's body flush against mine, his hand resting on my waist, my worries are temporarily put to rest. At the very least, I already know this one's not gay.

I fidget in my seat, trying to find a comfortable position. Glancing at my stiff posture, Parker slides his hand under my thighs, picking them up and draping them over his thighs, my body turning into his with the movement. With a sigh, I sink into his embrace, my eyes briefly closing as a sense of peace washes over me.

"Comfortable?" he whispers against the side of my face, goose bumps rising along my arms. I nod my head, snuggling deeper into his chest, resting my head in the space where his neck meets his shoulder. Tilting his head, his cheek comes to rest on the top of my head.

The screen flickers with the opening credits to a movie I've never heard of, but I couldn't care less about what we're watching. My attention is on everything but the movie as Parker's scent fills my nostrils, the butterflies in my stomach swarming into a frenzy. His arm flexes around me, reminding me of the strength he possesses and how he used it to hold me up against the wall our first night together.

Taking a deep breath, my eyes flit to the screen, doing my best to clear my head of the indecent images as I focus on the movie, but it's damn near impossible. The man sitting beneath me is temptation incarnate.

We're about thirty minutes into the movie when Parker's hand gently glides against my side. My attention snaps to the sweet sensation of his skin against mine as his fingers sneak under the hem of his borrowed shirt, dancing in a smooth rhythm along my waist. Peeking under my lashes, I glance up at his face, finding his attention still fully focused on the movie. I'm not sure he even realizes his hand is moving.

The longer he glides his fingers across my sensitive skin, the more distracted I become. His fingers dip, drifting lower to connect with my hip, and my breathing speeds up, growing heavier with each pass of his thumb against the sensitive area.

He must notice the effect he's having on me because soon enough, his body shifts away from mine. With the new space between us, Parker dips his head, a whisper of breath against my neck the only warning I have before his lips make contact, sending a bolt of pleasure straight to my clit. Goose bumps race down my arms, and my eyes fall closed as I tilt my neck to the left, giving him easier access.

His right hand moves to grip my thigh as his lips move down my neck and across my clavicle, leaving a trail of kisses in his path. With a soft kiss to my shoulder, his lips glide back to the juncture of my neck. My pulse flutters against his tongue as he licks the skin before gently biting down, a muffled groan vibrating against my skin before he licks the sting of his bite away. My hands tangle in his hair as his other hand creeps across my thigh, disappearing between my legs.

A whimper bubbles up my throat, brushing past my lips as his hand makes contact with my throbbing center. He scrapes his thumbnail across the seam of my denim, creating a vibration I didn't know I needed. My thighs clench around his hand, trapping it against me as desire floods my body.

With a harsh growl, Parker twists his body out from under mine and pushes me down, my back sinking into the couch cushions as he settles his heavy weight on top of me. My legs wrap around his lean hips as his lips zero in on my skin. His mouth wanders from my neck down to my heaving breasts, leaving me gasping for air. Leering at me with an excited glint in his eyes, he bites down on my hardened nipple, his teeth cutting through his shirt and the thin padding of my bra, sending a wave of heat directly to my core.

I squirm beneath him, desperate for more contact. Thankfully, he doesn't make me wait long. Sitting up, he pulls me with him, ridding me of his shirt and unsnapping my bra with little effort before pressing me back down into the cushions. His eyes glitter with lust as he latches his mouth on to my left nipple, swirling his tongue against the stiff peak. Using his fingers, he mimics the action on my right nipple, driving me absolutely insane with need. It's entirely possible that I'm about to combust from the nipple play alone—something I didn't know was possible until now.

Right when I'm on the edge, my orgasm threatening to shatter me, he pulls away, leaving me wanting. I cry out, reaching out to force his mouth back to my nipple, but pull back when I see he's moving his hands to the button of my jeans, unsnapping it. He pulls them down, along with my soaked panties, tossing them behind his shoulder. Leaning back on his haunches, he grabs the back of his shirt with one hand, ripping it over his head in that sexy way men do.

His muscles ripple with the effort, my pussy clenching at the view, desperate to feel him moving inside me. With a flick of his thumb, he releases the button holding his own jeans together, pushing them down his hips and kicking them off. He grips my thighs in each hand, spreading my legs wide open. If his eyes weren't so full of heat, feasting on the vision before him, I'd be embarrassed at the vulnerable position he's put me in.

He rubs one hand up my thigh, gliding straight to my center, right where I need him the most. Groaning, he swipes his thumb up and down my slit, gathering my wetness before gliding up to the tight bundle of nerves, swollen with desire. His first brush against my clit sends fire racing through my body, the room filling with my gasp. Blue eyes darkened with lust meet my gaze as a shudder racks my body, a moan falling from my lips from the pleasure he's pulling out of me.

Parker's tongue darts out of his mouth, swiping across his bottom lip before he bites down on it—*hard*. Maintaining eye contact, his fingers dance against my clit, my body climbing to heights it's never reached with battery-operated toys. His free hand wraps around the base of his hard cock, the head an angry purple as the blood pools at the tip. Without breaking rhythm against my swollen bundle of nerves, he works his hard length from root to tip with quick strokes. Pre-cum slips through his slit, beading on the head of his dick as a harsh grunt flies out of his mouth. The sight has my orgasm rushing to a crescendo, tipping over the edge and shooting bolts of pleasure throughout my body as I scream out his name. My legs tighten around his hips as my eyes slam shut, channeling all my energy into the ecstasy exploding throughout my body.

My chest heaves with haggard breaths, filling the room with my pants, and my hands clench the couch cushions as I float down from my blissed-out state. I barely register Parker's body moving against me, my eyes peeking open as the couch dips with his motion.

His muscular arm flexes as he snakes a hand under my leg, gripping my upper thigh tightly. With one swift tug, he pulls me closer to him, his other hand gripping the base of his hard cock, lining up with my entrance. I brace myself, expecting him to impale me roughly, but he surprises me, gently rubbing his dick up and down my slit, coating it in the wetness left behind from my orgasm.

"You're so fucking wet," he groans out, my core clenching at his husky voice. "I need to feel you grip me with that tight pussy of yours."

His dirty talk sends another wave of wetness crashing between my thighs, drenching his rigid member. The heat in his gaze sets my body on fire, and suddenly I'm as desperate to feel him as he is to feel me. His eyes drop to where we're connected, watching as he glides through my soaked petals.

With a gentle thrust of his hips, he pushes inside me, bringing his eyes back up to mine as he thrusts fully inside. I clench around him, my eyes rolling back as he fills me, my walls stretching to accommodate his size.

This is so different from our first time together. We were so desperate then, racing each other to the finish line. This time, he takes it nice and slow, allowing me time to cherish every powerful thrust his hips deliver.

Leaning down, his chest rubs against my tits as he snakes a hand under my back, wrapping his hand around the back of my neck, keeping me from sliding up the couch with the snap of his hips. His forehead drops to mine, his breathing ragged from the energy he's using to rock my world. I wrap my leg tightly around his hips, using the heel of my foot against his bare ass to speed up his tempo. My lips latch on to his neck, sucking on the vein that's pulsing with desire as my nails find purchase on his back, leaving crescent-shaped divots in his skin.

"Fuck, Riley," he growls against my ear. His dick pulses, hitting a spot deep inside me, and my walls flutter, clenching around him. His pleasure spurs mine on, my second climax ripping through me, milking his cock of every last drop of cum.

He collapses against me, our sweat soaked bodies sliding together as his arms give out. His breath is warm against my neck as we both float down from our high, my body tingling with euphoria. Lifting his head, he places a tender kiss on my lips before moving to my side, pulling me against his body.

We lie in a satiated silence on the couch, watching the movie credits roll on the screen as our breaths even out. My back rests against his front, and his arms are wrapped tightly around me, his heat enveloping me in a cocoon of pure happiness. My eyes drift shut, exhaustion settling over my body like a blanket as Parker's thumb brushes against my arm in a calming rhythm.

I'm on the edge of sleep when he opens his mouth and snatches my peace away with a few whispered words.

"Do you think Madison is going to be okay after tonight's game?"

My chest squeezes at his question, my heart turning to stone as disappointment invades every cell of my body. We just had hot, passionate sex, and now he's asking about my friend? My throat tightens with emotion as realization sets in. I know Maddie is gorgeous, wild, and crazy in all the right ways, but when he let her walk out of the arena and all but forced me to come home with him, I thought that was him choosing me.

Stupid, stupid, stupid. I should've known better.

33

RILEY

Pulling out of his arms, I reach for my jersey I placed on his end table earlier, struggling to pull it on while moving away from him. Avoiding Parker's questioning gaze, I search for my underwear and jeans. I can't look at him right now—not with the tears clouding my eyes, threatening to fall at the first blink.

"What do you think you're doing? Take that back off," he teases, reaching out to grab the hem of my jersey.

Ripping away from his grasp, I bend and grab my underwear, slipping it on despite his grunts of protest. I try to shield my face from him, but when he catches sight of my grief-stricken expression, the humor falls from his face in an instant. He surges into a sitting position and reaches out, pulling me back to the couch.

"Fuck, Riley. What's wrong?" His voice is full of genuine concern, but that's most likely just his fear of losing a booty call talking.

"Nothing," I lie, pulling out of his grip again. "I just didn't realize you were interested in Maddie. Although, you didn't need to sleep with me to get closer to her. I'll send her your number tomorrow. I'm sure she'll call you if she's interested," I choke out while snatching up my jeans.

I can't believe I didn't see the signs. *I always see the signs.* Every time I stand next to her, I'm lucky to get a quick glance over before their attention glues to Maddie and her beauty. I saw it tonight with all of Parker's friends, but just once...just this one goddamned time, I thought the guy wanted me instead.

"What the fuck are you talking about?" he demands harshly, grabbing my arm and pulling me back to face him. "I'm not interested in Maddie."

Face colored with anger, his brow pinches, furrowing his forehead.

"Don't lie to me, Parker. Why else would you be asking about my best friend while I'm naked in your arms?"

"I'm not lying. I asked because of her comment about depression at the arena, and I figured as her best friend, you'll be the one consoling her. I don't want to be an asshole and rush her grieving process, or whatever, but I fucking will if it keeps me from camping out in front of your apartment door just to spend time with you. I'm goddamned tired of sleeping on your floor."

My heart falters in my chest as I process his words. Falling back down to the couch, I blink a few times, clearing my eyes of the tears that had built up. Parker quickly reaches out to brush them away, his gaze never leaving my face.

Taking a deep breath, I choke out a watery, "You're not interested in Maddie?"

"Fuck no," he spits out in anger, his body turning toward me on the couch. "If I wanted Maddie, I wouldn't need your help getting her. But if tonight is any indication of where we stand, I apparently need her help to get to you. I thought I made my interest in you pretty fucking clear earlier, but I guess not."

Looking me dead in the eyes, he grabs my hands, holding them between his as he wrecks me with his next set of words. "I want *you*, Riley. I want you in my bed. I want you in my arms. I want you in my life. Any way I can get you, but preferably naked and happy," he suggests with a wink. "I'm done with the fake bullshit and the meaningless sex. I want to build a goddamned life with you if you'll let me."

Jamming his finger against his temple, he continues. "Despite every attempt to resist this fire between us, I can't seem to stay away. You're so deeply embedded in my head, I can't think straight unless I'm around you. You've got me forgetting plans and threatening to knock the lights out of any man that hits on you, even if they're my friends. Hell, *especially* if they're my dickhead friends. Shit, Riley. I knew you were a touch crazy, but you're downright psychotic if you can't see that I've only got eyes for you."

Dropping my hands, he grips my cheeks in a tight hold, smashing his lips against mine. Between his words and his claiming kiss, I almost forget how to breathe. He pulls away from me sooner than I'd like, resting his forehead against mine.

His breathing grows ragged, matching my own as my heart violently pounds against my chest. Only Parker could say something so sweet while also managing to sprinkle in a bit of asshole along the way. Now I'm sitting here half-naked, tears slowly falling down my cheeks while trying to commit every word to memory.

My throat is still tight from the emotions flooding through my body, but I finally manage to choke out a whispered, "Okay."

"Okay? O-fucking-kay?" he questions, his hands releasing my face as he falls backward, his back slumping against the couch. Raking one hand through his hair, he grips the ends and shakes his head. With confusion clouding his face, he demands, "What the hell does that mean?"

I do my best to choke it back, but it's pointless. A soft giggle escapes my mouth at his obvious distress. He stares at me with complete and utter confusion, probably thinking about committing me to the looney-bin, which makes me giggle harder.

Reaching over, I gently pry his grip off his hair and entwine my fingers with his. Swinging my leg over his powerful thighs, I straddle his legs, leaning in to pepper kisses across his cheek. My lips connect with his, molding together as I pour every ounce of emotion I have into one searing kiss. He drops his free hand to my back, pressing me tightly against him like he's afraid I might run away.

Reluctantly pulling back, I rest my forehead against his again as I whisper, "Okay. I'm sorry. I guess I was just nervous. Ever since our first time together, I've been waiting for you to realize I wasn't as good as all those models you've been with in the past. And then, with you meeting Maddie today, it brought out all of my biggest insecurities. I know she's gorgeous, and I thought maybe you'd want her instead. I'm sorry for doubting you."

Parker sighs heavily before leaning back, removing his forehead from mine. He grabs my cheeks in both hands, staring at me intently. A mixture of anger and sincerity flashes behind his eyes when he says, "Listen to me, and listen closely. I don't want those other women. The whole reason I'm so attracted to you is because of how goddamn real you are. Your beauty isn't just skin deep. Although, you're sexy as fuck, if you can't tell by what you're doing to me simply by sitting on my lap." He presses up against me, grinding his rapidly hardening erection into me. A soft moan slips up my throat at the contact, but it's short-lived.

He chuckles, winking at me before growing serious again. "Yes, Riley, you've got natural beauty. But you're so much fucking more than that. You're intelligent and capable of holding a conversation that doesn't revolve around the newest pair of Manolo Blahnik shoes or some designer's new fall line. You care about people and animals and how they're treated instead of how they can benefit you or enhance your clothing. You smile at every person you walk past on the sidewalk instead of scowling at anybody that gets too close to you, treating them like some viral disease. Jesus, Riley. You drive me fucking wild with your cartoon pajamas and your tendency to put clothes on inside out or backward. You've got something those women will never have. You've got a goddamn heart, and fuck, do I want it all for myself."

A tear leaks from the corner of my eye, his words fighting back every insecurity I've harbored for well over half my life. He brings his finger to my cheek, gently brushing away the wetness before replacing it with a kiss.

Swallowing harshly, I whisper the question battering against my skull, wondering how he could possibly know all of this when we've only been on one date. "But we barely know each other. Aren't you worried this is all moving too fast?"

A deep laugh rumbles up his chest as he shakes his head. "I know enough to know you're worth diving into the deep for. It's too late to slow down now, Riley. You're already under my skin, and I'll keep knocking on your door until I'm under yours too."

My heart beats harshly against my ribcage, almost like it's trying to beat right out of my chest and into his. There's no need for him to keep knocking, he's already under my skin too.

I mimic his hold, placing my hands on his cheeks before leaning down to brush a gentle kiss against his lips. "You're a good man, Parker. You know that? I don't care what anybody else says or how big of an asshole you think you are. You've got a good heart."

"I don't know about that, but I'll do my damnedest to be a good man if that's what it takes for you to give me an honest chance."

Smiling down at him, I wrap my arms around his neck, leaning my forehead against his to whisper the scariest words I've ever let cross my lips. "You have more than a chance, Parker. You have all of me until you decide otherwise."

His eyes crinkle at the corners with his smile, and in one swift motion, he stands, carrying me toward his room. Tossing me down on his bed, he wraps his fist around his hard cock. I'm tempted to watch the show, but instead, my eyes stay trained on his, watching the desire flood his irises.

"You're fucking gorgeous, Riley, and I'm about to show you exactly what you do to me."

The bed dips with his weight, just as my heart dips with his words. My mom always told me actions speak louder than words, but apparently, she never met a man like Parker because he has the power to wreck me with both.

OVER THE NEXT MONTH, PARKER AND I GROW CLOSER. IF WE aren't at work or with our friends, we're together. Sometimes he treats me to a night out on the town, spoiling me with extravagant dates he knows I don't need, and sometimes we stay in, curled up in each other's embrace as we watch a movie or read the latest publications in our own respective fields.

But one thing that doesn't change is the fact that we always spend the night together. Whether it's in his bed or mine, we end each night tangled up in the sheets. Up until last night, anyway.

He had to pull a late night at the office, and despite it being a Friday night, I was so tired from a busy week that I fell asleep before he could make it to my place. Waking up alone feels strange after weeks of starting my day with my body wrapped around Parker's. It's such a weird concept to consider. Before we met, I never had an issue sleeping alone. I loved spreading out across my bed, utilizing every available inch.

But now my bed feels cold and empty, my sheets recognizing the loss of heat his body normally provides. Not wanting to dwell on how dependent I am on Parker sharing my bed, I rip the sheets off my body and head to the shower to start my day.

A few hours later, I'm cleaning my apartment and putting laundry away when Parker finally stops by. I greet him at the door, spending our first five minutes together making out like horny teenagers.

"Mmm, I missed you last night," he growls out, the words vibrating against my neck before he sucks on the spot below my ear.

"Me too. I hated sleeping alone," I respond in a breathy whisper, forcing his lips back to mine.

His phone rings, the shrill tone breaking our kiss apart. He groans at the disruption before pulling the phone out of his pocket, his brow furrowing at the name flashing across his screen.

"Sorry, I should probably take this," he grunts with an apologetic expression.

"This is Parker," he barks into the phone, switching to what I call his "business tone." I leave him to his phone call, heading to my bedroom to finish putting away my laundry.

A few minutes later, he stalks into the bedroom, and I can tell by his face that any plans we might've had for tonight have been derailed.

"I'm sorry, babe. I need to head to the office to handle an urgent matter. Maybe we can get dinner when I'm done? Whatever you want," he begs, leaning in to brush a kiss against my cheek.

Disappointment swirls in my stomach, but I do my best to hide it from my face as he pulls away from me. I know what it's like to have to work on the weekend. Hell, I've even had to cancel a few of our plans while being on-call for the zoo. It sucks, but sometimes it's unavoidable.

"Of course. Do what you have to do. I'll be here when you're finished."

"Mmm, you better be. I wouldn't hate it if you were naked and spread out on your bed, wet and waiting for me." He finishes his sentence with a slap to my ass, and a laugh bubbles up my throat at his playfulness. "I'll go take care of these assholes, then I'll come take care of my girl."

"I love the sound of that," I agree, walking him to the door. He leans in for another kiss, groaning when I nip at his bottom lip, trying to extend our time together. He pulls back, adjusting himself in his pants before scolding me. "Don't be a cocktease, babe. I have no problem taking you to work and fucking you over my desk while I fix this problem."

I giggle, knowing he wouldn't dare fuck me with someone else in the room. He's too possessive to let anyone else see me in that vulnerable of a state.

When he turns to leave, I risk a slap to his ass, knowing I'm playing with fire. He whips around, growling while smashing his lips to mine. He backs me up against the wall—the same wall he fucked me on the first time we had sex—and pushes his thigh between my legs, expertly applying pressure right where I need it.

I'm panting with desire and clawing at his shirt, desperate to get him naked when he pulls back. Groaning out my disappointment, I resort to whining, "Are you sure you have to leave right now?"

Chuckling, he backs away. "Yeah, babe. The cock-blocker's already at my office. I'll charge him triple for my time, then I'll be back to fuck you into oblivion." He winks, and with that, he struts out of the apartment, leaving me alone with a dripping mess.

Doing my best not to mope, I go back to my bedroom, determined to finish cleaning before he gets home. I have plans for us, and they don't include doing chores.

A few hours later, a knock at my door halts my cleaning spree. I was hoping to get a shower in before Parker made it back home, but I won't complain about more time with my sexy man. Heck, maybe we can take a shower together.

My cheeks heat with a swirl of lust and excitement at the thought, and I pause at the door, reaching inside my shirt to readjust my boobs. I pull them to the top of my bra cups before pulling my shirt down, leaving my cleavage proudly on display.

I lick my lips and fluff my hair, then reach for the knob, swinging the door wide open. "I'm ready for my orgas—" the tease dies in my throat, my sentence cutting off as I realize it's not Parker standing on the other side of my door. My mouth drops open in surprise, my heart crashing down along with it.

What the hell is he doing here?

34

PARKER

The door to my office slams shut moments after I bring my fingers up to my temples, doing my best to massage the headache away after the shit-tastic news my client just delivered. My eyes snap open when my assistant clears her throat and starts speaking, bringing my attention to the fact that she just witnessed firsthand—again—how my own brother is trying to exact his revenge in the pettiest of ways.

"Well. That was…unexpected."

Mr. Klein—the asshole that demanded I meet him at my office on a Saturday, effectively squashing the plans I had to fuck Riley every which way imaginable this afternoon—just dropped a bomb on us before packing up and leaving.

We've been working with several of his companies over the last year, rebranding and doing a complete overhaul of his previous business structures. We've spent months pouring over his products, debating which ones would be carried moving forward and which were being trashed to minimize his costs and triple his profits. This project alone has brought in over a quarter mil, labeling them our biggest client right now.

Or at least he was, before my brother Rory swooped in and

low-balled us, offering promises I have no idea how he intends to deliver. Not unless he's partnered up with another one of our competitors to make this possible.

I snort, unable to stop the sneer from taking over my face. "Was it, though? Rory has been doing his damnedest to bring us down for the last year. Hell, I'm actually surprised he waited this fucking long to go after our biggest client."

Before I can think better of it, I pick up the phone and dial the asshole directly. As I wait for him to answer, I chance a peek at Haylee, considering asking her to leave for this conversation. My brow furrows slightly as I take in her rigid stance, her eyes glued to the floor as she fidgets nervously.

Rory's smug tone travels over the line, distracting me from my assistant's odd behavior. "Hello, brother. I'm assuming you're calling after meeting with a certain Mr. Klein this afternoon. Such a pity, I know how long you've been working with him."

"What the fuck do you think you're doing, Rory?" I roar, my anger vibrating through my voice.

He has the nerve to laugh, and my fingers tighten around the phone, damn near crushing the thing with my bare hand at the sound.

"What do you mean, brother? I'm just doing the same thing you love to do to me: take things that don't belong to you."

"Jesus Christ. I know you're still young, but it's time for you to grow up. There's a hell of a big difference between willingly stealing something and unknowingly having something thrust into your hands, and if you could step outside of your misguided hatred, you'd fucking know that."

"This isn't just about Sabrina, you egotistical fuck. This is about everything else you've stolen from me over the years. Not to mention the fact you've been on a high horse ever since you started your company. It's time someone knocks you the fuck down, and I won't stop until I'm the one to do it."

With that, he ends the call, the dial tone echoing through my ear. I slam the phone down on the receiver, positively seething with rage. His words bounce around in my brain, forcing me to review every memory I have with my brother in the last ten or so years.

It doesn't take long. We've drifted so far apart, there's only a handful of memories since I graduated college, and even less so after the misunderstanding with his fiancée.

So what the fuck else does he think I stole from him? I know he blames me for receiving most of Mom's attention after Dad died, but that's neither true nor fair, and it certainly doesn't warrant him sabotaging my company.

Haylee's phone beeps with a new text, pulling my attention back to the shit storm we need to fix.

After checking her phone, Haylee's eyes shoot to mine briefly before settling on the floor again. She squirms in her seat, twisting her hands together with nerves. Usually, she's a pillar of strength, never showing any fear or weakness in the office. She's always quick with a comeback and brushes off negativity like it's nothing but lint on her blouse. But right now, she looks pale and downright fearful.

Strange.

Did my fight with Rory make her uncomfortable? She's never been bothered by my anger before. Or is there something else going on? Something she's hiding from me? Hm. Either way, it's moving to the back burner. I can't worry about my assistant and my company at the same time.

"Get me everything we have on Mr. Klein's project. If we're going to fix this, we need to get started. It's already late."

"Sure, but you know there's nothing we can really do about this on a Saturday evening," she declares, straightening in her seat. She lifts her eyes to mine before continuing. "Unless, of course, you want me to start making calls to get the whole team in here. Though I should probably remind you of the last time we did that and how big of a waste of time it was. Half of them were borderline drunk, and the other half were so pissed at being pulled away from their weekend that they decided to be as unhelpful as humanly possible, and nothing was solved."

"Fuck. FUCK!" I run my hands through my hair, angry with the situation but knowing she's right. We need to get ahead of this as soon as possible and figure out just what the fuck Rory has up his sleeve. There's no way in hell his little revenge plan is going to work. I won't allow it to.

"Calm down, Parker. I'll clear our schedule for Monday and send out a memo for all essential employees on this project to meet in the conference room at eight-thirty Monday morning. I'll take the files home with me and review them, making notes of anything I think we can do to salvage this, and I'll brief you before the meeting. There's nothing Rory can do between now and then to further his chances at taking over this project. We'll pull together and prove why Mr. Klein chose us in the first place."

Haylee finishes the email she was furiously typing, hitting send at the same time a ding on my computer alerts me to the new memo. There's no need to read it—I know she's got it handled. She packs up her shit and stands, fixing me with a take-no-shit expression.

"Meanwhile, I suggest you go home and spend the evening with Riley. Forget about your brother and everything that's going on here for the rest of the weekend, and come back Monday with a clear head. Rory may be doing his best to tank this project, but you'll cost us the whole company if you end up in prison for murdering your brother."

"Fucking hell," I sigh, my fingers pinching the bridge of my nose. "Thanks, Haylee. Sorry to waste your weekend."

"Don't worry about it. I could use the distraction anyway," she mutters in a softer tone, making me wonder what she needs distracting from. This lady damn near runs every aspect of my life, but I barely know a thing about her outside of how she handles my business. She turns her back on me and walks toward the door, slightly looking over her shoulder as she calls out, "See you Monday, boss man."

Haylee shuts my office door behind her, leaving me alone to pull my shit together. Closing my eyes, I lean back in my chair, doing my best to calm the anger flowing through my veins. Taking a deep breath, I can't stop the slow smile that crosses my face as Riley's beautiful face pops into my head. The way she was panting with desire when I left her wanting in her apartment entryway distracts me from my earlier anger.

I shift in my seat, making room for my rapidly hardening cock as every dirty thing I wanted to do to her earlier flits through my mind. Soon enough, my anger with Rory is damn nearly forgotten, and the fact that just the thought of Riley can bring my anger down to manageable levels shows how wonderful she truly is. And not just the sex. *Everything* about her, from her brain to her body, drives me fucking wild.

She really is everything to me.

Grabbing my phone out of my pocket, I check the time before calling to make us a reservation at The Red Table. Riley mentioned it a few weeks back, but we haven't had the time to check it out. I can't think of a better way to turn this night around than by spoiling my woman with a nice meal before taking her home to deliver on my promise to fuck her brains out.

35

RILEY

"Liam? Wh-what are you doing here?"

A war between confusion and anger breaks out, overriding the lust previously surging through my body. The last time I saw this man, he was walking away from me, leaving me alone on a beach with a half-assed promise to call me. We had a wonderful date—arguably the best date of my life until I met Parker—and then he just…disappeared without another word.

So what the heck is he doing here now?

Sighing heavily, Liam bows his head, running his fingers through his messy strands as he stares at the ground. Dropping his hand, his head lifts, revealing a haunted expression.

With a slow, deep inhale, my eyes scan down his body, cataloging each noticeable change. Once bright and seductive, his ice-blue eyes are now dull and emotionless, rimmed with a dark purple that hints at bone-deep exhaustion. He's lost weight since we last saw each other. The suit that previously strained against his muscles now hangs loosely off his body. His sun-kissed skin that used to glow has been replaced with a pale shade of grey, resembling a shadow of his former self.

Despite his haggard appearance, he's still as handsome as he was the first night I met him. But it's also clear the last few months haven't been as great to him as they have been to me.

"I'm sorry I dropped by unannounced," he answers on an exhale, the deep timbre of his voice kissing my ears. "I just pulled into town after an extended trip and wanted to see you. I need to explain what happened after that night on the beach, and I figured you'd hang up if I tried doing it over the phone."

He peers at me nervously, almost like he's waiting for me to slam the door in his face. If I'm being honest, the thought crossed my mind. Anything he has to say will only relieve his own guilt over ghosting me. It won't change the fact I've already moved on.

Liam's ship sailed a long time ago.

However, as much as I'd love to slam the door in his face, showing him exactly how I feel about him after he wasted my time, there's something in his expression that's stopping me. He seems so far removed from the Liam I met that night, and his entire demeanor has my heart reaching out to him, begging me to hear him out.

Before I can think better of it, I move to the side, the door opening further with my movement. "Would you like to come in?"

Shoulders sagging with relief, the corners of his mouth tip up into a small smile as he nods, following me through the open door. "You look good, Riley. Beautiful as ever."

I stumble at his quiet words, a nervous blush stealing over my cheeks as I murmur a soft, "Thanks." He smiles back at me, the blush deepening as I turn my back on him, leading us to the living room.

Taking a seat in my recliner, I leave him with no other option but to sit alone on the couch. I'm more than willing to hear him out, but I don't want to give him the wrong impression or leave a door open for him to make a move. Crossing my legs, I lean forward and fold my arms against my stomach, taking up a defensive stance to shield myself from any emotions he might provoke.

When he doesn't make a move to start the conversation, choosing instead to sit there silently watching me, I clear my throat and blurt out, "So what happened, Liam? Why are you here?"

I'm not sure if he's trying to gauge my mood or if he's simply hoping I'll forgive and forget, letting him off the hook easily—something I refuse to do—but his face falls at my hardened tone. He releases a heavy sigh before leaning forward on the couch, resting his forearms against his thighs. Clasping his hands together, his eyes leave my face, dropping to fixate on his joined hands instead.

"I was hoping maybe we could start easy, maybe catch up a little before diving into the deep, but I can see you're not in the mood to pussyfoot around. The problem is, I don't know where to start. This isn't easy for me to discuss, and worse yet, I know I was wrong for how I handled things between us."

"Well, at least you know that. I didn't need a grand declaration or anything, you know. If you weren't interested in me, that's all you needed to say."

His head snaps up, his brow furrowing as he meets my stare. Air traps in my throat, stealing my breath from the emotion swirling in his eyes, the light blue transforming to a navy sea with his anger. "That's just it, Riley. I was interested! Hell, I still am," he barks out, his hoarse voice sending a shiver down my spine. "You're everything I'm looking for in a partner, and I was ready to make you mine. But I never could've foreseen the curveball life was about to throw at me. You have to understand, Riley. I meant everything I said to you that night, and I had every intention of calling you the next day."

"But you didn't, which is exactly why we're here now." My protective shield begins to crumble, allowing my emotions to spill out. All my anger and hurt from that night come rushing back in full force, tightening my stomach into a ball of emotion.

With a heavy sigh, I urge him to continue, needing, more than wanting, this visit to be over. "Why don't you just get to the point and tell me what really happened that night?"

His shoulders slump in defeat, and I fight hard not to cringe at my rudeness. It feels unnatural for me to be so blatantly harsh, but this man hurt me. He brought out every insecurity I've ever held over being unwanted and discarded, and I refuse to be that same girl I was in college who didn't stand up for herself when I had the chance. I won't make that mistake again. *Not this time.*

Staring intently into my eyes, he nods his head, taking another brief pause to seemingly gather his wits before he opens his mouth, breaking my heart in half with an almost unbelievable story. His words float through my ears, scrambling my brain the further he dives in. My head swims as it struggles to understand the simple phrases, "one-night stand in Florida," and "surprise baby," and "drugs," and "couldn't find her."

Just when I think things couldn't be worse, he drops the words, "underground sex trafficking ring," and my heart stops altogether.

Tears cascade down my cheeks, a hand held against my mouth in an attempt to muffle my cries. When Liam showed up at my door, I never in a million years could have predicted this was the reason he disappeared from my life.

"Liam, oh, my gosh…I'm so, s-sorry," I manage between sobs.

"I am too. I'm sorry I didn't think to include you from the beginning. But we had only been on one date, and things with my daughter were moving so fast. You were never far from my mind, though. Memories of our date gave me the strength I needed to continue when everything felt so bleak. And I know things are still uncertain with my life right now, and I'm sure this is more than you bargained for after our first date. But I was hoping you could maybe give me another chance? I promise to always include you from here on out—on everything. Please, Riley, give us another chance."

Reaching out, his fingers tangle with mine, his thumb brushing against my knuckles, and I feel...*nothing*. That spark of electricity and the butterflies I felt with him a few months ago have completely abandoned me. My heart aches for this man and what he and his daughter have been through, but the chemistry we once shared has evaporated, confirming that my relationship with Parker is stronger than ever. He's the only man I yearn for, and despite the pain Liam is already in, I can't give him false hope.

Had he told me what was going on in the beginning, things could've ended differently with us. I would've stuck by his side during this horrific, life-changing situation he found himself in. But I can't be sorry about finding Parker. Not with how happy he makes me—how hard he makes my heart beat every time he's near.

Gently withdrawing my hand from Liam's hold, I brush my tears away, gathering myself before further breaking this man's heart. "I'm so sorry for everything you've been through these last few months, Liam. You absolutely did the right thing, leaving as soon as you heard you were a father. I appreciate you stopping by to explain what happened, and I sincerely hope you find a happy ending with your daughter, but I can't be there to help you through this."

I close my eyes, blocking out the devastation falling over every inch of his usually handsome face. My chest rattles as I take a deep breath, the exhale shaky on its release.

"I see." His choked-out words drip with emotion, forcing my eyes back open to meet his sad stare.

"You're a wonderful man, Liam," I whisper, battling the emotion doing its best to choke me. "I was so hopeful after that first date, but when I never heard from you again, I moved on. I'm actually dating someone now, and I think it's pretty serious. I probably shouldn't have even let you in, but I could tell you really needed this."

His eyes are fixed on the floor between us, having dropped halfway through my explanation, but the simple nod of his head tells me he's listening. The silence stretches between us, and just when I'm about to ask him to leave, he shocks me once again.

"I can't say I'm surprised that you've found someone, but that doesn't mean it doesn't hurt. You're the full package, Riley, and you deserve someone who can give you the world. I just wish that someone was me."

A blush forms on my chest, traveling up my neck and into my cheeks over his sweetness. Swallowing the lump in my throat, my lips tip up in a soft smile. "Thanks, Liam. I hope you find someone who can help you through this. You absolutely deserve to find your other half, and I have no doubt in my mind that you will. The timing just wasn't right for us. Focus on finding your daughter, and everything will fall into place for you when it's meant to. I sincerely believe that."

When he doesn't say anything else, I stand, and he follows suit. Making a rash decision, I step forward, pulling him into a comforting hug. His arms wrap around my shoulders, hugging me tightly to his chest. My heart absolutely aches for him, and a few more tears slip out of the corners of my eyes, seeping into the shirt covering his chest.

I'm just pulling out of Liam's arms, ready to escort him out, when a loud knock sends my heart plummeting in my chest. There's no doubt in my mind who's at my door.

Guilt floods my body, knowing Parker is about to find me with another man in my home. I haven't done anything wrong, but I'm sure he won't see it that way—not at first. If the situation was reversed, and he opened the door with another woman there,

I would be just as upset as I'm sure he's bound to be. I can only hope he gives me a chance to explain the situation before things spiral out of control.

If only Liam had left a few minutes earlier.

I'd still have to tell Parker about this visit—I refuse to hide something like this from him—but it would've been easier to explain without the evidence staring him in the face.

Taking a deep breath, I open the door, bracing for the emotional onslaught I'm about to fight off, praying my relationship with Parker isn't about to end over a misunderstanding. I care for him way too much to lose him now, especially since I'm no longer interested in being with Liam romantically.

As soon as the door cracks open, Parker pushes inside, swooping in with a bouquet of roses clasped in his hands. He pulls me into a warm embrace, his arms wrapping around me as his hands find purchase on my ass. Lifting my feet off the floor, the cellophane wrapper crinkles around the flowers as he brings my face even with his before leaning in, gluing his lips to mine within seconds.

Liam clears his throat behind us, the unexpected noise alerting Parker to the fact we aren't alone. Eyes shooting open, Parker pins his gaze on our audience, his entire body hardening to stone as his lips halt their brutal assault on mine. A wave of tension ripples through the air, his anger practically palpable as he slowly lowers my feet back to the ground.

Parker's chest rumbles with a deep growl, the sound vibrating against my body as it travels up his throat and through his mouth. Frozen in fear at his expression, the introduction dies on my tongue, allowing Parker the time to make his own assumptions.

His heated glare shifts away from Liam, refocusing directly on me. I was expecting his anger—braced for it, even. But nothing could've prepared me for the murderous glare he levels me with. A deadly silence descends on the apartment, and my heart pounds violently in my chest as I swallow, trying desperately to coat my throat with enough saliva to speak the words I need to say.

Unfortunately, I'm too late. The silence breaks—Parker the first one to speak. He lashes me with his tongue, delivering a verbal punch to the gut with his stern tone.

"Who the fuck is this, Riley?"

Shit.

36

PARKER

"Who the fuck is this, Riley?" I demand in a harsh tone, hardened with the anger vibrating through my body. She stares up at me with wide, fearful eyes, her mouth dropped open in surprise.

The longer she stands there without explaining, the faster my brain jumps to fill in the silence. Every relationship I've been in the last few years flashes through my mind like a Rolodex of mistakes. I've been used for money, treated as a meal ticket, cast aside for a man that could take their fame higher than I could. But nothing—abso-fucking-lutely nothing—hurts quite like the idea of Riley cheating on me.

My heart thrashes against my ribcage, threatening to break itself with each violent pound as I stare Riley down, waiting for an explanation. Did she call some other fuckhead to take care of her needs because I had to work? Is this some sort of twisted fucking punishment for leaving her wanting? No, she said she understood. Or was that just some bullshit line she delivered to test me? Like her version of "it's fine" or "nothing's wrong."

Fuck! When I made the decision to revoke my celibacy pact, I did it for one reason and one reason only—I thought she was different. But staring at her face, covered in guilt, I can't help but wonder if maybe she was just better at hiding her disloyalty. *How the fuck could I get this so wrong?* A-fucking-gain.

Scooting around Riley, my feet move on their own accord, taking a few steps toward the strange man in disheveled clothing standing behind us. Riley moves with me, her hand rushing forward to wrap around my bicep, but I shrug her off as another growl works its way up my throat. My mind fills with unpleasant images of how he got those wrinkles in his suit, and rage courses like a river through my veins at the idea of some other man putting his filthy fucking hands all over the woman I love.

Yeah. I fucking love her.

Realized that on the drive home tonight. And look where the fuck that got me—standing here like some goddamn schmuck, holding a bouquet of flowers I stopped to buy, hoping she'd think it was romantic, while the woman I planned to confess my love to peers at me with guilt.

And just like that, I suddenly understand Rory's blind hatred for me over what happened last spring. My face twitches, remembering the pain from the punches he rained down on me when he thought I was messing around with his now ex-fiancée, Sabrina. My fists clench at the memory, wanting nothing more than to deliver the same punishment to this asshole for fucking around with my woman.

Taking a deep breath, I relax my grip on the flowers, allowing them to fall to the floor as I do my best to refrain from ending up with assault charges. I settle for a deep glare instead, glancing him over from head to foot. He looks familiar, but for the life of me, I can't place him. Right now, all he looks like is the man trying to take my woman from me.

The irony of a second man trying to steal from me less than an hour after I've been accused of being the thief isn't lost on me. If

I wasn't so pissed off right now, I'd probably even find the irony humorous.

"P-Parker," Riley stutters, my heated glare snapping to her pretty, pale face. She briefly closes her eyes, her spine straightening as she prepares to deliver her blow. Her lashes flutter open, her emerald green eyes filling with worry as she introduces us. "Parker, this is Liam. Liam, this is my boyfriend, Parker."

"I don't really give a damn *who* he is," I bark out, Riley jumping at my tone. "I want to know what the fuck he's doing here."

"Watch it, man," Liam growls, his own temper flaring. "There's no need to talk to her that way. She's done nothing wrong."

The asshole moves forward, putting himself in front of Riley like he's worried over her safety, which only serves to piss me off more. I'd never lay a hand on her. *Him, on the other hand...*

Riley steps forward, gently placing her hand on Liam's chest, pushing him away from me. Her delicate hand resting on his chest sends my blood pressure through the roof, and I'm not sure what hurts more right now—my fists from clenching so tightly or my heart from breaking at the sight in front of me. Closing my eyes, I take a deep breath, trying and failing to calm down.

Between my own brother trying to poach my best client and finding my girl in this apartment with some dude she clearly cares about, I'm hanging by a very thin thread here.

"Parker, please..." Riley whispers. I open my eyes to find she's no longer touching the dickhead. Her eyes plead with me to hear her out, and as much as I want to turn my back on her and leave, drowning myself in liquor at the nearest bar, I can't. Something in her gaze tethers my feet to her apartment floor. Call it hope or misguided trust, but every fiber in me screams with the need to hear her out.

She reaches out to me, clasping my hand in hers before finally giving me the explanation I've been waiting for. "I promise you, nothing is going on between Liam and me. We went on one date a few months back, before I ever met you. Then he ghosted me—"

Liam clears his throat, cutting her off. I snarl at him, both for interrupting her and for ghosting her. *Yeah, I'm confused by that too.* Obviously, I'm happy he fucked up. Otherwise, we might not be together today. But also, who the fuck does he think he is, hurting my girl like that?

He wisely averts his eyes, looking down at the floor. Riley spares him a sympathetic glance before aiming her full attention my way, continuing on.

"He stopped by today to explain what happened and why he did what he did. He's going through a hard time right now, and human to human, I care about him and his situation. But Parker, it doesn't change anything between us. I told him I was happily committed to you and made sure he understood he doesn't have a chance with me, nor will he ever. I was just escorting him to the door when you showed up."

Peering into Riley's beautiful green eyes, I gauge the truth in her words, finding nothing but sincere honesty. Little by little, the anger fades from my bloodstream as I digest her words, my pulse slowing the longer she holds my stare. Her eyes plead with me to believe her as her grip tightens on my hand, and fuck me, I do.

She turns to Liam, still holding my hand, and says, "I'm sorry for everything you're going through, Liam. I truly hope you find your daughter and things work out for the best. But I think it's best if you leave now."

His hand reaches up, rubbing back and forth across his chin as his gaze darts between the two of us. My chest inflates with a mixture of pride and love over her choosing me, filling me with a primal need to take her right here in her apartment entryway. *Liam be damned.*

Sighing, he nods his head and moves toward the door. I withdraw my hand from Riley's, following him out. He's barely across the threshold before he turns to me and mutters, "Take care of her. She's a good one." My eyes narrow at him, annoyed by the asshole trying to tell me what I already know. He's the one that fucked her over, not me.

I don't bother acknowledging him with words. Instead, I glare at him until he turns and leaves, walking down the hall with a slump in his shoulders.

Fucking finally.

The door slams shut between us, and without a moment's hesitation, I stalk toward Riley, the air between us thickening with tension. Her eyes widen in shock, but she doesn't shy away from me, and I'm thankful for that. I'm in no mood to chase after her right now.

"Parker," she breathes out.

Reaching out, I bring my hands up to her cheeks in a punishing grip. A gasp of surprise leaves her mouth moments before I slant my lips across hers, silencing any further discussion. The time for talking is over. I need to feel her body wrapped around mine, assuring me with every kiss and caress that she really is mine—only mine.

She hesitates for a split second before matching the ferocity of my kiss. Her hands run through my hair, tightly gripping the ends, forcing my mouth closer to hers. A growl rumbles up my throat as I nip her bottom lip before sucking it into my mouth, soothing the sting of my bite.

My fingers slowly travel up her light blue blouse, unhooking each button as they go. Moving my hands up to her shoulders, I ease the shirt down her arms until it falls away from her body. Her shorts are next to go, dropping down to the floor with a quick flick of a button, leaving her standing before me in nothing but a white lacy bra and matching thong.

I step back, bringing her body fully into view. All the blood coursing through my body drains to my cock as I lick my lips, desperate to taste her on my tongue. I bend, gripping her thighs and hauling her up against my body, her legs wrapping around my waist as I walk us back to her bedroom. The heat of her sex radiates against my abs, sending a bolt of lust straight to my balls. There's nowhere my cock would rather be than buried deep in her wet heat.

Our tongues are a tangled mess, fighting for dominance until my shins hit her mattress. I toss her down on the bed, watching as her tits bounce from the impact. Eyes full of lust stare back at me as I slowly undress, my eyes trained on hers as they dilate with each article of clothing I toss to the floor.

A groan leaves her lips once I'm down to my boxers, my muscles rippling as I grip the steel pipe through the fabric, stroking it while my eyes devour every inch of her skin bared to my view. Setting my knee on the bed, I dip low, crawling up her body, peppering her legs with kisses as I go. Pausing at the apex of her thighs, I brush my tongue up her thong-covered pussy, the material already drenched with her desire.

Her thighs tighten around my head, her body writhing against my tongue, hoping for more friction. She whines when my mouth leaves her heat, traveling up to her hip bone. Swiping my lips across the sensitive area, I nip at her skin, before trailing kisses up to her tits, goose bumps rising in my wake.

Pulling the cups of her bra down, I release her nipples from their prison. My tongue circles her left nipple, never quite landing where I know she desperately needs it. Moving to her right tit, I deliver the same torturous teasing until both are stiff peaks. Glancing up, I make eye contact as I bite down on her rosy red tip, finally giving her the relief she craves as I grind my erection against her hot center. Her eyes roll back, a loud moan of pleasure ripping from her throat. She rolls her hips against mine, searching for friction as I push her tits together, sucking on both nipples at once. Digging her nails into my shoulders, her body trembles, the first flutters of her orgasm building as I continue to devour her nipples and grind my dick against her sensitive nub.

A whimper falls from her luscious lips as I pull away at the last second, robbing her of her orgasm. "Parker, please," she whines, my dick jerking at her breathy voice. "I can't take any more teasing."

"You'll fucking take as much as I give you. And maybe next time, you'll remember this before you let another man inside your apartment. I'm the only man you need, Riley."

Crawling forward, I straddle her shoulders, forcing my boxers down to release my hard, angry cock. Gripping it at the base, I squeeze tightly before stroking up to the tip, purple in color and leaking pre-cum, desperate for relief. I place one hand against her headboard for stability while using my other hand to guide my dick to her mouth, swiping it across her fuckable lips, painting them with the desire leaking out of my tip.

Fuck, she's so sexy.

Her tongue peeks out, swiping against my sensitive head, and my control snaps, a hiss escaping through my clenched teeth at the pleasure pulsing through my cock. I thrust forward, pushing past her lips to hit the back of her throat.

Her mouth closes around my length, her cheeks hollowing out as she sucks me in deeper.

"That's it, baby. Suck my cock like a good little girl."

Her hands grab on to my ass, thrusting me deeper into her throat as her eyes latch on to mine. My groan fills the room as shivers of desire shoot down my spine, settling deep in my balls. The point was to tease her, but fuck if this isn't sweet, heavenly torture for me too.

Thrusting deep, I hit the back of her throat before popping out of her hot mouth with a hiss. She licks her lips, catching the drool leaking out from the corner. She reaches behind her back, unclasps her bra and flings it to the side as I kick my boxers the rest of the way off and settle between her thighs, right where I feel at home. Leaning down, I bite the material of her thong, tearing it with my teeth before leaning back up to rip the fabric the rest of the way off her body, discarding it on the floor.

She gasps in shock, but I can't find it in me to give a fuck. Gripping my hard length, I swipe it through her drenched center, coating my dick with her wetness. "Parker, please," she begs again. *Right there with ya, babe.*

Pushing past her lips, I sink into her tight heat, setting my nerves on fire. "Fuuuuck," I groan out, my hips slamming forward until I'm seated to the hilt.

My hands hold her hips in a bruising grip as I pull out and thrust back in with brutal force, claiming what's mine. Sweat forms along my brow as I watch her face contort in pleasure, her cries growing louder and louder each time my dick hits that sweet spot inside her. Leaning down, I nip at her skin, my lips traveling down her neck, latching on to the top of her breasts, sucking hard. I've never felt so possessive over someone. In fact, love bites usually repulse me. But with Riley…*fuck.* She brings the beast in me out to play, and he's ready to mark his territory.

My hand searches for hers, lacing our fingers together in an affectionate embrace as I raise them above her head. Her other hand moves to my back, her nails digging into my skin, as I pound into her. "Come on, baby. Come for me," I growl against her neck. The flames of desire lick at my veins, scorching a trail down my spine as my balls draw up tight, aching with the need to spill my seed inside her, but I can't let go until I know she's satisfied too.

The words have barely left my lips before her walls flutter with an orgasm, her legs squeezing around my torso as her body shakes. Her fingers tighten their grip on mine as her head falls back in ecstasy. I pound into her once. Twice. Three times before

I explode, our moans mingling together, reverberating against the walls as she pulses around my hard length.

I collapse against her, my head falling to the space between her neck and shoulder as my dick twitches inside her tight heat. Wrapping my arms around her, I breathe her in, her scent calming me as I place a soft kiss against her neck and roll off her. Heading to the bathroom, I clean myself up before grabbing a washcloth, wetting it down with warm water and walking back to Riley. She tips her legs open, allowing me to clean her up without protest, a practice that took some time for her to get used to.

Tossing the washcloth in the dirty clothes basket, I lie down beside her, pulling her into my arms. She rests her head on my chest, her fingers drawing lazy patterns against my skin. I lean down and place a gentle kiss against her forehead, savoring every minute with her.

"I'm sorry," she whispers. My arms tighten against her, holding her body tightly to mine. "I didn't mean to hurt you or make you doubt my feelings for you. Liam means nothing to me."

Sighing, I release the final thread of doubt tethering me to the past, setting it free as I choose to believe that Riley really is the woman for me. "I know, babe. I know."

A few minutes of silence pass before I realize Riley's breathing has deepened, falling into a peaceful rhythm. Staring up at the ceiling, I softly move my fingers up and down her arm, content to just lie here with her.

My stomach rumbles with hunger, reminding me of the dinner reservation we aren't going to make. I consider waking her but change my mind. We can order in later. Then I'll probably need to spend a few more hours working on this issue with Rory and Mr. Klein.

The last goddamn thing I need is for something to slip through my fingers right now. Especially when I'm still waiting on pins and needles to hear back from The Helping Haven. If news breaks that Parker Solutions is losing business, why the hell would their organization trust that I can handle taking them over? They fucking wouldn't, which is exactly why I need to spend the rest of the weekend making sure that doesn't happen.

I close my eyes, allowing myself a brief rest before returning to the chaos. My mind wanders as my body relaxes, drifting over today's events. I never got the chance to tell Riley I love her, but maybe that's for the best. It's still early in our relationship, and besides that, I don't want the first time she hears those words from me to be after the first threat to our relationship.

No, when she hears those words, I want her to believe it's because I love her and need her, not because I think the words will hold us together when our pasts are trying to rip us apart.

37

RILEY

After a drama-filled weekend, I'm glad to be back at work Monday morning. Although, I wouldn't be opposed to a few more hours of lying in Parker's arms. We made filthy, passionate love after the Liam misunderstanding, and I ended up falling asleep wrapped up in his embrace shortly after.

When I woke up a few hours later, though, Parker was missing from my bed. I stumbled out of my bedroom, worried he had fled my apartment after I fell asleep. Fear had nearly crippled me at that moment as negative thoughts flooded my brain. Was he still mad? Did he leave me? Was that break-up sex?

My fears were put to rest when I found him slumped over on my couch, piles of paperwork gathered in his lap. Noticing the late hour, I ordered us dinner, waking Parker after it had been delivered. The meal passed in a stifling silence, and for the life of me, I couldn't figure out if he was still angry with me or if it was because work had stolen his attention.

When eleven o'clock rolled around, I was almost sighing in relief at the idea of us turning in. At least then, we could allow our bodies to do the talking for us.

Unfortunately, Parker had other ideas, dashing my hopes of

rekindling our connection. He never did explain what happened at work that day, but I guess whatever it was demanded his attention. With a swift kiss to my forehead, Parker left, saying he needed to head back to work.

When I texted him Sunday morning, he said he was already on his way to the office. I spent the rest of the weekend alone, agonizing over the newfound distance between us. As horrible as I felt for Liam and his predicament, a small part of me hated him for the fracture he'd caused in Parker and I's foundation. Everything was going so well between us. But now...now I wasn't sure where we stood.

Was our trust broken? Or did he believe me when I said nothing happened? He said he knew, but never said he forgave me. And that's what worries me the most.

The morning flies by as I immerse myself in the challenging duties of my job, putting the troubles with my personal life on the back burner. Allie and I complete appointment after appointment, and before I know it, I'm sitting in my office, typing up an email before taking a break for lunch.

A knock sounds against my office door, interrupting my typing.

"Come in."

Allie pops her head through the door, wearing a shit-eating grin.

"There's a hottie up front asking for you. I suggest you go see what he wants, and quickly. Heather's already making her move."

With a laugh, Allie disappears, leaving me clueless. Nobody ever visits me at work. I walk to the front, irritation shooting through my body as soon as I clear the door. Parker stands at the counter, which is certainly a surprise but isn't the source of my irritation.

Nope, that would be Heather.

As Allie said, she's leaning against the counter smiling at

Parker, her bountiful cleavage on full display. She's the resident flirt of our office and constantly bats her freakishly long eyelashes at all the good-looking men on staff.

Parker smiles politely back at her but, thankfully, doesn't seem to be reciprocating her blatant lust. Clearing my throat, Parker's attention snaps to me, a megawatt smile transforming his entire face. He slowly scans me up and down before greeting me, a blush forming at his perusal. "Hey, beautiful."

Heather glares at me with a snort, lifting her nose into the air before she leans forward to recapture Parker's attention. He's having none of that, though, ignoring her completely as he walks past her, meeting me halfway for a hug. He leans down, brushing a kiss to my forehead as Heather scoffs behind him, annoyed at his snub.

Using his shoulder to hide my smirk, I squeeze my arms tighter. Relief floods through my system at the return of his affection after our crappy weekend.

"This is a nice surprise. What are you doing here?" I whisper, gazing up at him in adoration.

Smiling down at me, he mesmerizes me with deep, swirling pools of blue, resembling the deepest parts of the ocean. I could stare at this man's eyes forever and still be amazed at their range of color.

His chest rumbles against me, vibrating with his deep voice as he responds, "I had a meeting close by this morning and thought I'd stop to have lunch with you if you're free?" Leaning down, he softly brushes his lips against my neck, his lips burning a path up to my ear where he growls, "I missed you," under his breath, his words for only me to hear.

"I missed you too," I whisper, leaning up to give him a quick kiss. "Lunch sounds great. Let me just go grab my things. I'll be right back."

"Take your time. I'll wait."

He winks at me, and I turn, hurrying back to my office. I glance at my computer, remembering the email I was responding to before Parker's surprise visit. I finish typing my response and push send before grabbing my phone and wallet, shoving them in my scrub pockets, and rushing back to Parker.

He smiles and places his hand on the small of my back, leading me out of the office doors while asking, "Where do you want to eat?"

"We could grab some sandwiches from the Treetops Café? Maybe eat them while we walk around?"

"Lead the way," he agrees with a wink.

I take a few steps toward the path that leads to the café before a light slap on my ass startles me. Gasping, I whip around, my eyes wide as I whisper-yell, "Parker!"

Wearing a shit-eating grin, he shrugs, showing no signs of remorse. I quickly look around, searching for any zoo employees that could've seen his inappropriate gesture.

"What? I couldn't resist. Your ass looks so good in those scrubs," he groans. He reaches down, discreetly adjusting the large bulge growing underneath his business suit.

Closing my eyes, I shake my head at his crude actions. We're in public, for shit's sake. Does this man have no shame? Besides, these scrubs aren't "sexy." They don't hug my curves or show off my figure in a flattering way. Not to mention that I'm covered in several stains, courtesy of the bodily fluids animals tend to leave behind during their appointments.

"Oh, hush," I tease. "These scrubs are anything but flattering."

Parker glances over at me, his eyes traveling up and down my body before a sinister smirk covers his face. "Do you know what I see when I look at you right now?"

"Uh, yeah. A hot mess covered in animal boogers, tiger slobber, and...What is that, kangaroo blood?" I ponder, pulling the bottom of my scrub top away from my torso to get another look, picking at a dried mystery spot. "Jeez, sorry I'm such a mess. I probably shouldn't have hugged you in your nice suit."

Parker shakes his head with a laugh before stepping in front of me, forcing me to a stop.

"No, babe. Well—yeah, but no. I see a hard worker who isn't afraid to get down and dirty to help the animals she cares so much about. I see a sexy body hidden underneath scrubs that make you look smart as hell. I see your hair tied back," he adds, pausing to gently tuck a strand of stray hair behind my ear, "so it doesn't get in your way while you're hard at work. I see pure, natural beauty every single time I look at you, but even more so right now. You're hotter than hell when you're doing what you love, so don't give me that self-deprecating bullshit."

I fidget under his heated stare, his words squeezing my heart. Nobody has ever tried to make me feel pretty the way Parker does, but I'd be lying if I said it was easy to believe him.

My insecurities have lessened over time, no longer suffocating me. But they're still there, hiding just beneath the surface, waiting to rear their ugly heads at the first sign of weakness. And after watching Heather's blatant flirting this morning, they're pecking at my brain, begging to be heard.

"Well...to be fair, you caught me on a decent day. We weren't too busy this morning, so I don't look nearly as bad as I normally do at work. But I'm still a far cry from the supermodels you used to date before me," I admit with a forced giggle, trying and failing to pass it off as a joke.

"You still don't get it, Riley," he growls out, his voice taking on a hint of frustration. Heaving a deep sigh, he squeezes my hand in his before turning around, walking us toward the café in silence.

No, I guess I don't.

"Did you know I made a pact to stay celibate before I met you?" Parker questions, breaking the silence between us.

"Umm...no. You never told me that. Weren't you dating some model or something right before we met?"

"Not exactly," he growls, his face scrunching with distaste. "Regardless of what she thought, we were never dating. When I told her our fucking days were over, she trashed my house, as you know, which is how I came to meet you."

I cringe at his crass response, his ability to speak so harshly over their time together filling me with a shred of doubt, but before I can spend too much time worrying about how he'd label us, he continues, demanding my attention once again.

"Leigha was just the tip of the crazy iceberg, but she was the straw that broke the camel's back, if you will. The night I moved into the apartment next to yours, I decided I was done with dating. I made it my mission to stay far, far away from women. Especially the crazy kind," he admits with a fake side-eyed glare.

A giggle escapes my lips at what he's implying. I'd like to consider myself reasonably normal, but I'd be lying if I said I wasn't going through a little bit of a crazy phase when we met, having been on so many failed dates. It was enough to drive any woman a tad insane.

"Is that why you were such a jerk when we met?" I ask, curious if his decision to repel women was the reasoning behind how he treated me in those early days.

"It's part of it. For starters, I was fucking horny."

"Parker!" I gasp, my eyes widening in shock. I was expecting him to say he was lonely, maybe, but not...*horny.* Quickly glancing around, I'm grateful to find that the closest family to us is well out of earshot, but I steer us off the path and away from foot traffic, just to be safe.

"What? I was," Parker states, pulling my attention back to him as we reach a somewhat secluded area. "I was used to having a constant fuck buddy to relieve stress. So when I decided I was done with women, I lost my outlet, which made me irritable."

I scoff at his choice of wording, rolling my eyes. Irritable doesn't even begin to cover his attitude. "Okay, so what was the other part of it?"

"I was tired of being used and abused. I figured if I was a big enough asshole, women would stay away from me, saving me from any other chances to be screwed over." He shrugs his shoulders like his explanation is no big deal, but the fact he's avoiding my gaze tells me otherwise.

My face scrunches with confusion, my mind struggling to understand. *Wasn't he the user?*

"What do you mean, used and abused?"

"Well. Leigha was all about my wallet. She wanted to be a stay-at-home wife, living off my money without contributing anything to our situation. Before her, there was Aubri. She wanted her name splashed across the tabloids to gain some fame, and she had no problem using my name to do just that."

"How so?"

"She'd call the paparazzi and let them know where we were planning to be. Then she'd pick a fight or cause some sort of a scene, ensuring the paps got their payday. She's the fucking reason my reputation as San Diego's resident asshole was born. Meanwhile, she gained a following of people who worshipped her, treating her like some sort of Saint for 'putting up with Parker.' And when we broke up, they labeled me the villain, despite the fact she was the one caught with another man's dick inside her. Needless to say, I'm still trying to fix my piss-poor image in the press."

My eyes widen in disbelief. When I first saw Parker in our building's elevator, I had this feeling that I knew him from somewhere. There was an air of familiarity about him that I just couldn't place. It took me weeks to realize I had seen him in tabloids over several months, always showing him in a negative light. He was such a jerk when we first met. I always assumed the stories were true, never giving him the benefit of the doubt that the tabloids could be the ones lying.

"Parker, I'm so sorry. I had no idea."

Sighing, he runs a hand through his hair before quietly muttering, "Sadly, they weren't even the worst of the lot I've dated."

He falls silent, momentarily withdrawing his attention from me. After everything he's already shared, I can't even guess what could possibly be worse. Giving him a few moments to gather himself, I fix my eyes on the hippopotamus exhibit a few feet away. A few families walk by but thankfully don't stick around, leaving us in a private bubble of sorts. I watch the hippos wade through the water, chasing after a beach ball until Parker clears his throat, bringing my attention back to him.

With his eyes planted on the ground between our feet, he sighs, "Sadie. She was the one that had me fooled. We dated for nearly two years, shortly after I started my company. I thought she was everything I was looking for. She had her own money, she never caused a scene in the tabloids, she knew how to cook, didn't force me to buy her shit—which, ironically, made me want to buy her everything she ever wanted. I was nearing the point where I thought I'd marry that woman. Then, the curtain fell, revealing the truth behind her deceit."

Pausing to rake his hands through his hair in frustration, he looks away, still refusing to meet my eyes. "I was so busy with work and building my company that I didn't realize she was almost always busy on the weekends, only ever available to meet me for lunch or an early dinner. She'd usually come over for a while to hang out in my house, or use my pool, or cuddle. We'd fuck like bunnies, then she'd disappear into the night, always having some good excuse not to stay over—an early meeting, needing to feed her dog, laundry to do—it was always something."

I cringe at the image of him having sex with another woman, but I do my best to hide it. My jealousy isn't what's important here. Besides, I knew he had a healthy relationship with sex before we ever got involved. I can't fault him for his past, especially not now that he's painting an ugly image for why he is the way he is—*or was.*

"We never spent any time at her apartment, either. She claimed she'd rather spend time with me at my place because it was bigger and had more room, but I was just too fucking blinded by idiotic puppy love to see what was really going on."

With a shaky breath, he continues, my heart squeezing in anticipation of where I think this story is heading. "Then one weekend, my business trip got canceled, and I suddenly had the whole weekend off. I decided to surprise her at her apartment with a weekend getaway, which is where I found her cuddled up with her 'real' boyfriend. Turns out, she was hired by my competitor and arch-nemesis from college to be my fake girlfriend. Her 'job' was to distract me, pulling me off my game so my company would crumble within the first few years. And she almost had me too," he spits out, the venom coating his words forcing a shiver down my spine.

"She may have ripped my heart out of my chest with her deceit, but I ended up working harder than ever after learning the truth and came out on top. Over eighty-five percent of his clients jumped ship, signing on with my company instead. He went under about four months later and was forced to file for bankruptcy. I may have come out on top business-wise, but he sure as fuck took my heart with him when his business crumbled to the ground."

Silence stretches between us, my words trapped in my throat as my brain processes his story. The hand holding mine tightens its grip as he pulls us to a stop again. He turns and faces me, stepping into my personal space. My boobs brush against his hard chest as troubled blue eyes dart up from the ground, meeting my devastated greens. Parker brings his free hand up, cupping my cheek sweetly as he brings the topic full circle, explaining the relevance of his story.

"So you see, Riley. Every girl that came before you chipped away at my happiness—at my self-worth. They made me feel like I was nothing more than a hot piece of meat with money. So I decided to live up to that standard. I became a vile, inaccessible, asshole bachelor, determined to stay single in exchange for avoiding users. That is, until you came along with your hysterics and dramatics, offering cookies in exchange for a friendship truce," he says with a wink, "winning me over with each new interaction. For the first time in a long time, you made me feel guilty for how I treated you. Hell, you made me feel a lot of things I was desperate to never feel again."

Butterflies take flight deep in my stomach as Parker stares at me, his eyes shining with an emotion I've never seen before.

"So when you say you're nothing like the women I used to date, you're abso-fucking-lutely right, and I couldn't be happier about that if I tried. You're worlds above them. You're genuine, you work hard for your money, you literally never ask me for anything other than my time and affection, and you are absolutely brilliant. You're everything a guy could ever want. *Everything.* You don't look at me and diabolically plan out how I can boost your life financially or what being on my arm could do for your own fame. You look at me, and you see me—the real me. You look past the good looks and materialistic bullshit to find out what I have to offer on the inside, and you've made it clear that the only thing you care about is my brain, my heart, and my loyalty. You care about what's really important, and that means more to me than you'll ever know."

Pausing, Parker takes a deep breath, his chest expanding as it fills with air, pushing against my breasts. He drops my hand from his hold, moving it to grip both of my cheeks as he stares intently into my eyes, and suddenly, it feels like we're on the precipice of change. Like everything between us is about to shift with the next words out of his mouth.

The air around us thickens, my breath quickening along with it. He opens his mouth, then closes it again, swallowing harshly, never breaking eye contact. The anticipation of his next words feels like a hand slowly wrapping around my heart, squeezing tight and depriving me of its normal rhythm. *Is he about to say what I think?*

All signs point to yes…but am I ready for that? More importantly, do I believe him?

Yeah…I think I do.

Parker opens his mouth again, his deep voice shaking slightly as he says, "Riley, I—"

A nearby scream cuts him off, drawing both of our attention to the source. I have half a moment of frustration at the interruption, but then my eyes adjust, fully taking in the scene in front of me.

The scream that initially caught our attention doubles, then triples, and before I know it, we're rushed at by a herd of zoo-goers screaming their heads off. Some of them look angry, some of them look terrified, but all of them are covered in animal feces.

What the hell?

Parker is still holding my hand when I take my first few steps toward the screams, straining against his grip. I finally break free, shaking his hand off as I run straight into the thick of chaos alongside other staff members. Parker shouts my name, yelling at me to wait, but there's no time for me to waste. I need to find out what's going on, especially if the animals are involved.

The stampede of people rushing past me parts, giving me a direct view of the shit show—quite literally—happening in front of the monkey exhibit. Somehow, several monkeys have escaped their enclosure and are now throwing their feces at every attendee in range. A few monkeys are chasing the runners, swinging from the tree branches above them and dropping poo as they go, while the others run across the ground, slipping and sliding through the crap.

One of the caretakers tries to entice the escaped monkeys with bananas, attempting to coax them back into their enclosure, but they're too bright for that. It's a wasted effort.

A horrific screech sounds, sending shivers of terror down my spine. That's not a sound any animal lover ever wants to hear. My body comes to a halt, my eyes frantically darting in every direction, trying to locate the source of the wounded battle cry.

After several frantic moments of searching, my eyes land on an infant monkey lying on the ground a few yards away. Before I can make a single move toward him, I watch in horror as another fleeing attendee steps right on the infant monkey's leg, crushing it beneath their shoe.

The poor, injured infant releases another scream of tortured pain, sending my heart into a nosedive. Pushing against the throng of people still fleeing the shitty scene, I rush over to the monkey, arriving just as another caretaker drops to his knees, hunching over the monkey to protect him from further injury.

"What the hell happened here?" I scream, gently running my hand along the infant's leg, determining it's broken in several places.

The monkey releases a screech of pain while trying to escape our grasps, clearly terrified by the chaos surrounding us.

"A gate malfunctioned during feeding. None of the gates would close or lock, which led to a mass breakout of monkeys," he yells, his voice barely heard over the screams echoing around us.

Gently picking the infant up in my arms, I stand to my feet, ready to run to the vet clinic. Allie appears at my side, tears streaming down her face as she sees the monkey's leg. Her hands dart forward, helping me stabilize his leg.

"Jesus fuck," Parker shouts as he finally reaches us, his suit speckled with monkey shit. "What the fuck is happening here?"

"There was a gate malfunction. This little one, and possibly more, have been injured. I'm sorry, I have to go. He needs emergency surgery if he has any hope of surviving this trauma," I yell, Allie and I already moving toward the clinic. The caretaker from earlier darts in front of us, doing his best to part the crowd for us.

"Shit, of course. Go, go!" Parker blurts, his face riddled with concern as he urges me forward.

Allie and I take off at a brisk jog, rushing to save our little monkey friend's leg. We spend the rest of the afternoon fixing monkey injuries—some severe, some minor—before staying late to help clean up the area around the exhibit. Thankfully, all the monkeys were located and safely returned to their homes once the gate was fixed.

Several hours later, when I finally get home from work, I'm covered in monkey shit, smell awful, and my hair is an absolute disaster, matted to my head with sweat and feces. I'm absolutely exhausted, falling into bed after a record-fast hot shower, barely taking the time to wonder why I never heard from Parker the rest of the day.

THE REST OF THE WEEK PASSES SLOWLY, AND BY FRIDAY, THE entire staff is a bundle of nerves, waiting on pins and needles to see what's going to happen with the zoo.

Allie came back from lunch the other day, frantic and distraught, yammering on and on about how she overheard some of the administration members talking about possibly closing the doors. Every staff member knows the zoo has been struggling financially for a while now. After a decrease in state funding and the recent rise in taxes, the zoo "cut back" on staff a few months ago. Now with attendance at an all-time low after the shit-slinging monkey fiasco, everybody's on edge, worrying they're about to lose their job.

It doesn't help that all the news stations in the area have been running stories on the zoo all week, painting us in a horrible light and talking about how poorly we managed the situation. Several of the stations have pushed it further, interviewing zoo attendees from that day, giving them a platform to embellish the story, making matters worse.

Don't get me wrong, the situation was pretty bad, especially for those closest to the monkey exhibit when they escaped. Some of the attendees were hurt during the mass exodus from the zoo, but not too severely. A few scraped knees and one broken arm—which the zoo covered financially—but nothing even remotely close to the injuries some of the monkeys endured while being trampled by frantic guests.

According to the news, a few people have come forward with stories of being traumatized, requesting the zoo to pay for their visits to mental health institutions. On top of that, we've received several threats of lawsuits over destroyed clothing and personal belongings. It's a disaster of epic proportions, and I'd be lying if I said I wasn't worried over a possible closure.

Worse yet, I've hardly seen Parker since the incident. There's some big client that reached out to him with an emergency situation, and he's been working on it late every night this week. I understand him needing to focus on his company and the important work he does, but that doesn't mean his absence doesn't hurt.

I'd love nothing more than to go home after a long, worrisome day and cuddle up with my boyfriend, listening to him tell me everything will be alright. But that's not how this week has gone. Hell, we've barely even spoken since Monday. Just a few brief messages back and forth, long enough for him to tell me he won't be home until long after I've gone to bed. We never even finished our conversation from that day at the zoo, meaning I still have no idea what he was planning to say.

I genuinely thought he was going to tell me he loved me, but now I'm not so sure. He was distant with me after Liam showed up unannounced, and now this. It doesn't make any sense. We went from potentially saying those three little words to barely speaking at all when I need him the most.

My head swims with doubt, a revolving door of questions keeping me up at night as I toss and turn. Is this the beginning of the end? Will he always be too busy to offer me comfort in a time of need? Will his job always come before me? Am I being too needy? Is it too much to ask for him to be here for me?

I wish I knew the answer to those questions, but I just don't. All I know for sure is I could potentially be losing my job and he's nowhere to be found.

And what will I do if that happens? Sure, I could get a new job at a local clinic, but it won't be the same. I love working with the variety of animals. Between tiger cubs and koalas in the mornings, to giraffes and elephants in the afternoon, and every animal in between, I love everything about my job. I was made to work with these animals, and I can't imagine doing anything else with my life.

Which means...if we close down...I'll have to relocate to a new city.

Best case scenario? I find another zoo in California and pray they have an opening for a vet. Worst case? I could end up thousands of miles away at a zoo on the east coast.

On the bright side, I'd be closer to my parents and could possibly see them more than once or twice a year. But on the other hand, I'd have to leave Parker. A few months ago, that wouldn't have been an issue—I could hardly stand the guy. But now everything's changed. In fact, I'm pretty sure I love him, which would make leaving him incredibly hard.

I'm not so naive as to believe our relationship could handle long distance—in love or not. Some days I'm not even sure we're strong enough to survive the turbulent dating waters when we live in the same city—right next door to each other. We have so many differences, some we haven't been able to move past yet, so it's hard to know where we'll be in a year, let alone twenty. Not to mention the fact he's been missing all goddamn week, putting a new strain on our relationship.

I mean, seriously. *Where the fuck is my boyfriend?*

38

PARKER

My alarm blares to life at an ungodly hour for a Saturday morning, instantly dragging a loud, ragged moan from the depths of my throat. Rolling over, I slam my hand down against the off button, half tempted to throw the fucking thing against the wall.

For the past few weeks, weekends were spent waking up with Riley in my arms, our bodies tangled between the sheets. We'd indulge in a mind-blowing morning fuck before spending the two days together, doing whatever Riley felt like. I never gave a shit what we did, as long as we did it together.

Not today, though. *Nope*. These last two weekends have been fucking brutal. Between Rory trying to poach my clients, juggling several other client accounts, trying to secure the sale of The Helping Haven, and taking on the most recent, top-priority account, I've been swamped.

Jesus, that's not even an accurate description. I'm damn near drowning right now. Of course, all my late hours and early mornings mean I've hardly seen Riley this week. I'm lucky if I have time to sneak in a fucking text or two throughout the day.

The shit with the zoo couldn't have happened at a worse time.

I know she's stressed out and probably a little mad at me, given my lack of attention, but if I have any hope of keeping her in my life long-term, I need to focus on my job right now. I just hope she understands once I have permission to tell her what's going on.

Gathering all my strength, I pull myself out of bed and stumble into the bathroom. My brief morning routine is completed in a haze, my mind torn between wanting to go back to bed and trying to focus on everything I need to get done today. My balls ache as I finish my quick shower, protesting their recent neglect. They've become so accustomed to Riley's daily attention, going a week without has them heavy with need.

With any luck, I can wrap the majority of these client accounts up today so that I can spend tonight and tomorrow buried in Riley's honey pot. But finished or not, I need to make time for Riley this weekend. Even if it means I have to go to work early and work through lunch again for the rest of the week. I need to see her and make sure she's handling everything okay. Make sure she knows she's been on my mind all week, and I've fucking missed her.

Dressed and donning my briefcase, I leave my apartment, walking toward the elevator. I've just passed Riley's apartment door when I falter, my steps coming to a halt. Looking at my watch, I see it's already a quarter 'til nine. I sigh, knowing I need to get a move on and get to the office, but something tells me I need to make a quick stop at Riley's before leaving.

Turning back, I knock quietly on her door, just in case she's still sleeping. A few seconds later, the door clicks unlocked and slowly creaks open. My heart drops in my chest as Riley's face comes into view. Her hair resembles a rat's nest, and she's still in her pajamas, making it obvious she just woke up, but that's not what has my heart sinking in my chest, tightening with pain.

Her eyes are bloodshot and rimmed with red, making me

wonder if she's been crying. The bags drooping beneath her bottom eyelashes tell me she's definitely not sleeping. I knew she was stressed, but I had no idea she'd be taking things this hard.

There's no way she already lost her job. I would've known about that. *Right?*

When I spoke to the zoo director earlier this week, he assured me nobody would lose their jobs until we sat down and talked about a few options moving forward. Something I'd love to tell Riley but can't. The fucking non-disclosure agreement I signed really puts me in a bind here.

Rushing in, I drop my briefcase next to her door before wrapping her up in my arms.

"Riley. Christ! Are you okay?" I whisper against the side of her face.

Her head shakes against my chest, moments before a sad, "No," tumbles from her lips.

Placing a gentle kiss against the crown of her head, I bring my hands up to cradle her cheeks, tilting her face up toward mine. My thumbs wipe away a few rogue tears sliding down her cheeks as she refuses to meet my eyes, sending my nerves into overdrive.

Leaning down, I rest my forehead against hers, my voice a whisper as I question, "Did something happen? Have you been fired?"

Her chest expands, brushing against mine as she inhales a deep breath, a choked sob escaping on the release. "No. Not yet, at least. Things have just been extra hard this week."

"I know, babe. I'm sorry I haven't been around this week. Everything with the zoo just happened at the worst time possible. But I swear to you, Riley, everything is going to be okay, one way or another."

She pulls away from me before sweeping her fingertips below her eyes, clearing away the tears I missed. "You can't possibly know that, Parker. Do you even have the slightest clue what's been going on at the zoo this week? The shit they've been saying in the press?" She angrily demands. Her face contorts into a sneer before she answers her own question, cutting off any response I might've had. "No. Of course not. You've been so busy with your own business, you haven't even bothered to check in with me to see if I'm going to lose my job. Not that you seem to care about that."

"Shit, Riley, that's not true. You'd be surprised at how much I actually do know."

"What's that supposed to mean? Do you know something I don't?" She questions, a flare of hope filling her eyes.

Fuck. I shouldn't have said that.

"No. I just mean..." I pause, searching for something to say. "I just mean I've been following the press and the news. I know things look bleak, but I have a feeling things will work out. They always do."

She turns her back on me, walking into the kitchen to start her coffee pot. My hands tighten into fists at my side as I press my tongue to the roof of my mouth, doing my best to keep my mouth shut. As much as I would love to explain everything to her, I just can't. Not yet, at least.

"I know it doesn't seem like it, but I care a lot more than you probably realize," I try again, hoping she believes me.

"Oh, yeah. Sometimes I forget about your love of animals."

An unbidden growl of frustration travels up my throat at her words. How the hell can this woman think I don't care about her after everything we've been through? After everything I've done to prove my feelings for her?

"It's more than just that, babe. I care about what happens to you. Your friend too. Hell, everyone at the zoo. There are a lot of jobs at stake right now, and I know that. I'm sorry I haven't been around much this week, but I swear to you, it's not because I don't care. This is just part of owning a business, sometimes. I have to put in the work if I want to keep my company in the black."

"I understand your business comes first, Parker. You've made that clear. But I thought I meant a little more to you than a brief check-in or two while my life crumbles to the ground."

My head drops back, my eyes focusing on her ceiling as I do my best to remain calm. Taking a deep breath, I bring my gaze back to her, my tone softening as I agree with her.

"No, you're right. I'm sorry. I've been swamped this week, but I should've made more of an effort to be here for you."

Scoffing, she takes me in from head to toe, shaking her head as she turns back around to face the coffee pot.

"I see you're wearing your business attire. Spending another day at the office?"

Raking my hands through my hair, I tighten my fists, pulling hard on the ends before sighing in defeat. There's no way of fixing things right now. Especially not when she's in the mood she's in, and I'm about to run out of here again.

Swallowing my guilt, I clear my throat before saying, "Yeah. Not that I want to, but I have to finish these accounts this weekend. I'm on a massive deadline with a brand new account, and it's extremely time-sensitive. If I don't go in today, the job will fall through, and trust me when I say a large portion of San Diego's job force will be at risk."

I watch her closely, mentally praying she takes the time to read between the lines. I know she's smart enough to understand what I'm saying without me breaking the agreement, but she's too close to this to see things clearly.

Her shoulders slump before she turns to face me again, resting her back against the counter behind her. She brings her arms up, folding them across her chest as she shakes her head.

"I'm sorry, Parker. I know your company deals with a lot of important businesses, and I'm sure they need you. But I needed you this week too. So it's been tough to face the fact that you'll always put your business before me."

Fucking hell. I've never hated non-disclosure agreements more in my life.

Seeing the disappointed look on her face feels like a punch to the gut, and I'm close to spilling the truth. It's killing me to know she's losing faith in me, but if I tell her what I'm up to, it could ruin everything. And as much as I love her, I can't risk this job falling through. I just need her to hang on a little bit longer. She'll understand soon enough. And once she does, I know everything will be okay between us. *Or at least, I hope it will be.*

"My business doesn't always come before you, Riley. But just this once, I need it to." Sighing, I glance back down at my watch before saying, "I need to head out now, but I promise I'll be back tonight, and we can spend some quality time together. Okay?"

She looks at me with doubt, and I can hardly blame her. Fuck if she doesn't have every right to not believe me right now, but that doesn't make it any less frustrating that she still doubts me so much.

"Okay. Yeah," she finally agrees. I move closer to her, pulling her into a tight embrace. Lifting her chin with my fingers, I place a few gentle kisses on her lips before leaving.

39

PARKER

Raking my hand through my hair for the millionth time, I let out a series of curses and grunts. I've been at this for several hours now, but it feels like I've barely made any progress. After spending all week pushing every other job to the side to focus on saving the zoo, I'm spending the weekend catching up on all the other accounts I'm personally managing.

My phone rings, vibrating across the desk, breaking my concentration on the contract for a local boutique that uses recycled fabrics to make their clothing. Not bothering to look at the screen, I let it go to voicemail. I don't have time for any more distractions right now.

A few seconds of silence pass before the damn thing starts ringing again, sending my temper through the roof. Picking up my phone, I slam my finger against the answer button before yelling, "What?"

A throat clearing greets me before a masculine voice sounds through the line. "Um, yes. I'm calling for Mr. Adams?"

"Speaking. What the fuck do you want?"

"Sir. This is Derek with Wright Home Construction. I was calling to let you know the renovations on your house are complete. We've cleared out of the area, and it's ready for you to move back in at your convenience."

"Thank fuck. It's about time. Send the bill to my office." With that, I hang up. A combination of relief and excitement spreading through my body at the thought of finally going home. I can't wait to see how everything turned out, but more importantly, I can't wait for Riley to see my real home.

Reaching down, I rearrange the steel rod that's popped up at the thought of laying Riley's naked body across every single surface of my newly remodeled house. If I thought my balls were aching this morning, they're damn near threatening to fall off soon if I don't make good on these dirty thoughts running through my head.

Desperate to fill Riley in on the good news, I'm halfway through dialing her number when it hits me.

Son of a bitch.

Placing my phone back down on my desk, I turn my chair around to face the windows, staring out at the waves as I try to figure out what to do now. I've been waiting for what seems like years to be back in my own domain. Hell, had it been possible, I would've lived in the mess of a construction zone just to be able to stay home.

But now, with the all-clear to move back in, I can't imagine not living next to Riley. The convenience of walking fifteen steps next door to see her has been a benefit I've clearly taken for granted. What will happen when I move back home? Will this change everything between us? Or will we still see each other as often?

I don't see how we possibly could. For as long as I've been kicked out of my home, I can't imagine continuing to stay somewhere else every night. And it's not like I can expect her to stay at my house all the time.

Or can I?

Would it be insane to ask her to move in with me? We spend damn near every night together anyway, other than this week. Would living together be any different?

The idea takes root, digging itself deep into my mind and planting its ass in solid ground. I can picture it now: waking up to her beautiful face every morning, enjoying our morning coffee together before we each head to work, coming home to her every night. Then, this issue of not seeing each other when I'm bogged down with clients and spending extra time at work won't be an issue. No matter what, I'd still have her in my bed every night.

Besides, if the zoo doesn't accept the proposal I had Haylee submit on Friday, and she ends up losing her job, at least she wouldn't have to worry about bills while she finds another one. Unlike my previous relationships, I wouldn't mind providing for her, as long as it meant I didn't lose her in the end.

With a renewed excitement to rush home, I dive back into work. The sooner I can get home, the sooner I can take Riley out and tell her the good news. Shit, maybe we can go see it together tonight. If she loves it, it'll make it that much easier to ask her to move in with me.

After finishing the boutique contract, I move on to the next thing on my list. Searching for the financial documents I started last week, I dig through the heaps of client folders on my desk, my frustration growing when I come up empty-handed. Turning in my chair, I look for my briefcase to check in there, not finding it anywhere in my office.

Fuck. I probably left it downstairs in my car. I was so wrapped up inside my head, worried about Riley's reaction to me this morning, I must've forgotten to grab it before heading inside. Standing from my office chair, where my ass has been glued for the last six hours, I stretch my aching limbs and walk out of my office.

After a thorough search of my car, I realize with dread my

briefcase isn't there, either. Mentally retracing my steps from this morning, I determine the only place it could possibly be is at Riley's.

Releasing a sigh of frustration, I head back toward the elevators and up to my office. I dial Riley's number, praying she answers, and after a few long rings, her soft voice fills my ear.

"Hello?"

"Hey, babe. Do you know if I left my briefcase in your apartment this morning? I need it and can't find it anywhere, but I know I had it when I left my apartment."

"I don't know. Let me go look."

"Thanks. How's your afternoon going?"

"Fine."

Oh, fuck. I hate that goddamn word.

"Were you able to relax after I left?"

Ignoring my question completely, she answers with, "Yeah, it's here by the front door. Looks like it slid under my entryway table."

"Fuck. Of course, it did. Can you do me a favor? Look in the middle compartment, find the folder labeled Tasty Bakes Financials, and send me photos of the documents? It's the last account I need to finish up before I can call it a day."

"Sure."

"Thanks, babe. Hey, I should be done here in the next hour or two. What do you think about going out tonight? I think we could both use a date night."

"Are you sure you have the time?"

I deserve that.

My head falls to my desk, thumping hard against the wood. Cursing, I raise my head, rubbing the sore spot with my hand. *I deserved that too.*

"Come on, babe. I'm sorry, and I miss you. Let me make it up to you. Please."

Sighing, she concedes, "Okay. Sure."

A minuscule amount of relief washes over me. It's not much, but at least she isn't completely shutting me out. The need to bring back her smile is so strong, I'm half tempted to say fuck it and head home now, but I can't. This shit needs to get done, or I'll have to spend another week playing catch up, losing even more time with her.

Rustling sounds on the other end as she searches through my briefcase. Anxiety creeps up my spine, spurring a sheen of sweat to coat my skin as I remember what else is in there. Having her search through my client files is the epitome of risky business.

"Found it. I'll send the photos over now."

"Perfect. Thanks, babe. I can't wait for tonight," I answer honestly, trying to improve her mood.

"Yeah. When should I be ready?"

Looking at my watch, I do a few quick calculations. "I should be back home in the next two hours. So…six or six-thirty?"

"Okay."

"See you soon, beautiful."

"Mhm," she grunts before ending the call, forcing my shoulders to slump.

While waiting for the documents to come through, I spend a few minutes formulating a plan for tonight. The last few weeks have been like wading through the surf, getting knocked out and dragged down by wave after wave. Our relationship has suffered a bit of a divide, and tonight needs to be perfect if I have any hope of fixing things.

While I can't tell her exactly what's going on, I can do my best to convince her our relationship is worth battling the turbulent waters for. Fixing things isn't even an option—it's a must.

40

RILEY

Hitting the end call button, I place the documents on my entryway table. After snapping a few photos of the documents he asked for, I compose them into an email and send them off to him. Gathering all the documents, I place them back into their folder before my phone buzzes on the table, the screen lighting up with a new text.

Parker: *Thanks, babe.* ***Kiss Emoji***

As hard as I try to fight it, I can't stop the butterflies that fill my stomach, knowing I'll finally get to spend time with Parker tonight. Despite how upset I've been with him this week, I can't lie and say I haven't missed him.

Sinking to the floor, I kneel beside his briefcase to stuff the folder back inside, eager to take a hot, relaxing bath before getting ready. As I close his briefcase, a folder in the back catches in the zipper, halting my progress. My level of frustration rises the longer I have to fight with the zipper, trying to get the folder loose. After a few rough tugs, the folder frees itself from the greedy jaws of the zipper, but not before tearing off a large chunk from the corner.

"Ha!" I cheer out, happy with my half-win against the briefcase jaws of hell. I'm about to put the file back into its rightful spot when I catch a glimpse of the word "zoo" through the missing piece of the folder. My eyes dart to the label, where I find the words *"Zoo Solution"* written across the top.

My brows furrow together in confusion, and though it's none of my business, I can't ignore the niggling feeling that I should look at what's in this folder. Glancing around, I double-check to make sure I'm still alone. As I'm looking over my shoulder, a laugh bursts up my throat. Of course, I'm alone. Who else would be in my apartment?

Shaking my head in amusement, I flip open the folder, the smile on my face slowly vanishing as my brain struggles to comprehend what I'm seeing. It looks like a business proposal of some sort, but why is the Shoreline Safari Zoo listed at the top?

Turning the page, I find an entire section that proposes shutting the zoo down altogether, replacing it with a safari-themed amusement park that will draw in a ton of money. There are specifics listed out on how an amusement park caters to a more diverse crowd than a zoo and ultimately smells better, which would please the housing communities closest to the animal exhibits.

My heart races furiously as sweat beads along my forehead and upper lip. There's no way Parker would do something like this. *Absolutely not.* He knows how important this job is to me. It's my entire life's dream—something I've mentioned several times throughout our relationship.

Frantically flipping through the last few pages of the proposal, my heart sinks to the pit of my stomach like a boulder. There it is, in black and white, Parker's signature stamped across the bottom of the page.

What the fuck?

There are several other documents behind the proposal, most of them appearing to be financial reports that further prove that what Allie said on Friday was the truth. I'm not very business savvy, but from what I can see in these reports, the zoo is losing money hand over fist and has been for a while. But there has to be some other solution. *Right?* They can't just close down the zoo. What would they do with all of the animals? Where would they go?

Flipping back a few pages, I re-read the section about closing the zoo, just to make sure I didn't misunderstand his intentions, but no. Everything is clearly listed out, depicting in detail how each section of the zoo could be transformed into some sort of safari rollercoaster or interactive game for kids. Although, I don't see any mention of where the animals would be relocated to. The more I read, the more my heart breaks, and eventually, the page blurs as my eyes fill with tears.

How could he do this to me?

Clutching my excruciatingly tight chest, I try to take a deep breath but can't seem to get enough air. Feeling weak and lightheaded, my body sways from side to side before I lose my balance completely. Falling to my side, I land next to my entryway table, my back against the wall.

My hand flies up, clamping over my mouth as the first sob breaks loose, filling my apartment with a wounded cry. Sob after sob wrack my body as my mind rewinds our entire relationship, searching for an explanation for Parker's betrayal, coming up empty.

How could I be so stupid?

This is exactly why I chose to remain single for the last ten years. The saying, "if it's not broken, don't fix it," pops into my head, my fists clenching in anger. I mean, sure, it's been lonely at times, but loneliness was a hell of a lot better than this overwhelming heartache. I had my job, I had my girls, and I had my trusted vibrator—none of which have ever caused me the pain I'm feeling now.

Fuck my decision to give dating another shot, and fuck turning thirty. That stupid number sent me into a panic spiral, and for what? Who the hell cares if you're still single when you turn thirty? I know several women in their thirties who are unhappy in their marriage, proving that relationships aren't always what they're cracked up to be.

And you know what? Fuck Maddie for making me believe SinglesVille wasn't my forever home. Except for my dream of having children swirling down the drain, I was comfortable in my singleness. But there are other ways to have children. Ways that don't involve having my heart smashed to smithereens by another asshole. I can adopt, or foster, or even use a sperm donor if I need to. I don't *need* a man at all. In fact, maybe it's time I borrow a page from Parker's playbook and start a celibacy pact. Save myself a world of hurt.

With a few deep breaths, I calm the angry tears streaming down my face before standing from my position on the floor. I glance into the kitchen on my way to the couch, considering pouring myself a massive glass of wine to dull the pain and anger, but end up thinking better of that idea. As much as I would love to find an escape from the ache in my heart, I know I need to keep a clear head if I have any hope of confronting Parker when he shows up later.

Curling up, I wrap my arms around my legs and tuck my chin into my chest, determined to hold all the pieces of myself together. Now's not the time to fully break. There's a job to do first, and I'm the only one that can do it.

Honestly, it's almost too bad that he's my neighbor. Having him so close has prevented him from leaving a ton of his stuff in my apartment. Otherwise, it'd be kind of nice to pack all of his shit up and toss it out of my window like you see in the movies. Cathartic, even. But since that's not really an option, I guess I'll have to do the adult thing and break up with him in person.

Then, and only then, will I allow the pieces of my heart to fall where they may.

41

PARKER

Pulling into a parking space outside of our apartment building, I check the time on my dashboard and see I'm right on time. Hopefully, that'll earn me a few bonus points with Riley, along with the surprise I picked up for her on my way home.

Reaching over, I grab the bouquet of flowers off my seat before exiting my car. I stopped at the flower shop just down the street and found the perfect arrangement in the flower display. It's full of vibrant red roses and radiant sunflowers—a perfect combination of happiness for my girl. *I hope she loves them.*

My steps falter as those words run through my head. Goddamn, I sound like a pussy.

Shaking my head, I enter the building, my stomach growling as I wait for the elevator. I'm starving and can't wait for our date. After a bit of bribing, I was able to make another reservation at The Red Table since we never made it last week. They weren't thrilled, but a little money went a long way toward changing their mind.

Arriving at Riley's door, I glance down, making sure everything's in order. Taking one last deep breath, I tighten my hand around the bouquet of flowers before raising my fist to her door, giving it a few hard knocks.

The door immediately flies open, almost like she was waiting for me. Only, I'm not greeted with the sight I was expecting. She's not dressed yet, her hair's a little bit of a mess, and her face is void of any makeup. That's okay, though. She still has a little time before we need to leave. I gave us some wiggle room, just in case I could swindle her out of her panties before we left.

Taking a step forward, I lean in, ready to press a sweet kiss against her lips when she rears back, an angry snarl forming across her face. It's then that I notice her eyes are still rimmed with red, and there are fresh tear tracks down her cheeks.

Fuck.

The crying I can somewhat understand, but why does she look so angry? I don't think I've ever seen her wear this expression. Not even in the beginning, when we strongly disliked each other. She's practically shaking with fury, her face contorted with rage, and if I look close enough, I think I'll actually see the devil looking back at me.

"Babe, wha—"

Slamming my briefcase against my chest, Riley cuts my words off, the air leaving my chest with a grunt.

"Get the hell out of here. I never want to see your face again, you selfish fucking bastard," she yells at me, steam billowing from her ears.

Okay, not really. *But, what in the actual fuck?*

She tries to slam the door on me when my reflexes kick in, my body spurring into action as I slam my palm to the door, forcing it back open. My natural instinct is to immediately jump to anger, but my brain seems to be stuck in first gear, leaving me with nothing but confusion.

"Woah, what the hell? What's going on, Riley?"

She levels me a maniacal laugh, shivers of terror racing up my spine at the sound.

"Don't play dumb with me. You know exactly what's wrong. And to think I trusted you."

"I'm not playing anything. I *don't* know what's going on, so why don't you calm down and explain it to me."

She rips the briefcase out of my hands and unzips it, rifling through the folders I have stored in there. I start to panic, sweat forming along my brow as I put the pieces together. Although, that doesn't explain her anger. Yeah, I kept it from her, but if she saw the proposal, surely she saw the non-disclosure agreement? She should understand why I couldn't tell her what was going on.

Seemingly finding what she was after, she takes the folder and thrusts it into my chest, knocking me back a step or two with her second use of unnecessary force. Glancing down, my suspicions are confirmed when I see the folder's label.

A nervous chuckle travels up my throat, filling the space between us. "Well, that fucking sucks. Obviously, you weren't supposed to find out this way. But why the hell are you so angry? I thought this would make you happy?"

"Happy? *Happy?*" She screeches, my balls shriveling at her shrill tone. If it were possible for them to disappear inside me, I think they would. Clearly, we're in danger of bodily harm. I just wish I fucking understood why. "Are you out of your goddamn mind?"

My temper enters the conversation, rearing its ugly head as those last few words harshly shoot from her mouth. I've spent the last week putting myself through hell to save her job, and here I am, getting reamed out for my troubles.

"I sure as hell must be because I thought this would put a goddamned smile back on your face and ease your worries. Hell, not just that. I figured once you found out, I'd be in for a wild night of fucking, or at least a goddamn grateful blowjob or two. Not this bullshit."

Riley throws her head back with another evil laugh, and I'm downright terrified. I watch as she brings her hands up to her hair, pulling on it so hard I'm scared she's going to rip it straight out of her head.

What in the actual fuck is happening right now?

And more importantly, who the hell is this crazy lady, and what has she done with my sweet, loving girlfriend? This version of her is downright frightening.

Her head snaps back down, pinning me to the floor with a death glare. "Of-fucking-course you did, Parker! Of. Fucking. Course," she spits out at me, clapping between each word. "I guess that confirms my theory that all you ever care about is sex. But you're even more of an asshole than I realized if you seriously thought you could destroy my goddamn career and still get fucked afterward."

"That's fucking right, Riley. You caught me. I'm out to destroy your—wait. *What?*"

The rest of my angry, sarcastic retort falters on my tongue as her words register in my brain. My temper takes a sharp detour to the backseat, allowing my confusion to retake the wheel. My eyebrows furrow as I drop my gaze down to the folder she's thrust into my chest.

Opening it, I rapidly flip through the pages, my heart speeding up to dangerous levels before halting altogether, sinking like a ship when I find what she's referring to.

This isn't fucking right.

"Riley, wait. You don't understand—" I try to say before she cuts me off. *Again.*

"Oh, I fucking understand plenty. I may not be some billionaire businessman like you, but that doesn't make me an idiot. Is that what you've been aiming for this whole time? Shutting down the zoo?"

"What? *No!* There's been a serious fuck up here."

"Just shut up, Parker. The only 'fuck up' here is how I could possibly be with a man that cares so little about me. I knew from the beginning that there had to be some underlying reason you were dating me—some benefit or achievement you were angling for. I just thought it had to do with fixing your piss poor image in the tabloids by dating the proverbial 'good girl.' Not to fuck with my career."

My head snaps back at her words, spewed with so much hatred I feel like she just injected my heart with venom. Anger seeps through my veins, clouding my mind of what's really important here. My brain is so twisted trying to figure out what happened to this proposal that I can't even begin to defend myself right now, let alone calm Riley down. *Heads are going to fucking roll on Monday.*

"Tell me, Parker," Riley demands, bringing my attention back to her. "Did you ever actually give a damn about animals? Or did you fake all that to get close to me?"

Rolling my eyes at her outlandish accusation, my voice rises in anger as I snarl, "Are you fucking kidding me? For the love of God, Riley. Why would I use my love of animals to get close to you? What the hell kind of leg up do you think that would get me?"

"I don't know, but it sure as hell worked in your favor! So just answer the question, Parker. Were you gunning for shutting down the zoo all along? Or did you decide to do that after we started dating? Or hell, maybe that was your revenge for me being a— what did you call it? An annoying as fuck, dramatic neighbor?"

"Jesus Christ, Riley. Are you actually this psychotic? Who the fuck shuts down an entire zoo because they hate one of the employees that works there? Get real."

Judging by the look on her face, that was not the right thing to say right now, but shit! She's sure as hell acting psychotic.

"Oh, so you admit it, then. You *do* hate me."

And there goes my temper again. My emotions feel like they're on a goddamn rollercoaster. Huh. *Ironic.*

Growling with anger, I fist my hair instead of putting my fist through a wall like I want to. This entire situation is completely asinine. "No," I seethe. "I don't fucking hate you. Nor do I hate animals. The only thing I even remotely hate right now is the fact you won't listen to a goddamn word I say."

"I don't need to listen, Parker. All the evidence is right here in front of me," she shouts, pointing at the folder I'm clutching.

"The evidence," I snarl through my clenched teeth, using air quotes around the word, "is entirely wrong. This. Is. A. Misunderstanding." Despite my attempt to break through to her by enunciating each word, she disregards my explanation entirely, refusing to believe a word I say.

"Stop lying to me, Parker. All of this is just too goddamn convenient for you. Did you plan for a disaster to happen at the zoo while you just 'happened' to be visiting so your company could profit off shutting us down?"

My fist tightens around the bouquet of flowers I've managed to cling to throughout our fight. I've never met a woman more frustrating than Riley. I know I was an asshole initially, but how could she think so little of me to not even give me a chance to explain myself before automatically jumping to her own conclusions? Haven't I proved I'm not the man she thought I was in the beginning?

"That's not what happened, Riley. There was no fucking plan! Goddamn it, just give me a chance to explain."

"What did you do, pay someone to release the monkeys so you could be there to witness it and swoop in to secure another client?" She continues, ignoring me completely. "Or was that just a coincidence too? Not to mention the fact that you practically disappeared from my life immediately after. Dropped me like a hot fucking potato. You haven't been here all week, you've barely answered my messages, and then I find this proposal in YOUR briefcase to shut down the zoo, and suddenly it all makes sense. You got what you needed from me, so why stick around any longer, right? Am I getting closer to the truth yet?"

I open my mouth, trying to get a word in to defend myself when she cuts me off with more bullshit theories.

"What was your plan, Parker? Take me out somewhere nice tonight so you could break the news in public before dumping me? Make a spectacle out of me? All your ex-girlfriends did their best to make you look awful in the press, so why not do the same to me, right? Put all of your lessons to use and test out what you've learned? Or maybe you just decided to take their sins out on me in general? Destroy my career and my image, all in one shot? Well, brav-fucking-o, Parker. Consider your test completed."

Alright, that's fucking it. My patience for this bullshit packed up and left about fifty words ago. I'm done with this. Bringing my hands together in a slow clap, the flowers crumble with each impact. "Wooow," I mock, drawing out the word into three syllables. "You really have it all figured out, don't you, Riley. Nothing gets past you."

"Fuck you, Parker," she bellows out while a single tear cascades down her cheek. My heart squeezes in pain as I watch its journey down her face, but I can't find it in me to make her feel better right now. She could've let me explain instead of turning this into what it's become.

At some point during our fight, we moved into her apartment entryway. Hopefully, that has given us a little bit of privacy while our relationship burns to the fucking ground. Although, I highly doubt it. Not with these thin as hell walls. I bet everyone on this floor—and possibly the floor below us—heard the entire demise of our relationship.

That realization smacks me in the face as I realize that's exactly what's happened here. She was never going to give me a chance to explain, already having it cemented in her head that I'm guilty. She's just done—washing her hands of me, and our entire relationship, like it meant absolutely nothing. *Hell, maybe it didn't.*

"You were never going to believe me, were you?" I question as all the air leaves my lungs. I don't know why I bothered with the question, though. I already know the answer.

My shoulders deflate, the anger I was clinging to evaporating, leaving nothing but a hollow ache in my chest. "I've spent weeks telling you you're better than every woman I've dated. Telling you that you meant everything to me. But you just couldn't believe me, could you? Hell, I should've seen it weeks ago. You've been searching for reasons to end this since the very beginning. Doing your absolute best to sabotage any chance we had at a successful relationship."

"Yeah, and obviously with good reason. You're no better than the guys I dated in college. Using me for your own personal gain, then tossing me to the side as soon as you got it, never giving a single shit if you were hurting me in the process. I should've stuck to the Matches app. I was doing just fine before you stormed into my life and fucked everything up."

"Oh, please. You weren't fine. You were fumbling through a line of failed matches left and right before I walked into your life and put a stop to your tragic dating life. I did you a fucking favor when I deleted that godawful app."

"At least none of those dates hurt me the way you have! You've absolutely destroyed me and my career, Parker. And that's something I can never forgive. Now get the hell out of my life."

My heart falls to my stomach at her request. This may have

started out as a simple misunderstanding, but it's so far past that now, there's no fixing this. I can't make her trust me, and as proven today, I sure as hell can't make her believe me. Not to mention I'm no Cupid. I can't force her to love me—no matter how much I love her.

"Fine. If that's really what you want, I'll leave. But I promise you, Riley. You're making a colossal mistake. Right here, right now, you're the one ending us, not me. And someday—probably sooner than you think—you're going to realize exactly what you did. I just hope it won't be too late."

For a few seconds, I have a sliver of hope as her face shifts from anger to confusion while she considers my promise, but it's not enough. Her body stiffens in anger once again, robbing me of all hope as she points to the door, ending our relationship with a simple hand gesture.

Turning on my heel, I cross the threshold of her apartment seconds before the door slams behind me. Unlocking my own apartment, I head straight for the kitchen, dumping the flowers right where they belong—in the trash, along with my stupid fucking heart.

42

PARKER

Sitting in my office chair early Monday morning, my back to my desk, I watch as dawn breaks across the ocean. The weather channel predicted a storm today, and it looks like they weren't wrong. It's overcast and dreary as hell, matching my current mood perfectly. The only thing missing is the actual rain. Judging by the sky, though, it won't be long before it hits.

I spent all day Sunday packing up my apartment, moving my shit back home. As much as I hated to leave with things as they were, there was no point in sticking around. Riley made that perfectly clear. So instead of seeing her face light up with happiness as I asked her to move in with me, I dropped all my boxes inside the newly remodeled rooms, barely taking the time to see all the improvements before falling into my bed. *Alone.*

What should've been a happy moment for me was instead plagued with anger and heartbreak. All my newfound dreams of filling these rooms with love and laughter, of making new memories with Riley and building this house into a loving home were crushed when she kicked me out of her life without a second of hesitation. Now I'm right back to where I started—a miserable, grumpy bastard that never should've broken his celibacy pact.

I had a fail-proof plan in place: stay single, focus on my company, and fix my image in the public eye. Then I had to go and meet my crazy, dramatic, fucking gorgeous neighbor, and my plan was shot to shit in a matter of minutes. All it took was yet another pretty face to send my life into a goddamn tailspin.

Fuck, am I stupid or what?

Swiveling around in my chair, I turn my back on the thunderstorm brewing outside, focusing my attention on the shit storm that already hit my life Saturday.

Re-reading the zoo proposal for what seems like the hundredth time since Saturday night, my temper climbs with each word. Soon enough, my skin absolutely crawls with rage, begging for a target to aim my red-hot fury at.

The ding of the elevator sounds through the empty office floor, alerting me to Haylee's arrival.

Bingo.

Her keys have barely hit her office desk before I'm barking my order. "Haylee! Get your ass in here. *Now!*" I hear a gasp from outside of my office, and know she heard the wrath in my tone. Fucking good. I've been sitting in this goddamn office since four a.m., trying to put the pieces of this fucked up puzzle together with no luck. It's about time someone explains what the hell happened to this proposal.

The only—and I do fucking mean only—reason I didn't call every one of my employees into the office yesterday to sort this shit out is because I was busy packing up my life before allowing myself a few hours to be a miserable, broken-hearted fuck. But today's a new day, and I'll be damned if I leave this office before things are sorted.

The door to my office creaks open seconds before Haylee steps into the room. I briefly glance up at the sound of her high heels clicking against the floor before moving my eyes back to the folder on my desk, only to do a quick double-take.

Jesus, she looks like a fucking mess. There are dark circles under her eyes, and it looks like she forgot to brush her hair after climbing out of bed this morning. Her shirt is wrinkled, and her skirt doesn't match the rest of her outfit. Did she get dressed in the dark or some shit?

Whatever her problem is—and clearly there is one—it doesn't matter. I don't have time to focus on anything but the issue at hand. Besides, I didn't fucking ask for her personal shit to interfere with my company or my personal life. Which is why I can't seem to refrain from jumping down her throat the minute she's standing in front of my desk.

"Are you fucking *trying* to sabotage my life?" I belt out, causing her to jump with surprise.

"W-what?" Haylee stutters, looking at me with wide, fearful eyes as the blood drains from her face.

Not that I blame her. I haven't raised my voice at her like this since her first week here, but her previous work ethics won't excuse this major fuck up. And there's no doubt in my mind she's the one responsible for this mess.

After retracing my steps a million times, I remembered handing these documents to her myself on Friday, asking her to make the appropriate changes. Even if she handed them off to someone else, she was in charge of making sure this proposal went through without a hitch.

Throwing the papers down on my desk, I growl out, "I told you on Friday to sign off on the zoo proposal once it reflected the list of changes I handed you. You were supposed to add the mini safari-themed amusement park in the center of the zoo to the proposal, moving a few of the smellier exhibits to the outer perimeter so people wouldn't get sick while on the rides. So imagine my fucking shock when I saw my signature at the bottom of a proposal to shut down the entire goddamn zoo and replace it with a theme park. What in the actual fuck, Haylee? Tell me you didn't send this shit off to the city!"

She's frantically shaking her head before I even finish asking the question.

"N-no. No, no, no. There's no way I messed that up. I know I was distracted Friday, bu—"

"Distracted?" I shout, cutting off her response. *"Distracted?* Jesus fucking Christ, Haylee. This is a hell of a lot more than the product of distraction. Your mistake not only put this entire project and thousands of jobs at risk, but it also ended my fucking relationship."

"What?" she cries out, her eyes doubling in size.

Bringing my hand up, I clutch my head, attempting to cut off the headache that's been blooming all morning, gaining strength as each hour passes. I watch as a few tears slip down Haylee's face—something I've never seen before—as she shakes her head and glances down at the proposals scattered across my desk.

"Just," I start, heaving a deep sigh, "get the fuck out of my office, and don't come back until you have the correct proposal in your hands. I can't even look at you right now. This may have cost you your job."

She sucks in a deep breath before turning on her heels, practically running out of my office. Sinking into my chair, I brace my elbows on my desk and let my head fall into my hands. My whole body sags as the exhaustion and stress from the last forty-eight hours finally catches up to me.

Running my hands through my hair, I grip the ends in an iron fist, tugging until the sting of pain grounds me. I need to clear my head, so I can focus on fixing this problem. I wasn't joking when I said this mistake could cost us this contract, especially if they have a proposal from another company that gives them a way to save the zoo—the very thing I was trying to do.

In all my years of running this company, I've never had a mistake like this happen. For several reasons. The first being that when Parker Solutions proposes a solution, it's in a face-to-face meeting with the business in question, which means all mistakes are caught before the presentation, or worst-case scenario, during the presentation, and are promptly fixed. The second reason being I employ a team that damn near never makes mistakes—especially Haylee.

Unfortunately, because this solution required major construction, we had to obtain a permit from the city, which means the proposal had to be submitted to the City of San Diego for approval before it could be passed on to the zoo itself. I trusted Haylee to make the appropriate changes and submit it without me looking it over again because she's never fucked up like this before, and we were on a massive time crunch. The proposal and permit request had to be submitted by four p.m. on Friday to make it on to the Monday morning docket. I've never prayed so hard for Haylee to miss a fucking deadline. It might be the only thing that saves us now.

Swiveling my chair around once again, I face my floor-to-ceiling windows, staring out at the rain that's now coming down in sheets, mixing with the angry ocean waters. Suddenly I find myself wishing like hell it could just swallow me whole. Drowning would probably hurt a hell of a lot less than the current stress and heartache I'm battling now.

As I watch the ocean rage, the waves crashing against the shoreline, I review my options. I'm contemplating calling the city myself when my phone dings with a new text. I immediately try to dig the phone out of my pocket, fumbling a few times before freeing it from its confines, praying it's Riley wanting to talk.

My prayers go unanswered when I see the sender's name flash across my screen, but a reluctant smirk crosses my face anyway.

If there's one thing I can count on, it's my idiotic boys providing a distraction.

Colton: *Pick up game. Tomorrow night at 7. I expect you all to be there.*

Rhett: *Yes, DAD.*

Hell yeah, that's exactly what I need. Taking my anger out on the other team will do me some fucking wonders, keeping my ass out of jail for pounding the shit out of my employees.

Parker: *I'll be there.*

Wesley: **gif of a man bowing down on both knees* Can't wait for you to grace us with your presence, Master.*

Jesus Christ. What a fucking toolbag.

A boom of thunder rattles the windows behind me, sending a wave of nausea through my system as I silence my phone and drop it to the desk. Despite the fair warning I had, every muscle in my body tightens with anxiety. Closing my eyes, I do my best to breathe through it, but it's a wasted effort. Riley is the only one who can calm me when I'm lost to the storm.

Resting in bed, Riley draped across me after our third round of orgasms, my muscles tense as thunder shakes the walls. We damn near broke the bed, but even my sexual exhaustion doesn't rid my body of the mounting tension. There's an afternoon storm raging outside, and it's got me ten shades of fucked up.

Riley stirs against my body, lifting her head off my shoulder as she peeks up at me through her lashes.

"You okay, babe?" she whispers, her breath tickling my skin.

I do my best to inhale her calm and exhale my panic, heaving a deep sigh when it doesn't work.

"Yes. No. Fuck, I don't know."

I tighten my arms around her to keep her where she is, but it's pointless. She wiggles around until she's propped up against my chest, her eyes meeting mine.

"What's wrong? And don't say 'it's nothing.' I can practically feel your body vibrating with tension."

The room falls silent as she waits for my answer, her eyes pleading with mine to give her honesty. Looking at the window, I watch as rain pelts the glass, wincing as another ominous boom of thunder sounds in the distance.

"It's the storm," I sigh, turning to face her.

Confusion flits across her face seconds before understanding dawns, her eyes filling with sadness as she whispers, "Your dad."

Riley shifts against me, settling back into her original position. I wrap my arms around her again, pulling her deeper into my embrace. She nuzzles her cheek against my heated skin, turning to place a gentle kiss on my chest, directly above my heart.

"Yeah," I choke out, emotion clogging my throat. "Unexpected storms stress me out. If I know they're coming, I can usually plan for them. Build my walls up to keep the doom and gloom out. But the storms that come out of nowhere...Well. They remind me of my father. How he must've felt standing under that palm tree. I imagine it's a lot like I feel when I'm waiting for the storm to pass. You're sure it will. It has to, right? Only question is, will you still be here when it does?"

Wetness glides across my chest where Riley's head is lying. I can't see her face, but I know without a doubt she's crying softly at my words. That's my girl for ya. She wears her heart on her sleeve. It's one of the things I love about her—her ability to feel so strongly, even for those she's never met.

The tension in me slowly fades, giving way to peace as her arms tighten against me, lending me her strength. Her legs move to tangle with mine, wrapping me up in a Riley cocoon. Every inch of her naked skin caresses mine, doing wonders to soothe my aching heart.

Her fingers gently trace patterns across my skin, their lazy dance calming my mind as I focus on nothing but the tingling sensation. Finally at peace, my eyes drift shut as I slip into an easy slumber.

THE DOOR TO MY OFFICE CREAKS OPEN, ROBBING ME OF THE soothing memory. My eyes pop open, focusing on Haylee. She slowly ambles to the front of my desk, her face a sheet of white as her hands tremble.

"Parker...I'm so sorry..." she whispers, remorse dripping from her words.

My eyes slam shut again, my shoulders dropping with disappointment as I sense the words before she says them.

"I just got off the phone with the city office. The proposal and permits were received Friday afternoon and already went through processing this morning. The secretary told me they're in a meeting discussing the zoo's shut down right now, per our proposal. I'm so sorry. I was distracted by a call from my mother's care facility. I was rushing to get out of here so I could get to her sooner...."

Ignoring the rest of her explanation, I lurch forward, picking my office phone up off the receiver. Dialing the city office, I glare up at Haylee, dismissing her as the call rings out. "You can leave now."

Her head dips, her chin falling to her chest as she turns and hurries out of the room.

"Thanks for calling the City of San Diego; how can I direct your call?" a chipper voice answers.

"Permits and approvals office, please," I bark out, barely remembering my manners.

"One moment, please."

Stupid ass elevator music meets my ear, my grip clenching around the phone as my headache worsens. A few minutes pass before, "Permits and approvals, this is Sherry speaking."

"Sherry, put me through to Tom, please."

"I'm sorry, Mr. King is in a meeting. Can I take a message?"

"This is Parker Adams regarding an urgent matter. Put me through to him. Now."

She sputters, taken back by my tone. She doesn't bother answering, simply putting me on hold yet again.

What feels like ten years later, but is more likely a handful of minutes, a brusk voice fills the line. "Tom speaking. What can I do for you, Mr. Adams?"

Tom and I are well-acquainted. He's been in the city office for as long as my business has been open, approving all of my building permits with ease—something I typically love but fear today.

"Tom, tell me you haven't approved the permit we submitted last week for the zoo."

"Erm, well. It's been agreed upon, pending inspection. We have a guy out walking the zone right now to make sure there aren't any issues with water or electrical lines."

"Call him and cancel. Right now. There was a massive error with the proposal we submitted. Lines were crossed. We never intended to replace the entire zoo. The amusement park was only supposed to be an addition to the zoo. Do me a solid and ignore the original proposal. We can have a new one submitted within the hour."

"Oh, um...I'm not sure I can do that, Parker. The committee already voted. It was a unanimous vote to shut down the zoo, as long as the inspection was approved."

"I don't give a fuck what you have to do, Tom. Squash this. I'll pay off the inspector to fail the permit if I need to. Hell, I'll pay off every member on the approval board to pretend like they never fucking saw that proposal. Don't. Push it. Through," I seethe through clenched teeth.

Silence greets me on the other end of the line.

"You know bribery of a city office is a punishable offense, Mr. Adams. Are you sure you want to risk this?"

My throat tightens with his words, a brief image of The Helping Haven's building flashing through my mind at his reminder. Fear spikes through my heart, knowing I could lose this deal if they find out what I'm doing, especially if I end up in jail. I'm risking everything by doing this, but I don't have a choice.

Clearing my throat, I announce, "I'm aware of the possible consequences. They're worth it to save the animals and the love of my life's career."

A clucking of sorts travels through the line before Tom chuckles. "Awfully chivalrous of you to do all of this for a woman."

"I don't know about that, but there's nothing I wouldn't do for her."

"Even jail time?"

"Even jail time."

"Let's hope it doesn't come to that. I'll be in touch."

The phone clicks off, silence ringing through the air of my office. What the fuck am I doing? She doesn't even want me, yet here I am, possibly throwing my entire life away for one woman. My mother's going to kick my fucking ass if I end up in prison.

I sit in silence, stewing in my anger as I wait for a response. Twenty minutes later, my phone pings with a message from Tom.

Tom King: *Consider it forgotten. You have one hour to re-submit.*
Parker: *Thank you.*
Tom King: *It's going to cost you, but not in the way you think.*

Parker: *What do you need.*

Tom King: *An anonymous donation to the city for the parks and recreation project.*

Parker: *How much?*

Tom King: *$1.7 million. Today.*

Fucking Christ. This is turning out to be a costly mistake—monetarily and emotionally. Sighing, I rub at my chest, trying to physically soothe my aching heart as I shoot off a response before I can change my mind.

Parker: *Consider it done.*

Dropping my cell, I hit the intercom button on my office phone, barking at Haylee to get into my office. She appears less than thirty seconds later, fear written across her face.

"Sit down. We have a job to do."

"W-What? You're not firing me?"

"Consider yourself lucky you're normally a damn good employee. You're on probation. Now sit down. We have one hour to fix this fucking proposal."

Her eyes widen, her head nodding rapidly as she sinks into the chair, ready to work. Forty-seven minutes later, the proposal and permit are updated and signed after I personally re-read the contents. *Twice.*

"Go scan and submit this. Now." I grunt, thrusting the papers in her direction. She takes them from my hand and rushes to the door, her signature sass nowhere to be found.

"Oh, and Haylee," I add, stopping her before she leaves.

"Yes, sir?"

"After you submit the proposal, send an anonymous donation for one point seven fucking million to the city office for their parks and recreation project. That'll be all."

Her eyes widen to the size of saucers, her face paling as she understands my words and exactly how much her mistake is costing me. Briefly closing her eyes, her shoulders slouch before she shakes her head and meekly responds, "Yes, sir."

The door clicks shut behind her, leaving me alone to sink into my chair. We fixed the proposal, but I'm not sure there's any way of fixing my heart. My only hope is that Riley comes to her senses when she realizes how wrong she was.

But how long will that take?

43

PARKER

Sweat drips from my body as I rush down the ice, crossing the blue line with the puck seconds before Rhett. We're halfway through the third period, and we trail by one point, which is mostly my fault. My head hasn't been in the game, and the whole team knows it.

Rhett slaps his stick against the ice, begging for the puck, but there's no way I'm passing to him right now. Not when I have a clear opening for a slap shot. All I have to do is sneak the puck past the goalie. I fake a pass to Rhett before shooting the puck toward the upper left corner of the goal.

Holding my breath, I watch as the goalie doesn't fall for my dangle. He tracks the movement, easily snatching the puck out of the air with his glove. *Fuck.* Another failed shot. That makes seven in this game alone.

A defenseman on the other team snickers, despite the fact I fucking beat him down the ice. "Your mom called. She said you left your game at home," he taunts.

Anger filters through my veins at his stupid fucking chirp. I know I should brush it off, but I can't. He picked the wrong week to mess with me. My temper has been following me around like a fucking storm cloud, waiting to dump on everyone around me.

I pick up speed, chasing his ass down the ice while shouting, "You've missed every pass in your direction, and you want to chirp at me? I've seen better hands on a fucking digital clock, asshole."

The defenseman whips around, raising his gloved fist like he's going to attempt to land a punch. Fortunately for him—because, let's face it, I'd pound his ass into the ice—Wesley skates in out of nowhere and interferes, sending the dude flying into the boards before I can start a brawl.

Rhett skates up on my left, using his body to herd me back down the ice toward our bench. "Come on, bro. Take a breather," he demands before swinging his own legs over the boards.

Rolling my eyes, I follow his lead, letting some other dude take the ice in my place. With a scowl, I pick up my water bottle, filling my mouth and swishing it around before spitting it on the ice. Thankfully, Rhett chooses to watch the game in silence instead of trying to talk. I'm in no mood for meaningless chit-chat.

The game clock dwindles down, Rhett and I both taking the ice for our final shift. After a few good hits and several failed shots on goal, the buzzer sounds, signaling the end of the game. I don't need to look at the Jumbotron to know we lost. We were down by one going into the third period, and we didn't do jack shit to change that score.

Stalking off the ice, I head down the tunnel toward the locker room, where I slam my ass down on the bench. Bending over, I remove both my skates and toss them in my bag before Rhett and Wesley join me on the bench. They're joking around, making plans to head to the bar for wing night, but I'm having none of that. Ignoring them, I continue to undress so I can get the fuck out of here.

Colton lumbers into the room, still fully decked out in his gear. He levels a cold glare my way before he reaches back with one hand and grabs the back of his sweat-soaked sweater, pulling it over his head and tossing it to the floor in front of his locker.

He runs his hand through his hair before he slams his fist against the locker in front of him. Wesley and Rhett jump at his anger, their banter dying down as they glance between Colton and me.

"What's your problem?" I taunt in a snide tone, knowing I'm picking yet another fight.

Sure enough, Colton whips around and shoves his finger in my direction before shouting, "You! You're my fucking problem. What the hell was that out there?"

"Looked like a hockey game to me," I mock with a shrug.

Out of the corner of my eye, I see Wesley shake his head before he drops it to his chest. Rhett just sighs. Colton, on the other hand, takes another step closer to me, raising my hackles.

"Stop with the bitchy attitude and tell us what's going on. I just had to have a talk with the captain of the other team. He said if you can't keep your temper out of the rink, they're done playing with us. The last time you showed up for a game, you started a brawl with Brad. Now you're trying to throw punches at defensemen for calling you out on your piss-poor game. And he wasn't wrong. You're better than how you played tonight, so I'll ask again. What the fuck's your problem?"

The anger I've been holding on to slowly seeps from my body, along with my energy. Leaning forward, I brace my elbows on my knees and sink my head into my hands, pressing the heels of my palms into my eyes.

"Riley and I had a misunderstanding last weekend and she dumped me. Told me to get the fuck out of her life without bothering to hear my side of shit."

Silence descends on the locker room as I take a few deep

breaths, trying like hell to swallow the bile forcing its way up my throat. A hand clamps down on my shoulder before Colton says, "I wondered if she had anything to do with your shit mood. Nothing like a woman to completely turn your life upside down."

"Ain't that the fucking truth," Rhett grunts.

Wesley's dumbass has the nerve to ask, "What'd you do to piss her off?"

"Nothing, asshole. That's the point," I shout, my temper flaring back to life.

"Well, obviously, that's not true. Otherwise, she wouldn't have dumped your sorry ass."

"I didn't fucking do anything wrong. She stumbled across some documents that she wasn't supposed to see, and instead of letting me explain the misunderstanding, she just ended shit. Chucked my heart in the trash and set the fucker on fire. Then I had to drop a cool one point seven mil to fix the mistake she brought to my attention."

"Damn, dude. That's brutal," Wesley hisses.

Nodding my head, I agree, my eyes flickering to Rhett as I watch him dig around in his bag, looking for something. His hand finally shoots up, holding his phone.

"What's her number, man? I've gotta move fast if I'm gonna sweep in as the rebound."

A deadly growl rips from my throat as visions of Rhett and Riley cloud my vision. The thought of her naked body riding his makes me fucking ill, and before I know it, I'm springing into action. Grabbing him by his sweater, I throw him against the lockers, shoving my face within an inch of his.

Spit flies out of my mouth as I shout, "Don't even fucking think about it. I swear to God, I'll rearrange your ugly fucking face if you lay a single finger on her."

Rhett has the nerve to sneer at me before he tips his head back and laughs, stopping long enough to say, "I was wondering when you were going to stop being such a goddamn pussy."

I rear back in shock before my anger tips over, boiling out of every pore. My fist cocks back, ready to send this jackwagon's head into the fucking lockers. Sadly, a set of hands clamp down on each of my arms, pulling me away from Rhett before my fist can connect with his face.

"Let me the fuck go," I roar out, doing my best to shake their grasp. It's useless, though. Colton has a death grip on my arm, and as much as I hate to admit it, Wesley has about fifteen pounds of muscle on me.

Backing me up against a locker, Colton gets in my face, yelling at me to calm down. I watch as Rhett straightens up, righting his clothes before cleaning my spit off his face with a smirk.

Colton raises his voice, forcing me to look in his direction when he says, "Grow the fuck up, man. We lost that game out there because you were too focused on punching everyone instead of worrying about shooting the puck. Now you're in here trying to knock your best friend's teeth in over a joke. The fuck's the matter with you?"

"Nah, fuck that. He's no friend of mine."

"That's where you're fucking wrong, Parker," Rhett fumes, matching my hardened glare. "I'm the best kind of friend there is, because while these guys will hold your hand and let you bitch, that's not me. I'll gladly be the asshole to slap you with a dose of reality. And if how you just reacted is any indication, you're not over her. Not by a fucking long shot. So what the hell are you doing here, trying to beat the shit out of everyone in your path to deal with the pain you're feeling? We," he grunts, pointing at the three of them, "aren't the enemy, and you know it. You need to channel all this pain you're feeling and throw it into the fight of your fucking life to win Riley back. Pull your head out of your ass and fight *for* your girl instead of *over* her."

"Don't you think I tried?" I bellow out, stepping toward Rhett. "I did fight for her. But she made it clear that she wanted nothing to do with me. Told me I was just another piece of shit using her."

"Well, were you?" Rhett dares to question.

"No! I fucking love her."

"Then stop being a pussy and fight for her. And don't stop until you have her in your arms again. Because trust me when I say if you don't fix this, and soon, some other schmuck will swoop in and steal her away from you. It won't be me, but it will be someone. She's too good of a girl to stay single forever."

"He's right, man," Colton agrees while handing me my gym bag. "Using your fists in this arena won't do shit to win her back. Go to her. Make her listen to you. You're too good of a man to just give up because your back's against the wall."

"Alright, fuck!" Taking my bag from him, I finish changing before heading for the door. Steps away from leaving, I halt and close my eyes, letting out a deep sigh. Looking over my shoulder, I meet Rhett's eyes and mutter, "Thanks."

He tips his chin up at me and says, "You're good, man. Just go get your girl. Don't let her get away."

Colton and Wesley both nod their heads in agreement. Readjusting my bag, I square my shoulders and leave, ready for a battle.

About thirty minutes later, I pull into a parking spot outside of my old apartment complex. I'm about to exit my car when movement at the front of the building catches my attention. Glancing through the windshield, I watch in awe as a redheaded beauty struts out, my heart clenching at the sight of her. Goddamn, I miss her.

Grabbing the door handle, I take a deep breath, a relieved smile tipping my lips up as I watch a brilliant smile take over her entire face. It takes me entirely too long to realize the smile isn't for me, though. It's for the douchebag following her through the door.

I sit there and watch as they come to a stop, standing outside the building, facing each other. His smile matches hers, and I want to punch it right off his smug fucking face. My fists fly to the steering wheel, damn near ripping it from the dashboard when the fuckhead leans down and kisses Riley on her cheek before pulling her into a hug.

I know Colton was right when he said I can't fight my way through this heartbreak, but fuck if I want to listen to his advice right now. My vision turns red, and I swear on every penny I own, if this asshole doesn't remove his gorilla paws from her body, I will remove them for him, right before I beat him with them.

Before I can resort to more violence, he steps away from her. She smiles and nods her head, and he takes off. Riley stands there for a few more minutes, staring after him with a soft smile before she turns and walks back inside, never sparing me a glance.

I can't fucking believe she moved on so fast. She had me fooled, pretending to be heartbroken during our breakup. If I hurt her as bad as she claimed, how could she just shut off those feelings and jump right into a new relationship? I can't even stomach the idea of another woman lying next to me, but apparently, she isn't suffering from the same issue.

My head falls back against the headrest, my eyes closing as a painful realization hits me full force. She probably redownloaded her dating app as soon as the door shut behind me.

I knew she wouldn't stay single long, but I genuinely thought she'd wait at least a week before moving on.

Guess I was wrong about a lot of fucking things.

Waves crash against the shore as I look on from my office the following afternoon. I haven't got shit done today. I've been too busy sitting here, staring at the waves as Riley's betrayal plays on a loop in my mind. Reaching behind me, I grab my half-empty glass of bourbon off my desk, downing the rest of its contents.

I'm not usually one to drink during business hours, not wanting alcohol to cloud my judgment, but when you're a broken-hearted fuck like I am, who really gives a shit. I can't believe I paid over a million dollars for a woman that's already moved on. The only bright side to that is saving the animals. At least they won't lose their home over a mistake.

Haylee knocks on the door before popping her head into my office, disrupting me from my moping. "There's a Sarah from The Helping Haven on line one. She said you'd take her call, but I couldn't find a folder for their company. Should I start one, or do you have one you forgot to give me?"

My heart falters in my chest, the alcohol previously clouding my brain clearing in an instant as I turn to face my assistant. A tinge of anger heats my blood at them using my business line. I gave them my personal number for a reason.

"No. This is a personal call."

"Oh, okay. Line one, then."

She turns to leave, but I halt her, calling out, "Hold all my calls and push my next appointment. I don't want to be bothered by anyone during this call. And I do mean everyone."

She raises her eyebrows at me, her signature sass making an appearance as she understands my meaning.

"You got it, *boss*." With that, she turns and leaves, shutting the door behind her.

Clearing my throat, I make sure the door has latched tightly before answering the call. "Parker," I bark out.

"Mr. Adams, hello. This is Sarah calling on behalf of Noelle from The Helping Haven. I'm sorry to call you on your company line. It would appear I've lost your personal number."

Frustration creeps up my throat at her admission, but I do my best to lock that shit down tight. I can't afford to lose this deal by being an asshole now, no matter how negligent their actions are. This offer is the only thing keeping me afloat right now, and the distraction it would provide is desperately needed.

"That's alright. Did you come to a decision on my offer, then?"

She clears her throat, stalling for half a second too long. "Not quite, sir. We are so grateful for your interest in The Helping Haven. Unfortunately, there seems to be some…dissent…between Noelle and the board, and they've taken up two issues with selling to you."

My fingers drum impatiently against my desk as my heart clenches. My offer was more than generous to buy out their building and take over all official business proceedings moving forward, and each board member was offered a fair severance package, ensuring they'd be happy to sell.

"Such as?"

"Well, um. They're worried you might not have the sufficient time to dedicate to the organization, and we'd hate for our families in need to fall through the cracks due to a lack of time and focus."

Anger seeps through my veins as her words find their mark, but as my brain processes her statement, my brow furrows, confusion replacing my rage.

"And may I ask what gave them the notion I'd lack time or focus, should the sale go through?"

She clears her throat again, seemingly steeling her nerves. "Have you, or have you not submitted a proposal to save the Shoreline Safari Zoo?"

What the fuck? The proposal is still supposed to be confidential, per the zoo's request, and I paid way too much bribery money and lost way too fucking much personally for this shit to blow up in my face again.

"I have—"

"Precisely," she states, cutting me off, my irritation spiking a bit higher. "That is quite the undertaking when coupled with the twenty-seven other accounts your company is in the process of acquiring or restructuring, six of which you are handling personally, are you not?"

How the fuck do they know that?

Wiggling my mouse, I bring my computer screen to life before doing a quick count of the open accounts with Parker Solutions.

"Yes, that's correct," I bark out, my anger getting the best of me.

With a soft sigh, Sarah's voice comes through the phone, "So you see our fears, Mr. Adams. The zoo project alone will take a massive amount of focus. Add in the time you'll need to focus on your other accounts, as well as running your company, and you should understand why we fear your time won't be dedicated to our beloved organization."

"The details of the zoo account haven't been made public yet. How did you know it was my company handling the restructure?"

"Oh, um. Noelle's husband is friends with someone in the City of San Diego office. Once she knew you were the owner of Parker Solutions and heard about the proposal, she brought the information to the board to make an informed decision."

Of fucking course, because why wouldn't something else in my life go to shit right now. *Does anybody know what confidential means these days?* Running my hand along the lower half of my face, I swivel around in my chair to focus on the waves again, doing my best to temper my emotions. At least nobody mentioned the bribery.

"Ms. Tilling,"

"Sarah, please," she cuts me off. *A-fucking-gain.*

"Sarah," I spit out between clenched teeth, annoyed by the interruption. "I assure you, my company has successfully handled numerous accounts simultaneously in the past. This will be no different."

"Accounts of the zoo's size?"

I hesitate briefly, debating how honest to be. "Admittedly, no," I slowly admit, bracing for impact. "The zoo will most likely end up being our biggest account."

"Are you prepared to hand that account off to your staff to dedicate your focus to the running of The Helping Haven?"

The line falls silent as I consider her question. *Am I willing to do that?*

Initially, I took on the zoo account for two reasons: to save the animals and to save Riley's career. But now that seems like a moot point, considering she left me regardless of my intentions.

I could probably hand this job over, should the proposal be accepted, ensuring I have the time to take over The Helping Haven, but doing so would feel like giving up on Riley entirely. And call me fucking stupid, but I'm not sure I'm ready to do that.

Sarah takes my silence as a definitive answer. "That's what I was afraid of," she gently mutters.

Unable to confirm or deny her assumption, I redirect the conversation. "You said there were two issues with my offer. What was the second?"

"Oh. Well, there was just some hesitation due to your negative press."

"Your hesitation is unjustified. My name hasn't been in the press for months."

"That may be so, but the stories from the past were rather unfavorable. We would hate to see our families hesitate to come to The Helping Haven for help due to the negative connotation associated with your name."

"I understand how the biased stories shed me in a negative light, but I can assure you, this is why I asked for the sale to push through anonymously. It doesn't matter to me whether the people of California know I'm the new owner or not. It was always my intention to take over silently, and I would gladly run the company from behind the curtain. There's not a single business associate or friend that knows of my intention to buy out the organization."

"If you're not doing this for some sort of redemption in the public eye, then why are you doing this?" Sarah asks, her voice muddled with confusion.

"As I told Noelle, it's personal."

"Yes, she did say that, but I'm afraid if you have any hope of this deal going through, you're going to need to give us more of an explanation."

Sighing heavily, I bring my fingers to my face, pinching the bridge of my nose to stave off my headache. My reasoning for wanting to buy them out shouldn't fucking matter. I've promised to keep their doors open, and that should be enough. But I'm not prepared to lose this deal just to be a stubborn fuck, refusing to tell them what they want to know.

"I was twelve years old when my father died in a freak accident. My brother was barely ten. For years following his death, my mother struggled to raise us as a single parent because nobody gave us a helping hand. We nearly lost our childhood home when she lost her job. It was nearing foreclosure when she finally found a new job and was able to bounce back in the nick of time. But that didn't end her suffering. I was forced to watch her grieve on her own because she couldn't afford the mental health sessions she needed. I couldn't do anything back then—I was too young. But I can now, and I'll be damned if I sit back and watch this organization die. Not when I have the funds and the means to do something. Like I said. This isn't business—it's personal."

"I see. I wish someone could've been there for you back then, and I'm very sorry for your loss, Mr. Adams. Nonetheless, thank you for sharing with me. I can assure you, this is very personal to us too. Let me talk to Noelle and see what I can do. I'm not sure if I can change their minds, but I'll give it a try. We'll be in touch."

"Thank you. And Sarah?"

"Yes?"

"Be sure to use my personal number next time."

With that, I hang up the phone, slamming it down on the receiver. For the next several minutes, I sit in silence, staring at my desk. My rage continues to bubble at the prospect of losing this project, my mind at war with which is more important.

Personally being the one to save Riley's career out of love or saving the lives of thousands of suffering families?

I know which way my brain is leaning.

It's my fucking heart that won't fold.

44

RILEY

Two long, excruciating weeks have passed since I've seen or heard from Parker. It's been absolute radio silence—from both of our ends. Part of me keeps hoping I'll run into him when I get home from work or when I'm heading out in the morning, but nothing. Not even a glimpse of his profile since the night he walked out of here.

After months of consistent communication or seeing him almost every night, going weeks without him is damn near killing me. I might as well be missing a limb from the way his loss has been affecting me.

My heart feels like it's been ripped from my chest. Like if I don't hold myself tightly enough, all of my pieces will crumble, leaving me with nothing but a shriveled-up corpse. I just can't figure out if I feel this way from missing him or if it's from the pain he caused with his betrayal. I've spent many nights crying myself to sleep over the entire ordeal—if I sleep at all.

On top of that, my brain and my heart have been at war with each other. While my brain is adamant that leaving him was the right thing to do, my heart wants me to pick up the phone and beg him to come back to me. Hell, I've even drafted a few messages to him, only to delete them at the last minute. He's the one who messed up here, so why should I be the one to try to fix things?

Hence, the war.

I've gone over that whole week several times in my head, trying to piece everything together and gain some clarity, but no matter how I look at things, it just doesn't make any sense. I was so sure he was in love with me. Everything from his body language to his sweet gestures screamed love. The only thing missing were his actual words.

So how the hell could he do something so evil? So calculated? There's no way in hell he didn't know what that proposal would do to my life, as well as every other staff member at the zoo. Which leads me to believe his betrayal was intentional, and that's something I just can't forgive. No matter how much my heart thinks it misses him.

I'm sitting on my couch, snuggled up with a blanket and the latest journal on zoo medicine when something bangs into the wall next door. Dropping the journal to the couch, I sit up, my ears trained on the wall that connects my apartment to Parker's.

This is the first time I've heard any noise from his side of the wall, and it's got my heart in my throat, begging for any confirmation that Parker's finally home. I'm practically holding my breath just to make sure I don't miss anything over the sound of my racing heart.

Finally, another bang rings through the room, followed by voices. I jump to my feet, grabbing my keys and mindlessly rushing out of my apartment, my heart making the decision for me. I take the few steps to Parker's door and knock. A split second of indecision forms as footsteps walk toward the door. What am I going to say to him?

I'm not sure, but all I know is, a part of me has been dying since he walked out of my apartment. I'm still so angry, but the need to see him is stronger than the need to hate him.

Or at least, it was...

The door swings open, and my heart stops dead in my chest as a beautiful, slender brunette with perfectly curled hair opens the door. Her radiant smile takes up her entire face, revealing perfectly straight, white teeth. "Hey! I'm sorry, were we being too loud?"

My mouth drops open, my heart re-breaking as I take her in from head to toe. She's my exact opposite and everything I'd expect Parker to be attracted to, which only serves to hurt me more. Clearing my throat, I peek around her, doing my best to lay eyes on Parker, but it's useless. He's nowhere in sight.

"N-no, no. I-I'm sorry," I stutter out, doing everything I can to hold back the tears threatening to fall. "I was just looking for Parker, but I guess he's busy. Sorry."

I whip around, rushing toward my apartment, when the beautiful brunette follows me into the hallway and gently grabs my arm.

"Wait, there must be some confusion. I'm not sure who Parker is, but I'm Amy. My friend, Cara, and I just moved in. We're your new neighbors! The leasing office contacted us a week ago and let us know they had a sudden opening for the apartment."

My emotions are torn between relief and sadness as I process the news. While I'm certainly happy this means Parker hasn't moved *on*, I'm equally confused and hurt, wondering when the hell he moved out. How could he just leave like that without me knowing?

Attempting to pull myself together, I force a smile in Amy's direction. "Oh, wow! I'm sorry, I didn't know Parker moved out." Reaching my hand out to hers, I grasp it in a soft shake and smile. "I'm Riley. It's nice to meet you." The first tear sneaks out of the corner of my eye, forcing me to rush our meeting. "I'm sorry, if you'll excuse me, I need to run."

Her smile falters as she watches the tear trail down my face. She takes her hand from mine and mutters, "Sure, we'll see you later…"

Hurrying into my apartment, I barely have time to shut the door before the dam breaks. Tears fall from my eyes like rain as I realize our relationship really is over, any chance of us repairing the damage disappearing along with all of his things.

My phone chimes from its spot on my coffee table, interrupting my breakdown at the door. That'll be Maddie. She's been sending daily check-ins since the breakup. Walking over, I pick up my phone, confirming my theory.

Maddie: *Hey, babe. I just got off work and could use a drink. You up for some company?*

Relief filters through me at her message. If there was ever a time I needed a friend, it's now.

Riley: *I would love that. More than you know. I'm going to invite Allie if that's okay?*

Maddie: *Sure. I'll be there soon. I'll bring the wine.*

Pulling up my message thread with Allie, I shoot her off a quick text, hoping she isn't busy.

Riley: *Hey, Maddie is on her way over with wine for an impromptu girl's night. I could really use a friend right now. You in?*

Falling to the couch, I curl back up, content to sulk as I wait for the cavalry to show up with reinforcements. I drank my last bottle of wine last night while crying in the bathtub.

I consider picking up Iannah Roberts' romance novel while waiting for the girls to show up but decide against it. I finally started reading it a few weeks ago, and while the book is heartbreakingly beautiful so far, I'm just not in the right frame of mind tonight. Reading about Elle's healing while I'm so broken myself doesn't sound appealing. I'd rather wait and read it when I can fully appreciate Fin and Elle's angsty journey to love. So instead, I lie here, blankly staring at the wall.

Twenty minutes later, Maddie lets herself into my apartment with her spare key. She sets her stuff down on the kitchen table, pulling out bottles of wine. Glancing over at me on the couch, she takes me in from head to toe and slowly draws out, "Yeeeah, definitely a three bottle kind of night."

Like a freaking modern-day Mary Poppins, she reaches into her bag and pulls out a third bottle of wine and two glasses, bringing all of it to the coffee table in front of me. She pours me a full glass and hands it to me before pouring her own, plopping down on the couch next to me.

It isn't until she asks me when Allie will be here that I realize she never responded to my text, which is weird. She almost always responds. Shrugging my shoulders, I sigh, "I don't know, she never answered."

Maddie nods her head and takes another sip, an action I'm all too eager to copy. We sit in silence for a while, each of us sipping our wine. I manage to make it halfway through my glass before Maddie faces me.

And, cue the inquisition.

"Alright, spill. You've kept shit bottled up for too long. What's the update with Parker?"

Nailed it.

With a heavy sigh, I take another sip before answering, "There isn't one, really. We haven't spoken since he left my apartment two weeks ago—"

"You mean since you kicked him out," she interjects, cutting me off. I glare out of the side of my eye before continuing on like she never interrupted.

"And I just found out about an hour ago that he moved out. I heard voices next door and went to see him. Turns out, he packed up and left, leaving me with two new neighbors. He's gone, Maddie," I choke out around a sob.

She reaches over, resting her hand on my shoulder. "You didn't know he moved out?" she questions, her face full of confusion. "How the hell did you miss that? These walls are paper thin."

"I don't know. Maybe he did it while I was at work or staying with you those first few days? There's no way I was here. I would've heard it."

"Where would he have gone so fast?"

"I don't know. I know we didn't talk much that week leading up to the breakup, but surely he would've told me if his house was finished, right?"

"I don't know, Riles. The way you talked, you thought he was hiding a lot from you."

"Yeah. Or do you think he just moved somewhere else to get away from me? Maybe that was his plan all along? Bolt as soon as the damage was done?"

Glancing over, I see her shrug her shoulders while refusing to make eye contact with me. She lifts her glass to her lips and downs the whole thing, my eyebrows raising as she moves for a refill.

"You alright, Mads?"

"Uh, yeah. Sure," she shrugs.

I stare her down in disbelief, waiting for her to crack. She's never been one to hold back with me before, and I'll be damned if I let her start now.

"Alright, alright. Fine. I don't believe that for a minute."

"What?"

"Parker. All of it. I can't wrap my head around this whole situation. It doesn't make sense."

"I know. I told you—"

"Yeah, yeah. I know what you said," Maddie huffs, cutting me off again. "I just don't believe he did this on purpose."

"Well, believe it. He's had plenty of time to reach out to me if this wasn't what he wanted, and he hasn't."

"And what's stopping you from reaching out to him? Besides the anger, I mean."

Turning an incredulous look on her, I waffle at her question. Why is she sitting here pushing for me to talk to him? She's my best friend. She's supposed to be on my side here.

"He hurt me, Maddie. More than any other man ever has."

"Well, no shit. You've never given any other man the chance to hurt you."

My heart squeezes at her statement, the secrets I've kept from her rattling their cages, begging to be released. *Maybe it's time she knows the truth.*

Staring into my wine glass, I avoid all eye contact as I mumble out, "That's not entirely true."

"Hmm? What do you mean? Other than Parker, you've been holed up in SinglesVille for as long as I've known you."

"Well, yeah. I've been single, but that doesn't mean men haven't hurt me."

Glancing at her, I take in her puzzled face, confirming my decision to finally be honest with her. "There's something I've never told you," I whisper, looking back down at my glass of wine, wishing it was something stronger.

"What is it, babe?" Her voice is full of concern, and I'm glad we have that third bottle of wine. We're going to need it after I rock the foundation of our friendship with my best-kept secret.

"Part of the reason I have so many insecurities is because of you."

She rears back, her brow furrowing as her cheeks heat with emotion. "Me? What the fuck? I've never done anything but try to build you up, so how is it my fault you're insecure? I tell you you're beautiful all the time!"

"No, no. That's not what I mean. You've never intentionally made me feel insecure, but that doesn't mean my feelings are baseless." Taking a deep breath, I shed light on our past, explaining why she's half the reason I've been single all these years. "Back in college, I loved being your roommate. We got along so well, and you always felt like the sister I'd been missing. But what you never seemed to notice was how many men you hooked up with because I introduced you to them."

Her brow sinks over her eyes, confusion written clearly on her face. "Ooh-kayyy?"

"You didn't think it was weird that I never went out to parties or social gatherings but somehow always had a new boy for you to meet?"

Her eyes flit back and forth between mine as she thinks back on our time at college, ten years ago, trying to put the pieces together. "Yeah, I guess that is a little weird. What were you doing, standing out on a corner, hookin' for my men?" She jokes, shoving my shoulder with a laugh as she tries to lighten the mood.

I spare her half a smile as I clarify, "Well, not exactly. It's more like they would find me."

"Huh? What the hell does that mean?"

Sighing, I take a hefty drink of my wine before mumbling, "Do you remember that party we went to together?"

"You mean the one and only party you ever joined me at? Yeah, I remember. Parts of it, anyway," she jokes with another laugh, and I know exactly what she means.

She had quite a bit to drink that night and ended up hooking up with some man she had spent the night dancing with. And who wouldn't? The man was gorgeous. Not that it really mattered in my case. Just like every other man I met in college, the dude only had eyes for Maddie.

I, on the other hand, ended up going back to our dorm. *Alone.*

"Didn't you meet someone that night? I distinctly remember you talking to a really cute guy in the kitchen. You were still with him when I headed for the dance floor," she questions excitedly.

"Yeah, I met someone. If you can call it that. But you don't remember hooking up with that very same guy the next week?"

Her eyes widen in shock, a gasp ripping from her throat. She shakes her head and shouts, "What? No way. That wasn't the same guy. There's no way I'd do that to you."

"It was the same guy, but I know you didn't do it to me on purpose. In fact, I introduced you to him that next week at the coffee shop. You two hit it off, and you wham-bammed him shortly after."

She gives my shoulder another shove—this one rougher than the last. "What the hell, Riley. Why'd you set us up, then? You practically shoved me on his lap. Why would you do that if you wanted him for yourself?"

"Because he asked me to," I yell, the feelings I've kept bottled up over the years finally exploding.

She rears back, shocked by my anger. We've never fought before, not even when we lived together in college, so this is a first for both of us.

Sighing, I look away, a few sneaky tears leaking from my eyes.

A couple moments of silence pass between us before Maddie places her hand gently on my arm, whispering, "Riley, I didn't know. Why didn't you say anything?"

"I didn't know what to say. The truth is, once that guy realized I was your roommate at the party, our entire conversation shifted. Any interest he had in me flew out the window when he figured out he could use me to get to you. He started asking all these questions, trying to get to know you through me, and when he asked me if I could introduce you two, my heart was crushed. I loved you so much, and I knew you were gorgeous. The problem is, so did every other man on campus. There was no doubt in my mind why men would choose you over me.

"And the worst part is, it didn't end there. After Shawn—that was his name, by the way, in case you forgot. After he hooked up with you that week, news spread like a wildfire that I could hook any guy on campus up with you. And sure enough, one man turned to two, and then five, and then I started to lose track. Men would seek me out and ask for your number or ask where you were planning on hanging out that night. Hell, some of them were even bold enough to ask me to introduce you to them personally, which is exactly what I did."

"But why?" she demands angrily. Jumping up from the couch, she faces me, her posture stiff and her face flushed. "Why the hell would you do that to yourself?"

"Because it's not me they wanted! It was you," I shout again, the lid I've kept on my pain all these years finally blowing off. Standing, I face her, tears streaming down my face as I cry out, "It was always you. I've never held a candle to you, so why bother trying to keep any of them for myself when it wasn't me they wanted?"

"Because you deserved them more than me! You had so much more to offer than I did. Hell, you still do. You're beautiful and smart and loyal. You're not afraid to commit, and that's more than I could ever say for myself." I watch as she smashes her finger into her chest, a tear slipping down her cheek, shocking me to the bone. In all the years I've known her, I've never seen her cry, and watching that one single tear fall down my best friend's face drains the fight right out of me.

Flinging myself down on the couch, I tip my head back, resting it against the couch. My eyes close as I answer her, exhaustion coating my voice. "Well, it doesn't matter now. Eventually, I just gave up. Finding a boyfriend was impossible when they were all interested in my best friend. I didn't want to have to worry about whether or not the man I was dating was just trying to get to you through me. Or fret over whether he was checking you out every time you walked into the room."

Several minutes of silence pass between us, but I can't bear to open my eyes and see Maddie's reaction. I knew this would hurt her, but I can't let her pain distract me from my own. I've been holding this in for so long, I refuse to push my pain to the side any longer.

The couch dips beside me as Maddie sinks beside me. Her hand falls gently to my lap, squeezing my leg as I continue. "I've spent the last several years feeling unlovable because I wasn't pretty enough for those guys. I wasn't worth them sparing me a second glance once they saw you. I wasn't funny enough to hold their attention, or wild enough to demand it. Simply put, I was never enough. I always came in last place, and I didn't want to feel that way anymore. So I just avoided it entirely, choosing to focus on my studies and my career instead."

With a trembling voice, Maddie whispers, "I'm so sorry, Riley. I had no idea you felt that way. Why didn't you ever say something?"

"I don't know. I guess I was scared to lose your friendship. You were one of my only friends in college, and I didn't want you to think I was just jealous. I never wanted boys to come between us. It was so much easier to just let them have you than to threaten the bond we had."

"But that's the thing, Riley. They never would have. Hell, if I knew the boys were using you to get to me, I wouldn't have touched them with a ten-foot pole. Instead, you just let me step all over your heart by sleeping with all of them, never speaking up over how that was hurting you. I mean, what the fuck, boo? You've gotta stand up for yourself! No one else can do that for you."

"I know, Maddie. But that doesn't make it any easier."

Sighing, she leans back, resting against the couch as she stares up at the ceiling. I take a drink of my wine, giving her time to reflect on my giant truth bomb. Eventually, her head moves against the couch as she tilts her face toward me.

"But what about Parker?"

"What about him?" I ask, confusion lacing my voice.

"Where does he fit in with all of this?"

"I don't know what you mean, exactly. But that's why I was so scared to introduce you two that night after the game. I had this overwhelming fear that he'd be yet another man that'd leave me for you. I've seen the beautiful women he's had on his arm in the past. I knew for a fact that you fit that image more than I ever could, so I tried to hide you away, hoping you two wouldn't meet until I knew for sure he wanted me for me. And even then, I knew there was a chance he'd leave me. I just hoped for once, he'd be the man that chose me instead."

"And he did, Riley," she huffs. Sitting up, she turns her body to face me, her eyes pleading with mine. "That man barely spared me a glance. He only had eyes for you, babe."

"His friends sure did, though," I counter with a forced laugh. "You should've heard what they were all saying after you walked away that night at the arena."

Her voice kicks up a notch as she argues, "But Parker didn't. Who cares what his friends think, as long as he's only interested in you."

"That's what you're missing here, Maddie! Clearly, he wasn't interested in me. He was using me too. He just did it differently than the other men." My voice rises alongside my frustration, making me feel slightly guilty. None of this is Maddie's fault. *Not really, anyway.*

"What? Oh, hell no. There's no way that man was just using you, Riley. He had hearts in his eyes, and anyone that looked at him could see it. Anybody but you, apparently," she spits out sarcastically.

"You're wrong." *How the hell does she still not understand?*

"Alright, Riley. If I'm wrong, then what the hell was he using you for? Because it sure as hell wasn't to get to me. Not once did he make any sort of advance toward me, and you two broke up over two weeks ago and I haven't so much as received a friend request on Facebook. So what was he using you for?"

"He might not have been using me to get to you, but he was definitely using me. I just haven't figured out how exactly. It could've been to fix his image in the press or to somehow use my connection to the zoo to profit his business."

"MMM, yeah. I don't think either of those theories are right," she spits out with sass, mocking me.

Whipping my head toward her, I frown. "How could you possibly say that? I told you about the zoo proposal. The man was trying to shut down the entire zoo. He knew that'd mean I'd lose my job. Why would he do that if he gave a damn about me?"

"That's the thing, Riley. He wouldn't. And you said yourself he said there was a misunderstanding, but you never gave him a chance to explain. You just booted him out of your life with zero hesitation."

Silence descends upon us as I digest her words, wondering if maybe she's right. Should I have let him explain? The evidence was pretty damning against him, written there in black and white, so how could that have been misunderstood? My head swims with the same questions I've been fighting with for weeks now, wondering if I did the right thing at all.

Taking my silence as an agreement, Maddie moves closer to me, grabbing my hand in hers.

"Look, I understand now why you feel the way you do, and I get why you may have jumped to conclusions here, but Parker's different from those guys in college. You need to give him a chance to explain. And while you're at it, stop doubting your worth. You'll never know love if you spend every minute of your life comparing yourself to others. There's no need to try to be anybody else when you're you! You have your own flaws and your own beautiful qualities, and you're worthy of an epic love. And I genuinely believe Parker is that love for you. You just have to be willing to put your trust in him. Open your heart to the possibility that that man wants you and only you, despite having access to every beautiful woman in and out of San Diego. That man chose you, and until you threw him out, he chose you every day. Remember that when you want to compare yourself to the cover models that came before you. Parker. Chose. You."

My heart squeezes at the conviction in her voice, begging me to believe her as a few tears slide down my cheeks. I've spent years hating myself for every flaw I possess, when the truth is, I do have my own beauty. It might not be cover model beauty, but it's beauty, nonetheless.

"You're right. He did choose me. And I do love him, Maddie. I do. But I'm scared. What if it wasn't a misunderstanding? What if he really did mean to close down the zoo?"

"You'll never know unless you talk to him. Besides, you've been broken up for two weeks, and I haven't heard anything about the zoo closing. Have you? Surely he would've moved forward with that by now if that was his true intention, especially since you aren't together anymore. What is there to hold him back, if not you?"

My eyes widen as I realize she's right. I haven't heard a word about the zoo closing, nor have I heard of anybody losing their job.

Holy shit.

"Exactly. You need to reach out to him. Figure out what really happened."

"I know, I know. I will," I promise, meaning every word.

"Soon, Riley. Before he moves on for good."

Nodding my head, I agree to reach out to him tomorrow. As much as I'd love to call him right now, I need to clear my mind and approach this with a level head. Between my talk with Maddie and the realization that I might've put us both through this hurt for nothing, I'm way too emotionally raw tonight. But tomorrow...tomorrow I'll get my man back.

45

PARKER

Slouching in my office chair, I stare at the bottle of bourbon sitting on my shelf, contemplating a drunken bender. The clock on the wall audibly ticks, the sound echoing off my empty walls, driving me fucking mad. Settling on a decision, I twist the top off the bottle, pouring the contents into a tumbler.

Raising the glass, I swirl the contents, inhaling the smoky scent of the bourbon. The first sip has barely passed my lips when the door to my office swings open, Haylee bounding in like she's on a mission.

"What the hell is this?" She demands, waving her hand that's clutching today's newspaper.

"A newspaper," I answer, my tone dripping with sarcasm. Haylee rolls her eyes and flips the newspaper around, reading the headline out loud.

"Reputation Redeemed: Parker Adams Saves the Families of California."

Taking another sip of my bourbon, I roll my eyes at the headline splashed across every tabloid and newspaper today. For once, it's for a good cause—something I wished for months ago. If only I could find it in me to give a fuck now.

"What are they talking about? Why didn't I know about this?" Haylee screeches at me, still waving the newspaper around like a psycho.

"Because you weren't supposed to. Nobody was, but much to my dismay, nobody fucking knows how to keep shit quiet these days."

"Parker, why the hell would you want to keep this quiet? This is PR gold."

"I didn't want it to be PR gold," I shout, slamming my tumbler down on my desk.

Haylee's eyes snap up to mine, her face paling at my anger. "Parker," she whispers, dropping the newspaper to her side.

"Just get out."

She stands there watching me for a moment before her head bows, nodding a few times before she glances back up at me. "Okay, okay. I'll leave you for now, but this discussion isn't over."

The fuck it isn't.

Picking up my glass, I swivel around in my chair, dismissing her as I face the windows. The door softly clicks behind her before I release a heavy sigh, the anger inside me deflating in a rush as sadness creeps back in.

A few nights ago, I received a call from Noelle herself, agreeing to the terms of the sale. We met halfway between Anaheim and San Diego last night to finalize the deal.

I should be happy right now. Hell, I should be out fucking celebrating. This is what I've been working toward for the last several years. Every dollar I made was for this exact purpose—to give my life the meaning it craved.

But it means nothing without Riley here to bask in the success with me.

Suddenly, the thing I wanted most isn't even at the top of my list. Now, whenever I think of success, I see a pretty little redhead at the forefront of my mind. A house full of mini-Rileys running around. A goddamn dog barking in the backyard as it chases around our happy children.

I see a fucking future I'll never have.

My phone rings, the shrill tone replacing the annoying ticks of the clock I was listening to, but I ignore it, knowing it's nobody I want to talk to right now.

The ringing ends, only to start back up a second later. I know that, because the clock only ticked once. Growling loudly, I whip around, picking the phone up and yelling, "What?"

"Parker, honey, I saw the newspaper. Is it true? Did you purchase The Helping Haven?"

For once, my mom's soothing tone does nothing to calm my inner suffering. I love her dearly, but there's only one person in the world I want to talk to, and she hates my fucking guts.

"Yes. I'm sorry, Mom, but now's not a good time. I'll call you later."

"Don't you dare hang up on me, young man," my mother's sharp tone barks down the line, forcing a sigh up my throat as I bring the phone back to my ear.

I don't bother responding because she knows I didn't hang up, but if she's so inclined to speak to me right now, she can carry this conversation.

"What is going on with you, Parker? This is the most selfless thing I've ever seen you do, and I've never been so proud. Aren't you happy?"

"No."

She's quiet for a few blessed moments, and I'm ready to risk it all and hang up, just to avoid what I know is coming next.

"Is this about Riley?" she whispers, her voice returning to a soothing tone.

I don't answer her—there's no need to.

"Have you spoken to her since the break-up?"

"It's a break-up for a reason, Mother. Of course, we haven't spoken." *Not that I haven't tried.*

"You need to fight for her, Parker," she begs from her end of the call, her words an echo of Rhett's from weeks ago.

"Why, so love can continue to wreck me the way it wrecked you? No fucking thanks."

I close my eyes as my words escape my mouth. Not that I don't mean them, but this isn't her battle, and she shouldn't have to be reminded of her own heartache just because I'm hurting.

"Is that what you think?" she whispers, her sadness seeping through the phone, wrapping a fist around my throat.

She's silent, waiting me out as I do my best to choke back the hurt in my voice. "Love is trash, Mom. I never should've broken my damn celibacy pact. I could've been at the top of the world right now instead of in the goddamn pits of heartbreak hell."

"Parker Adams. Love isn't trash. It's anything but. How could you say that?"

"It is fucking trash, Mom! It wrecked you, and now it's wrecking me."

"Honey. Love didn't wreck me. It wounded me, sure, but it didn't wreck me. Love gave me your father. It gave me you and your brother. And when your father died, love gave me pain. Pain that reminded me every single day that I was still here, that I still had a reason to live—two of them, actually."

Her voice wavers with emotion as she continues on. "Do I wish your father was still with us? Of course. Every day. But I wouldn't trade a single day of the love we shared to be able to avoid that earth-shattering agony when he died. Love made the suffering worth it because I know without our love, my life wouldn't look the way it does now. Love gave me memories I wouldn't trade for the world, and I would suffer the hurt of losing your father every single day, over and over again, if it meant I got to experience one day of the love we shared."

Her words break my heart all over again because I know deep in my soul, she's right. If given a chance, I'd go back in time, just to relive every happy day Riley and I did have together.

"This pain you're feeling, all it means is that Riley is it for you. She's the one. I've known it for some time now, and I think you have too. You're clearly not over her if your attitude is any indication. Which means you need to buck up and save your relationship before it's too late."

"I'm not the one that should be doing the saving, Mom. I didn't do anything wrong."

"That's where you're wrong, Parker. You may not have done the breaking up, but you're letting your pride stop you from fixing things, and that's just as bad as what she did."

With a final sigh, my mother sadly begs, "Don't let the clock expire on your love before it was meant to. Life is too short to be alone and unhappy when you still have the ability to change that. Not everybody is lucky enough to do the same."

The soft click of her hanging up on me forces an unwanted tear to fall from my eye. She's right. Life is too fucking short for this. But Riley isn't the only relationship that needs repairing. And something deep inside me tells me there's a different bond that needs fixing before I can fix everything else that's broken.

46

RILEY

Hanging my purse on a hook, I plop down at my desk. My computer whirls to life as I sip on my coffee, waiting for my schedule to load. Once it does, I sigh in relief. I've never been so grateful for a slow day.

It's been a few days since Maddie and I talked, and with each night that passes, I lose more and more sleep. I know I told Maddie I'd talk to Parker that next day, but after tossing and turning that whole night, trying to figure out what I'd say, I chickened out. I'm just not sure I'm ready to see him yet. Our fight was so nasty, I'm not sure how to climb the mountain of hurt between us now. But I know I need to try, which is why I plan on talking to him tonight. He has no reason to give me a second chance, but every cell in my body prays he still feels something for me and will hear me out.

Closing out my schedule, I bring up my email, tapping my fingers against the desk as I wait for the page to load. Raising my cup to my mouth, I click on the administration inbox with a flag, indicating I have a new email from the higher-ups.

My hand halts halfway to my mouth, my coffee cup suspended in the air as I read the subject line of their email.

Subject: Zoo Closure Beginning Next Week

I stare at the words, my gut clenching as anger courses through my blood. Maddie damn near had me convinced this was a misunderstanding the other night, that this wasn't really happening, but this proves I was stupid to listen to her. I can't believe I was going to call him tonight, giving him another chance to rip my fucking heart out.

I sit in a daze, staring at my computer, refusing to open the email. I'm not ready to face the fact that my entire life is about to change. Where will I go? What will I do? What's going to happen to the animals? Who's going to take care of them? Will they stay together?

Some of these animals have been together since birth. Splitting them up from their current habitat mates could be devastating to their health. People tend to forget that animals are fully capable of developing depression, which is exactly what will happen to these animals when they're torn from their animal friends and shipped off to different zoos. These poor, defenseless animals are going to suffer because some selfish asshole decided to put his company before them. *And to think he claimed to be an animal lover.*

I'm still staring at my computer, avoiding the email when my office door crashes open, bouncing off the wall. Allie rushes in, excitement shining on her face.

"Have you seen the email?" She squeals, bouncing with joy.

My brow furrows, confused over her excitement. Why is she so happy over losing her job? I thought she loved it here as much as I did.

"No. I read the subject line and couldn't bring myself to read an email that will end my career with this zoo. I have so many memories here. I can't believe this is how it all ends."

Her excitement quickly transforms to confusion as she blurts out, "What? No. Riley, read the email. This is the best news we could've hoped for."

"How could the zoo closing be good news? Are you high? And where were you last night? You never answered my text."

"Never mind that," she brushes off while running around my desk. She shoves my hand out of the way and opens the very email I've been ignoring. "You have to read this. The zoo isn't closing, it's expanding!"

"What?" I shout, sitting up in my chair to get a better look at my screen.

My eyes shoot back and forth at Mach speed as I read the email, word for word. Phrases like "safari-themed mini-park" and "zoo closed for construction" jump out at me as my mind works to understand what's happening.

"Isn't this great, Riley? Think of all the people this will bring to the zoo. And we get a paid vacation! Can you believe it?"

"I don't understand…"

"We aren't closing. They're going to restructure sections of the zoo to add a mini safari-themed amusement park. The entire monkey exhibit will be moving to the eastern part of the zoo, along with the Panda Trek. This is going to be so cool. And they added additional security features to the exhibits, so there's no chance of animals escaping again," she squeals.

"They scheduled the red-ribbon cutting for a little over two months. I guess whoever was behind this proposal hired all the crews they could, paying extra money to have this project completed in a quarter of the time it would normally take. And they're giving us a paid vacation while they shut down for construction. Essential personnel will be allowed to come and go to make sure the animals are all cared for, but otherwise, we get two weeks off while they set up the construction zone and break ground on the new exhibits!"

I didn't need Allie to explain it all—I can read just fine. What

I don't understand…is how I could be so wrong. It feels like there's a boa constrictor wrapping around my chest, squeezing the breath right out of my lungs as realization sets in. The words from Parker's proposal I saw a few weeks ago flit through my mind as I work to piece things together.

He kept saying there was a misunderstanding, but I refused to believe him. Now here I am, staring at the evidence of my wrongful accusations. *He really wasn't lying.*

Which means I was wrong. So, so fucking wrong.

Standing, I grab my purse, rushing to my door.

"Where are you going?" Allie questions, halting me in my tracks. I was so focused on fixing my mistake, I forgot I was still at work.

Turning back, I explain, "I have to go see Parker. He was telling the truth the whole time, and I really messed up. I need to see him and try to fix this. I'm so sorry. Can you cover for me today? I promise I'll make it up to you. Just tell everyone I went home sick or something, I don't care. I need to go," I plead with urgency.

A giant smile takes over Allie's face as she rushes toward me, pushing me out the door. I nearly stumble over my feet at her force but manage to stay upright.

"Of course. Go, go! Maddie is going to be so excited. She knew you were wrong."

Despite my eagerness to see Parker and set all this straight, a small part of me is riddled with fear. What if he doesn't want to see me? The things I said to him… *Ugh.* I was so horrible. He has every right to hate me now. I just hope he still wants me too.

47

PARKER

"Thank you for joining me today, gentlemen." Mr. Klein nods his head while Rory aims a scowl in my direction as I take a seat behind my desk. I've called this meeting because, no matter how badly I want to mend things with my brother, I can't allow him to take away one of my clients. The last thing I need is for my reputation to start suffering again.

That, and I need this company to continue funding my plans for The Helping Haven, which includes the money I'll rake in with Mr. Klein's business.

"Mr. Klein, would you like to fill Rory in on our conversation from yesterday? Or would you like me to?"

Crossing his legs, he rests an ankle against his opposite knee, leaning back in the chair across from my desk. "Go ahead," he draws out in a bored, lazy tone, unaware my next words will cause yet another strain on my brother and me. Not that that matters to him. As long as his account is taken care of, he couldn't give a shit less what happens in my personal life—business is business.

"Right. Okay, then. Rory, despite your brave attempt to poach my client, Mr. Klein has decided to remain with my company."

Rory's face flushes at my words, his temper rising, just like I knew it would. Hopefully, what I have to offer him will help smooth things over.

"Is that right?" he sneers, his gaze briefly moving to Mr. Klein before returning his glare to me. *Or, maybe not.*

"That's right," Mr. Klein responds with a dip of his head. "Don't get me wrong, boy, I admire your balls for going against your brother, and while I was thrilled with what you were offering, my board feels it's best to stick with a company that hasn't led us astray thus far."

"We haven't led you astray thus far, either," Rory spits out, barely concealing his anger. "And we wouldn't if you'd just give us a chance."

"That may be true, but now's not a good time to switch sides, if you get what I'm saying. Parker and his team already know the ins and outs of my company. Taking the time to familiarize you and your company with our practices would do nothing but lose us ground—ground we have no time to lose."

Rory's lip curls in disgust as he continues to glare at me, ignoring Mr. Klein's words. "What did he do, use his filthy money to bribe you into staying?"

My eyebrows raise in annoyance. It's one thing to insult me in private, but doing so in front of a client is unacceptable. I know my brother's a better businessman than that. He's just too blinded by his misguided hatred toward me. Clearing my throat, I pin him with an unforgiving stare while maintaining a level tone with my response. "I assure you, I did nothing of the sort. Mr. Klein's board simply knows what's best for their company."

Rory opens his mouth to respond before he's cut off by Mr. Klein, who's watched our interaction like a spectator at a tennis match, his eyes bouncing back and forth between Rory and me. "Well, if you'll excuse me, boys," he announces, standing from his seat and buttoning his suit jacket. "I have things to do, and this meeting no longer pertains to me."

"Of course. Thanks for your time, Mr. Klein." Standing, I button my own suit jacket before reaching my hand out to shake his own. "My assistant, Haylee, will be in touch with the details of our agreement."

He nods his head once and exits the room, leaving me alone with a fuming Rory.

"Are we fucking finished here?" He sneers, standing from his seat in a rush.

"Actually, we aren't. I have something else I want to discuss with you."

"I assure you," he snarls, mocking my earlier words, "There's nothing else I'd like to discuss with you. You can keep your brainwashed clients. I'll find a different way to bring you down."

"Would you drop the fucking attitude, Rory? You don't even want this career. You're just acting like a child, trying to take back a toy you don't even want. Let it the fuck go and move on."

"Are you shitting me?" he roars, his face turning an ugly shade of red.

"Lower your voice. Right now," I quietly seethe, spitting the words from between clenched teeth as his immature behavior grates on my nerves.

The door to my office swings open as Haylee peeks her head in with a worried look. "Is everything okay here, boys?"

"Leave the room, Haylee. We're fine," I bark out, my eyes never leaving Rory. The thick vein at his temple pulses, and the last thing I need is my assistant to witness my brother punching me.

She hesitates briefly, her eyes flickering between the two of us before she nods. The door clicks softly behind her, leaving us alone to face off.

"No. I'm not shitting you. I've been watching you for the last several years, Rory, and you can lie to yourself all you want, but you can't lie to me. You don't even want this career. You're not happy with it, but instead of accepting that and finding something else you'd actually enjoy, you're hanging on to it with a death grip to try and hurt me with shady-ass business tactics. You're better than that, Rory, and the only one you're hurting is yourself."

"Who the hell do you think you are to tell me what I do or don't enjoy? I love it just as much as I did back as a kid. You and I both fucking know this was my career choice before it was ever yours."

"That may be true, but you don't want it nearly enough, and it fucking shows."

"Wrong again, brother. If anything, I want it even more now."

"No, you don't. This isn't even a career to you anymore. It's a fucking job that you wake up and dread going to. All you want is to bring me down and make me suffer for the pain you're feeling —pain that isn't my doing—and every time you fail, you hate your job a little more. Just fucking admit it so we can end this pointless feud and move on. I have a plan for you, one that I know you'll actually enjoy."

"Fuck you and your plan. You think you can just run everybody's lives, taking over whatever the hell you want, but you can't take over my life. You've taken everything else from me, but you won't take my choice. I don't want a single fucking part of any 'plan' you think you have."

"For the last time, I didn't take shit from you. I won't apologize for pursuing the same field as you in college, because unlike you, I love this career. I wake up every single morning and breathe life into my company while you do the bare minimum to keep your job. Despite what you think, it's possible for two members of a family to work the same fucking career and both be successful, as long as they both want it—which clearly, they don't.

"As for your misguided assumption that you were the outcast of our family after Dad died, you're wrong, and I won't apologize for that either because that's your cross to bear. If you'd lower your goddamn guard, you'd see that Mom loves you just as much as she loves me. If anything, she tried to love you harder because she could see how lost you were when Dad died. It was no secret that you two were as thick as thieves, and when we lost him, we lost you to your grief. You pushed everyone away, rejecting the idea that you still had two other family members that loved you. You dealt with your suffering in your own way, which is more than acceptable, but you can't blame others for how you fixed yourself. You built a goddamn fortress around you, keeping everyone else out. So don't blame me for the love you think you were lacking.

"And as for Sabrina, I never took her from you. I never wanted her in the goddamn first place, but if anything, I saved you from a fucking slut that never deserved you. She was willing to wear your ring and use your love for her gain, all the while trying to sleep with your brother—a brother that never even had her on his radar. I'll apologize for not seeing the signs of her unfaithfulness earlier, but I won't apologize for your relationship crumbling. If it didn't end that day, it would have ended when you caught her cheating with some other weak fuck. I wasn't to blame for your relationship falling apart. She was."

With a heavy sigh, I lower my voice, desperately trying to reach my brother with these last words. "I don't hate you, Rory, and I've never conspired to destroy your life, as you seem to think. Open your eyes and see that I am trying my damnedest to help you right now. All I want is for you to get out of your own way and be happy."

The room falls into silence, the air between us thickening with tension. I wait with bated breath as Rory's eyes bore into mine, his brow furrowing as he considers the sincerity in my words.

Just as I think he's about to forgive me, allowing us both to move past this, his face clouds with renewed anger, venom dripping from his words as he spits out, "Fuck you and your bullshit lies, Parker. I don't want your help, and I sure as hell don't need it. Especially not to be happy, considering you're the reason I'm not. I'm not some naive client with eyes you can pull the wool over. I see you for the slimeball you truly are, and I'll never forgive you for what you've done to me. I may not be able to take Mom's love from you, and I'll never try to take Riley from you because that's a line only a selfish asshole would cross, but I can fucking destroy you and this company. I'll take back my dream if it's the last thing I do, just to fucking prove you wrong."

With that, he turns his back on me and storms out, the door slamming behind him. My shoulders slump with exhaustion, a sense of defeat filling my heart. That's not how I wanted this to go, but I should've known he'd never listen to me or accept the truth in my words. Anger is a powerful thing, and he's been holding on to it for well over half our lives, allowing it to poison his mind and his heart. It's going to take a hell of a lot more than a few emotional words for him to drop his weapons and see things for how they really are.

I'd give anything to have my brother back, but I can't fix this on my own, and I refuse to accept fault for crimes I didn't commit just so he can claim victory over a war I want no part of.

When I signed my name on those final checks for The Helping Haven, effectively taking over and switching the board-ran organization to a partnership, I had a dream for what came next. I knew exactly who I wanted beside me to run the new company.

But as I stand here with my hands in my pockets, my back

turned on the door my spiteful brother just stormed out of, I realize that's all it was.

A giant fucking pipe-dream.

48

RILEY

Stepping out of my parked car, I look up at the tall building that houses Parker's company. The sky behind his office has darkened with an impending storm, setting my nerves on edge. The air feels charged with electricity, and fat raindrops pepper the ground around me, turning the sidewalk a dark grey.

The wind picks up, whipping my hair around my face as I rush toward the building doors to escape the sky's wrath. Once inside, I do my best to tame my wild hair while I cross to the elevators. Pressing the button, I wait impatiently for it to arrive, my nerves growing as each second ticks by. A howling outside catches my ear, and I turn toward the front windows, watching as the strong wind bows the few palm trees in front of the building.

A shiver runs down my spine as I watch the storm gather speed, praying it isn't a foreboding sign of what's to come.

The ding of the elevator sounds, pulling my attention forward. The steel doors are barely open when a tall, attractive man barrels out, rudely brushing against my shoulder as he storms past me. I barely catch a glimpse of him, but it's enough to make a lasting impression. He has dark hair, broad shoulders, gorgeous green eyes, and wears an angry expression beautifully.

Looking over my shoulder, I watch as the mystery man shoves his way past the entrance doors and into the raging storm, leaving a path of anger in his wake. There's something oddly familiar about him, but I'm sure I've never met him—he has a face you'd never forget.

Turning back, I hurry through the closing elevator doors, settling into a corner of the empty cart. My stomach fills with manic butterflies as I arrive on Parker's floor a short ride later, but I know this is where I'm supposed to be. There's not a single doubt in my mind that Parker is the love of my life. Now I just have to convince him of that too, no matter how much of an uphill battle it may be.

Parker's assistant is nowhere to be found when I reach his office. Not knowing whether I should wait for her to return or push forward, I stand there like an idiot, wringing my hands with nerves. Looking down at the floor, I take a few deep breaths, trying my best to steady my racing heart.

A few minutes pass as I stand there and wait, but Haylee doesn't return. Taking one last deep breath, I lift my head and straighten my spine before walking up to Parker's door, ready to face the firing squad.

It's now or never.

Turning the door handle, I quietly push the door open, making sure he isn't on the phone or in a meeting. Thankfully, the room is quiet and empty, save for Parker. He's standing at his floor-to-ceiling windows, his strong back facing me as he stares out at the raging sea.

Tension rolls off him in waves, matching the ocean's energy, and I wish for nothing more than to run to him—to soothe the anguish he appears to be suffering. He lifts both of his hands, running them through his hair roughly before gripping the ends, his white, long-sleeved shirt straining against his biceps with the movement.

I manage to take two hesitant steps toward Parker before the door softly clicks behind me, alerting him to my presence. I'm halted in my tracks by a level of rage I wasn't expecting, his voice booming through the room as he yells, "Get the fuck out!"

I knew he might not be thrilled to see me. Hell, I was expecting some sort of anger, but I didn't prepare for such hostility.

"O-oh. Okay. S-Sorry," I manage to squeak out, ready to run from his office.

Parker whips around at my voice, his face morphing from angry to shocked. His eyes widen, and his hands drop from his hair, leaving it a wild mess. His body is still rigid and tense, but his mood seems slightly more relaxed than it was moments before.

"Riley? What the hell are you doing here?" He questions, his face twisting in confusion. The mere sight of him nearly takes my breath away. He looks so mean and broody, much like he was when I first met him. Just an angry, lost soul, searching for a reason to exist.

"Are you okay?" I whisper, ignoring his question.

Releasing a heavy sigh, he turns his head, looking back over his shoulder at the violent storm. Without making eye contact, he gruffly answers, "The storm…it came out of nowhere."

Despite all the mixed-up, confusing feelings I have for this man right now, my heart breaks for him as I remember his post-coitus confession months ago. "I'm sorry," I sigh. "I can't imagine how much you must miss your dad."

Still facing the window, I watch as his body tenses at my words. Clearing his throat, he turns to face me again before demanding, "You didn't answer my question. Why are you here?"

Breaking eye contact, I peer at the floor between us as I gather my thoughts. I do my best not to fidget under his hard stare as I glance back up at him, meeting his confused eyes. My voice wavers slightly with nerves as I answer honestly. "I'm sorry for dropping by unannounced, but I was hoping we could talk."

"Yeah, because that went so well last time," he scoffs. My cheeks heat with embarrassment, but I can't deny the truth to his words. Last time was a disaster.

"I can't take back what happened last time we were together, but I'm here now, and I'm ready to listen this time."

Refusing to look away, I watch as his temper rises, coloring his face. He shoves his hands in the pockets of his designer suit pants, rocking back on his heels as he shakes his head. "And why the hell should I bother explaining shit now? You discarded our entire relationship without a second thought, but now you want to hear my side? After weeks of silence?"

"I was wrong. I know that—"

"You're damn right you were wrong, Riley," he yells, cutting me off. "Jesus. I did nothing but try to spoil you and show you how much you meant to me. But you had no problem labeling me a user and a liar before tossing me out the door. You cheapened everything we had, all because of a misunderstanding. Something I tried to tell you over and over, but you just wouldn't listen."

"I know, and I'm sorry for that. But that's why I'm here. What's really going on, Parker? I got an email today from the zoo owners talking about new construction? I don't understand," I say, my voice pleading with him.

Scoffing, he snidely says, "Yeah, I'm sure you don't."

"Please, Parker," I beg, trying and failing to keep the tremble out of my voice. "I'm sorry. I never should've said those things about you. I was angry and hurt, and I wasn't thinking clearly. My feelings for you are stronger than any I've ever had, and I was devastated over being hurt by the only man I've ever let close to me, so when I saw those papers, I jumped the gun and hurt you back. It was childish and wrong, and I'm so, so sorry."

A moment of silence passes as he continues to scowl at me.

There's a good chance he's not going to give me a second chance, and the thought of losing him forever has fear strangling my heart. I never should've treated him the way I did, and judging by his silence, it might end up being the biggest mistake of my life.

I watch in silence as his eyes travel up and down my body, never giving me an inkling as to what he may be thinking.

Finally, he releases a heavy sigh and unfolds his arms, taking a step closer to his desk. Pulling a side drawer open, he grabs a stack of papers that look like they've seen better days. They're creased, crinkled, and torn in a few places. He tosses them down on the desk between us before slamming the desk drawer closed, folding his arms once again. A few of the papers scatter, but looking down at them, I know it's the same proposal I saw that night in my apartment.

He nudges his chin toward the stack of papers, but I don't bother picking them up. I already know what they say.

"Like I tried to explain the night you found this, the entire proposal was bullshit. I spent that entire week before coming up with a plan to save the zoo, but I'd signed a non-disclosure agreement and couldn't tell you anything. It was the hardest secret to keep because I knew how stressed and worried you were over the possibility of losing your job. But, despite the shitty way you thought of me, I was never going to let that happen."

Heat blooms in my cheeks, and I peer down at the mess of papers between us, avoiding his gaze. Once again, he's right. I did everything I could to force myself to believe he was the enemy that night, when in all reality, it was me who caused our downfall.

Clearing his throat, he continues, but I can't find it in me to look him in the face as he breaks down what really happened. "The file you saw wasn't what I spent all week putting together. Haylee made a giant mistake and messed up the proposal. I found out later that she was worried over her mother's health and rushed through the changes I requested. She fucked up and submitted a proposal full of wrong information. I had to bribe the city office with a shit ton of money to get them to reconsider the new, corrected proposal. I just got confirmation a few days ago that the job is moving forward. Crews were hired, and work should be starting next week. Congratulations, you get to keep your job," he sneers, his voice void of emotion.

Finally looking up at him, I wince at the anger swirling deep in his blue eyes, but it's not enough to stop me from asking the question that's been burning my tongue since I walked in.

"So the zoo isn't closing down?"

"No, Riley. The zoo isn't closing. It was never going to," he sasses, irritation coating his words.

Tears fill the bottom of my eyelids, but I do everything I can to keep them from falling. Swallowing the lump of emotion in my throat, I whisper, "You were trying to save the zoo? For me?"

"Yep," he retorts, popping the "p" at the end of his word.

"Why didn't you come back and tell me? Or try harder to explain?"

Tossing his hands into the air, his voice rises in anger as he barks out, "What the fuck was the point? You had your mind made up. Not to mention when I did come back to talk to you, you had already moved on."

What on earth is he talking about? "What? I haven't moved on," I argue, my brow furrowed with confusion.

"Don't fuck with me, Riley. I know you had some asshole at your apartment days after we broke up."

Rearing back at the venom lacing his words, my eyes widen with shock.

"That's right," he sneers, mistaking my reaction. "I stopped by to try and talk to you, and instead, I found you standing outside with *him*. I watched you stand there and let him kiss you, so don't bother trying to lie to me."

Understanding dawns as he describes what he saw, but once again, our relationship is being threatened by a misunderstanding.

"No, wait. You don't understand—"

"Don't bullshit me, Riley. I know what I saw. I just didn't know you could move on so fast. Tell me. How long did you wait for the door to shut behind me before downloading your stupid little dating app?"

"Parker, stop," I yell, frustrated with his refusal to listen. Now I know exactly how he felt the night of our fight, and I can't say I blame him for his hostility now. But he needs to know the truth before he says anything else he might regret—before he's the one standing in my shoes.

"You don't understand. That was Allie's husband. He came by to help me move some furniture around. We've been friends for a while, and he was just being kind. Allie was there with us the whole time, but she left before him to pick up their dinner. You didn't see what you thought you saw. It was just another misunderstanding, and I'm so sorry you thought otherwise."

After a moment of hesitation, I watch as the anger melts from Parker's expression, his shoulders sinking with relief. I can't help the laugh that bubbles up my throat over our situation. For two people who seem to care about each other as much as we do, we sure have a hell of a time communicating. I've never been riddled with so many misunderstandings in my life.

Stepping to the side, I make my way around his desk, stopping once I'm standing next to him. He turns to face me, and I reach down, grabbing his hand with mine.

"I was wrong, Parker. About everything, and I know that now. I should have let you explain, but I was just so scared. I've been used so many times in my life, I jumped to conclusions and assumed you were doing the same thing. I never understood how a man like you could fall for someone like me, but what I couldn't understand in my head, I now know without a doubt in my heart,"

I admit, pulling his hand up to my chest and placing it over my rapidly beating heart. "We were meant for each other. You make me feel loved, and I see you for your inner-worth. I have no need for a worthless dating app when I've already found the perfect match—*my* perfect match."

Parker opens his mouth to respond, but I hurry on, cutting him off before he can answer. "A year ago, I was alone, yearning for a life I felt I would never have because I was too afraid to open my heart to someone that would ultimately hold the power to destroy it. But it took me going through this hurt the last few weeks to realize you can't have an epic love if you aren't willing to go through the pain first, and there's nobody I'd rather suffer the growing pains of love for than you."

The tears I've been holding in for so long finally crest, spilling from my eyes as I continue. "When I met you, you were everything I wasn't looking for. You were a hardened, angry jerk," I choke out around a watery laugh. "But then you did what I couldn't do. You opened your heart to me, allowing me to see the beauty inside you. The world may see you as San Diego's Resident Asshole, but I see the real you—the kind, funny, playful, intelligent, loving you. And that's the you I never want to lose again because I know now without a doubt in my heart that you aren't everything I was searching for in life. You're more."

Parker's face breaks out into a radiant smile, banishing his previous mask of anger. His hands move up to cradle my face with a gentleness he's never given me before. Staring intently into my eyes, his thumbs caress my cheeks lovingly.

"Fuck, Riley," he whispers hoarsely, his voice cracking with emotion. "I love you. I love you so goddamn much. I've known for a while now, and I should've said it sooner. Maybe it would have saved us from all this hurt."

Raising my hands, I wrap them around his wrists, holding him in place as I whisper, "Maybe, maybe not. I'm not so sure I would've believed in us until we went through this suffering. It took us being separated for me to understand the depth of my love for you. And I do love you, Parker. More than I ever knew was possible."

Another tear falls from the corner of my eye, cascading down my cheek before Parker lowers his face, slanting his lips across mine. He slides his tongue across the seam of my lips, demanding entrance. With a passionate sigh, I part my lips, allowing his tongue to seek out mine in a dance of desire.

With a step forward, Parker backs me up against his desk before removing his hands from my face. He bends slightly and wraps his hands around my thighs, lifting me up and settling me on top of his desk, all without breaking our connection. As he steps between my parted thighs, I wrap my legs around his back, bringing his body flush against mine. Despite everywhere our bodies are touching, it feels like we still aren't close enough. I need more—so, so much more.

My hands move to the back of his neck before traveling north, tangling in the strands of his hair. Gripping my hips, he rocks his pelvis against mine, the evidence of his arousal pushing against me as he continues devouring my lips.

Gasping for air, I break our kiss, turning my head toward his office door. He takes the opportunity to move his lips across my cheek and down my neck, ripping a moan from deep in my chest as he places wet kisses along the column of my throat.

"Wait," I cry out in a breathy voice, the realization of where we are pushing past the haze of lust. "The door's not locked."

"Ignore it," he pants, placing another kiss against my neck. Brushing his mouth up to my ear, he whispers, "Anybody that comes in without an invitation will be a dead man walking."

He doesn't wait for me to answer. Instead, he grabs the hem of my scrub top, lifting it up and over my head, tossing it behind him. He makes quick work of my bra, reaching behind me to unsnap the clasp before dragging it down my arms, adding it to the growing pile. Parker releases a deep groan, licking his lips as my heavy breasts come into view. The sound sends a spark of lust directly to my core, every inch of me clenching in anticipation of what's to come.

Parker grabs my hands, placing them on his shirt buttons before focusing his attention on my pants. Fumbling a few times, I manage to unbutton his shirt and push it off his broad shoulders as he lifts my ass and tugs my bottoms down my legs.

His pants are the next to go, although he doesn't wait for my clumsy hands. Stepping back, he unsnaps the clasp and pushes his pants and boxers to the ground, releasing his monstrous erection. I watch as it bobs up and down, heavy with desire. Gripping it at the base, Parker slides his stiff crown up my wet slit, briefly rubbing against my throbbing clit.

A groan slips past my kiss-swollen lips as Parker's hoarse growl meets my ears. "I need to be inside you. *Now.*"

"Yes. Please," I beg, my voice dripping with need.

Coated in my desire, he lines himself up with my center. A breathy moan escapes my lips the second he pushes past my entrance, pleasure radiating through my limbs as he fills me.

"Fuck, I've missed you," he growls against my ear, sinking his rigid member deep into my wet heat. My walls tighten, clenching around him, desperate to keep him inside me, and I know this won't take long. I've been desperate for his touch for weeks now.

Agonizingly slow, he pulls out to the tip, revealing his hard dick that's now glistening with my juices. His gaze glues to our connection as he sinks back into the hilt, ripping another moan from my throat when he hits my sweet spot.

Leaning forward, he places a rough kiss against my lips before resting his forehead against mine. With his eyes peering into mine, glittering with emotion, he hoarsely demands, "Don't ever leave me again."

"Never," I pant out before sealing my promise with a kiss.

My words unleash his desire, his hips plunging in and out of my tight, wet slit with force. The desk feels like it's about to tip over from the power behind his thrusts, but nothing could stop us now. We're chasing a high that's just barely beyond our reach.

"Yes, right there," I purr, tossing my head back as pleasure radiates through every inch of my body.

"Fuck," he growls, sweat forming at his hairline as his cock pulses deep inside me.

Our orgasms crest simultaneously, each of us tumbling over that cliff as ecstasy soars through our bodies. His hot breath fans against my ear as he groans through his release, my nipples brushing across his bare chest, extending my climax.

"I fucking love you," Parker whispers against the side of my face. I nod my head in agreement, unable to form words as my brain remains focused on our physical connection.

Slowing his thrusts, he grinds into me twice more, riding out the end of his orgasm before slowly pulling out with a grunt. His lips briefly find mine before he steps away to grab a tissue from his desk, cleaning himself up before pulling his boxers and pants up from around his ankles. Tossing his used tissue in the trash, he grabs a few more before turning to me. Forcing my legs apart, he cleans the sticky mess between my thighs, clearing away the evidence of our lovemaking.

Hopping down from the desk, I gather my clothes, both of us dressing in silence. I've barely secured my pants on my hips when thunder booms behind us, a startled yelp falling from my lips as the unexpected sound rattles the glass windows. A shadow falls across Parker's previously relaxed face, his body tightening with tension before my eyes.

"Hey, look at me," I gently whisper, pressing my body against his. His eyes flash to mine, pleading for help as I wrap my hands around his waist, pulling him into a tight embrace. "I know what these storms do to you—how they cripple you with fear and remind you of memories you can't change. But everything's going to be okay, Parker. I'm here." Running my hands up and down his back, I do my best to soothe his anguish, hoping my words are penetrating his anxiety. "I'll always be here, standing beside you to weather the storm. Rain, thunder, wind, a full-on hurricane, it doesn't matter. From here on out, it's you and me. I won't run from this or search for an escape. I'll always be right here next to you. And no matter what the future brings, we'll face it together. Just you and me."

With a heavy sigh, his chest deflates, the tension releasing its hold on his body. His eyes fill with love, slowly replacing the anxiety as I hold his gaze. Wrapping his hand around the back of my neck, he brings my face within an inch of his, his lips brushing against mine as he whispers, "Thank you."

Placing a sweet kiss on my lips, he pulls back, resting his forehead against mine. "Ever since my dad died, creating a divide in my family, it's felt like my life has been one giant storm. I had no idea I was searching for an umbrella until the day I met you. You came along and pulled me from the eye of the storm, sheltering over me with your love and brightness. You gave me a reason to do better—to be better. I never thought I'd say these words, but I'm so glad I was forced to move in next door to you, Riley. My life would be so empty without you."

"Mine too, Parker. I've missed you so much."

Laying my head against his chest, I close my eyes, my arms still wound securely around his waist. A moment of silence passes, nothing but the sound of his steady heartbeat and our breathing filling the space between us. Parker's arms wrap around me, his cheek coming to rest against the top of my head. I listen as his heart picks up speed, racing with each second that passes.

I'm about to pull away to ask what's wrong when he beats me to the punch, answering me before I can ask.

"Move in with me, Riley," he whispers, my heart stopping with his words. Tears I couldn't stop if I wanted to leak from my eyes, soaking into his shirt as my heart kickstarts, beating furiously in my chest. Everything I've ever wanted—everything I thought I'd never have—is finally coming true, and I've never been so happy.

49

PARKER

Her head lifts from my chest as bright emerald eyes, shining with tears, meet my nervous gaze. When she doesn't say anything, I press forward, doing my best to convince her. "Build a life with me. Kids, dogs, cats, elephants, I don't care, I want it all with you. These last few weeks without you have been some of the worst days of my life. I can't stand to be away from you for one more day—I fucking won't. Please, Riley, come home with me."

I'm careful not to mention marriage, although I'd marry her tomorrow if it meant she'd never fucking leave me again. But she deserves a proposal a hell of a lot better than us standing in my office, the scent of our make-up sex permeating the air.

Just when my panic rises with her silence, thoughts of kidnapping her and tying her to my bed running through my mind, her face breaks out into a radiant smile as she squeals, "Yes, Parker! I'd love to."

Her hands grab my cheeks, forcing my lips down to hers as she slams her mouth to mine. Happiness and excitement fill every inch of my heart, effectively silencing my doubts and anxiety.

Breaking the kiss entirely too soon, she leans back, her smile still firmly in place as she adds, "Although, we can probably leave the elephants at the zoo. That's a lot of poo I don't want to clean up."

Her answer forces a laugh to barrel up my throat, the sound foreign to my ears as it bursts out of my mouth. It's been weeks since anything in my life has been worthy of a laugh, but standing here with Riley in my arms, I'm finally fucking home.

"Whatever you want, babe. It's fucking yours."

"Don't get any grand ideas. If I come home to a damn elephant in our backyard, I'll move back out. You're all I need, Parker. You, my family and friends, my job, a kid or two, eventually. But nothing else."

Her response damn near brings me to my knees. I know she doesn't want me for my money—she never has. But the fact she'd turn down anything my money could buy her is the exact reason I'm in love with her.

"Hey, who was that angry man storming out of your building earlier? He looked really familiar," she asks, changing the subject and stealing an ounce of my joy, all in one swoop.

With a heavy sigh, I answer her honestly. "That was my brother, Rory. He's been trying to poach one of my best clients for the last few months but just found out they're sticking with Parker Solutions."

"Oh," she mutters softly. "I guess that explains why he looks familiar. He looks a lot like you. But, what happened between you two? Why is he trying to steal your clients?"

Her question has my heart clenching with fear in my chest. I've been avoiding this topic for so long, always brushing it under the rug. But after everything we've been through, I can't keep another secret from her—especially one that could tear us apart if she didn't hear it straight from me.

"He blames me for a lot of things I didn't do, but the biggest misunderstanding is his belief that his fiancée cheated on him with me."

Her eyes widen with shock, her gasp filling the space between us. She drops her hands from around me as she takes a step backward, her arms folding across her chest. My hands clench at my sides, my heart speeding up as nerves steal over my body. I know it sounds bad, but it's not the fucking truth, which is exactly what I do my best to explain. Her bottom lip trembles before she bites down on it, my eyes tracking the movement as sweat forms along my brow.

She slowly nods her head as the words tumble from my lips, her eyes flickering back and forth between mine as the entire story comes to light. Taking a deep breath, I finish, "I tried to make him understand today, but he stormed out, once again refusing to listen to reason. He wouldn't even listen to the plan I have for him."

"What plan?" she asks, interest coloring her face. She hasn't said anything about the misunderstanding, which I don't miss. I'm sure she's still processing my words. It's a lot to take in.

"I bought out a non-profit organization recently—"

"The Helping Haven," she cuts me off, nodding her head with understanding.

"Oh, you heard about that?"

"Of course, I heard about it, Parker. Everyone in California probably heard about it. It's a wonderful thing you're doing, and I'm so proud of you."

My throat swells with emotion at her words, but I do my best to swallow it down. I have yet to cry in front of her, and I won't, no matter how much her words mean to me.

"Thank you. Anyway, I bought that out with the hopes Rory and I could run it together, with him handling the brunt of the business. I know he's not happy with his current job, and I know this would bring him a lot of joy. Or, it would have if he would've listened to me."

"Wow. That's amazing, especially after how he's been treating you lately." Breaking eye contact, she glances down, her eyes fixed on the floor between us. A few agonizing seconds pass before she looks back up at me, her shoulders dipping with a sigh as she encourages, "I know it's hard, but give it time. One of these days, he'll realize he was wrong, and maybe then you can fulfill that dream."

"So you believe me, then? That I'd never fuck around with my brother's fiancée?"

"Of course, I believe you," she scoffs, relief filling every inch of my six-foot-two frame. "You're a lot of things, Parker, but a cheater isn't one of them."

If only my brother believed that too.

I never should've doubted her, but I know how things looked. Hell, my own brother doesn't believe me, and neither did the press when that particular story circulated in the tabloids. I paid a lot of hush money for that to go away, but it didn't matter at the time. Enough people read about it before it was pulled from the headlines, and it did nothing but further damage my reputation as the news continued to spread like wildfire by word of mouth. Hell, there was even a time I questioned whether my own mother believed me. But fuck if I'm not relieved Riley knows the truth. Her trust in me is all I need—fuck what anybody else thinks.

Folding her back into my embrace, I kiss the top of her head before asking, "Do you need to go back to work?"

She shakes her head against my chest, her words slightly muffled when she admits, "No. I took the rest of the day off to come talk to you. Actually, I asked Allie to tell them I was sick. Either way, I don't have to go back."

Excitement courses through me as I drop my arms from around her body. Leaning over, I jab my finger down on the intercom sitting on the corner of my desk. Nothing else on my schedule is more important than taking Riley home. "Haylee," I bark out, my voice booming around us. "Reschedule the rest of my appointments for today. I'm leaving."

"Consider it done," she answers right away, her professionalism making me roll my eyes. Ever since her screw-up, she's been on edge, doing whatever she can to protect her job. Every task has been completed flawlessly, she beats me to work every morning and stays until I leave, and she jumps at the chance to do my bidding. If I'm being honest, it's annoying the shit out of me.

While I appreciate what she's doing to ensure she doesn't fuck up again, I've come to miss her sassy personality and willingness to spar with me. It was one of the reasons we got along so well, and now everything feels stuffy and unenjoyable. It's a lot harder to be a formidable asshole when Haylee's walking around like a scared puppy, wilting under my glare. It makes my skin itchy and uncomfortable, which pisses me off.

Now that I have Riley back and things with the zoo are settled, I'll have to work on getting things back to normal around here, that way I can go back to being an asshole, free of guilt. But that's a problem for another day.

Grabbing my cell phone and keys off my desk, I shove them in my pocket before grabbing Riley's hand, pulling her behind me as I head to the door.

"Where are we going?" she questions, her tone full of amusement.

Looking at her over my shoulder, I tighten my grip on her hand and aim a devilish smirk her way. "I think it's time you see your new home. We have some rooms to christen, don't you think?" I ask with a wink, the crotch of my pants tightening at the dirty thoughts running through my head.

A brilliant smile transforms her face, her own pace quickening when she giggles, "Yes, let's go home."

EPILOGUE
RORY

Ice rattles against my empty glass as I slam it down on the sticky, scarred bar top. The thunderous noise level of the packed sports bar assaults my ears as a sudden cheer travels around the room. Glancing up at one of the six television screens above the bar, I watch an instant replay of a batter for our local Major League Baseball team hitting a home run.

Who gives a shit?

The only sport worth watching is hockey, and that season ended a few months back. Rolling my eyes, I nod to the bartender, silently demanding a refill. Two drinks deep with no intention of stopping anytime soon, I'm well on my way to drowning my anger in a bottle of scotch.

My brother's words from earlier in his office bounce around in my brain, reverberating against my skull as I wait for the bartender to pour my drink. *You don't even want this career. You're not happy with it.*

With a shake of my head, I easily dismiss Parker's words. He's fucking wrong — grasping at straws and trying to manipulate me into believing he's doing what's best for me. And while that may have been true at one point, it hasn't been the case for a long time. Not since the first dagger he stabbed in my back during our childhood.

As hard as I've tried the last several months, I've yet to inflict an ounce of pain on my brother. Pain he more than deserves after constantly fucking me over, filling my heart with hatred with each new twist of his knife.

After our dad died, Parker did everything he could to become the man of the house — a job I wasn't ready for. I was only ten, suffering from grief I didn't know how to manage.

The day death stole our father from us, it robbed me of my best friend too. While Parker and our mom were close, my father and I were thick as thieves. He understood me, relating to me on a level nobody else could, mainly because they never tried. Our bond was unbreakable — or at least, it was, up until the day it was severed altogether.

My first spark of hatred flared to life when my asshole brother commandeered our only surviving parent's love, hogging it all for himself. I watched from the sidelines as they continued to lean on each other, just as they always had, while I struggled to handle the pain on my own.

As grief-filled days passed, turning into months of suffering, the poison of hate continued to spread as I was left out in the rain, with no room under their two-person umbrella.

The second strain on our relationship came when he stole my future career, running off to college two years before I could. He listened to me rant and rave for years about my dreams of helping failing businesses find their stride again. I thrived on showing people how they could turn their weaknesses into strengths, turning the tides of failure into waves of success.

Parker never once showed an interest in my plan, so imagine my surprise when he came home from college on fall break, boasting to our mother about declaring a major in business. When she asked him what he planned to do with that major, he recited the words I had shared with him in the past, marking them as his own while he prattled off a career plan that mirrored mine.

I stood in the dining room, my jaw dropped in shock, as my mom hugged and praised him, ignoring her awareness of his thievery. She knew that was my dream, and she did nothing to deter him. That was the day my resentment toward her began to grow alongside my hatred for him.

In time, I probably could have forgiven him for those two offenses, but my brother's betrayal didn't end there. With a final twist of his knife, Parker stole my fucking fiancée.

He has everyone fooled, playing the role of an innocent bystander in Sabrina's unfaithful activities, but I know better. I saw the fucking proof with my own two eyes. Photo after photo of Sabrina in varying levels of clothing, ranging from sexy black lingerie to every inch of her naked, flawless porcelain skin on display.

Leaning against my bedroom door frame, the strap of her lingerie seductively hanging off one shoulder as her tits strained against the material.

Naked in the shower, water cascading down her body as she caressed her full tits, two fingers wrapped around her right nipple in a pinch.

Draped across my fucking bed, her legs spread wide open as her fingers disappeared into the same wet heat I'd sunk my hard cock into the night before.

Each image flits through my mind once again, my blood rolling to a boil as I remember thinking there was a mistake. There was no way the name at the top of her message thread was Parker Adams — no way she had been sending these images to anybody but the man who bought that three-carat diamond rock on her left hand. But those thoughts were put to rest after I clicked on the name and slowly raised the phone to my ear, that first shrill ring echoing through the phone.

"Parker," he had answered. The familiar husk to his voice sent a shiver of rage down my spine, and my eyes fell closed when the reality of my situation crashed down around me.

My own goddamn brother had stolen the last bit of happiness I had carved out for my life.

I remember hanging up and tossing the phone down on my bed right as Sabrina walked out of my bathroom, draped in nothing but one of my fluffy white towels, her hair piled on top of her head, hidden inside a second towel wrapped up like a cone. Beads of water rolled down her shoulders, traveling down her bare arms and dropping from her elbows, seeping into my plush cream-colored carpet.

"Should we have Thai or Italian for dinner, babe?" she had asked, her slightly high-pitched voice replacing the whooshing in my ears as my blood furiously rushed through my body.

"Get the fuck out."

The harsh whisper had fallen from my lips, circling the air around us as she peered up at me beneath wet lashes, her face clouding with confusion.

"What, babe?"

"Get. The fuck. Out."

One look at the rage coloring my face, and she knew. She had glanced from me to the phone tossed down on my bed, then to the spot where it had lain before she waltzed into the bathroom, a seductive sway to her hips after begging me to join her. Her gaze flickered back to mine, eyes widened with horror as she realized what I must have seen.

I had no intentions of rifling through my fiancée's phone, but when I couldn't find mine to call my boss, solidifying our plans for the following morning, I picked her phone up to dial mine. With the messaging app still pulled up on her screen, my focus flew to my brother's name like a heat-seeking missile, one thread below her best friend Natasha's name, forcing me to click on it.

"Wait, Rory. It-it's not..." she had stuttered, her face as pale as a white sheet as she tried and failed to explain. There was no need to. She couldn't deny photo evidence.

Without another word, I shook my head and turned my back on her, grabbing my keys and wallet off the dresser and slamming the front door behind me as I left.

Speeding down the busy streets of San Diego that night, I barreled toward the restaurant I knew my brother was dining at, hosting a business meeting with a potential client. My mother — bless her soul — had mentioned his plans for the evening when I spoke with her earlier that afternoon, a random tidbit of information I was grateful for then.

As I sit at the busy bar, a replenished drink now cradled in my left hand, my right fist clenches with the ghost of pain from that night. I had stormed through the restaurant and punched my older brother straight in the nose — twice — before finishing him off with a mean right hook.

To say he was shocked doesn't begin to cover Parker's reaction as my fist plowed into his face that night, but I didn't waste time letting him talk his way out of the truth. I turned around and stalked out of the restaurant while faces of horror reflected at me as I left Parker bleeding on the floor.

He still swears that it was all a misunderstanding, but I'm not as stupid as he seems to think I am. I saw all the evidence I needed to, and that was the final stab to the back. That was the day I decided to do whatever it took to pull that knife out and turn it on him, and I won't stop until he feels the pain of it slicing through his own back.

Figuratively speaking, of course. I'm too fucking pretty for prison.

A familiar tinkling sound rises above the racket of the bar, a smile stealing over my face as the distinct laugh reaches my ears. Swiveling my chair toward the noise, I raise the glass of cheap scotch to my lips, welcoming the burn of alcohol as it sears my throat. My eyes track the movements of a blond bombshell as she struts across the room to the dartboards.

I watch as she yanks her darts out of the electronic game, her tits swaying with the movement before she turns on her heel and struts back to her table.

I peruse her lean body, cataloging every dip and curve I've overlooked in the past. My mouth waters as her hips sway back and forth, and my dick twitches with excitement from the view of her tight ass in that skirt. He wouldn't mind burying himself between those deliciously round cheeks of hers, slipping down the crack until her silky heat greets him with a wet embrace.

A new idea for revenge ignites, each step stoking the flame as the plan sparks to life. The thought of exacting my vengeance sends a fire of excitement coursing through my blood until it's a raging inferno, unable to be tamed. A wicked smile transforms my face, and the corners of my lips slowly tick up as the final plan of action clicks into place.

I can't believe I didn't think of this sooner.

I'm not stupid. I've seen how she looks at me, and if I have to exploit her desire for me to get what I want, I fucking will. She's the ticket to revenge on my selfish prick of a brother. She just doesn't know it — yet.

Swallowing down the last of my scotch, I turn and slam the glass down on the bar top before standing from my seat. I toss a few twenties on the bar and rake my hand through my hair, tousling the ends.

I heave in a deep breath before sauntering across the room, each step full of confidence. Stamping my signature smirk across my lips, I prepare to flirt until she falls into the palm of my hand, even if it takes all night. Nothing will stop me until I bring that asshole down.

I'll flirt my way into her life tonight, and soon, retribution will be mine.

Game on, brother.

Game. On.

INTERESTED IN WHO RORY'S TICKET TO REVENGE MIGHT BE? FIND out in book two of the San Diego Alphas series, The Wicked Secret.

JOIN BROOKLYN'S BRAZEN BOOKMATES, FOLLOW BROOKLYN ON Instagram, or sign up for her monthly newsletter for more book-related updates!

ACKNOWLEDGMENTS

Is this the Oscars? I feel like it's the Oscars. I have so many people to thank.

First off, thank YOU! Thank you for taking a chance on a debut author and for reading up to this point! Without readers, books would be pointless, so thank you for your love of reading and for giving me the chance to follow my dreams!

#56, thank you for your unconditional support and your entertaining feedback on the steamy scenes. Our love of hockey brought us closer together, and your support with my first ever novel will forever be appreciated. P.S. Happy 70th birthday!

To my family, thank you for believing in me and encouraging me. Thanks for loving me enough to read my book, even when romance isn't your favorite genre, and for always understanding when I had to cancel plans.

Jess L. and Taylor E., thank you for being my original Alphas! Thank you for your endless support. It means more to me than you'll ever know.

Emily, Stalina, and Haley, thank you for being my Beta readers. Your invaluable feedback and hilarious commentary saved my butt. The Perfect Match wouldn't be what it is today without your help!

Jeff K. and Ashley L., thank you for listening to my harebrained ideas and for providing motivation when I was lacking.

A very special thanks to my book mom, Iannah Roberts. Thanks for holding my hand and guiding me through this journey. Thanks for taking the time to answer stupid questions (turns out they really do exist) and for never getting irritated when I ask you to explain them a week later. Thank you for reading an early copy, in all of its ugly glory, and for loving it anyway. I love you endlessly and am so grateful for your support and encouragement. The Perfect Match wouldn't exist without you and all of your help.

And finally, to the Brain Dump and RWR, y'all are my MF tribe. Thanks for holding me up when I was drowning. Thank you for your unconditional support and wisdom, for the daily laughs, and for simply being unapologetically you.

ABOUT THE AUTHOR

Residing in Eastern Nebraska, Brooklyn is an author of contemporary romances that will either make you laugh or cry. Maybe even both. When she's not writing, editing, crying over her keyboard, working, or reading, you can probably find her watching hockey games, napping, drinking coffee, or cuddling with her lovable fur child.

With a life-long passion for turning the pages, it's always been Brooklyn's dream to write a romance she'd love to read, and she's eternally grateful to YOU for giving her a chance to do so.

Made in the USA
Columbia, SC
19 September 2022